"I Hate You!" She Cried. "I Never Asked You to Come After Me."

Suddenly he caught her by the shoulders, his lips seeking her out in the darkness. A fresh gust of wind lashed them together, their bodies molding one to the other. A flash of lightning illumined her up-turned face, and he saw her eyes were half-closed, her lips lifted expectantly to his. He could feel her rain-soaked body swaying in his arms, readily yielding herself to him.

"You're just a child in love with love."

She cringed as though he had struck her. "You arrogant scoundrel," she exclaimed angrily.

Silently Miguel turned away from her, grateful now for the darkness. He couldn't bear to see the hatred in her eyes, nor did he want her to know how those brief moments of intimacy with her had really affected him.

Dear Reader,

We, the editors of Tapestry Romances, are committed to bringing you two outstanding original romantic historical novels each and every month.

From Kentucky in the 1850s to the court of Louis XIII, from the deck of a pirate ship within sight of Gibraltar to a mining camp high in the Sierra Nevadas, our heroines experience life and love, romance and adventure.

Our aim is to give you the kind of historical romances that you want to read. We would enjoy hearing your thoughts about this book and all future Tapestry Romances. Please write to us at the address below.

The Editors
Tapestry Romances
POCKET BOOKS
1230 Avenue of the Americas
Box TAP
New York, N.Y. 10020

IRON LACE

Lorena Dureau

A TAPESTRY BOOK
PUBLISHED BY POCKET BOOKS NEW YORK

This novel is a work of historical fiction. Names, characters, places and incidents relating to non-historical figures are either the product of the author's imagination or are used fictitiously. Any resemblance of such non-historical incidents, places or figures to actual events or locales or persons, living or dead, is entirely coincidental.

An *Original* publication of TAPESTRY BOOKS

A Tapestry Book published by
POCKET BOOKS, a Simon & Schuster division of
GULF & WESTERN CORPORATION
1230 Avenue of the Americas, New York, N.Y. 10020

ISBN: 0-671-46052-8

First Tapestry Books printing February, 1983

10 9 8 7 6 5 4 3 2 1

POCKET and colophon are registered trademarks
of Simon & Schuster.

TAPESTRY is a trademark of Simon & Schuster.

Printed in the U.S.A.

To my many friends in Mexico who taught me to know and love their country—and most of all, to those very special *amigas* who were always there to help and encourage me over the years:

Alicia Kamel Ortega
Adela Dinorah Ponce de Mejia
Josefina Saldana de Marin

—and the late, but dearly remembered—
Bertha Valencia U.
and
Sally Zeitlin

Acknowledgments

Besides the usual sources of information consulted while researching such a book, the author wishes to give special thanks to
the following people for their invaluable assistance:

Miss Florence Jumonville, Head Librarian
The Historic New Orleans Collection

Dan Gill, Asst. Area Agent, Horticulture
The Louisiana Cooperative Extension Service

Vaughn L. Glasgow, Chief Curator
Louisiana State Museum

Dr. Charles Nolan, Associate Archivist
Archives of Archdiocese of New Orleans

Sidney Villere, Louisiana historian and author

Dr. Joseph A. Polack
Audubon Sugar Institute
Louisiana State University, Baton Rouge, La.

Chapter One

"*MON DIEU*, MONIQUE! WE SHOULDN'T BE OUT ALONE on the street like this. There will be the devil to pay when we get home!"

"Oh, stop your fretting, Celeste. Grandmother will still be dozing when we get back. She'll never know we've been gone."

The traveling marionette troupe had already begun its show, and the two young girls had run all the way to the plaza, not wanting to miss any of it.

The Plaza de Armas was bustling this afternoon, yet the Chausson sisters attracted considerable attention as they wended their way breathlessly through the clusters of townsfolk milling around the large square. Seventeen-year-old Monique and her sister Celeste, younger by less than two years, were a delight to behold as they darted about in the warm spring sunshine like bright-winged butterflies fresh out of their cocoons. Beneath their tiny ruffled parasols, their golden curls bobbed merrily about their shoulders as they swished along in their full-skirted gowns of diaphanous white muslin draped over colorful petticoats of rustling taffeta, their wide satin sashes streaming behind them. They fancied themselves quite the grand ladies of fashion, even though they were surrounded mostly by other youngsters.

"Heaven knows we have little enough distraction these days now that Papa's gone," sighed Monique, the rosy glow of her deep pink underskirts momentarily opposed by the shadow of sadness that flitted across her round doll-like face. "Grandmother never likes to go anywhere these days except to mass or the cemetery, and now we don't even have a chaperon to accompany us if we want to go somewhere. I'm afraid we're well on our way to becoming old maids!"

Celeste smiled as she adjusted a fold in her sash of crushed green satin. She was accustomed to her elder sister's tendency to dramatize. "Oh, I doubt that, my dear. You already have more than your share of beaux. Every time we go promenading on the levee, there are always more young men around you than there are orange trees along the walk. Grandmother will have to let you begin going out with them before too long."

But Monique had her doubts. Although her grandmother often boasted that her nieces were among the most outstanding beauties of the Louisiana colony, Monique was far from satisfied with herself. Secretly she hated the babylike chubbiness of her cheeks that were not pale enough to be fashionable, and that silly button nose of hers that made her look more like a child than the classic-featured Parisian lady she so yearned to be.

Of course, beaux like Maurice Foucher insisted that the dimples in the middle of her cheeks made her all the more charming, but then he was always reciting pretty phrases. She knew better. Her face was too round, her nose too small, and her mouth often made her look as if she were about to go into a pout. There was absolutely nothing classic about her at all!

What's more, her eyes had a way of changing color. Instead of being an intense violet or emerald-green, they mirrored whatever happened to be near them at the moment. Although they were a strikingly clear gray, heavily lashed and well set apart, they had no color of their own as far as she was concerned, and Maurice's assuring her they were all the more fascinating because of their unpredictability didn't do much to console her.

About the only thing she could really be proud of was her generous mane of pale gold hair. Sometimes she was not above calling attention to it by giving her head an extra toss or two. She was doubly glad, therefore, that it was no longer the style to powder the hair now except for formal occasions.

Monique cast an affectionate glance down at her younger sister. At fifteen, dainty little Celeste might still be immature in many ways—an inch or two shorter and not very developed yet under her fichu —but the girl had a beauty all her own. Her hair was of a darker gold, more honey-colored, and she had inherited her father's hazel eyes, giving her a doelike appearance that seemed to match that air of calm about her that often bordered on timidity.

The bond between the sisters was a strong one. Six years before, their mother and younger brother had died in the epidemic that had followed the Great Fire of 1788, when four-fifths of New Orleans had burned to the ground. Since then the girls had been raised under a loose rein. Their father had been engrossed with the rebuilding of their partially destroyed town house and trying to get the family plantation upriver on a better-paying basis. He had left them to the vigilance of their doting grandmother and their well-meaning but easily manipulated governess.

Six months ago, however, Louis Chausson had suddenly been killed in a freak accident when his horse, startled by a snake, had thrown him to the ground and broken his neck. The shock of losing her son so tragically and without warning aged Aimee Chausson almost overnight. Now she left the running of the plantation almost entirely to the overseer. Most of the time she just sat sighing or dozing over her sewing, murmuring that the burden that had been left on her shoulders was more than she could bear.

As luck would have it, two months after the death of Louis Chausson the girls' governess had suddenly resigned to marry a simple but hardworking planter on the German Coast farther up the Mississippi. Since then, Grandmother had not been able to find a suitable replacement for her, so Monique and her sister had been enjoying even greater freedom than ever lately.

Sometimes Aimee Chausson even spoke of closing up the town house and going to live permanently at their plantation upriver. Monique hoped they wouldn't move. She much preferred the more active life of New Orleans to that of the plantation. In the city there was always something exciting going on. She especially loved to come to the Plaza de Armas. There was always so much to see: elegantly clad noblemen and uniformed soldiers with long slender swords swinging impressively at their sides . . . street vendors hawking their wares in singsong voices . . . hooded friars gliding calmly through the busy throng in dark homespun robes and bare sandaled feet . . . buckskinned rivermen who had poled down from the Ohio Territory to sell their produce in New Orleans . . . and in the midst of all this activity, the laborers working feverishly away on the new cathedral.

The broad expanse of the mighty Mississippi could even be glimpsed from the plaza. From one of her favorite spots, Los Naranjos, Monique would often sit for hours on the levee, just watching the continuous parade of vessels going by—as imaginative a collection of man-powered or mule-drawn barques as was ever contrived by merchants to get their wares to market.

Although the loading and unloading docks were farther down the embankment, a distance away from the main plaza, the sounds of the activities going on there could be heard. The shouted orders, the squeaking of the pulleys, the warning cries, occasional grunts and curses . . . they all drifted into the square to mingle with that reverberating symphony of innumerable sounds that made up the thriving little port of Nueva Orleans, political and ecclesiastical seat of His Catholic Majesty Carlos IV's Louisiana colony. Of course, it was still better known as Nouvelle Orleans by the majority of its citizens, who continued to be passionately French at heart, despite the fact that well over a generation had gone by since they had become a Spanish colony.

Although many of the townspeople continued to cling to the old-type buildings, like those of the original French settlement, some were slowly changing over from the wooden structures to the more solidly built ones of plastered brick, neatly painted in white or pastel colors and frosted with black iron-lace balconies and gateways. Much as Monique hated to admit it, the new Spanish style of architecture was giving New Orleans a more elegant air than it had ever had before. Her father had even adopted the style for the Chausson town house when he had rebuilt it after the fire.

Their more or less unwelcome rulers were making other improvements, too. New Orleans had a newspaper of its own now, and the newly appointed governor, the Baron de Carondelet, was planning to put up street lights and organize a permanent police force for the city in the near future.

Only a few months ago, the governor had signed a peace treaty with the Indians and reinforced the five forts guarding its palisades, although Maurice had observed that the Spanish had probably taken such measures more to keep its subjects inside the walls than protect them from any dangers without!

Monique cast a disdainful glance up at the royal red and yellow flag lightly fluttering in the mild afternoon breeze. It was one of the few things she didn't like about the plaza, but she hoped the day would come soon when that Spanish banner would be replaced by the fleur-de-lis of France.

Celeste nudged her sister nervously and whispered, "Look, there's Padre Sebastian. I'm sure he's spotted us. See how he's looking this way? Now we're going to get it for sure!"

Monique crinkled up her tiny nose until it almost disappeared from sight between her rosy cheeks.

"I hope he doesn't come over here," she moaned. "That Spanish friar gives me goose pimples every time he comes near me. He always seems to be peering down my fichu!"

"He's writing something down on that piece of slate he always has stuck in his prayer book. I wager it's something about us!"

Monique gave a toss of her wheat-colored curls. "Don't be silly!" She laughed lightheartedly.

But Celeste cast another anxious glance at the

hooded figure standing in front of the church. "I'm sure Fray Sebastian will say something to Grandmother this Sunday about having seen us without a chaperon."

"You fret too much, my dear," insisted Monique merrily, but she pulled her sister deeper into the crowd, hoping they were no longer in range of the Spanish monk's disturbingly penetrating gaze.

As they stood on tiptoe, stretching their necks as far as they could to see what antics the Harlequin was up to just then that had the people laughing so much, their view was suddenly blocked by two stockily built figures in dirty buckskins.

The unsightly pair stood there facing them, and the men's bearded, suntanned countenances suddenly broke into broad, mocking grins as they saw the consternation they were causing the two young girls.

Chapter Two

"WELL, LOOKIE HERE, WILL! WE DONE STUMBLED ON two pretty little French *feeyahs!*" exclaimed the older of the two while he shifted his wad of tobacco from one side of his mouth to the other.

Instinctively Monique caught her sister's hand in hers and drew herself up indignantly, feigning a bravado she was far from feeling at that moment.

"Will you please step aside, messieurs? You're blocking our view of the show," she protested, trying to keep her voice steady despite the growing apprehension within her.

"But the view right here is sure better than any old puppet show, isn't it, Will?" snickered the same man as his pale bloodshot eyes swept approvingly over Monique's fully developed figure. "I want this one for myself," he added with a sly wink to his companion. "I'll bet there's a lot of tit under there holding out that fichu!"

The younger man flashed a row of crooked yellow teeth behind his scraggly beard. "What luck to find choice ones like this without any leashes on them," he replied. "They look like real quality, too. A pair of dainty little Frogs like this would make a trip downriver worthwhile anytime!"

Monique recognized them as flatboatmen—the type of men that the colonists in New Orleans referred to contemptuously as "Kaintocks" from the

8

Ohio and Kentucky territories to the north. They were carefully cutting the bewildered young girls off from the knot of spectators gathered around the marionette show and easing them over to a less busy part of the square.

Monique continued to hold tenaciously on to Celeste's trembling hand, pulling the frightened youngster along with her as she tried to walk away from their unwanted admirers.

"Come now, my *chayrees*, don't run off on us like that!" coaxed the older man as he laughingly placed himself in their path once more. "We can show you two one hell of a good time if you let us."

There was the strong odor of alcohol about them, and the one who was speaking teetered a little as he tried to balance himself in front of her.

"That's right, girlies," interjected the younger man. "We just sold our flatboat, cargo and all, so we have a bagful of money now to spend on the lucky wenches who give us a little loving before we have to start back up the trail."

"Please, messieurs, let us be on our way," insisted Monique, wishing she could keep her voice from sounding so tremulous.

The older man detained her with a large callused hand.

"Come on, dearie, don't put your airs on with us," he chided. "You two came out to have a good time, didn't you? Well, we're the ones to give it to you. I promise you that."

"Let go my arm, you smelly old man!" snapped Monique, stamping her foot impatiently. The pink of her dimpled cheeks was turning to apple red as she struggled to break free from that ironlike grip, all the while trying to hide how frightened she really was.

The man reeled back unsteadily as though she had struck him. "Smelly? Did you hear that, Will? She called us smelly! And us that just paid out good money for a bath up the street!"

Celeste, on the brink of tears, went white as a sheet as the younger man caught her by the arm.

"Now, ladies, don't be so finicky!" he scolded. "Although we may not look it, me and my partner here are all nice and washed up, so don't go calling us names. Of course, we didn't bring no change of wardrobe with us, but I don't see where that ought to matter much. We'll be only too glad to peel it all off for you as soon as we get to a more private place. Right, Jeb?" He chuckled meaningfully and pulled Celeste in closer to him. The poor girl looked as though she were going to faint away at any moment.

The feel of her little sister's hand trembling in hers fired Monique all the more. She let Celeste go and tried to place herself protectively in front of the girl.

"You let us go, or I'll start scratching your eyes out and screaming for help," she warned, holding up a threatening fist.

But the grip on her other arm only tightened, and the man named Jeb seemed to find her threats all the more humorous as he toyed with her as a cat might with a mouse trapped within its paws.

"For myself, lassie, I'm not so particular." He grinned. "I don't give a damn whether *you* just took a bath or not." He poked a curious finger into the folds of her neatly crossed collar. "From the feel of you, I wager you'll be something to keep me going all night, once you've shed these trappings!"

Monique was so horrified at the feel of a man's hand testing the fullness of her breasts that her fury fanned her desperation all the more. She tried again to free herself. She was about to let out a cry for help when suddenly she heard a cutting masculine voice coming from behind her.

"Perhaps you ruffians would prefer tilting swords instead of ladies' parasols?"

The roustabouts paled beneath their suntans, but they continued to hold fast to their prey.

"This is none of your concern, sir," retorted the older man. "These wenches here gave us every reason to think our attentions would be well received."

"That's right," seconded the other, but his bloodshot eyes were blinking nervously. "We was just discussing where to go."

Monique turned quickly around to face that unfamiliar but very welcome voice. For a second she was taken aback to see that her savior was a tall, elegantly dressed Spaniard in a claw-hammer tailed frock coat of mulberry-colored velvet with black satin breeches and vest. He had probably just exited from Don Almonester's house, the huge mansion extending along one side of the plaza where the governor and the city council were temporarily holding most of their meetings until adequate chambers for the Most Illustrious Cabildo would be ready.

"Oh, no, monsieur, that's not true!" she exclaimed, the spots in her cheeks burning redder than ever as her large gray eyes widened in dismay at the drunken boatman's words. "I assure you we did nothing—"

"Say no more," the stranger bade her with a wave of his long, discreetly cuffed hand. "I can see the situation at a glance, although what possible reason such ruffians could have for molesting children in the street, I can't for the life of me understand." He turned contemptuously to the two men once more.

"Surely, senores, you can find wenches more suited to your needs in any tavern or bawdy house. From what they tell me, the town abounds with them."

Monique didn't especially appreciate the reference to her and her sister as "children," but she was in no mood to quibble over the point. She tried again to pull herself free from the boatman's grip, and this time he offered no resistance.

"Now don't go getting your dander up, *seenyour*," the older riverman ventured sheepishly. "We was under the wrong impression, that's all."

"That's right," echoed the younger man, releasing Celeste's arm of his own accord. "You can't blame us for thinking the wenches was out looking for some fun. After all, they was running around loose here like they wanted someone to come on to them."

The dark-eyed young Spaniard gave them such a glaring look that they quickly decided to withdraw any further protestations of innocence.

"All right, all right, sir, we'll be on our way," the older man assured him, tugging at the sleeve of his partner to leave with him. "Our apologies, ladies. No offense meant. We only wanted to show you a good time. Come on, Will, there's nothing here for us. Let's go to the Maison Coquet. We'll be more appreciated there."

For a moment Monique and Celeste stood there beside their unexpected deliverer, watching the two flatboatmen walk rather unsteadily across the square and disappear into a cluster of people standing near the river side of the plaza.

Monique was trying to think of some appropriate words of gratitude to say to the stranger, but before she could speak, he had turned back to her and, with the easy bow of one accustomed to such courtly manners, removed his high-crowned black beaver hat and addressed them. "And now, little ladies, if you'll tell me where you last saw your chaperon, I'll be glad to help you find her. She must be looking frantically for you by now."

The two girls lowered their eyes in confusion. For a moment they could only stammer, feeling suddenly very young and foolish.

Monique was the first to regain her aplomb. "Oh, we're not lost, monsieur," she replied, deciding to brazen it out as best she could. "We live only a few blocks from here, on the Rue Royale just past Dumaine Street."

The Spaniard narrowed his dark eyes and scrutinized her more closely. "Then those men spoke the truth. You really are unaccompanied. You were . . . as they so aptly put it . . . running around loose?"

"We were doing no such thing!" protested Monique indignantly. "That is, it's not the way they made it sound. We only wanted to see the marionettes. Then we would have gone right back home. After all, we're not *children!*"

The tall, ebony-haired stranger kept a stony, disapproving look on his lean face, but a faint twinkle flickered momentarily in the depths of his dark eyes.

"Indeed? Well, permit me, then, to accompany you to your home. I didn't realize things were so lax in the colonies, but then I'm newly arrived here. Where I come from a lady doesn't go about unaccompanied, especially not to the plaza!"

"But we're not really unaccompanied," insisted Monique with a firm set to her fleshy little mouth. "After all, my sister and I are accompanying each other, aren't we?"

The twinkle flashed again in the Spaniard's eyes as he bowed. "Very well . . . if you say so," he acquiesced. "And now, if you'll show me where you live . . ."

He offered them each an arm, but Monique hung back hesitantly. She dreaded arriving home escorted by someone who might call attention to the fact that she and Celeste had been out. She had hoped they could sneak back in through the carriage entrance without anyone's being the wiser.

"Please don't bother," she said, giving him her most gracious smile. "We've already caused you enough trouble. We can return home all right. Thank you, sir."

"It's no trouble at all," he assured her politely. "My own destination is on the Rue Royale. Perhaps you'd be so kind as to direct me to where I'm going once I leave you and your sister off at your home?"

Monique cast a reluctant glance in the direction of the still-performing marionettes and, with a sigh of resignation, accepted his proffered arm, whereupon Celeste, following suit, took the other.

But they had no sooner turned to go toward the Rue Royale than they nearly collided with the dark, silent form of a hooded Capuchin monk. Monique recognized him at once as Padre Sebastian and realized uneasily that he had probably been standing nearby all the while observing the whole incident.

"By your leave," began the monk, his clasped hands lost in the loose folds of his long sleeves, his wizened face barely visible in the shadowy recess between the peak of his hood and his equally pointed beard. "I've been watching these two young girls for several minutes now, curious to see just how far their brazenness would lead them astray," came the monk's acrid voice from out of the dark hollow of his hood—a voice so dry that it seemed about to break off at any moment from the very brittleness of it. "I was just about to intervene when you, like the gentleman you obviously are, stepped in and put an end to such scandalous goings-on."

"It was a simple matter, Padre," replied the stranger politely. "They were molesting these young ladies, so I sent them on their way."

"We're going home now, Padre," Monique quickly assured the monk.

The Capuchin turned toward her, and although she couldn't see his face clearly since he was standing with his back to the sun, she could feel the accusation in his gaze. "I can't help wondering what you and your sister were doing here on the square without a chaperon in the first place," he admonished sharply. "Looking for mischief, I daresay!"

"Oh, no, Padre," exclaimed Monique in dismay. "It was all perfectly innocent, I assure you."

"We only wanted to see the marionettes," ventured Celeste timidly.

"It's not enough to shun evil," cautioned the friar. "One should avoid the appearance of it, as well."

Monique hung her golden head, and the frilly little white parasol on her shoulder drooped, too.

"Yes, Padre, we realize now how wrong we were to have come out alone as we did," she admitted. "But it was as my sister says. We wanted to see the puppet show, that was all."

"And meanwhile you are letting the devil make puppets of you!" scolded the Capuchin mercilessly.

The Spanish gentleman felt the poor girls had suffered enough and came to their rescue a second time. "I promise they won't get into any more mischief today, Padre," he assured the priest. "My own business takes me to Royal Street, so I will personally escort the senoritas to their home if you have no objections."

The monk hesitated, while Monique squirmed uncomfortably.

The young man, sensing the monk's vacillation, continued. "Permit me to introduce myself, Padre. I'm Miguel Vidal de la Fuente, at your service. I arrived in *Nuēva Orleans* only a couple of hours ago on the *María de la Concepción,* but I'll probably be making my home here for a while. I've just come from presenting my credentials to His Excellency the Governor."

The monk stepped back, obviously impressed. "A pleasure to meet you, Don Miguel. Welcome to our humble city. I see that the señoritas are in good hands. Don't hesitate to call on me if you should ever have need of the Holy Church in the colony. Just ask for Padre Sebastian Montez de Barcelona. I'm at your service."

He cast a scathing glance once more toward the two blushing sinners and added, "As for you, girls, I'll speak to your grandmother about this incident at mass. For now, go with God." He made a sweeping sign of the cross over their bowed heads.

Then, with a second benediction for the aristocratic young Spaniard, he directed his parting words to the latter. "I hope to see you attending our church services while you are here in the city, sir. Meanwhile, God be with you."

Vidal and the two girls stood there staring after the monk as he moved silently across the flagstones of the plaza in his bare sandaled feet and disappeared into the crowd. It took them a moment to recover from the impact of that strangely phantom-like presence, but finally the aristocratic Spaniard turned his attention back to his bewildered young companions.

"And now, ladies, if you'll be so kind as to show

me the way . . ." He offered them each a velvet-sleeved arm once more, and without further objections they allowed him to escort them from the plaza and over to Rue Royale, only a block away behind the cathedral.

As they neared an attractive little white two-story house, Monique paused. She hoped she could be rid of their solicitous escort without having to alert the entire household to their arrival.

"This is where we live," she told him. "We'll be all right now, sir. . . . Did you say your name was de la Fuente? I'm sorry, but I was so upset before . . . I don't believe I caught your full name."

She extended her hand toward him in her most ladylike manner. "My sister and I are eternally grateful to you for your timely intervention on our behalf today. I assure you, you'll be remembered in our prayers tonight."

He gave her a polite bow and quickly replied, "Miguel Vidal y de la Fuente, ladies, at your feet."

"Vidal?" she echoed with arched brows. "My late aunt married a Vidal. Perhaps you know the family? She and my uncle lived in Madrid, and I understand they were quite well known there until their untimely death in a boating accident a couple of years ago. My uncle's name was Roberto Vidal y Flores."

The Spaniard was taken aback.

"By all the saints! But I think you're speaking of my father!" Disbelief bathed his angular face. "Your aunt . . . what was her name? By any chance, was it Isabella?"

"Isabelle Chausson, my father's sister."

"And my stepmother! It's incredible!" A flood of rapid Spanish surged to his lips and he spoke excitedly, his dark eyes glowing with emotion, until he saw the looks of bewilderment on the two young faces and realized they didn't understand a word he had been saying. With a smile he continued a little more slowly in French. "I'm sure you're speaking of my poor dear stepmother," he explained. "Now tell me, little ones, do you have a grandmother by the name of Madame Aimee Chausson?"

Now it was the young girls' turn to be taken by surprise.

"Why, yes," replied Monique confusedly. "That's Grandmother!"

"Then this . . . this, I suppose, is the Chausson residence?"

"Yes."

"The saints be praised! Then you have unwittingly led me to my destination, for I have come to New Orleans specifically to see Dona Aimee!"

The three of them stood there in front of the entrance to the whitewashed house in the shadow of the iron-lace balcony hanging above them, staring at one another with mouths agape.

"Then . . . then we are . . . in a manner of speaking . . ." Monique was still unable to digest the unexpected development and its implications completely.

"Yes, we're cousins!" Vidal assured her. "You, your little sister here, and I are cousins. At least we are by law, and although I'm Roberto Vidal's son by his first marriage, your aunt was really the only mother I ever knew, bless her. But please, take me to your grandmother at once. There's no need for us to be standing here in the street, is there? Take me to Dona Aimee, little cousins . . . my pretty little cousins!" He threw back his dark handsome head and burst out laughing as the humor of the situation struck him.

Monique and Celeste watched in bewilderment as he took the huge brass knocker in his hand and sounded it against the large oak door. Then they stood there, continuing to stare at one another in amazement while they waited for someone to come let them in.

Chapter Three

THE ARRIVAL OF DON MIGUEL VIDAL DE LA FUENTE from Madrid had taken the Chausson town house so by surprise that Monique and Celeste's escapade earlier that afternoon would be soon forgotten.

Fortunately Vidal had thought it prudent to skim lightly over the girls' disagreeable encounter with the rivermen so as not to upset their grandmother.

"You can see for yourself, Miguel, just how desperate the situation is here these days!" she exclaimed as she ordered her abashed granddaughters to their room so she could continue talking to her late daughter's stepson in private.

Monique and Celeste were beside themselves with curiosity, but they obediently went to the upstairs bedchamber they shared. Confused by the latest developments, they sat apprehensively on the side of one of the two four-poster beds in the room, trying to analyze what it all might mean.

"I can't understand why Grandmother never said anything about a cousin from Spain coming here," mused Monique. "Yet from the way she received him, it's obvious she invited him."

Celeste seemed not only ready to accept Miguel Vidal as a member of the family but to be rather pleased with the prospect.

"It might not be so bad to have him as a cousin,"

she observed, more dreamy-eyed than ever. "He's quite handsome, don't you think?"

Monique tossed her head nonchalantly. "I hadn't noticed. I suppose he is . . . for a Spaniard, that is," she conceded halfheartedly.

"You can't say it wasn't very gallant of him to come up and chase those horrid men away from us with his sword," said the young girl as she smoothed over her golden-brown curls and puffed out her fichu just a little more.

"Yes, but did you hear the way he called us children?" Monique reminded her indignantly. Then, after a moment's thought, she added, "How old do you think he is?"

"Oh, I don't think he's middle-aged yet. Cousin Miguel can't be more than twenty-seven or so."

"Don't call him cousin! He's not really any relation of ours," chided Monique, annoyed with even the idea that they could be related to a Spaniard.

"I rather like him," insisted Celeste. "After all, he tried to soften things for us with Grandmother. He could have told her a lot more than he did, you know, and we'd be in worse trouble now if he had!"

"Yes, he has been unusually kind, especially when you consider where he's from."

"There you go again!" scolded Celeste. "Just because the man is Spanish and not French . . ."

"You're too young to remember all the things Mama used to tell us about what those horrid Spaniards did when they took over this colony, but I can," Monique declared, her gray eyes suddenly flashing sparks of flint. "That monster—that Spanish mercenary O'Reilly—used trickery to trap our grandfather and those other French patriots. He promised them amnesty if they surrendered, and then, once they came out into the open to make their peace, O'Reilly had the leaders shot or sent to prison. So much for taking Spaniards at their word!"

"Actually, O'Reilly wasn't Spanish. He was Irish," ventured Celeste timidly.

"But he was acting on orders from Madrid, and came with two thousand Spanish troops! Thanks to him, Mama's father died!"

"At least he wasn't among those executed," sighed Celeste. "He was finally pardoned and released, wasn't he?"

"A lot of good that did!" snapped Monique angrily. "After those horrid Spanish dungeons in Havana, he came out a broken man and died only a few weeks after he returned home. They killed him just as much as if they had stood him up against the wall and shot him. Believe me, our family has good reason to hate them!"

"But all that happened so long ago," sighed Celeste. "The governors we've had since then—at least the ones we can remember—have been good."

Monique gave an exasperated shrug of her shoulders. "You're just too young to understand such things, Celeste. New Orleans is French, and the Spaniards have no right to be here in the first place. Now that Spain and France are at war, that even makes us enemies! Didn't you see those leaflets Maurice gave me, the ones calling on the citizens of Louisiana to overthrow the Spanish government? You should read them."

"Oh, Monique, it's all to complicated for me!" exclaimed Celeste, shaking her dark blond head wearily. "Only the good Lord knows how it will all end! But meanwhile, Cousin Miguel is here, and I think we should try to remember he's Aunt Isabelle's stepson and treat him as part of the family, which I'm sure is the way she would have wished us to receive him."

"I remember only too well how Mama always lamented Aunt Isabelle's poor taste in not only choosing a Spaniard for a husband, but one who was a widower with a child, as well!" Monique replied. "Papa wasn't too pleased, either, about his only sister having married a Spaniard and gone off to live in Madrid like that."

"Oh, well, all of that happened before we were even born," observed Celeste. "Neither of us really knew Aunt Isabelle or Uncle Roberto, anyway."

"Exactly, so why should we be so quick to receive their son with open arms? After all, what do we really know about him?"

Celeste sighed again. At least what she did know, she liked, but she knew better than to argue with her sister.

They must have been sitting there talking for over an hour before a knock sounded on the door and one of the housemaids announced that she had been sent to call the girls back down to the parlor.

"And your grandma says not to dally," the pert young Negress cautioned them. "She's waiting there to see you with that elegant Spanish gent who came in with you."

The girls rose nervously and, hastily smoothing their multiple skirts over their little bustle pads, descended the polished oak staircase with mounting apprehension, fearful that a second, more severe scolding still awaited them for their recent mischief.

As they entered the parlor, they found their grandmother seated in her favorite upholstered chair finishing a cup of hot chocolate, while Miguel Vidal sat on one of the red velvet couches sipping a glass of claret and instructing the houseboy to go to the

docks with a note for the captain of the newly
arrived *María de la Concepción*.

"You are to show the men how to get here with my
luggage," Vidal was saying as he handed a sealed
envelope to the little black boy.

On seeing his young cousins entering, Vidal quickly gave his messenger a few final words and rose to
greet them.

"Ah, my charming little cousins," he saluted them
pleasantly but said nothing more.

Aimee Chausson, in black silk frosted with snowy
linen, lifted her white-capped head and motioned to
the girls to draw nearer.

"My dears, I'll come directly to the point," she
said with an obviously contented smile on her broad,
benign countenance. "I sent for your cousin Miguel
to come to New Orleans because I want him to take
over the management of our affairs from now on, or
at least until you become of age or marry and are
able to look out for yourselves."

For a moment there was silence in the sun-
speckled parlor, while the still-bright light of the
lengthening spring day filtered in cheerfully through
the open shutters and the two young girls stood there
staring bewilderedly at their grandmother and their
newly discovered cousin.

Finally Monique found her voice. "But, Grandmother, we've been managing well enough without
any help until now, haven't we? Why have you
suddenly asked someone who is really a stranger to
us to come here and handle our affairs?" She turned
quickly to Miguel, flushing a little as she realized he
might take offense at her words. "Please, I mean no
discredit to you," she assured him. "It's only that,
despite the fact that we're cousins, we're really not

blood relatives. Why, we'd never even met until today!"

A faint smile flickered across Vidal's face as he nodded in agreement. "What you say is quite true. That same fact has also occurred to me, I assure you."

"Be that as it may," continued Aimee Chausson, waving aside their verbal exchange, "after weighing the circumstances very carefully and consulting with your late father's attorney, I have appointed your cousin to be your curator—that is, for all practical purposes, your guardian. You and Celeste may not know Miguel, but I have heard much of him over the years from your Aunt Isabelle's letters, and, of course, the lawyers who handled your father's will made investigations as well, so I can assure you that your cousin is a fine, upright gentleman of impeccable reputation whom I trust completely. If it were otherwise, I would have never turned your guardianship over to him."

Monique was more confused than ever. "But, Grandmother, you . . . you are our guardian. Don't you want to take care of Celeste and me anymore?"

"Of course, my dear, I'll still be here—at least for as long as the good Lord permits me to linger," the elderly woman assured her with a tender smile. "But I need . . . we need the help of a man . . ."

Vidal continued to stand beside the wing-back chair, prudently silent as he fixed his dark eyes deliberately on the rim of his wineglass. He had anticipated this moment might be difficult, and for a moment he regretted having let himself be wheedled into such an awkward position.

"But why . . . why?" Monique persisted, still vigorously rejecting the idea. "If we have you to care

for us, Grandmother, why should we need anyone
else? If it's because you're vexed with me, I promise
I'll be good. But please, don't turn us over to
someone else. We love you, Grandmother, truly we
do!''

Suddenly a sob escaped Celeste's lips as a horrible
thought occurred to her. "Merciful heavens! Are
you ill? Are you going to . . . to . . .?" Panic filled
the young girl's hazel eyes, and she didn't dare put
her fears into words.

Grandmother Chausson began to laugh, but tears
were also glistening in her pale blue eyes. "Ah, my
dear sweet girls!" she exclaimed. "Bless you for
caring! But don't worry, little ones, I'm not expect-
ing to leave you for quite a while. To the contrary,
with the peace of mind that Miguel's presence will
give me, I hope to live on to a ripe old age. Now,
now, my dears, stop crying. Come here and let me
give you each a hug and a kiss. There, my little ones,
everything is all right. Don't fret.''

With a rustling flutter of colorful skirts, the girls
ran over to their grandmother and sank down beside
her in a sea of billowing muslin and taffeta while the
elderly woman affectionately patted their pretty
young faces.

Vidal shifted uneasily behind the chair and turned
aside to drain the last drops of wine from his glass.

"Now listen to me carefully, you silly geese,"
Aimee Chausson continued. "As your guardian, I
have a right to delegate my responsibilities to someone who I feel might do a better job than I can of
looking after you and your inheritance. The task is
simply too much for a poor inexperienced old
woman like me. This household needs the firm hand
of a man at its helm, and I thank God we're

fortunate enough to have someone like Miguel in the family to help see us through this difficult period."

But Monique was still having trouble digesting the news. This stranger—and a Spaniard, besides!—was to be Celeste's and her guardian! Curator ad bona . . . tutor . . . judges . . . lawyers . . . yearly accountings . . . Aimee Chausson was explaining some of the official details, but Monique was too angry to hear, much less understand, all her grandmother was saying. She was still trying to absorb just one bare fact: Miguel Vidal was going to be controlling her life from there on out, and she didn't like the prospect at all!

Chapter Four

"BELIEVE ME, MY DEARS, I THOUGHT ALL THIS OVER very carefully before I contacted your cousin," Aimee Chausson went on. "After all, this is a big step for Miguel to take, too—to leave his life of ease and plenty in Madrid to come here to what must seem like a very primitive land to him and take on the burden of a failing plantation and two mischievous young girls. I'm sure he hesitated considerably before deciding to accept my pleas to come to New Orleans."

From where she still knelt beside her grandmother, Monique cast a quizzical look up at the tall, silent figure standing beside the large upholstered chair, and Vidal couldn't help but catch the martial look in her eyes.

"I confess I've accepted this chore that Dona Aimee has thrust on me with some reservations," he admitted, deciding to speak at last. "Frankly, the idea doesn't appeal to me any more than it does to you and your sister. But, in all conscience, I could hardly refuse, once I knew the predicament you were in, knowing that I was the only person in the family to whom your grandmother—our grandmother—could turn to in her hour of need."

He came forward as he spoke and, setting his empty glass down on the serving table, sat on the couch once more, while he continued in a well-modulated voice, his perfect French only tinged with the dulcet tones of his native Castilian. "I think you should know that I really feel much more a part of your family than you might imagine under the circumstances," he explained, his eyes softening as he looked down at his distraught cousins, who seemed so small and unhappy at their grandmother's knee. "You see, my mother died giving me birth, so your Aunt Isabella really filled a very important niche in my life. When my father remarried, I was only seven or eight years old, and until that time my mother's family, the de la Fuentes of Cadiz, had been rather inadequately trying to care for me. I'll never forget that first day I arrived at my father's villa . . . how my stepmother took me in her arms and welcomed me 'home' . . . that was the way she put it, and that was the way she made me feel it was from that moment on. I soon came to look on her as my real mother, for we couldn't have been closer had she given me birth from her own womb. So you see, although we may not be blood cousins, I assure you I feel a true bond with my stepmother and her family and will try to fulfill my obligations to you to the best of my ability, as I know she would have wanted me to do, and as I myself would like to do in memory of the woman who did so much for me."

For a moment the ring of sincerity in his voice disarmed Monique, and some of the hostility in her eyes melted.

"But . . . but Le Rêve has been getting along well enough all this time with the overseer who has been running it since before Father died," she ventured, a little more defensively now than belligerently. "He should know what to do, shouldn't he?"

Vidal smiled patiently from the sofa. "My dear child, no matter how good an overseer your man might be, he is still only hired help and needs someone to make the important decisions for him," he reminded her. "From what I understand, your plantation, which is called Le Rêve—The Dream, is that right?—is really more of a nightmare for you these days, now that the place has lost its indigo crops for two years running and is in danger of losing another one this year."

"But what experience have you had in such matters?" asked Monique challengingly. "I didn't know they had plantations like ours in Madrid."

"Don't be impertinent!" scolded her grandmother, nudging the softly rounded little arm resting on her knee.

"No, senora," interrupted Vidal. "Don't be annoyed with her. The girl is intelligent and does well to ask questions. After all, I have been appointed to look after her affairs. She has a right to know the facts."

He turned again to Monique. "I confess I know very little about plantations, little cousin, especially the sort they have in these parts," he continued. "But after a few weeks of intense investigation and consultation with those who *do* know, I hope I'll be able to make some reasonable decisions about what ought to be done to try to save your property."

Celeste smiled approvingly at her new guardian. "I trust you, Cousin Miguel," she said shyly. Then she looked at her sister across their grandmother's knees. "I think we should give him our support, Monique. He has a difficult job ahead of him and will need all the help we can give him."

"Well said, little one" declared Aimee Chausson with an approving pat on her granddaughter's honey-colored curls. "You girls should be grateful to Miguel for taking on so thankless a task. Most of the

planters here have been having a run of bad luck
lately with their crops. We're not the only ones in
difficulties these days."

"I suppose we do need a man to help us out with
the plantation," conceded Monique at last, rising
agilely from the midst of her frothy pink and white
skirts and leaning lightly against the arm of her
grandmother's chair. "And you can count on our
cooperation . . . and gratitude, as well . . . if you're
successful in taking that burden off grandmother's
shoulders, at least until my sister and I become of
age and are in a better position to take such matters
in hand ourselves."

"I'm happy to hear you are agreeable to my being
your curator," Vidal said with a smile. "I hope I can
expect the same cooperation from you and your
sister concerning my authority over your personal
welfare as well."

Monique was taken aback. "What . . . what do
you mean? Is there more?" She looked down questioningly at her grandmother sitting beside her.

"Yes, my dear," the latter replied quickly. "I
thought you understood what I was explaining to
you. Your cousin Miguel is your legal guardian now.
You and Celeste should accept his authority in *all*
things. I'm still in the picture, of course, and I'm
sure he will always take my wishes into consideration, but I have asked him to be your guardian in the
full sense of the word, for not only are you both
sorely in need of discipline, but you also should have
more protection than I, as a poor aging matron, can
possibly give you."

Vidal had listened attentively. "Frankly, when
you wrote and explained your situation to me, Dona
Aimee, I didn't realize the two orphaned grandchildren you were talking about were quite as grown up

as they are. I pictured younger girls—not young ladies old enough to be courted. Be that as it may, if I'm to be responsible for them, I'll have to insist that they obey me in what I say. I'll try not to make my guardianship weigh too heavily, but I must lay down certain rules. I'm sure you understand."

"Rules?" interrupted Monique, a martial look creeping into her eyes.

He turned sternly to her. "Yes, little cousin, rules. To begin with, there will be no more leaving this house without either your grandmother's or my permission. Under no circumstances will I ever consent to your running around the streets without a chaperon—a chaperon of my approval, I might add."

"Mon Dieu! We may as well go to a convent!" Monique exclaimed, while Celeste stood by in tragic silence.

"I'd hardly go so far as to say that," Vidal hastily assured them. "You can count on a reasonable amount of diversion. Since you seem to like puppet shows so much, perhaps you would enjoy an evening at a real theater. When I asked the governor what there was to do for entertainment here in New Orleans, he told me there was a new theater in the city, still in its formative stages but featuring a few actors from the Cap-Français. Give me a week or two to get settled, and I'll take you and your sister—and your grandmother, too, of course—to one of their performances."

He turned quickly to Madame Chausson. "That is, if it meets with your approval, Dona Aimee," he added politely.

The elderly woman nodded her white-capped head approvingly but held up a detaining hand before he could continue. "I'll be glad to see the girls going out so well protected," she replied, "and perhaps if they have more social life they'll be less restless, but please don't include me in such plans. It's too much trouble to climb into my stays and bustle and get all dressed up and coiffured just for a few hours of distraction. Young girls love taking all day to ready themselves for such outings, but I'm beyond that point, thank you."

Vidal smiled understandingly and turned back to his two wards. "Then I hope I'll at least have the pleasure of your company, little ladies?" he said in his most gallant manner.

"Oh, yes!" exclaimed Celeste quickly, her hazel eyes already aglow at the prospect.

Monique, however, was a little less enthusiastic. "I suppose anything would be better than staying home," she acquiesced begrudgingly.

Celeste shook her head disapprovingly in one of those rare moments of annoyance with her older sister.

"Now, Monique, don't be a bore," she chided. "You know very well how you were wishing only the other day that we could find some way to go to the new theater."

Monique flushed crimson. "Hush Celeste!" she scolded crossly. "You know it's unmaidenly to accept a gentleman's invitation too eagerly."

Vidal's eyes remained impassive, but the corners of his mouth were tugging despite his efforts to control them. "I'm happy to see you are making some attempt to behave like a well-bred young lady, my little cousin," he said smoothly. "For a moment I almost mistook your ladylike acceptance of my invitation as a refusal."

Monique shifted uneasily beneath those dark, enigmatic eyes. Although he seemed as unperturbed as ever, she had the disagreeable feeling that he was secretly laughing at her.

"My granddaughters sorely need a governess," sighed Madame Chausson, "but since Mlle. Fortier left us, I haven't been able to find a suitable replacement. I do the best I can with them, but I confess they are getting to be too much for me. They need a younger, more energetic woman to keep up with them and teach them the niceties of social behavior. The poor dears have been without a mother these past six years, and their *gardienne*—old Zizi, who had been their nanny since they were born—died about a year or so ago."

"Don't fret yourself, senora," Vidal consoled her. "The first thing tomorrow morning I'll begin looking for some suitable woman to hire as governess for the girls."

Monique's indignation finally exploded. "Really, Grandmother, I hardly need a governess anymore!" she protested. "I could already add and subtract twice as fast as Mlle. Fortier could by the time she left us, and, as you know, I can read and write fluently in both French and Latin."

Grandmother Chausson smiled and turned momentarily to Miguel. "Monique really is well versed," she told him proudly. "The child has always devoured every book she can get her hands on, and I'm sure she can hold her own with most of the learned men of the colony."

She turned then to Monique. "But there are always new things a governess can teach you, my dear. Under the circumstances, it wouldn't hurt you to learn to speak Spanish better, for example, and although you play the harpsichord very well, I'm sure one never really reaches perfection in such things. But most of all, as I said before, there are still so many more things you should be learning social-ly."

Vidal immediately seconded her.

"Your grandmother is right, Monica. Besides, Celeste undoubtedly still needs some instruction in scholarly things, and if we only hired a companion for you, the woman might not be well versed enough to serve as governess for your sister. On the other hand, a governess can always serve as a companion."

"But a governess! Why, many women my age are already married and have one or two children, and here we are talking about a governess for me!"

"You may refer to her any way you wish— governess or companion, it's all the same to me—but you're never too old to learn, and at any age you're going to need a chaperon, so enough said on the subject. That's my decision, and if I'm to be your guardian, I'll have to ask you to abide by it."

Monique's stubby nose crinkled up as her brow lowered to meet it in a disapproving frown. Things were taking a very unpleasant turn, indeed!

Chapter Five

IN THE DAYS THAT FOLLOWED, MONIQUE CHAFED under what she repeatedly referred to as "the Spanish yoke," which she declared weighed down not only on the Louisiana colony but on her own shoulders now as well.

After having been under little or no restrictions for so long, it was difficult to have to yield suddenly to another will—a will that she was discovering with each passing day was as strong as or stronger than her own.

From the very beginning, her cousin took charge with the air of one accustomed to exerting authority and who expected to be obeyed. Although he was not nearly so tyrannical and heartless as Monique made him out to be, Vidal did put a closer rein on his restless little wards and, living up to his word, would not tolerate their leaving the premises unless they were well chaperoned.

On more than one occasion Monique angrily accused him of setting the servants to "spying" on her, but he simply gave that maddening half-smile of his and admitted he had indeed ordered them to "keep an eye on her."

Late that first day and all the following morning, there had been a steady stream of traveling trunks and crates coming into the town house from the *María de la Concepción*, which the new head of the

36

Chausson family had immediately set about unpacking with the help of the Negro servants.

The upstairs front bedroom, which had been kept locked off from the rest of the house since Louis Chausson's death six months before, had been reopened for Vidal. It seemed strange to Monique to go past its door and catch glimpses of her cousin's personal belongings strewn about amid the familiar furnishings that had once been her father's.

Cousin Miguel also had a few pleasant surprises for his new family. One of the first trunks he had unpacked from among the mountain of suitcases and trunks he had brought with him produced a colorful array of gaily embroidered white fringed shawls and a wide assortment of black lace mantillas, from the tiny triangular headscarfs for church to the regal full-length ones to be worn on more festive occasions.

Celeste and her grandmother were delighted, and even Monique had to admit somewhat reluctantly that her guardian had exquisite taste, but she was certainly far from ready to relinquish the misgivings she still felt about him and the entire arrangement.

As for Cousin Miguel, he might have found many aspects of his new position not to his liking, but if he did, he kept his feelings to himself, going about his new responsibilities in his characteristically unruffled manner. It seemed as though, having once decided to take on the management of the Chausson affairs, he was determined to do so as efficiently as possible. He might have missed the pomp and glitter of his former life in Madrid, but he also seemed to find the challenge of his new life rather invigorating.

He spent much of his time going around town

getting to know its prominant citizens as well as the geographical terrain of the region. By the end of his first week, he probably knew more about the city than the residents themselves did. What's more, because of the lofty position he had held in Madrid society, the doors of New Orleans were readily opened to him wherever he went, and when he asked questions, he usually received answers.

Before that first week there was out, he had also paid a two-day visit to the Chausson plantation, but on his return, he had had little to say except that he was afraid the worms were going to get the indigo crops in the colony again that year. Whenever the women asked him what he thought should be done to save the plantation, however, he simply replied it was too soon to come to any conclusions and either changed the subject or sank into a pensive mood.

On more than one occasion Monique and her new guardian had their clashes. They especially had a confrontation the day he returned from the plantation and caught her trying to sneak out, as was her custom, through the carriage entrance just as he was entering the courtyard on horseback.

"And where might you be going, my little cousin?" he asked tartly as he dismounted his mare and turned it over to the stableboy.

Monique tossed her pale gold mane defiantly as she glared back at him. "I was only going as far as the gate," she replied, making no effort to hide her annoyance.

"And do you have your grandmother's permission?" He stood there towering above her as he tapped his riding crop impatiently against the top of his black leather boots and waited for her to think of a suitable reply. "Of course you don't," he finally answered for her, "for why would you be sneaking out of the entrance to the stables if you did?"

"But you weren't here to ask, and grandmother is sleeping," she retorted defensively. "What should I do under such circumstances?"

"Well, in the future if I'm not around, you will simply have to decide whether your reasons for wanting to go out are important enough to awaken your grandmother to ask her for permission or not. If they aren't, then just stay home and find something else to do."

With an exasperated sigh, Monique spun around on her heelless slipper of pale blue satin and began to walk back across the palmetto-lined patio.

"It's so boring to be locked up in the house all the time!" she flung back at him, pausing momentarily by the little brick well, as though dreading returning inside.

"Well, all of that will soon change," he assured her. "Come Monday, you'll have a governess to keep you busy once more. I just hired one for you and your sister today on the way back from the plantation."

Vidal looked at her standing there bareheaded in the bright daylight. How dazzling her hair was in the sun, he thought. And that shapely little doll mouth of hers between a pout and a dimpled smile, just begging to be kissed. He wondered whether she had ever been kissed . . . really kissed, the way a man kisses a woman. How he would love to savor the taste of that fleshy little lower lip and probe into the sweet recesses beyond to meet the tip of that saucy little tongue!

He caught himself quickly. What was wrong with him? He knew better than to think such things about, of all people, his ward! Besides, despite her pleasingly rounded little figure, it was evident she was still more of a child than a woman. He was annoyed with himself for having thought of her in such a way even for a moment.

Suddenly he remembered the way those ruffians had looked at her that day on the square, and the memory chilled him. The girl might still be a child, but she was certainly highly desirable. Unfortunately, she didn't seem to have the slightest idea of how much just the sight of her could rouse a man. He felt a sudden urge to protect her. He must think of her and Celeste as the sisters he had never had. . . .

"Just a minute, Monica," he called after her as she continued now to walk on ahead of him toward the house that embraced the patio from three sides.

Pausing, she looked at him in surprise.

"Come, sit here for a moment," he invited, motioning toward the bench beneath the shade of the tree. "I'd like to talk to you."

She hesitated, the petticoats beneath her light blue muslin skirts still swaying from the rhythm of her gait.

"Please, little cousin," he insisted, his voice taking on a less impersonal tone than usual.

Reluctantly she sank down on the bench, her dress billowing about her, leaving little room for him to sit beside her, but he didn't seem to mind. He came nearer and, removing his high-crowned felt hat, he rested a booted foot on the partially exposed edge of the bench and stood there looking down curiously at her.

For a moment, as his eyes lingered on the fullness of those firm young breasts rising up beyond the ruffling that edged the deep square neckline of her dress, he found it difficult to continue thinking of her as his ward. Despite himself, he could feel the desire suddenly rushing through his veins and swelling to a burning hardness that he knew could not be fulfilled. *Qué barbaridad!* He'd have to tell the new governess to see to it that the girl cover herself more. . . .

Monique lowered her lashes, feeling suddenly self-conscious beneath his penetrating gaze. She prepared herself for another scolding.

But when he spoke there was a gentleness in his voice she had never heard before. "Now tell me, little cousin, why are you so bored? I was an only child, and I confess I sometimes missed the company of a brother or sister with whom to while away the hours. But you at least have Celeste. What's she doing now? Is she so bored, too?"

"No, I don't think so. She's working on her sampler."

"And don't you have something like that to work on, too?"

Monique puckered up her tiny nose. "Of course, but I'm not especially fond of needlepoint."

"I see." Vidal smiled sympathetically. "But there must be other things you could do. How do young ladies your age usually pass your leisure time? Your grandmother said you liked to read, didn't she?"

"I was reading to Grandmother when she fell asleep."

"But what do you personally like to read?"

"Just about anything, but I especially like the new French philosophers, and, of course, I've read some of Molière's plays and . . . and translations of one or two Shakespeare works, as well."

"My! That's commendable, and heavy reading for

one so young. I had no idea a girl your age could be interested in such things."

"Perhaps I'm not as much the child you think I am," she retorted, tilting her upturned nose even higher. "Oh, of course, I like the romantic novels, too," she added quickly, "but I seldom get to read any, since Grandmother doesn't care for them, and Mlle. Fortier, our former governess, used to forbid Celeste and me to read them. She said they filled young girls' heads with silly notions."

Vidal looked at the drooping head of pale gold ringlets and chuckled. "Well, we'll have to see what we can arrange for you with your new governess—or, if you prefer, companion—when she begins next week," he promised. "But surely there must be something you enjoy doing—I mean really enjoy. It's a calamity to be only seventeen and already so bored with the world!"

Monique was pensive for a moment. "I . . . I used to like to play the harpsichord," she confessed at last. "People said I was rather good at it."

"Used to? Don't you play anymore?"

"Not very much since we lost the one we had here in the fire. Of course, there's still one at the plantation, but we only go there a couple of months in the summer, that's all."

"Well, I'll have to see about getting another one for the town house, or have the one at the plantation brought down to New Orleans whenever you're here," he told her.

"When the town house was finally rebuilt and we began to stay here again in the winters, Papa promised to get me another one, but then the crops started going bad, and I hated to keep bothering him about it."

"Well, I think we can find a way of getting you a

harpsichord for here at the town house, too. Would you like that?"

She lifted her head, and at that moment her eyes seemed like a pair of enormous aquamarines as they reflected the pale blue of her gown with its wide satin sash and large flounce running around the edge of the skirt.

"Oh, yes, I would . . . I . . ." But the impact of his direct gaze suddenly inhibited her, and she immediately lowered her lids once more. She was annoyed with herself for letting this enigmatic guardian of hers affect her so. Her thoughts were always so confused when she was near him. "Yes, that would be nice," she concluded lamely and fell into an uneasy silence.

"And I haven't forgotten my promise to take you and your sister to the theater, either," Vidal continued, hoping he could put their relationship on a more friendly basis. "If I get good reports from your governess about you, I'll take you the end of next week."

"That would be nice," Monique repeated as she shifted self-consciously on the bench, acutely aware of his nearness as he bent his knee and leaned forward slightly on his booted foot and a disturbing masculine scent of tobacco and lavender tickled her nostrils. It was a pleasant odor, strangely appealing. Celeste had been right to call him handsome, and he was especially so in his brown riding habit, with the tousled locks of his blue-black hair cut stylishly short about his face and the slightly longer back neatly braided with a black ribbon into a short queue at the nape of his neck. It was difficult to continue hating someone who had brought her such lovely gifts, had just promised to buy her a new harpsichord, and was going to take her to the theater!

But suddenly she felt guilty, as though she were betraying the memory of her mother. She could well imagine what Eugenie Chausson would have said at that moment. The latter would have called Miguel Vidal an overbearing, presumptuous Spaniard, intruding on their lives and dispensing favors which, for the most part, could have been obtained sooner or later with or without him as her guardian.

"You know, Monica," he was saying, "although music and the theater may both be important to gracious living, you shouldn't scorn your sewing and other household activities so completely. Granted, you have servants, but you should know how to do such things for yourself, if only to be able to better instruct those under you when the time comes for you to be mistress of your own house. I'm sure you'd like to marry someday and have your own home . . . a husband . . . children . . . right?"

She shrugged her blue puff sleeves listlessly. "That's what Maurice keeps saying, too," she sighed.

Vidal put his booted foot back on the ground and planted himself in front of her. "Maurice? And who, pray tell, is Maurice?"

"Oh, just a young man I know."

"You must know him quite well if he has already spoken of marriage to you."

Monique sensed a sudden sternness creeping into his tone once more. "Oh, he's a beau of mine," she replied with a flippant toss of her head, suddenly enjoying the opportunity to boast a little of a suitor. Now perhaps her pompous guardian would stop thinking of her as only a child and treat her more like the grown-up woman she really was.

"Well, this Maurice had better present himself in

the proper manner and ask permission first to call on you before he even entertains any thoughts of marriage," he snapped. "Are you interested in this young man?"

"Oh, I guess I like him the best of all my beaux," she replied pertly. "I have several, you know." She could sense she was ruffling that usually frustrating calm of his and was rather enjoying it.

"I don't doubt you do," he retorted dryly, "but, of course, you realize you're too young to take any of them seriously yet."

"Oh, I don't know. . . . After all, I'm seventeen. Many women my age are already married and have a couple of children."

"Well, I do know, my little cousin, and you may look like a woman outwardly, but you're far from being one inwardly. There will be time enough to think of matrimony once you're of age."

"But that's almost four years away!"

"You're exaggerating, but it only goes to show how much growing up you have to do yet."

"Do you mean I have to be tied to your will all that time before I can do as I please?"

"The only way you could contest my authority over you would be to go to the courts and ask that they emancipate you before you're twenty-one, but before they would even consider your petition, your grandmother and I would have to testify that we feel you're old enough to be responsible for your actions. Since I couldn't say such a thing in all honesty, I'm afraid you'll just have to reconcile yourself to the situation and let time take care of it. Meanwhile, please bear in mind that, from now on, your regiment of beaux will have to line up to pass inspection before they can pay you court. Is that clear?"

Monique tossed her head angrily. "If I decide to marry, I'll do so when and with whom I please," she declared airily.

"Don't try me, Monica," Vidal warned her, his voice taking on a sharp edge. "I have no intention of letting you make a fool of yourself or of me."

"And stop calling me Monica!" she retorted. "That's Spanish, and I'm French!" She rose indignantly, pulling herself up to her full height, which unfortunately was only to his shoulder.

"What an incorrigible little brat you are!" exclaimed Vidal in exasperation. "I've been trying to make allowances for you, reminding myself that you've had no mother for so many years and have been allowed to run about with very little discipline until now, but even my patience has its limits."

"And so has mine!" retorted Monique, venting her fury with her slippered foot on the flagstones beneath her feet. "I don't like any part of this arrangement!"

There was a faint touch of sarcasm in his smile. "Believe me, we all have to do things sometimes we don't like to do," he replied. "I can't say I especially relish this role of guardian that has been pressed upon me, but someone has to take the responsibility for the welfare of you and your sister. And since it seems the burden has fallen on my shoulders, I suppose I have to accept it with as good a grace as possible, although your hostility toward me doesn't make it any easier."

"You don't have to sacrifice yourself on our account. We were doing quite well before you came."

"Ah, yes, I've seen how well you were doing!" He laughed sardonically. "You and your sister were running fancy-free in the streets with drunken riff-raff at your heels, and the plantation was losing its crops to the worms! One more season like this last one, and you and poor little Celeste would have probably found yourselves bankrupt as well as dishonored or worse. A pretty prospect indeed!"

Monique flushed angrily. "Oh, but you're despicable! Why don't you and all your kind go back to Spain where you came from and leave us here in peace?"

"I'm thinking on it," he replied with maddening tranquility in the face of her fury. "One thing is certain, I didn't change my whole way of life and come across the ocean to this island in the swamplands to be sassed by a spoiled brat. So you'd better mend your ways, little cousin, or you'll find yourself with even shorter reins than at present. Meantime, while I ponder on the temptations of returning to Spain, as you've so kindly suggested, will you please go to your room and stay there until you're called?"

Monique turned to leave but then hesitated.

"What is the matter?" he asked sharply. "Why don't you obey?"

"I . . . I was hoping to see Maurice this afternoon," she confessed, regretting now that she had goaded her guardian as far as she had. "He usually comes by on Saturdays around this time."

"Aha! Now I see the reason for all that talk about being bored. You simply wanted to get out of the house to go meet your beau!"

"And why not? We do nothing wrong. All we do is talk a little and perhaps take a stroll on the Orange Tree Walk along the levee. Is that so terrible?"

"It's certainly not proper that you meet any young man alone on the sly, no matter how innocent it

might be. You know better than that. I'm sorry, but
I can't give you permission to go out like that
without a chaperon. Perhaps later on, once your new
governess is here and I've met the young man, I
might be willing to let him call on you sometimes. In
the meantime, I'm afraid you'll just have to remain
'bored' and find something else to do closer to home
that doesn't involve clandestine meetings with young
men."

"If . . . if I'm not waiting for him at the courtyard gate, he'll probably knock to see what's
wrong."

"Then let him knock," snapped Vidal. "I'm anxious to meet that young man, anyway. The sooner he
knows he can't come sneaking around to the servants' entrance to meet you, the better. Now will
you please go to your room as I said? You won't be
seeing your beau or anyone else today."

"I'm not a child to be treated this way!"

"Then stop acting like one, and you'll be treated
accordingly."

For a moment she still hesitated.

"Don't worry, I'll meet this friend of yours and
tell him he can't see you today or any other day
unless he presents himself at the front door like a
gentleman and asks for permission to call on you in
the proper manner."

He stood tall and unrelenting, his hat and riding
crop in hand, until she had swished past him, her
long skirts and satin sash flying in a haze of blue,
delicately scented with crushed rose petals.

Only after the door had slammed behind her did
he finally heave a deep sigh and follow his wayward
ward into the house at a more leisurely pace. How
he longed to catch that delightful half-child, half-

woman in his arms and awaken her to life! What a pity he was in so awkward a position! If he weren't her guardian, how different things might be between them. More and more he found himself drawn to the fascinating woman he suspected lay hidden just below the surface of that restless, defiant child.

Chapter Six

MIGUEL VIDAL DE LA FUENTE SAT UNCOMFORTABLY IN the pew reserved for His Excellency the Governor and his family. Between the exaggeratedly full skirts of the ladies and the Baron de Carondelet's plump figure, space was at a premium, so Vidal felt obliged to extend one of his long booted legs discreetly out into the side aisle in order to balance himself on the edge of the bench.

Vidal cast a glance back to where he knew his two pretty wards and their grandmother were seated. He had intended to sit with them, but he and the governor had been in the midst of talking crops and politics when mass had begun, so the latter had insisted that Vidal join him. It would have been impolite not to have accepted the invitation.

The padre was giving one of his fire-and-brimstone sermons, and Miguel shifted uneasily in his precarious seat. He had to admit, at least to himself, that he wasn't the best of the Church's followers. Not that he didn't consider himself a good Catholic or a loyal subject of the Spanish realm, but he sometimes found himself plagued with feelings of guilt because he didn't always like the way his religion was practiced in his country, especially when it came to making converts.

Of course, he would never dare voice such "dangerous thoughts" aloud. Who was he to question the methods of the Holy Office? But after he had spent those three years traveling about on the Continent and had had an opportunity to see the way his religion was practiced in other lands, he couldn't help wondering whether the Spanish Inquisition, despite its centuries of existence, might not have hurt more than helped the overall cause of Catholicism. Religion, he felt, should be based on faith, not fear.

He had been happy to learn that the Holy Tribunal was not active in Louisiana. At least that was one of the redeeming features of New Orleans. If it weren't for the heat, the city would be quite bearable.

This crowded guardhouse next to the cathedral was especially stifling. Poorly ventilated, it had never been meant to accommodate so many people under such conditions, but until the new church was ready, this was the only place in New Orleans large enough to hold a sizable congregation.

Vidal cast another glance back at his newly adopted family and thought how they were at least nearer the door and might be getting a little more air than he was. He couldn't see Monique at that moment and craned his neck a little farther out of the folds of his cravat, trying to catch a glimpse of that glorious halo of bright gold hair that not even the black lace of the little headscarf he had given her could completely hide. There were too many heads, however, swaying restlessly between him and the object of his search.

He smiled inwardly as he thought of that rebellious little ward of his. What an adorable little thing she was, with her round, impish face and huge, defiant eyes! Sometimes, when she was angry, which was practically always when he was around, that tiny upturned nose of hers would crinkle up almost out of sight, and those budlike lips would become all the more pronounced. She was a sensuous child, unaware as yet of the woman dormant within her. . . .

He checked himself. It was becoming more and more necessary to remind himself that the girl was his ward. How different things might be if he could court her openly. But he was a fool! Why look on her as anything more than the spoiled brat she was? Even if he weren't her guardian, what difference would it make? She obviously couldn't stand the sight of him. She preferred that pale, freckle-faced Maurice!

The boy had been polite enough when he had spoken to him yesterday afternoon. Maurice had accepted without protest the announcement that in the future it would be necessary to ask for permission first before seeing Monique, but Vidal had sensed a guarded hostility beneath the young man's courteous exterior that foreboded possible problems. He sighed. Whatever could a girl like Monique see in a popinjay like that?

Of course, she was still so young and inexperienced. What did she know about judging men? He was sure she had never known such emotions as love and desire. He wondered how she'd react if the woman in her were really roused. She was so intense, so impulsive in everything she did. He sensed there were great wells of passion waiting there within her to be explored. The thought both pleased and frightened him. Most certainly it was all the more reason to keep a short rein on her, for the girl really did need someone to look after her . . . someone to protect her not only from those around her but from herself, as well.

He tried to catch a glimpse of her once more, and

this time he realized that the seat at the end of the row where she had been sitting was vacant. Now where had that skittish little ward of his gone off to this time? Perhaps she, too, had found the room overly close and felt the need for fresh air. She might not be feeling well. . . . But no, if she were really ill, her sister would have accompanied her, yet there was Celeste still sitting quietly next to her dozing grandmother, appearing rather nervous, but not as though her older sister might be fainting away outside.

No, Monique had probably just wanted a little fresh air . . . or perhaps there was another reason?

Vidal felt the sudden urge to investigate. Knowing his impetuous ward as he did, he found himself wondering what new mischief she might be up to at that very moment.

Feigning a few discreet coughs into the linen handkerchief he had been using to keep his brow dry, he murmured his excuses to the governor and slipped off down the side aisle of the improvised church toward the rear exit. The sonorous tones of the priest's voice resounded throughout the room as his thunderous tirade continued to barrage the assembly.

As Vidal reached the arched doorway he nearly collided with the drab figure of Padre Sebastian, who was standing there staring out into the bright morning sunlight with fixed fascination. Whatever the friar was looking at seemed to be holding his undivided attention.

Vidal followed the Capuchin's intense gaze to where Monique stood in the shadow of an arch engaged in earnest conversation with a slim, sandy-haired young man whom he immediately recognized as Maurice Foucher. In her long flowing gown of pale yellow lawn, topped by the burst of her bright gold hair, no longer hidden beneath the black lace of her headscarf, the young girl seemed like a blazing torch in the dazzling light of the noonday sun.

Vidal couldn't blame the padre for staring at so delightful a picture, yet there was something in those deep-socketed eyes that made him uneasy. Even as he made his way angrily toward his capricious little ward, Vidal found himself fleetingly thinking how strange it was that this somber monk so often seemed to be around wherever his cousin Monique happened to be.

Chapter Seven

"I'M SO GLAD YOU UNDERSTOOD MY SIGNAL TO COME outside," Monique was commending the freckle-faced young man standing tall and gangly before her in his Sunday finery. He held his high-crowned felt hat respectfully in his hand as he gaped adoringly at her.

"You know I'm always at your beck and call," he assured her. "I've been desolate all this past week, now that you can no longer come out of your house at will."

"I know. I feel like a prisoner these days."

"I'd like to visit you, but frankly, my dear, your guardian doesn't strike me as the type of person who will welcome many callers. I don't know what to do."

"He's promised to allow my friends to come to the house, but I'm sure he'll only frighten most of them away," lamented Monique, tragedy written across her dimpled face.

"Perhaps you could sneak out as you used to do?"

"No, that's impossible now. Celeste and I are going to have a new governess beginning tomorrow."

"Is he abusive? I mean, he hasn't tried to strike you or anything, has he?"

"Oh, no, he's never done anything like that. To the contrary, sometimes I've had the impression that he goes out of his way not to touch me."

"Well, after all, he is a man, and there are no real blood ties between you."

Monique was thoughtful for a moment. The fact that Miguel Vidal was a man had also occurred to her, and it was rather disquieting. Actually, it often aroused strange, confusing feelings within her. Celeste was always saying how handsome he was, and Monique had to admit that, even if he was a Spaniard, he could hold his own with any of her French beaux, perhaps even surpass them.

It was true about his never touching her, and his seeming hesitancy to do so only made her wonder all the more how it might feel if he ever did. She had never before thought about any man the way she did about Miguel Vidal.

At that moment the object of her curious musings came marching over to them and, with no preamble, proceeded directly to the point.

"I thought I'd made myself clear yesterday afternoon, Senor Foucher, yet here I find you sneaking behind my back again, trying to see my ward."

Before the startled Maurice could reply, however, Monique sprang to his defense. "Please, Cousin Miguel, it's my fault. He came out because he saw me leave the church and was afraid I was ill."

Her guardian cast a skeptical look at both of them. "Indeed? Don't tell me!" he quipped. "Well, I'm not interested in arguing the point. The important thing is I want these impromptu meetings of yours to stop. You're not to see my cousin again for any reason, senor, without my permission. Is that understood?"

Maurice had regained his composure now, and, pulling himself up to his full height, he met Vidal's dark, penetrating gaze with his own unflinching blue one.

"Yes, Don Miguel, I understand perfectly," he replied calmly, "And since you say I cannot see your cousin without your permission, I am requesting that permission here and now. Tell me a time when I may call on Mlle. Monique that will meet with your approval, and I'll be there."

"Frankly, senor, it's not that simple," retorted Vidal, although he liked the boy better now for this new stand he was taking. "You see, I'd prefer that my cousin have no young men calling on her at the moment. Believe me, there's nothing personal when I say I'd like you to wait at least a few months before asking for permission to visit her. It's simply that I'd like to be certain first that my ward is mature enough to be receiving calls from members of the opposite sex. Actually, much will depend on her deportment in the future."

Monique was fuming. "I told you, Maurice. I may as well be in a convent!" she murmured between clenched teeth.

"Not at all," Vidal assured her. "The only thing I'm asking is that you wait a little until you're more accustomed to your new mode of life and have demonstrated that you're a well-disciplined young lady instead of just an irresponsible child."

The final blessing of the church service was just beginning, and Padre Sebastian, abandoning his post in the doorway where he had been watching their discussion, made his way toward them. His eyes were fixed on Monique as he spoke. "I see you flee from the sermon, my child," he said, a recriminating tone in his dry, cracked voice. "It's a pity, for one should never turn a deaf ear to the word of the Lord."

Monique's rosy cheeks flushed to a deeper shade as she lowered her gold-tipped lashes and acknowledged her guilt.

"Forgive me, Padre," she replied meekly. "I meant no disrespect. It's just that I . . . I felt faint from the closeness of the room and came out for a breath of air."

The monk gave a smile that bordered on a sneer. "Don't add lying to your list of sins, Monique Chausson, for the Lord is looking down on us and can see all."

Vidal suddenly felt sorry for his poor ward as she stood there so obviously uncomfortable beneath the monk's accusing gaze.

"Don't worry, Padre. I'll get to the bottom of this," he quickly assured the friar. "After all, Monique is still quite young and unfortunately has been without much discipline until now. But things will soon be different. I've finally found another governess for the girls—a fine Christian woman, fluent in both French and Spanish, who will start with us tomorrow. My ward is not really a bad girl, Padre. She may be a little too frisky sometimes, but she's really good at heart, I assure you."

"Don't be too certain of that," snapped Fray Sebastian, still not taking his dark, accusing eyes from the girl's highly colored face. "A pretty girl is always easy prey for the devil. She makes a handy instrument for Satan."

He turned suddenly to Maurice, who was standing back abashed now, not knowing quite what to say. "And you, young man," the monk added stonily. "If you value your immortal soul, stop letting pretty young girls distract you from the word of the Lord."

The congregation was beginning to pour out of the building now, so Vidal welcomed the excuse to be free of the monk's disturbing presence. Celeste came anxiously toward them, carefully leading her grandmother by the arm, while the latter blinked dazedly in the bright sunlight.

Just as Miguel was trying to think of some way to break away from the overzealous friar, the latter suddenly murmured a quick blessing and walked abruptly off, losing himself in the tide of dispersing townsfolk.

Miguel paused only long enough to catch the eye of Celeste and her grandmother. Monique felt his hand tighten on her arm, and the strength she sensed behind it awed her. So he was touching her at last, but in anger. For some inexplicable reason, her legs seemed to be buckling beneath her. She stumbled in momentary confusion as he pulled her in the direction of Rue Royale.

Vidal looked down questioningly at her. Perhaps the girl really didn't feel well, after all. "Are you all right?" he asked, his voice suddenly less stern.

She nodded her head feebly, unable to find enough voice to reply at that moment. The spot where his hand circled her arm seemed to be on fire.

"Then come along," he urged. "When we get home, we'll talk further." He didn't want to say anything more for fear of upsetting Grandmother Chausson, who fortunately seemed unaware of anything having been amiss.

As they walked back to the town house Miguel kept a firm grip on Monique's arm, as though half afraid she might try to slip away from him even then. By the time they had reached the town house, however, the annoyance he had felt earlier had subsided somewhat. After all, it was true what he had said to Padre Sebastian in the girl's defense. She was really still so young and naive. She simply didn't realize the consequences of some of her impulsive actions.

How smooth and sensuous that little arm felt! Here was a skin that invited caresses. In spite of himself, he couldn't help thinking that the rest of her body must be like that, too. If she had been any other woman but his ward, he would have permitted the desire he felt for her to continue to mount unchecked, anticipating with delight the moment when he could at last share it with her in a paroxysm of delight in each other's arms; but quickly he quenched his thoughts with the cold water of reality. Why let a passion that could never be slaked go on building up within him?

Deliberately he reminded himself how soft and small that same arm was . . . how fragile and vulnerable. Even as he released it he noted how a red ring still marked the spot where he had held her so tightly. Above all, he didn't want to see her hurt— not by anyone, not even himself. He must try to be more patient with her, less emotional. He couldn't bear it when those disturbing gray eyes of hers looked at him with such contempt. Sadly he recognized that with each passing day his little ward's opinion of him mattered far more than he cared to admit even to himself.

Chapter Eight

MUCH TO THE CHAGRIN OF HER UNHAPPY CHARGES, Mlle. Arthemise Baudier was a martial-looking matron who took her post very seriously. A tall, angular woman with bulging eyes, beak nose, and firmly set jaw, the middle-aged spinster had long since resigned herself to being a governess for life, so she practiced her profession with the utmost zeal.

After a long talk behind closed doors with the head of the Chausson household, Mlle. Baudier had sallied forth with an uncompromising resolve to obey to the letter Vidal's instructions concerning the education of his wards. Actually, she was so over-zealous that even Vidal had to tone her down a bit on several occasions.

There was the time he had asked Mlle. Baudier to send for the dressmaker to make the girls some new gowns and had suggested discreetly that she see to it that the necklines not be cut too low. The conscientious governess had immediately ordered chin-high yokes of white lawn added to all the girls' dresses. The shrieks of protest had so filled the house that Vidal had rushed up the stairs two at a time to see what was happening.

"She's trying to suffocate us in mosquito netting!" wailed Monique indignantly. She stood in the center of the room, draped in white lawn and green-striped cotton, amid a sea of multicolored bolts of cloth, while Celeste stood beside her draped in flowered muslin, looking equally woebegone.

Vidal was utterly bewildered to find himself suddenly confronted by a tangled maze of female flippantries instead of a sinister adversary waiting to meet his half-drawn sword. He listened awkwardly to the reason for the young girls' noisy rebellion, flushing all the while beneath his smooth olive complexion as he tried to straighten out the problem as quickly as possible so he could be gone from that confusing world of muslins and lace that he had so unwittingly invaded.

"But you said to cover them up more, señor," the governess explained defensively, while the poor dressmaker, in peril of swallowing her mouthful of pins, continued to stare in dismay at Vidal's tall, imposing figure standing there before her with his hand still on his sword hilt.

From the expression on the girls' tear-streaked faces, they gave the impression that their virtue had been about to be violated instead of protected.

"I . . . I only meant a . . . an extra ruffle or two perhaps," he faltered. "I don't know how to explain . . . but I'm sure you can think of something appropriate that will meet with my cousins' approval and yet not be too . . . too provocative . . ." He searched for the right phrases, while the women gaped at him in silence, offering little assistance. "Something stylish, you understand . . . yet decent . . ." His voice trailed off lamely. Quickly he backed himself out the door.

A couple of days later Vidal made one of those impromptu visits of his to Mlle. Baudier's classes. The governess was in the middle of teaching Celeste some new chords on the guitar as he entered. Celeste had taken readily to the string instruments and was progressing with surprising rapidity in the mastery of them. The young girl especially seemed to like the Spanish guitar that Vidal had bought for them.

"Ah, Mlle. Baudier and my lovely little cousins," he greeted them with a trifle less formality than he customarily addressed them. "And how goes the music lesson today?"

He had just returned from his morning rounds about town and was especially striking in his rust-colored frock coat and black leather riding boots that rose up smartly to cover the knees of his sleek nankeen breeches.

"Our little Celeste is doing splendidly with the guitar." The governess beamed as she looked up from where she was putting the young girl's slim fingers into the correct position on the strings for the next chord. "Monique, on the other hand, seems to prefer the mandolin," she added with a smile, although it was evident that her pet was little Celeste, whom she found more docile and studious than her restless elder charge.

Vidal cast a curious glance over to where his more troublesome ward sat with a mandolin lying listlessly in her lap. She looked cool and fresh in her soft flowered muslin with tiny rosebuds spilling generously over her long flowing skirts and an upstanding ruffle discreetly veiling the low sweep of her decolletage.

"The thought occurred to me as I rode back home just now that my cousins here might like to learn some of the dance steps that are popular around Europe right now," he offered.

The girls immediately perked up at the mention of dancing.

"If Mlle. Baudier will play a cotillion for us, I'll show you the way it's being done these days," he suggested.

Celeste quickly handed the guitar to her governess and rose eagerly to put herself at Vidal's disposal as a partner. Just the thought of dancing with her handsome guardian brought an excited flush to her delicately chiseled features.

"Better yet, the quadrille!" exclaimed Monique, setting aside her mandolin and also rising with a new surge of energy.

"Of course, you know whichever you do, it should be with at least a set of four couples," began Vidal, who had already taken Celeste's outstretched hand into his. "Let's see how you do the two-hand turn," he invited the delighted young girl.

Mlle. Baudier struck up an appropriate tune, and Celeste let him swing her around in a two-hand turn, her bright skirts of jonquil-flowered muslin swirling along to the rhythm.

"Fine! Fine!" declared Vidal approvingly. "And now you, Monica, let's see if you can do as well as your sister just did."

He caught the tiny dimpled hands that Monique hesitantly extended toward him. They felt softer, fleshier, than Celeste's slimmer ones had been. There was a sensuousness about them that made him want to squeeze tighter. . . .

Not to be outdone by her younger sister, Monique whirled around with her guardian in a two-hand turn that sent her full skirts flying in a cloud of rosebuds. "Very good!" came Vidal's cry of approval. "Now, if this were a quadrille, and you had to go into a ladies' chain, which hand would you offer the lady opposite you to pass her?"

Monique stood there for a second, finding it difficult to think while her hand still rested in his.

"Why, the right one, of course," she finally replied and extended her hand daintily in the direction of the imaginary girl across from her.

"Correct. And then which hand would you give to the man opposite you?"

"The left."

"Good," approved Vidal. "And now another turn in place with your partner, right?" he caught both her hands and whirled her around once more.

Monique's breath was coming more rapidly now, but she knew it was more from the fact that her guardian was holding her hands than because of the turns. In spite of herself, she couldn't help admiring the sinewy grace of those long, athletic limbs as the smooth, clinging breeches encasing his thighs set off to advantage the fascinating ripple of the muscles beneath them.

Celeste was applauding merrily. "Oh, please, Cousin Miguel, let me do the turns again!" she begged excitedly.

Almost reluctantly Monique yielded her guardian to her sister, but she continued to watch him through veiled eyes while he caught the younger girl's hand and repeated the steps with her. Afterward, he proceeded to show them other geometrical patterns for both the cotillion and the quadrille, which he told them were in vogue in Europe at that moment.

Monique found herself looking forward to her turn with her agile guardian. That aroma of lavender and tobacco that she had come to associate with his nearness . . . the feel of his hands holding hers tightly as he whirled her around . . . it all left her giddy, as though she had been inbibing too much wine.

When finally, after another half hour or so, Vidal brought his impromptu dancing lesson to a close, his tireless wards seemed to be bounding with more energy than when they had begun. Despite their protests, however, he insisted that he should withdraw and allow them to go on with their more serious studies of Spanish and French grammar which still had to be hurdled that day, urging them to put some of their revived energies into their forthcoming language lessons.

As Monique watched her guardian walk across the room to the exit, admiring the disturbing rhythm of those fascinating thighs once more, she found herself thinking how different things had seemed between them when they had been dancing together. The memory of his presence lingered. There was something about that proximity that always disconcerted her. It was so difficult to tell what her guardian was really like. Every time she thought she knew, he'd say or do something so completely unexpected. . . .

That afternoon, for the first time, Monique paid a little more attention than usual to her Spanish lesson. Perhaps if she learned more about Miguel Vidal's language, she could understand him a little better, too.

Chapter Nine

MONIQUE AND CELESTE HAD BEEN GETTING READY ALL day. Since early that morning, they had had the upstairs maid running in and out of their room keeping the coals hot in the brazier for the curling iron.

Every time the door opened or closed, snatches of girlish giggles could be heard, and there was such an air of excitement in the household that Mlle. Baudier had finally agreed to suspend classes for that day so the girls could devote themselves entirely to their elaborate preparations for what was to be their first outing to a real theatrical performance.

Grandmother Chausson sent up two large tortoiseshell combs for them to use with the full-sized black lace mantillas that Cousin Miguel had brought them from Spain. Despite Monique's momentary resistance to wearing something so "unpatriotic" as a typically Spanish headdress to the performance, once she saw how elegant and ladylike the graceful black lace mantilla made her look, she offered no further objections.

Vidal had dressed in his royal-blue silk frock coat and breeches, tastefully trimmed with a silver and blue brocade vest and his finest white cravat and cuffs. Then he had gone down to enjoy a glass of wine with Grandmother Chausson in the parlor while he waited for his cousins to finish getting ready.

Five-thirty in the afternoon seemed like an unusually early hour to him for a theatrical performance, but Grandmother Chausson had explained that many of the theatergoers liked to finish out the night—sometimes until dawn—at the festivities offered on the ground floor of the theater itself or the nearby Condé Ballroom.

Since the city's first and only theater was only a few blocks away and it was still daylight, Vidal planned to walk there but to return in the carriage.

Celeste was the first to emerge from her "cocoon." She entered the parlor blushing with pleasure as Vidal and her grandmother duly greeted her with exclamations over how lovely she looked in her bouffant gown of pale pink muslin trimmed with a deep rose velvet sash streaming down the back from the bustle of her generous overskirt. With her honey-colored hair caught up high to support the curved comb and long black lace veil draped over it, the girl seemed to have turned into a woman overnight.

When Vidal and Grandmother Chausson asked for Monique, however, Celeste suddenly lost her newly acquired aplomb. She explained uncomfortably that her sister had had a last-minute idea. "She should be down shortly," the young girl assured them uneasily.

At that moment Monique appeared at the head of the staircase. Grandmother Chausson let out a little cry of amazement, but Vidal was absolutely speechless, as they both stared at the voluptuous little figure in the long flowing white gown, relieved only by the black lace mantilla, slowly descending, wraithlike, toward them.

"My God! But the child has gone daft!" exclaimed Aimee Chausson in dismay.

Vidal, however, could only stare in dumbfounded fascination at the way the thin silk gown, free now of the usual side and back padding and layers of starched petticoats, cascaded gently over the sensuously rounded body beneath it, caressing every curve and indentation as it undulated to the girl's rhythmic movements.

"Don't you like it?" She smiled, quite pleased by the attention her entrance had won from all of them. "It looks Grecian, doesn't it? It's so classic! They say this is the latest style in France these days."

"Merciful God in heaven! You might as well be naked!" gasped her grandmother. "You can see *everything!*"

"Monica . . . if you don't want to give your grandmother a heart attack, you'd better go right back upstairs and put on your *tournure* or *cul* or whatever you call it," advised Vidal, finding his voice at last.

"And your petticoats, too!" snapped Grandmother Chausson quickly.

"But it's so warm tonight," Monique protested, obviously disappointed. Celeste was standing to one side grinning away with an "I-told-you-so" look dancing in her soft brown eyes.

Just then Mlle. Baudier came dashing down the stairs, her usual implacable calm completely gone and her eyes popping out of her head more than ever.

"I assure you, I have nothing to do with this!" she exclaimed as she spotted Monique standing in the parlor still indignantly trying to defend her dubious efforts to be the vanguard of high fashion in New Orleans. "Only ten minutes ago I checked the girls, and they were all ready to leave, dressed the way any decent woman going out on the street should be. I can't imagine what came over the child. . . ."

"I tell you this is the latest fashion," insisted Monique, her cheeks coloring with frustration and embarrassment. "It's called the Greek Revival—the return to classicism. I read about it in one of the journals the dressmaker brought with her."

Vidal was smiling condescendingly at her now. "My dear cousin, I'm sure you mean well," he conceded, "but I'm afraid New Orleans isn't ready yet for such an extreme mode." He was beginning to see more humor in the situation now than scandal. "I'm afraid such a style really is beginning to gain some popularity in Europe," he assured the skeptical elderly ladies.

"No respectable woman would ever go out on the streets without her padding or petticoats," insisted Grandmother Chausson emphatically, while Mlle. Baudier nodded in agreement. "It simply wouldn't be decent for a female to show off the natural shape of her body like that in public! What is this world coming to, anyway?"

Monique was silent now, but it was evident she was still bristling beneath that drooping surface. It was only after the repeated urgings of her inappreciative audience and Vidal's firm stand that she couldn't go to the theater until she was dressed properly that the young girl finally acquiesced. Reluctantly she allowed Mlle. Baudier to lead her back upstairs.

As for Vidal, he poured himself another glass of wine and sat back down in the parlor to wait for his imaginative little ward to repair her toilette, while he continued making occasional comments to help soothe poor Grandmother Chausson's ruffled nerves.

But between the sips of wine and those soothing phrases, Miguel was anything but calm himself. He knew it wasn't the liqueur warming his blood and swelling the desire in him at that moment as he savored the memory of how the soft white silk of Monique's loosely hanging gown had marked all the more the firm roundness of those high young breasts and the tantalizing outline of those softly curved thighs and buttocks in motion. Try as he would, he couldn't stop wondering how it might feel to have those magnificent young breasts pulsating in his hands and those softly undulating hips stirring passionately beneath him. *Qué barbaridad!* It was becoming increasingly difficult to continue thinking of Monique Chausson as nothing more than a capricious child. Her actions might be immature at times, but his impetuous little ward had certainly looked every inch a woman as she had come down those stairs that night, and he could no longer deny that he wanted her with every fiber of his being.

Chapter Ten

MIGUEL VIDAL SLUMPED BACK IN THE BOX THAT THE
Baron de Carondelet had so graciously permitted
him to use for the evening in the Salle de Comédie.
He had resigned himself to a dull couple of hours.
There was only one actor in the cast from the
Cap-Français, and the leading lady, a rather attractive quadroon whom Monique recognized as a milli-
ner around town, wasn't too bad in her part, but the
rest of the performers were rank amateurs.

Fortunately, however, from the way his young
wards' eyes were glowing in their flushed faces, it
was evident they were quite fascinated by everything
they saw and were in no mood to criticize anything.
After all, thought Vidal, it shouldn't take much to
please them. The year-old theater they were attending was not simply the only one in New Orleans, it
was also the city's first.

It was hard for him to realize sometimes just how
sheltered and unsophisticated the girls' lives had
been until now. Despite their lack of discipline in
certain things, they had really lived so little. He had
to keep reminding himself that only a few blocks
away lay vast stretches of untamed wilderness and
that little Monique and Celeste were seeing a theatrical performance for the first time in their lives that
night.

He looked at the two girls sitting there beside him

in the box, so prim and proper now in their voluminous skirts and black lace mantillas perched atop mountains of carefully piled curls, and decided that the radiant look on their faces made the boredom of the evening worthwhile.

He almost chuckled aloud as he recalled once more the way Monique had looked when she had made her entrance earlier that evening in her makeshift chemise, wanting so desperately to be "classic," as she had phrased it. What an adorable little doll she was, with her huge gray eyes and pale spun-gold hair! Part of her charm was that she didn't seem to realize how truly beautiful she was, or how devastatingly provocative just the sight of her could be. His desire for her was a constant knot embedded in his loins. He knew it shouldn't be that way, but what good did it do to deny its existence, when that knot continued to grow with each passing day? Neither her contempt for him nor his common sense could melt it.

He looked at her doll-like profile as she sat there caught up in the spectacle. She seemed completely enthralled by the performance, the earlier skirmish completely forgotten now. There were so many things she didn't know . . . a whole world of concepts and sensations yet to be explored. How he wished he could be the one to take that little hand and lead her through those new experiences . . . sharing them with her . . . awakening her to the warm, sensuous woman he sensed she could be!

The night was warm and sticky, and the small, narrow hall, though decorated lavishly enough, was poorly ventilated. As he dabbed at his forehead with his monogrammed handkerchief he wondered why the citizens of New Orleans persisted in using wood for their buildings instead of the bricks and tile recommended by the authorities, especially after the disastrous experiences the city had already had with fires. What a firetrap the theater was!

Although the play had been billed as Molière's *Tartuffe*, it bore little resemblance to any performance Vidal had ever seen of that work. It soon became a hodgepodge of sudden quotations from Voltaire, Locke, and Rousseau to generous rounds of applause and shouted interjections of "Liberty, Equality, Brotherhood!" from the more demonstrative spectators. The audience was obviously as anti-Spanish as the actors.

Miguel never ceased to marvel at the laxity of the authorities there in the colony. Why did they permit such open expressions of hostility and downright treason to go unchecked? How was it possible that the words of the most radical philosophers of the day could be spouted publicly from the officially recognized theater of the town, while in Spain and the rest of its colonies they were forbidden by both the Crown and the Church as being too "dangerous and inflammatory" even to read in the privacy of one's own home, much less express aloud?

He remembered how he himself had wrestled with his conscience when he had finally succumbed to reading some of the works of those popular French leaders of the Enlightenment while he had been traveling around Europe. It had been hard for him at first to ignore the years of strict upbringing in his native land, where such books could only be circulated clandestinely, since they were on the ever-growing list of hundreds of similar works banned by the Inquisition. Even now he didn't dare admit to anyone that he had delved into such prohibited literature for fear he might be thought a heretic or a traitor. For one never really knew. The powerful tentacles of La Suprema stretched out even to the remotest corners of the world. No one was too far away from the all-knowing eyes and ears of the Holy Tribunal. Once its interest was aroused, it could be relentless and pursue a prospective victim for a lifetime, even beyond the grave.

In his opinion, such zealous persecution was absurd. It was ridiculous to try to control a man's thoughts. What was in his heart would always win out in the end, no matter how suppressed he might momentarily be.

Miguel was soon roused from his musings. The mood of the audience was becoming restless. The boisterous slogans and ready applause that greeted every florid speech made against "tyranny" and in praise of "freedom and democracy" seemed to inspire the actors to even greater heights of oratory, and more and more they deliberately added impromptu lines.

Of course, Vidal's two intensely French cousins were also among those who were being swept along on the emotional current of the moment, and once Monique even let the cry of *"Liberté!"* escape from her lips as she joined heartily in the applause of an especially moving speech, but her guardian had quickly put a restraining hand on her arm and motioned with a discreet finger to his lips that she should be quiet.

The atmosphere, however, was beginning to be so rowdy that Vidal considered walking out on the performance. He hated to cut short his wards' first theatrical experience, but he could see the emotionally charged atmosphere was already beginning to affect his impressionable little cousins, especially

Monique, who obviously was being increasingly carried away by the inflammatory speeches. Most certainly she didn't need anything else to make her more rebellious than she already was!

He bent toward her, hat in hand, and whispered that they had best be leaving, but she turned an elated, shining face breathlessly to him and protested vehemently.

Suddenly one of the actors, completely out of character now, took a step forward to the edge of the stage and, his face ruddy in the glow of the blazing candles of the footlights, extended his arms dramatically toward the audience and boomed out in his most resonant tones the first lines of the new French anthem:

> *"Allons, enfants de la patrie!*
> *Le jour de gloire est arrivé!"*

A thunderous response greeted the declamation. With cries of "Liberty, Equality, and Brotherhood," many of the young men in the audience rose instinctively to their feet.

A small voice off somewhere below began to intone "La Marseillaise," picking up the words of the song from where the actor had left off reciting it. Soon others were joining in.

> *"Contre nous de la tyrannie*
> *L'entendaré ranglant est levé!"*

Like wildfire, the impromptu song spread across the hall, sweeping along with it everyone in its path.

Completely transported now, Monique suddenly jumped to her feet and joined that exhilarating wave of patriotism, her high, lilting voice singing enthusiastically along with the others as the theater literally reverberated to the rafters.

"Aux armes, citoyens!"

Vidal rose angrily and tugged impatiently on Monique's arm, ordering her to behave herself, his voice barely audible above the din. "Come, Monica . . . Celeste . . . we must leave."

But Monique only turned wide, glazed eyes toward him, her flushed cheeks streaming with tears of emotion, as she stubbornly held her ground and continued to sing ecstatically along with her "fellow Frenchmen."

"Marchons! Marchons! . . ."

The occupants in the neighboring loge had long since abandoned the theater, and Vidal, sensing a riot in the making, decided that he should get his wards out of there, too, as quickly as possible.

Literally dragging Monique along with him, even while she continued to sing fervently at the top of her voice, he made his way out of the box and down the stairs to the exit.

Although the song died from her lips as the warm, humid night air hit her face, Monique still had a lightheaded feeling, as though she had drunk too much wine. Even as they turned off St. Peter Street into Rue Royale, they could hear the singing and shouting emanating from the brightly lit second-story theater.

Ironically enough, as they walked along that street behind the Plaza de Armas, they were just passing the calabozo, which, flanked by the arsenal, stood directly behind the guardhouse on the square, to the left of the cathedral.

"This is where those fools are going to end up!" he grumbled while he dragged his highly elated wards along with him. It was too early for the carriage he had ordered to be waiting for them, so he decided to walk back home.

Like an ominous giant crouching in the shadows ready to spring, the two-story calaboose lay far back from the street behind the massive brick wall that surrounded it, a huge blob barely glimpsed in the moonlight behind the ponderous wrought-iron gateway.

Vidal was doubly glad he had decided to abandon the theater when he had, for at the final notes of that extemporaneous rendition of the "Marseillaise," someone could be heard enthusiastically beginning a chorus of the offensive "Ça Ira," that song of many verses, set to the air of "La Carmagnole," which the French revolutionists and their sympathizers especially liked to sing to taunt the royalists.

> *"Ça ira . . . Ça ira,*
> *les aristocrates à la lanterne . . ."*

Now they were asking for trouble, thought Vidal. The guard will soon put an end to that boisterous performance, for they were going too far. The Baron de Carondelet was a proud man, and much as he might want to be lenient with the colonists, he was not to be provoked lightly. He could hardly overlook it when they were calling him a "suckling pig" . . . a clever play on words with the governor's name when pronounced exaggeratedly in French. Even from a block away, Vidal could catch the innuendo when they sang the words.

His rebellious young wards, however, still filled with the emotion of what for them had been an uplifting moment of pure, unadulterated patriotism, walked along reluctantly beside him. Although Celeste wasn't resisting him as Monique was, he nevertheless had to pull the girl along with him, too, for it was more than she could do to keep up with his long, angry stride. Even the usually docile Celeste, it seemed, had been moved by the demonstration, and although she hadn't participated in the vocal part of it, she, too, had obviously been quite impressed by it all.

"Oh, Cousin Miguel, wasn't it exciting?" she exclaimed breathlessly. "I had no idea a performance in a real theater was going to be like that!"

"Nor did I!" mumbled her guardian with open annoyance. It was evident, however, that the young girl hadn't caught many of the more delicate aspects of what had happened.

"Oh, I hope you'll take us again soon. What a pity we couldn't stay to see how it ended!"

"I know very well how this particular performance will end!" snapped Vidal. "The gendarmes will see to that!"

"But it was all so thrilling! I've never seen anything like it before in my life!"

Monique, who had been completely caught up in her own exhilarating thoughts, suddenly called out to her sister from the other side of Miguel's formidable figure as he dragged the two of them along, one on each side of him.

"You see, Celeste, I told you, I told you!" she exclaimed, her voice still tremulous from the recent excitement.

"Oh, yes, it's just the way you said!" agreed

Celeste. "It was all exactly like the leaflets, even down to the same words!"

Vidal came to an abrupt halt and stood there on the wooden banquette looking down with sudden curiosity at the deceivingly innocent faces of the two little radicals staring back at him in the light of the rising moon.

"Leaflets?" he echoed suspiciously, still holding firmly on to their arms. "What leaflets?"

With a startled gasp, Celeste put her hand belatedly to her lips. *"Mon Dieu!"* she exclaimed in dismay as Monique shot her an accusing glance.

"Answer me," insisted Vidal. "What leaflets? Has someone been giving you Jacobin propaganda?"

"Only . . . only some printed circulars that were thrown around the city a few weeks ago . . ." stammered Celeste.

But Vidal suspected there was more to it than that. For a moment he stood there trying to fathom the wide-eyed, confused little countenances looking up so fearfully at him. Then he continued down the Rue Royale once more, but at a slightly slower pace, while his suddenly abashed cousins walked in silence beside him. They were passing by the grounds behind the cathedral now, and most of the huts were already dark and silent, although a few had candles flickering like restless fireflies in their tiny cloth-covered windows.

Miguel resolved to investigate the matter further once they got back home. God help him! Here he was with two hotheaded little rebels on his hands! Something had to be done before his young wards got themselves into more trouble than they bargained for!

Chapter Eleven

THERE WAS QUITE A TEMPEST IN THE CHAUSSON household for the next few days. The aftermath of the theatrical outing had begun with a complete search of the girls' room. Amid a flood of tears and protests, Mlle. Baudier, on Vidal's orders, had gone methodically through every nook and corner of that frilly little bedchamber until her search finally had come to an end underneath Monique's four-poster bed.

Then, while his two wards had stood by squirming helplessly as they watched his mounting fury, their guardian read over the half-dozen throw-sheets that had been unearthed from below a pile of dog-eared volumes by Voltaire and Rousseau and a Dufoe novel rated as "scandalous" by the shocked Mlle. Baudier.

Vidal's voice fluctuated from a hasty mumble to indignant exclamations whenever he came to parts of the leaflets that especially enraged him.

" 'Liberty, Equality, Brotherhood . . . The Freemen of France to their brothers in Louisiana . . . second year of the French Republic," read Vidal. "The moment has arrived when despotism must disappear from the earth. France, having obtained her freedom . . . is not satisfied with successes by which she alone would profit, but declares to all nations that she is ready to give her powerful assistance to those that may be disposed to follow her virtuous example. . . .

" 'Frenchmen of Louisiana, you still love your mother country; such a feeling is innate in your hearts. The French nation, knowing your sentiments, and indignant at seeing you the victims of the tyrants by whom you have been so long oppressed, can and will avenge your wrongs. . . .'

"By all the saints! What rubbish!" Vidal began to pace the room angrily as he continued. " 'The hour has struck, Frenchmen of Louisiana. Hasten to profit by the great lesson you have received. Now is the time to cease being the slaves of a government to which you were shamefully sold. . . .' " He looked up, angrier than ever.

"I notice they say nothing about the French government that did the 'shameful selling'! But I might add that Louisiana was not sold, but rather given to Spain in payment for its having lost part of its own colonies while helping out France as its ally, no less!"

He read on, his anger increasing by the minute. " 'The Spanish despotism has surpassed in atrocity and stupidity all the other despotisms that have ever been known. Has not barbarism always been the companion of that government, which has rendered the Spanish name execrable and horrible in the whole continent of America? Is it not that nation who, under the hypocritical mask of religion, ordered or permitted the sacrifice of more than twenty millions of men? . . .'

"*Qué barbaridad!* As if France has been so lily-white! What about that bloodbath that's been going on there with the guillotine for years now under the hypocritical name of justice?" he asked indignantly. Then he continued, his voice dropping again to a mumble for a few more paragraphs, while his wards nervously waited in dread for his next outburst.

"'. . . all that you possess depends on the caprice of a viceroy, who is always unjust, avaricious, and vindictive.' That's not true! To the contrary, I daresay the baron has been a better, more conscientious governor than most of those you had while under French rule. Most certainly he's been incredibly patient with these rebels around town! You people here in the Louisiana colony don't realize how much more freedom you enjoy than any place in Europe or even the other Spanish colonies here in America.

"'. . . know ye that your brethren, who have attacked with success the Spanish government in Europe, will in a short time present themselves on your coast with naval forces; that the republicans of the western portion of the United States are ready to come down the Ohio and Mississippi in company with a considerable number of French republicans and to rush to your assistance under the banners of France and liberty. . . .'

"God in heaven! But this is treasonous—inciting open rebellion!" he exclaimed in amazement as his dark, flashing eyes raced ahead over the paragraphs that followed. Suddenly his voice rose again.

"'. . . it will be in your power to unite voluntarily with France and your neighbors—the United States —forming with these two republics an alliance to our mutual political and commercial interest.' Aha! Now we come to the *grano*—the real motives behind all of this high-sounding poppycock!

"'Your country will derive the greatest advantages from so auspicious a revolution. . . .' Of course, and so will France and the United States! Those French Jacobins of Philadelphia, who are behind all this propaganda, don't give a fig for you people here in Louisiana. What they want is to get control of the Mississippi River and the whole valley with it." He read on rapidly now to the fiery conclusion.

"'Gather up your courage, Frenchmen of Louisiana. Away with pusillanimity . . . *Ça ira . . . Ça ira!*'"

Vidal let out a roar. *"Vaya!* So this is where you've been getting all those foolish ideas of yours, little cousins! Do you realize this is treasonous material? Foolish children! You could be arrested for hoarding inflammatory propaganda like this. Leaflets like these are being sent into the colony by secret agents of the French Jacobins in Philadelphia who are trying to incite rebellion here to serve their own ends. Where on earth did you get such literature?"

But despite what Monique termed an "Inquisition" by her irate guardian, she steadfastly refused to say how she had come by her private cache of rebellious material. Although Vidal was fairly positive that it had been given to her by Maurice Foucher, he couldn't get her to admit it.

"Frankly, I'm at a loss to know what to do about your granddaughters, especially Monique," he confessed later to Grandmother Chausson. "Given a little time, I could probably handle Celeste, but Monica is another story. She seems so dead set against me. No matter what I say or do, she takes offense to it or goes deliberately contrary to my wishes, even to her own detriment, just to spite me.

"I'd hoped to win her over little by little, but I'm beginning to see now just how deep-seated her resentment against me really is, and sometimes I wonder whether I'll ever be able to surmount it."

"I know it's difficult for you, Miguel," agreed Aimee Chausson with a sigh, "but please try to be patient with the girl. Her mother was a good, pious woman, but she was obsessed with her hatred for the Spaniards. That mercenary O'Reilly really did cause a tremendous amount of ill feeling here toward the Spanish when he took over the colony. He used trickery to capture the French rebels, and once they fell into his hands, instead of being generous and perhaps winning over the populace by being lenient with their misguided patriots, O'Reilly executed six of them and imprisoned the others. At least Monique's grandfather wasn't one of those who was shot, but he might as well have been, for he returned from the dungeons of Havana a broken man and died only a few weeks after his release. Eugenie, my son's wife, adored her father, and it made a lasting impression on her. She never forgave the Spaniards and never let the girls forget what their grandfather had suffered, either. They grew up hearing the story over and over again, and every tale of Spanish cruelty was repeated to them.

"Monique, being older than Celeste, understood and remembered better what her mother said than her sister did, and sometimes the poor child used to wake up crying in the middle of the night after Eugenie had been exaggeratedly vivid about some gory detail. But no matter how I begged my daughter-in-law to stop frightening the children like that, she was too obsessed with the subject to let it rest.

"Of course, after Eugenie died and the girls grew older, they didn't seem to think much about those old tales anymore, but I guess the resentment was always there, although I confess I never suspected how deep-rooted it was with Monique until now. But give her time, Miguel. Frankly, I suspect that much of her hostility simply stems from the fact that you're pulling the reins in more tightly on her. Unfortunately, she's been spoiled and is headstrong—accustomed to saying and doing as she pleases—so I'm afraid she would resist anyone who tried to discipline her, although the fact that you happen to be a Spaniard has probably resurrected some of those old childhood memories that her mother seeded in her. But believe me, Miguel, Monique is basically a good-hearted girl. I'm sure she'll come around. You'll see."

Vidal was pensive. He wanted so much to believe that Aimee Chausson was right.

"God knows I hope it'll be as you say," he replied. "But if you could have seen her the other night singing that revolutionary song in the theater! She was so carried away."

Grandmother Chausson smiled and shook her white-capped head. "I can well imagine," she agreed. "Monique has a tendency to be overly romantic sometimes. This unpopular war between Spain and France has awakened all the girl's patriotism. Despite Spanish rule here, Monique is typical of the way most of the people of New Orleans feel. She still considers herself French and has deluded herself into thinking that France can do no wrong. The girl doesn't realize, of course, that if we were living in that unfortunate country right now, we'd be going to the guillotine ourselves!" She shook her head. "Our young people are so easily inflamed. Take Monique's friend Maurice. He's not really a bad boy. I'm sure he's fired by the noblest of sentiments, but he's being influenced by those Jacobin agents who have been filtering into town. I'd hate to see the boy get in trouble."

"Rest easy," Vidal assured her. "I mean the boy no harm, but I do intend to remove Monique from his questionable influence. If you permit me to make a suggestion, I think it might be advisable to take up summer residence at the plantation a little early this year."

Aimee Chausson sighed resignedly. "I really prefer living in the town house," she confessed, "but if it's best for the girls, I'll go, of course."

"I really think it might be wiser, especially where Monique is concerned," he assured her. "A change of scene for a while, away from the temptations and unrest of the city, might do her some good. By the time September comes and you're ready to return to New Orleans for the social season, she may see things in an entirely different light. Monique is at a transitory age right now . . . a period where a few months could make a great deal of difference."

Chapter Twelve

WHEN THE PLANS TO TAKE UP IMMEDIATE RESIDENCE AT the Chausson plantation were announced, Vidal's wards received the news with more protests. Monique, already smarting from the episode of the confiscated leaflets, was especially furious over what she called her guardian's "arbitrary manipulating of her life" and became more petulant than ever. The fact that Miguel showed her an article in the *Moniteur* that the governor was threatening to close the theater if the performances continued to be so disorderly didn't seem to impress her, nor did she feel especially eager to obey when Vidal asked her to leave her packing for a moment to have a few words with him.

He began with a conciliatory approach.

"Monica . . ." he said cautiously, but when he saw the way she immediately glared at him, he quickly corrected himself. "Monique, I've been wanting to tell you how much I truly regret having had to order your room searched. I can understand you resented having Mlle. Baudier go through your things that way, and I'm truly sorry it was necessary."

"You had no right to invade my privacy," she reproached him, her fleshy little lips in more of a pout than ever.

"It wouldn't have been necessary if you'd have been more cooperative," he reminded her. "All

considered, it was far better that it was someone like
me or your governess who searched your room than
an officer of the law. Don't you realize that those
leaflets are treasonable, inciting rebellion against the
Spanish Crown? You should tell that foolish Foucher
boy to watch his step, or he'll find himself in a pack
of trouble one of these days."

"I didn't say Maurice gave them to me," she
immediately protested. "I found them on the
street."

Vidal sighed. He was sure she was lying to defend
her friend, yet he couldn't help admiring her loyalty.

"I won't pursue that point with you now," he
conceded, "except to say that I don't want you to see
that young man anymore. At least not for the time
being, until he proves himself to be more prudent.
He's headed for trouble, and I wouldn't want to see
you mixed up in it. Governor Carondelet tells me
that, when the news of Louis XVI's execution
reached New Orleans, there were such open manifestations and signs of rebellion around the city that
he was forced to arrest six of the ringleaders and
imprison them in Havana for a year. But, under the
circumstances, I think the government has been
extremely lenient until now. Everything has its limits, however, and you and your hotheaded friends
like Foucher don't seem to realize the dangerous
ground you're treading when you persist in so openly
expressing your misplaced patriotism. After all, no
government can ignore open rebellion in its streets."

Monique lifted big doleful eyes toward him, and
for a moment there was more fear in them than
anger. Memories of her grandfather's fate had come
flooding back to her.

"Oh, please, Cousin Miguel, don't say anything to

the authorities!" she pleaded. "I wouldn't want Maurice to die in one of those horrid dungeons of Havana because of me!"

Vidal tried not to smile. At that moment she was just a frightened child. "Don't worry," he said a little more gently. "I have no intention of publicizing your rebellious inclinations to anyone, and if you obey me in the future and avoid associating with gentlemen of such dubious political leanings, there should be no need for me ever to concern myself over that young man's affairs, either."

Hostility flared up in her eyes once more, and the gray tinged with the reflection of her green-striped cotton suddenly became a stormy sea. "In other words, you're threatening me—*chantaje* is the word in Spanish for blackmail, isn't it? You're saying that either I bend to your will, or you'll have my friend, and perhaps even me, put in prison!"

Vidal was taken aback. "Good heavens, no! What kind of monster do you think I am? Do you really think me capable of sending you or that foolish freckle-faced boy to prison?"

"I don't know. . . . After all, you're Spanish. . . ."

Miguel ran his hand exasperatedly through the waves of his thick black hair, nearly pulling the ends loose from where he had neatly tied them back with a black velvet ribbon at the nape of his neck.

"Dios mío! But why do you hate us so much? I know the story about your grandfather, but how can you continue to hold so much rancor for something that happened a quarter of a century ago, before you were even born? It seems to me that at least some of the anger you French feel toward us Spaniards should be directed toward your so-called mother country, as well. After all, France was the one who

rejected you. Spain didn't especially want this colony, you know, but, for the most part, I'd say we've been trying to make the best of an unwanted gift. In many ways, Louisiana has been more of a costly headache for us than a boon."

"Indeed? Then why did Spain accept us and go to so much trouble to keep us, even after patriots like my grandfather made it clear we didn't want to belong to you?"

Vidal sighed but tried to keep the impatience out of his voice as he replied. "I see where Mlle. Baudier is going to have to give you another history lesson. Unfortunately, you are still sadly lacking in knowledge of world history. Tomorrow please ask your governess to tell you about the Treaty of Paris in 1763. You see, my dear cousin, Spain didn't take you away from France. We didn't conquer Louisiana, you know, despite what your Jacobin friends would like you to believe. My country was given this colony to help compensate us for the territory we lost while fighting on the side of France during the Seven Years' War back in the middle of this century. Actually, Spain has been as much the victim of an unfortunate set of circumstances as you have been. I can assure you Spain would have liked nothing better than to have gotten back the territory that had originally belonged to it, rather than getting a rebellious colony of Frenchmen in its stead!"

"If your country and mine have always been such good allies, why, then, did you go to war against France last year? Technically that makes us enemies, you know."

Her guardian laughed, finding her attitude more humorous than exasperating at this point. "When will you ever face the fact that you are no longer a colony of France but of Spain? Do you realize that, like it or not, you are really a Spanish citizen, since you were born here in a Spanish colony? As for this ridiculous war between Spain and France, you can thank your French revolutionaries for that. Traditionally, Spain and France have been more allies than enemies, but when rabble rule took over in Paris and they began beheading everyone in sight, including even their anointed king and queen, our King Carlos had little choice except to go to war against the ones in power now. After all, Spain is a monarchy. It could hardly condone the destruction of another monarchy. But the war is with the new political regime—the leaders of that reign of terror they are calling a revolution—not with the real French nation."

Monique gave a disdainful toss of her head. "Some blood must always be spilled when old evils have to be uprooted," she replied, "but once the new government settles down, things will be better, you'll see. Then perhaps France will want us back. It was a king who gave us away, but now that the old regime has been overthrown, perhaps the wrong that was done us will be righted by the new ones in power and we here in Louisiana will be accepted again by our mother country."

Vidal smiled patiently. "Now you're just repeating things you've read in those leaflets. Louisiana was given to Spain in an honorable treaty as payment of a debt that could hardly be ignored. It's wishful thinking on the part of your people to go on dreaming of belonging to France once more. Even if Louisiana were ever to return to French rule, I'm willing to bet that France would be using the colony to barter for something else before too long. I hate to disillusion you, but unfortunately the country you people here so passionately persist in clinging to doesn't really give a fig for you. That's a fact all you hotheaded young rebels will have to face sooner or later.

"But enough of politics. I want to talk to you about the plantation. I understand that you and Celeste aren't too happy over our going there to spend a few months. It will probably only be until the fall—just a month or so more than what you've been accustomed to spending at Le Rêve every year. Is that so terrible? I'd hoped you might welcome the change for a little while."

"But there's nothing going on there," she lamented tragically. "I've always found the summers at the plantation rather boring."

"Well, I hope this year will be different," ventured Vidal. "For one thing, I think it's time you become a little more familiar with the operation of the plantation itself. Since it will pass into your and Celeste's hands when you become of age, I think it'd be wise for you to start learning something about running it so that you'll be more prepared when that time comes."

Monique shrugged her shoulders nonchalantly. "Oh, I doubt I'll have to worry about such things," she quipped. "I'll probably entrust the management of the property and crops to a good administrator, or, more than likely, my husband."

"Of course," agreed Vidal. "I'm sure you will, but it still wouldn't hurt for you to know at least enough about such things to be able to know whether your affairs are being handled wisely or not. After all, you wouldn't want to be cheated."

Monique tossed her pale gold ringlets flippantly. "But if you are to be both my teacher and my administrator, with what criterion should I judge you, then?"

The color heightened in Vidal's cheeks. "As your guardian, I'm answerable to the courts," he replied, a sharp edge cutting into his usually well modulated voice. "If you think I'm being wasteful or dishonest with your inheritance, you and your grandmother have a right to press charges against me."

It was her turn to blush now. She lowered her eyes quickly, already regretting her taunt. Her cousin was a proud man, and she knew she had gone too far this time. "I'm not accusing you of anything," she assured him hastily. "But sometimes you can be so maddeningly pedantic!"

"And you, my ill-mannered child, can be so maddeningly impertinent!" he retorted angrily. "You should learn to curb that rattle you have for a tongue. If you had been a man, I'd have taken my sword to you for questioning my honor as you just did. You should weigh your words more carefully before you speak."

"You and your arrogant Spanish ways!" she fumed, all the more vehemently because she felt the need to cover up the fact that she knew she had overstepped herself. "You take offense too easily."

"Perhaps, but being courteous and controlling that spiteful temper of yours would certainly do you no harm. I'm afraid that impulsive nature of yours will get you into trouble someday, and, as your guardian, I feel it's my duty to insist that you mend your manners. You might keep in mind that, although I may not be able to use my sword on you, I most certainly wouldn't be above using the palm of my hand if you continue to be so incorrigible."

She paled. "You . . . you wouldn't dare!" she

exclaimed in tremulous defiance. "You . . . the epitome of Spanish manhood . . . you'd hit a woman?"

"No, I wouldn't dream of hitting a woman," he assured her dryly, "but I most certainly would feel no qualms about spanking a spoiled brat!"

Monique drew herself up indignantly. "You're being impertinent!" she sputtered.

"I'm afraid the impertinence is yours," he contested. "I've been trying to be patient with you, for I realize it's not your fault if your father and grandmother haven't disciplined you better. I know you look on me as an intruder, but I can assure you I didn't leave my comfortable life in Madrid to come to this sweltering pesthole just to wrestle with a failing plantation and two wayward brats!"

"Then perhaps the best solution would be for me to marry as soon as possible," she retorted angrily, "and put an end to a situation that's intolerable for both of us."

"Don't count on it," he snapped. "I doubt I'll give my consent for you to marry anyone for quite a while. Matrimony is for a woman, not a child."

"I'll be eighteen in January of next year," she reminded him. "That ought to be old enough for me to do as I please."

"I'm sorry, but you'll have to wait until you're at least twenty-one. Of course, if you're not satisfied with the way I'm managing your affairs, you're free to go to the courts and ask them to appoint someone else as your curator."

"I don't see why I couldn't run things myself. With the help of an experienced overseer like Roselle, things should go smoothly enough."

"The management of a plantation is much more complicated than you think, young lady, especially now that we're converting to sugarcane. The truth is, it's even a struggle for Roselle and me to learn all there is to know. I'll have to teach you a lot before you're ready to take over for yourself. Meantime, it seems we're stuck with each other, my little ward, so we may as well make the best of things while we're at it!"

Chapter Thirteen

LIFE SOON SETTLED DOWN TO A LEISURELY PACE AT LE
Rêve as the weeks wore on. Lifted high on eight-foot
brick piers, which were walled in now for storage
space, the large whitewashed plantation with its
overhanging gallery looked out toward the river
through a lane of whispering trees. It offered a
serene haven for Vidal and his adopted family. He
continued to make frequent trips into New Orleans,
where he often stayed for the weekend or overnight
at the town house. Monique and Celeste remained
undisturbed in their routine of daily classes with
Mlle. Baudier and sewing and cooking sessions with
Grandmother Chausson.

Monique found some degree of consolation in the
lovely new hand-painted harpsichord, and she often
gave informal recitals for her little family by candlelight to while away the lonely evening hours. Vidal
frequently brought back new pieces of music upon
returning from one of his excursions to New Orleans.

Miguel felt relieved knowing that his little cousins
were safely ensconced at the plantation. A young
girl barely two years older than Monique had recently vanished from the city and it wasn't known
whether she had fallen victim to foul play or simply
run off. It chilled Vidal to the marrow to think what
could have happened to his naive little wards had
they continued to run around New Orleans without a
chaperon.

Vidal found himself looking forward more and more to his visits to Le Rêve, now that he knew he had his grandmother and two young cousins waiting there for him. As an only child, he had led a rather solitary life until he had come to New Orleans to take charge of the Chausson family's affairs. He rather enjoyed the sharp contrast of the provincial life he was leading these days with the more sophisticated one he had always led in the courts of Spain and Europe. One of the things he especially liked was the feeling of freedom that the open spaces of the plantation gave him; but when darkness fell, he resented it when the shutters had to be closed tightly against the "evils of the night," foremost of which were the droves of mosquitoes that came out en masse from the nearby swamplands to lay siege to those who had dared invade what the insects evidently still considered to be their private domains.

The stuffiness of his room was intolerable, since he not only had to barricade himself behind closed doors but retreat even further behind yards of netting, as well, in order to keep the bloodthirsty little pests from feeding off him while he slept and leaving only stinging welts in return for favors received.

At least Grandmother Chausson and the girls seemed to take such inconveniences in their stride, accepting them as a natural part of life there in the Louisiana colony. Not that Monique was content. Vidal, who had come to recognize the signs of impending disaster where his ward was concerned, had noted lately how she was beginning to chafe at the bit and look for something to break the monotony of her daily routine.

He decided, therefore, that it was time for him to

begin introducing her to the more technical aspects of plantation life.

"Perhaps you've been wondering what I've been doing these past few months," he ventured one morning right after breakfast.

Monique had always been curious about her guardian's comings and goings. "I've never really given the matter much thought," she replied airily, trying to keep her eyes from focusing too noticeably on the patch of dark hairs glimpsed through the opening of his shirt collar. Until now she had mostly seen him with his fasionable chin-high cravat, impeccably draped down to the number of its folds.

The soft fabric of his shirt clung to the sinewy cords of the muscles beneath it—long, lean muscles hardened by years of fencing, horseback riding, and constant travel.

"Well, I think you should know I've been meeting and talking with the authorities in New Orleans and some of the experienced planters in these parts," he said, ignoring her tone of indifference, "and I've come to the conclusion that indigo is not the best crop for a region like this."

"But my father always planted indigo."

"And most of the others around here, but these past two years have surely demonstrated that the caterpillar makes more profit from it than the planters do."

"Then what do you plan to grow?"

"Sugarcane. You see, I think the future lies with sugar, or perhaps cotton. Most certainly not indigo."

"Is that what the other plantation owners are going to plant, too, now?"

Vidal paused a second before replying. "No," he

finally said cautiously. "Most of them are staying
with indigo, but I'm afraid they're going to lose their
crops to the worms again this year. Only a few of us,
like Etienne de Boré and me, along with one or two
émigrés from Santo Domingo, have gone over to
sugar. Perhaps because we who are newer to this
region can see things with a broader perspective than
those who can no longer see the forest for the trees."

"But if the majority still think that indigo—"

"Just being in the majority doesn't necessarily
make one right, little cousin. The cane grows very
well here as long as it's kept drained. What has really
been holding back the production of sugarcane in
Louisiana is the difficulty in successfully granulating
it. But a young French aristocrat, Henri Ducole, has
agreed to sell me some of his cane cuttings so I can
get a crop started and then, when the time comes to
granulate it next year, to share his expert with me to
ensure it's done correctly. I'm paying him a handsome fee, of course, but our relationship is a friendly
one. He has already given me some very helpful
advice. Perhaps you've noticed the sheds going up in
the back? I'd like to show you and Celeste what I'm
doing."

She shrugged her shoulders. "Why bother? It
seems you've already made all the decisions and are
doing as you please without any approval from us,
anyway."

"I've talked it all over with your grandmother, of
course, and, frankly, I wanted to include you in
those discussions, but she seemed to think you were
still too young to understand such details. Personally, I disagree, for I'd like to think you're old enough
to take some interest in at least the overall scheme of
things around here."

"Well, if Grandmother has put the control of our

money in your hands, there's little else we can do now, I suppose, except pray you're doing the right thing with it."

Her guardian made an almost visible effort to bite his tongue. His ward could be so exasperating at times. "Well, I certainly hope so," he conceded, "since I've advanced considerable money from my own funds to make most of the necessary investments. If the plan fails, I stand to lose a sizable amount of money on this new enterprise myself. You seem to forget that my father left me quite well off in my own right. I can assure you I have little need of going out my way to pocket any of your own dwindling funds.

"I'd like to show you the changes I've been making and how I'm preparing the fields for the cane. I thought we might ride around the plantation today."

Monique couldn't help smiling to herself. The prospect of going horseback riding always appealed to her, but doubly so now. She welcomed the opportunity it would offer her to observe her detestable guardian at closer range. After all, the better one knows an enemy, the easier it is to defeat him.

Chapter Fourteen

MONIQUE LISTENED INTENTLY WHILE HER GUARDIAN waxed enthusiastic over all he had been doing and still hoped to do before he was through. Suddenly, empty sheds, huge iron kettles, smelly cattle pens, half-plowed fields, and a mill still under construction all seemed to be fascinating topics of conversation. She had never seen Miguel's dark eyes shining like that, and the extent of his exuberance surprised her. It made him suddenly seem more human, for she hadn't imagined a dour Spaniard could be emotional about anything.

She had to admit, too, that her guardian had literally performed miracles in just the few months since he had taken over Le Rêve. Never before had she seen the place so well organized. She was still skeptical about changing over to sugarcane, but he seemed so sure. . . . Although she felt tempted to taunt him, as she'd so often done in the past, she couldn't bring herself to belittle his efforts now.

While they were in the vegetable patch Alphonse Roselle, the Cajun overseer, came over to talk to them. Smiling down at him from where she sat sidesaddle atop her black-spotted gelding, Monique greeted his familiar figure in its coarse homespun shirt and breeches with the nickname she had called him long ago as a toddler.

"Good day, Phonse, I see we're still in your very reliable hands, right?"

Vidal sat drawn up to one side on his own chestnut-colored gelding, watching her with a slight lift of his brows, accustomed as he was to seeing only the more contrary side of her nature.

"Yes, mam'selle, it's still my pleasure to serve you and your family. Senor Vidal here keeps me busy these days, but I'm trying to follow his instructions as best I can. I hope you carry back my best regards to that fine lady, your grandmother, and your little sister."

"I will, Phonse," she assured him, "and I know I speak for them as well as myself when I tell you how grateful we are for the way you've worked so hard to hold Le Rêve together for us ever since my father died last year."

Roselle invited her to have a closer look at how large the beans and squash were that year. She and Vidal dismounted. There was the same glow of pride in the old man's pale eyes that she had seen in her guardian's all that morning as Alphonse praised the merits of "good delta soil" to Miguel. The two men hovered over the plants like mother hens with their chicks, exchanging observations on the progress of each one's growth. As she bent over and touched one of those bulging pods, bursting with the exuberance of life, she suddenly sensed what they felt looking down at their first tangible yield for that year.

After exchanging a few more brief comments with them, Roselle finally put his tattered hat back on and respectfully took his leave.

She turned now toward her gelding but was suddenly aware of her guardian's dark, inquisitive gaze fixed intently on her.

"What . . . what's the matter?" she asked him, feeling uncomfortable beneath those disturbing eyes.

"Nothing," he replied, but he still didn't take his gaze from her. "You just surprised me a little, that's all."

"In what way?"

"It was nice of you to take such a kindly attitude with old Roselle," he observed. "It meant a lot to him, I'm sure."

"Why should that surprise you?" she asked saucily. "Don't you think I'm capable of being nice?"

"Well, you must admit, little cousin, you couldn't always prove it by me." Vidal smiled.

With an exasperated toss of her bonneted head, Monique lifted the ruffled skirts of her flowered cotton and took another step toward her mount. Suddenly she felt something sharp jabbing into the flesh of her right foot as she stepped down on it. With a cry of pain, she tried to regain her balance.

Vidal quickly lunged forward to break her fall. Momentarily he stood swaying with her, holding firmly like the trunk of a tree holding fast in a storm.

For a long, suspended moment, they clung instinctively to each other, vibrating in the midsummer air from the impact of their collision, even as a pendulum continues to swing once it has been set into motion.

Stunned, Monique suddenly realized she was in her guardian's arms. Those dark hairs in the opening of his shirt were brushing her chin, and the scent of lavender and tobacco, mingled with the heat of his body, filled her nostrils. It was an exciting masculine aroma that made her feel as though she were sipping wine. More shaken from the unexpected impact of his nearness than from the fall itself, she reeled unsteadily. Instinctively he tightened his arm about her waist and drew her closer, partially balancing her against his thighs . . . those fascinating thighs she had so often secretly watched flexing beneath the tight sheath of his breeches. Now they were sustaining her, and the feel of them—warm and pulsating—set her pulses pounding wildly. Once more her legs were buckling beneath her. She knew she'd surely fall to the ground if he let her go.

"Are you all right?" she heard him asking, his voice strangely muffled and labored in her ear.

"I . . . I don't know," she replied truthfully, clinging tightly to him, bewildered by the flood of sensations overwhelming her. She felt a strong desire to arch her body against the long, hard leanness of him as she clung to the thin fabric of his shirt and delighted in the feel of the firm expanse of the bare chest beneath it.

Was this the way it was to be in a man's arms? She felt strangely alive, with an uncontrollable exuberance racing through her veins. Shyly she lifted her eyes toward her guardian's face, wondering whether he was feeling all those exhilarating emotions, as well; but, aside from his quickened breathing and the deep flush on his countenance, he seemed unusually tense and his jaw was surprisingly clenched.

"What's the matter?" he asked her again. "Are you ill?"

She had cried out as if in pain when she had fallen forward and was trembling so in his arms now that he didn't know what to think. "I'm sorry if I've kept you in the heat too long."

He was caught in the dilemma of longing to prolong this moment, yet fearful of the consequences if it did continue. To feel those soft, sensuous curves molded against him and not be able to run his hands caressingly over them was more than he could bear. Even now he could feel the cones of her breasts pressing through the thin fabric of their summer garments and boring maddeningly into his chest. *Qué barbaridad!* How much could a man take without reacting? The palms of his hands were sore from digging his nails into them to keep from cupping them over those delightful tormentors. He only hoped she wasn't aware of just how much he was quickening with desire for her. Yet he was loath to let her go just yet. After months of wanting her, of longing to hold her precisely like this, here she was finally in his arms!

He pressed his loins yearningly against the sweet warmth of her and bit his tongue to stop from murmuring endearments that came rushing to his lips. Now that her bonnet had slipped back and was hanging behind her by its ribbons, he could at least brush his lips against that glorious mane of golden ringlets and leave a kiss undetected there in its perfumed midst. The scent of her inebriated him. He could taste it in his mouth as he momentarily nestled there in the gold of her hair.

"It's my foot," she was saying. "I can't put my weight on it. Something seems to be cutting it."

She was trying to draw back from him now, her cheeks burning hotter than the noonday sun. "There must be a stone or burr in my slipper." Her voice was breathless, but she reached down inside the soft leather of her shoe and sought out the cause of her discomfort.

"At last! Here it is!" she declared triumphantly, holding up the offending pebble. Impatiently she threw it off to one side among the rows of squash and then, with a sigh of relief, broke away from his sustaining arm. She hoped he hadn't been aware of what she had been feeling . . . of the emotions that had racked her body only a few moments before. How was it possible that a man she hated so much could have such a devastating effect on her whenever he got less than two feet from her?

"But are you sure you're all right now?" he asked, taking a step toward her again anxiously.

"Of course I am!" she snapped crossly, drawing back quickly in an effort to hide how confused she still felt.

But even after Vidal had helped her back up on her horse, she found it hard to act nonchalant. Her heart wouldn't stop pounding. Of course, she noted that her guardian seemed rather flustered himself as he swung up quickly into his own saddle and proceeded to ride back to the main house beside her in silence.

Although they kept their mounts at a casual pace, the air between them seemed charged and ready to crackle at any moment, even as the atmosphere right before a storm hangs tense and still in anticipation of the thunder and lightning yet to come.

Chapter Fifteen

ALTHOUGH MONIQUE CONTINUED TO WAGE HER PRI-
vate war against Spain, conveniently embodied in
the person of Miguel Vidal de la Fuente, there were
moments in the weeks that followed when she found it
difficult to hate her guardian quite so intensely,
especially when she recalled the disquieting reality
of his taut body pressed tightly against her own. At
such moments he was no longer an enemy, no longer
the arrogant Spanish don—he was just a man.

At night in that private little world of hers beneath
the mosquito netting of her bed, she would recall
those moments she had spent in her guardian's arms.
In spite of her efforts to blot them out of her mind,
she found herself reliving every vivid detail and
taking pleasure in the recollection.

In the past she had sometimes lain awake at night
wondering what it would be like to have a man that
close to her. There had been times when she had
gone even further and dared try to imagine how it
would feel to lie with a man . . . to have him actually make love to her. Until now, however, that
phantom lover of her dreams had always been
vague, his features indistinguishable or perhaps only
fleetingly reminiscent of some attractive young man
with whom she might have had a passing acquaintance. But now the man in her fantasies, awake or

dreaming, was always Miguel Vidal, down to every last disturbing detail of him!

Sometimes when she was really in her guardian's presence, she would blush crimson at just the thought that he might suspect some of the things she had been dreaming about him. But now that she had felt the touch of his hands and been close to his lips and sensed the hard warmth of his body, it was difficult not to wonder how it might feel if those same hands were caressing her breasts, or those same lips were kissing her mouth, or that same body were pressed close to her own.

Although she accompanied her guardian on his rounds of the plantation on several occasions after that first rather disconcerting one, Vidal never took her out alone with him again. Monique suspected he was deliberately avoiding her, and she realized with surprise that she was disappointed by this.

Nevertheless, there were times when, of necessity, Vidal would have to touch her while helping her up into the saddle or to alight, and then their eyes would meet, and she'd sense that he was remembering, too, those moments when he had held her in his arms, for the color would suddenly spring to his cheeks and he'd quickly turn away.

There were times, however, when Monique reminded herself that it might be easier just to go on regarding her guardian as her enemy and leave off trying to understand those more complicated emotions he awakened in her whenever she permitted herself to think of him as a man. Often she felt guilty, even angry with herself, for not being able to keep her thoughts about Miguel Vidal under better control. How was it possible to detest a man so much by day, yet dream so passionately about him at night? He represented everything she had been taught to hate. Why, France and Spain were even at war at that moment, and her guardian had no more right to be there meddling in her life than Spain had to be ruling over the Louisiana colony!

When Bastille Day came around in midsummer, she welcomed the opportunity to display openly to her guardian where her loyalties still lay. On the morning of July 14, therefore, she awakened in an especially martial mood and, together with Celeste, donned the French tricolors.

When her astonished guardian ventured to ask what might be the cause of that sudden resurgence of patriotism, she instantly informed him that they were celebrating the Fête de la Révolution, when the people of Paris took the Bastille in 1789.

"When Frenchmen struck their first blow for freedom against tyranny," she added meaningly.

Although Vidal didn't particularly relish the sight of his two treasonous wards parading around the house the rest of that day with red, white, and blue cockades on their frilly white caps, he kept his silence, deciding there was no harm in letting them have their moment of "patriotism" as long as they had it there in the privacy of the plantation.

After all, he didn't want to widen the breach between him and Monique with any more arguments than necessary. Whenever he remembered the feel of that soft, sensuous body in his arms, he lost his urge to discuss politics. He had carried the scent of her perfumed warmth in his nostrils for days after their encounter in the vegetable patch; even now, just the sight of her could conjure the memory of that aroma and all the other sensations he had experienced during those brief moments of proximity he had shared with her.

It was becoming increasingly difficult to be casual around Monique. The faint odor of rose petals emanating from her as she whisked past him . . . a fleeting glimpse into the shadowy depths of her bosom . . . an unexpected play of light as it sifted through the gold of her hair . . . they would all set his pulses pounding and reawaken his desire for her. Just the sight of her familiar profile with its saucy upturned nose and those bold uplifted breasts pushing exuberantly against the tight confines of her bodice would immediately set him to remembering the feel of those hard tips boring into his chest begging to be caressed . . . robbing him of his slumber. Sometimes his desire for her would swell until he felt he would burst for want of her.

In an effort to lessen the tension, Vidal readily consented to Monique's suggestion that she and Celeste be allowed to invite some of their friends to the plantation for a party.

There were difficulties when the girls presented their guest list to him and he felt obliged to strike off Maurice Foucher's name. Monique flared up again so vehemently that he began to doubt the wisdom of having agreed to the idea of the fiesta in the first place.

Thankfully, the overall excitement of planning for the party so swept Monique and her sister along that they were far too busy to fret over any single detail for long. Nevertheless, Monique resented her guardian's refusal to let her invite her favorite beau, and although she knew it would be useless to argue the point further with Vidal, she chalked up the incident as simply one more reason to continue her resistance to his "constant meddling" in her life.

Taking advantage of the fact that their guardian was off on another one of his weekends in New

Orleans, the girls prevailed upon their more lenient grandmother to let them go into town the Saturday before their party to buy some last-minute things for the coming festivities.

Overjoyed at being in the city once more, the girls led their governess a merry chase as they flitted about from shop to shop, counter to counter, merrily testing the exotic perfumes they longed to be given permission to wear, laughingly inhaling the different kinds of snuff that made them gasp and sneeze, wistfully fingering the softly scented silks and satins that they yearned to wear to the first ball of the next social season, and curiously stopping to investigate every pretty fan, bonnet, muff, and sundry item that attracted their attention along the way. Even the huge, sprawling market by the levee, with its more pungent odors and colorful merchandise, had a lusty, earthy atmosphere that the girls knew and loved.

Their poor bewildered governess did her best to keep up with them, but whenever her charges put their curly heads together to contrive effective ways to extend their purchases beyond those originally agreed upon or to slip away alone for a few seconds, the two young girls usually won out.

Consequently, as soon as Monique spotted her friend Maurice, it only took one of her "secret signals" to her sister to enlist the latter's ready assistance in getting Mlle. Pop-Eyes out of the way for a minute.

Understanding immediately what was required of her, Celeste proceeded to go into action, deftly pulling the unsuspecting governess along with her to another arcade at the far end of the market so they could purchase bonbons and dried fruit.

Monique rapidly brought Maurice up to date, telling him first how her guardian had discovered the leaflets under her bed and suspected who had given them to her.

"But I wouldn't own up to it," she assured her friend vehemently as he blinked rather bewilderedly at her over his chin-high cravat, trying to digest all she was trying to relate to him in a flood of breathless phrases before Mlle. Pop-Eyes would begin looking for her.

The sandy-haired young man had chopped his hair into the shaggy "dog-ears" that characterized the latest style of the revolutionaries in France at that moment, and although he didn't dare go so far as to go around New Orleans flaunting a red knitted tasseled cap and sansculotte trousers in the faces of the Spanish authorities, he did presume to tack a tricolor cockade on the folded back brim of his black felt tricorne, as so many other young men of the colony were doing those days, just to remind everyone where his loyalties really lay.

Without waiting for Maurice to reply, however, Monique raced on to tell him about the party she and her sister were planning to give at Le Rêve that coming Tuesday afternoon. Apologizing profusely, and not without a surge of anger, she explained to him how she had had his name on the invitation list but Vidal had struck it off.

"Don't fret yourself about it, my dear," Foucher consoled her. "I understand perfectly. Besides, from the looks of things, you may be seeing less and less of your guardian anyway."

Monique was taken aback. "What . . . what do you mean?" she faltered.

"Don't tell me you don't know where he goes

every time he comes to New Orleans? Why, he spends more time at the Ducole town house than he does at yours, I can assure you."

She tried to give the impression of complete nonchalance. "Oh, I remember he mentioned the name Ducole," she said glibly. "The man is an émigré from Saint Domingue who is advising him on how to raise sugarcane."

But her friend chuckled in a sly manner that suggested he knew more than he was telling. "And what is Ducole's pretty young sister Azema advising your guardian about?" he asked meaningly.

Monique nervously fingered the ruffled edge of her white starched fichu. "A-Azema?" she echoed incredulously. An icy chill was slowly beginning to creep over her.

"Yes. She and Henri Ducole have one of the most expensive town houses in the city and a plantation near Lake Pontchartrain that they say is like a sultan's court, where they lavishly entertain only the cream of New Orleans society. Your cousin is one of their most frequent guests, of course, at both the town house and their plantation, since it seems he and Azema have quite a *tendre* for each other. Some people think there's just a flirtation between them, but others speculate that your guardian might marry her, even if she is already his mistress, since she's as rich as she is beautiful and probably has a handsome dowry to compensate for any laxity she might have in her morals."

Monique's wide gray eyes were popping almost as much as Mlle. Baudier's at that moment.

"I . . . I'm sure you're mistaken," she insisted indignantly. The thought that her guardian might have a mistress tucked away somewhere so shattered her that she refused to accept it.

It didn't matter just then whether she had a right to be angry or not. She was. She felt betrayed. Maurice was saying something else to her, but his words were indistinguishable . . . far away. In the midst of the chaos within her, the core of her had suddenly gone numb. The threads of her thoughts seemed to have snagged and knotted over that one fact—her guardian had a mistress! Somewhere there was a woman he held in his arms and made love to. While she had been dreaming of the touch of his hand, he had been caressing some other woman's breasts. While she had wondered how his lips might feel cupped over hers, he had been kissing someone else. And those long, lean thighs of his that had pressed against hers so excitingly had held that other woman between them. What a fool she had been to think that she had pressed against a part of him known only to her!

Maurice had been babbling on and on, and suddenly she realized by his silence and the expectant look on his face that he was waiting for her to reply. But she had no idea what he'd been saying. It was impossible to hold a conversation with him or anyone else at that moment. There was only one thought in her mind and it overwhelmed all others.

"I . . . I'm sorry, Maurice," she apologized, "but I really have to go." Her breath was coming in such labored gasps she could hardly get the words out. "I . . . I don't want Mlle. Pop-Eyes to see me talking to you. There would be the devil to pay if she did."

The freckles on Maurice's face were more noticeable as he paled behind them.

"You don't think your guardian would be capable of going to the authorities and causing me trouble, do you?" he asked.

"What? Oh, no, I don't think so. He said he wouldn't, but then you can never tell about a Spaniard!" she replied absently as she thought that she certainly didn't know what to think about one particular Spaniard at all.

She handed the half-filled glass back to Foucher and murmured a hasty goodbye, leaving the young man staring after her in bewilderment.

The picture of her guardian holding some faceless woman in his arms was all she could see in vivid relief against the kaleidoscopic backdrop of the busy marketplace as hot tears scalded her flushed cheeks. Rage was churning inside of her as she ran back down the length of the aisle to rejoin Celeste and the governess. She was furious with Maurice for having told her such disquieting news, furious with her guardian for having had the effrontery to take a mistress, and, most of all, furious with herself for having let the news upset her so much!

Chapter Sixteen

MONIQUE'S FURY INCREASED AS THE EVENING PRO-
gressed and their guardian didn't arrive at the town
house.

Celeste sensed that something was drastically
wrong, but it wasn't until the girls had retired to the
privacy of their second-floor bedchamber in the
town house, where they were to spend the night
before returning to the plantation, that they could
really talk.

It didn't take Celeste long to wheedle the news out
of her sister. Brimming over with rage, Monique
blurted out the momentous announcement that their
guardian had a mistress.

"He's probably with her this very minute," she
fumed, "and that's why he hasn't come home yet."

Celeste sighed sadly but, with all the worldliness
of her fifteen years, seemed to be taking the news
more philosophically.

"Well, all considered, I guess it's to be expected,"
she declared resignedly as she sat upright in her
four-poster bed with the mosquito netting hanging
from the tester drawn tightly closed around her.
"After all, our guardian is a man, and a very
handsome one, at that."

"I . . . I'm just surprised, that's all," said Monique with studied indifference. "I didn't think he was
the type. After all, he's usually so cold, so
distant. . . ."

In the privacy of her mosquito net, Monique was remembering with mixed emotions how tense and stiff he had been, despite the warm pulsating of his body, when he had held her so close to him in the vegetable patch. "He's either a hypocrite or a cold fish," she declared suddenly, with ever-increasing annoyance.

Celeste laughed at her sister's extremes. "He doesn't strike me as either one," she insisted. "I suspect he's simply tried to be discreet around us. I heard grandmother and one of her lady friends talking once in the parlor, and they were saying that just about any bachelor, once he's of age, has at least one mistress—sometimes even more than one— hidden away somewhere."

Monique tossed her pale blond mane angrily as the nightcandle on the table between their two beds caught the steel glints flashing in her eyes, despite the tent of misty netting hanging around her.

"Ah, yes! And I wager our seemingly straight-laced guardian has had more than his share of mistresses over the years, too!" she observed sarcastically. "He probably made the rounds of every courtesan in the king's court in Madrid, and then some while he was traveling around Europe!"

Celeste couldn't help smiling at the bundle of contradictions her older sister seemed to be at that moment. "Well, I wouldn't say anything to grandmother about what Maurice told you," she warned Monique. "She'd be angry if she heard us talking about such things, and what's more, she'd probably say our guardian's love life isn't any of our business, which would be right, of course, for it really isn't."

A hush fell over the dimly lit room as the two girls lay back in their respective four-posters, each in her own little island of mosquito netting, lost in her private world of thoughts.

The minutes ticked slowly by. Then suddenly Celeste heaved a long, deep sigh and her eyes had a soft dreamy look in the flickering candlelight—a look they so often had when she spoke of her guardian.

"He must be a splendid lover," she murmured wistfully.

"Celeste! Hush, you naughty girl!" exclaimed Monique, sitting bolt upright in her bed once more. "What a scandalous thing to say!"

"But he . . . he's so masculine . . . so virile!"

"I think he's horrid . . . absolutely repulsive!"

Her young sister giggled. "I bet if he ever kissed you, you wouldn't say such a thing!" She gave a little shiver of delight at the very thought of Cousin Miguel kissing her, but Monique only gave an angry grunt for a reply and flopped back exasperatedly against her pillow.

Flipping over then to her side, Monique turned her back toward her sister and closed her eyes, trying to blot all thoughts of Miguel Vidal de la Fuente from her mind. Try as she would, she couldn't get the picture of him lying with that wanton Azema Ducole out of her mind. She couldn't check the thoughts of him holding that woman naked in his arms, kissing and caressing her as he passionately pressed her against that fascinating long hard body of his that she could still feel imprinted against the length and breadth of her own being.

She wondered whether Azema's body was better than hers. Did the sight of that woman's breasts set him on fire? Was he passionate with Azema Ducole, instead of tense and controlled as he had been with her? She tried to push back the picture of him holding another woman's breasts and finding them more desirable than her own.

Her stomach was tied in a thousand knots. Hour after hour she lay awake, unable to check the torrent of thoughts racing through her mind, each one torturing her more than the other. Then she would be furious with herself for having allowed the news to have affected her that way. Why should she care what Miguel Vidal did in his leisure moments?

The night candle was sputtering in its holder before she finally dozed off, exhausted from the emotions that had racked her for so many hours. But even then she found no peace, for Miguel Vidal was there again disturbing her dreams. This time, however, it was a sweet torment, for now she was the one he was making love to. Once again she could feel his arms encircling her as they had that day in the fields, but in her fantasy his hands were sweeping up and down her body and lingering on her breasts.

Even in her slumber, her breasts were swelling to that phantom touch and she could feel the cords of his thighs holding her fast as he pressed them against hers. He was showering her with kisses and telling her what a beautiful, desirable woman he thought she was, when suddenly some brazen naked woman pushed between them and, with mocking laughter, took her place in Miguel's arms . . . and he went right on making love to her!

With a start, Monique awakened sobbing and trembling, her breath coming in sharp gasps and her pulse pounding wildly. She cast a sheepish glance over in Celeste's direction, but her sister was sleeping peacefully. The candle had burned out and only a thin wisp of smoke still wafted upward from it, barely visible in the first streaks of dawn filtering in through the shutters.

She continued to lie there, listening and starting at every noise . . . waiting . . . hoping . . . hoping against hope that her guardian might still arrive and somehow disprove everything Maurice had said about him.

Chapter Seventeen

MONIQUE AWAKENED CROSS AND SLEEPY. MLLE. Baudier noted the girl's sullen mood and scolded her more than usual, commenting that she hoped their stopping off at Sunday mass before returning to the plantation would do her some good, even if it only served to inspire her to mend her ways a little.

When Celeste and Monique passed in front of the impressive new cathedral, they cast curious glances at it, noting how the work had progressed with surprising rapidity in just those few months since they had been away at the plantation and wondering how much longer it would be before the dedication.

With the little black lace headscarf that her guardian had given her when he had first arrived from Spain weighing heavily on her head that morning, Monique filed into the makeshift church in the guardhouse and sat fanning herself dejectedly in the Chausson pew beside Celeste and Mlle. Baudier. She hated the prospect of having to sit for at least an hour in that stuffy hall listening to one of those "pangs of hell" sermons she knew to be forthcoming. Nor did she especially look forward to the long, hot ride back to Le Rêve on the dusty, bumpy river road in the scorching heat of that typical August day.

Maurice was seated with his family in the pew reserved for them on the other side of the nave, and Monique wished she could get him aside to talk to him again so she could question him about Azema

Ducole, but Mlle. Pop-Eyes was watching her too closely.

The service was just about to begin when suddenly Celeste squeezed her sister's arm and signaled with wide, eloquent eyes to follow her gaze, which was fixed on the entrance at the back of the hall.

There, momentarily silhouetted in the archway, with the dazzling sunlight behind him, stood the familiar tall figure of Miguel Vidal de la Fuente, and beside him one of the most beautiful women his wards had ever seen. Her bright red-gold hair shone like a flaming halo around her head, which not even the tiny triangle of black lace atop her cascading curls could quench.

Vidal had seen them, too, and was coming down the nave now directly to their pew, looking impeccably cool and crisp in his wine-colored riding habit and freshly starched cravat and cuffs, despite the heat of the midsummer morning.

His tall, willowy companion, apparently equally untouched by such commonplace concerns as the weather, floated gracefully along with him, a slender tapered hand resting possessively on his arm. There was an air of self-confidence in the young woman's bearing, and the calm, almost bored expression on that perfectly chiseled, fashionably pale countenance suggested an aplomb born of the knowledge that few could excel her in beauty or poise. Monique bit her lip in vexation as she was forced to recognize that Azema Ducole was everything Maurice had said she was and more.

"Why, what's this? My little cousins!" their guardian greeted them with what appeared to be pleasant surprise. "I didn't know you were coming into town!" He directed himself now specifically to their governess. "I hope there's nothing wrong?"

"Oh, no, señor," she assured him quickly. "It's just that the girls insisted so much that they needed some last-minute things for their fiesta that Madame Chausson gave her permission for them to come to the city to do some shopping. I hope you have no objections?"

"Of course not. If their grandmother said it was all right and they are here in New Orleans with you and, I suppose, Gustave, the coachman, as well, they're well chaperoned."

"We came in yesterday and spent the night at the town house. After mass, we plan to go straight back to Le Rêve . . . if that meets with your approval, Señor Vidal?"

"Yes, yes, of course." He turned his dark gaze back to his unusually mute wards, who were sitting with their eyes still glued with hostile curiosity on his lovely companion. "I'm sorry I wasn't at the town house to see you last night," he told them without even a hint of uneasiness, "but I was at the Ducole plantation, and they graciously extended me the hospitality of one of their guest rooms for the night."

He turned momentarily to the vision in emerald-green silk at his side and added apologetically, "Please forgive me, my dear, but these are the two little cousins I've spoken to you about. Seeing them here in the city has taken me so by surprise that I'm forgetting my manners. Monique . . . Celeste . . . this lovely lady is Mlle. Azema Ducole, the sister of my friend Henri from Santo Domingo, who has been such a great help to me in converting Le Rêve to sugarcane production."

The two girls squirmed uncomfortably in their seats and murmured a polite acknowledgment to the introduction. Monique could feel the vivid green eyes of Vidal's companion looking curiously down at them along the length of her perfect classic nose, and the young girl suddenly felt as though she were only ten years old. Azema may have only been in her mid-twenties, but as far as Monique was concerned, there was at least twenty years' difference between her and her guardian's companion in poise and experience.

"Heavens, Miguel! I had no idea your cousins were such full-grown young ladies!" exclaimed Azema Ducole in exactly the melodious, well-modulated voice one would expect to hear coming from such delicately molded lips. "The way you spoke of them, I'd have thought they were much younger!"

For the first time Vidal seemed a little embarrassed. "Perhaps I do think of them as younger than they are," he admitted with a smile, "but they've lived such a sheltered life here in the colony that they really are quite young and inexperienced in so many ways."

Monique was glaring at him with such intensity that Vidal was suddenly afraid she might have taken offense from their comments. He sometimes forgot how the very young tend to consider any reference to their youth an insult.

He was about to add a few words that he hoped would soothe his ward's ego, but the priest was already entering the hall with his entourage of altar boys on his heels, so everyone was scurrying to his or her respective place. Out of deference to his lovely companion, Vidal escorted her to the pew reserved for the Ducole family and remained there with her throughout the service.

Monique paid little attention to what was going on around her. During the sermon, which she usually found terribly boring, anyway, she kept her eyes fixed on her guardian's tall, erect figure sitting across the nave several rows in front of her. Curiously, she studied the proud auburn head of his companion, wishing she could at least find one defect so she could have some justification for the immediate dislike she had taken for Azema Ducole. The latter was probably like those courtesans her guardian had become accustomed to while he was frolicking around Europe's courts. One thing was certain, there was a sophistication about Azema that came from having been on her own, thought Monique enviously. Mlle. Ducole had probably never had an eagle-eyed governess and a despot guardian to stifle her every womanly impulse.

After her brief but impressive encounter with her cousin's mistress, Monique felt shorter and dumpier than ever. She wondered whether she could suck in her cheeks a little to give their roundness a slimmer look. . . . A little more rice powder might at least make them more fashionably pale. . . . And perhaps a henna rinse in her hair . . . but no, Grandmother would never permit it. As always, she was subject to someone else's will! Besides, there was nothing whatsoever she could do about that button nose of hers! And although her eyes could reflect green fairly well, they could never reach that height of intensity . . . the gray would always be there to temper them. No, she had to admit, if only to herself, that Azema Ducole was everything she had always wanted to be but wasn't!

As she and her sister exited from mass into the blinding sunlight and opened their parasols to protect their complexions, Vidal joined them once more. His companion had opened a ruffled green silk parasol but was still clinging to his arm with her free hand. Monique sensed that Mlle. Ducole was slightly annoyed over her escort's continued preoccupation with his wards, but since she always managed to smile prettily every time Miguel looked her way, he seemed completely unaware of any impatience on her part.

As for Mlle. Baudier, she continued to adopt her complacent attitude, having long ago decided that, if she hoped to be a highly recommended governess, she should do her duty to the letter but question nothing around her that didn't directly concern her.

"So you're returning to the plantation now, is that right?" Vidal asked the governess.

"Yes, Senor Vidal, unless you would prefer otherwise."

"No, no. Do you think you can get off all right, or would you like me to accompany you back to the town house and help you prepare for your departure?"

"Oh, no, senor. Feel free to go on about your business. Gustave is there waiting for us with the coach and horses all ready to go. There's no need for you to bother yourself over us."

But Vidal vacillated a moment longer. "Are you certain, then, that you need nothing? Do you have enough money? Any problems that require my attention?"

"Everything is fine, senor," Mlle. Baudier assured him. "Don't fret yourself on our account. I'll tell Madame Chausson that we saw you and that everything is fine here with you, too."

"You might also tell my grandmother that, unless something unforeseen happens, I'll be returning to the plantation tomorrow sometime before dusk. I need to finish discussing some business with Mlle. Ducole's brother today, but I should be able to leave here sometime tomorrow. I wouldn't want to miss the girls' fiesta. It's this Tuesday afternoon, right?" He turned with a questioning smile toward his wards, but they only nodded glumly back at him.

"Well, I'll be there. I promise. And I hope your governess will have only good things to say about your progress in your studies when I have my weekly report from her." He seemed to be unaware of their belligerent attitude.

Azema Ducole, however, was giving signs of becoming restless in the increasingly hot sun and gave a discreetly audible sigh as she shifted her parasol on the bare shoulder that the low sweep of her decolletage so prettily exposed. Monique wondered why her guardian hadn't insisted that his mistress put some extra ruffles or a fichu on *her* neckline!

Vidal immediately apologized to his companion for having kept her standing there in the sun for so long and brought his conversation with his cousins and their governess to a hasty close.

As he walked away from them, still offering apologies to Azema for the delay, Monique caught the latter's melodious voice sweetly suggesting that perhaps he was "spoiling" his little wards with "too much attention."

With an angry pout, Monique pushed apart the two sides of the white starched fichu tucked discreetly into the decolletage of her tightly laced bodice. Even if she had taken her collar off altogether, her neckline wouldn't have been quite as low as the one Azema Ducole had been flaunting without any adornment at all. But Monique consoled herself with the thought that at least she could hold her own with that long-legged, green-eyed cat where bosoms were concerned, although no one would ever know it the way her elders had her muffled up to the chin with fichus and ruffles!

She twirled her frilly white parasol almost defiantly and, with a swish of her flounced skirts, turned to follow her sister and Mlle. Baudier across the square. But suddenly she froze in her tracks, for there was Padre Sebastian standing only a few yards away from her in the shadowy recess of the arched columns in front of the guardhouse. She realized with horror that he must have been silently watching her all along and colored to the roots of her hair at the thought that the monk must have witnessed her little act of defiance with the fichu. What a shameless hussy he must think she was!

Quickly pulling the two sides of her double collar closer together again over her partially exposed bosom, Monique shielded her crimson face from the accusing eyes of the monk with her open parasol and hurried after her sister and Mlle. Baudier in a delicate mist of white flounced organdy skirts.

Chapter Eighteen

MIGUEL VIDAL COULDN'T IMAGINE WHAT HAD POS-
sessed his young wards these past few days. Although they had never really been easy to control, he had always been able to reach them sooner
or later, and recently he had even begun to hope
he had been making some definite progress toward
bettering his relationship with them.

Now, all of a sudden, they were more incorrigible
than ever. Even gentle Celeste had been acting
strangely toward him since he had returned for the
fiesta, and Monique, who had always been as unpredictable as those delightfully changeable eyes of
hers, had become openly hostile again. He had
expected to find his young cousins in a party mood
when he arrived that Monday afternoon and had
even hoped they might be more kindly disposed
toward him after he had given them permission to
put all the servants on the plantation, if need be, to
work helping with the preparations. But there was a
prolonged sullenness in Monique now that couldn't
be dispelled, and this surprised him, for although the
girl might be given to frequent rebellious outbursts,
she was basically too good-natured to nurse them for
long.

He asked Grandmother Chausson and Mlle.
Baudier if they knew what might be ailing the girls,
but the two women admitted they were as mystified

as he was over the latest unexpected change in them.

It did occur to him that they didn't like the idea of his having a lady friend. Young girls their age with so little experience in life could sometimes be overly prudish. But he had been very discreet, simply presenting Azema as the sister of a business associate, which, after all, was the truth. Why would the girls think there was something more between the two of them? And if they did, why should they care? They couldn't be so naive as to think he was a celibate.

For a fleeting moment he found himself wondering whether Monique might like him more than she pretended, but he immediately dismissed the thought, laughing at his own foolish vanity. How could she know how much she meant to him . . . how his desire for her was mounting with each passing day until he feared he could no longer control it? How could she possibly imagine the burning knot he carried in his loins for her that only she could relieve? He could lie with a dozen women and it would still be there, yearning for her.

In a way, it had been mostly because of her that he had let himself slip into a light relationship with Ducole's sister. After that incident in the vegetable patch, he had realized how easy it would be for things to get out of hand, especially if there was no other woman in his life to fill at least his carnal needs.

Those intimate moments he had accidentally shared with his ward had only served to increase the desire he had already felt for her and, until then, been fighting to control. But the feel of that voluptuous little body soft and yielding in his arms had only fanned the flame all the more. For he had glimpsed the passionate woman lying so close to the surface of that as yet childlike innocence. Despite the girl's naiveté, he had felt the fullness of those splendid breasts responding to his proximity and the curves of that sweet young body arching instinctively against his. God as his witness, he didn't want to seduce the vulnerable child that inhabited that delightful body of a woman!

As her guardian, he had been entrusted with the child, and he dared not betray that trust, but what he longed to be was the lover, the mate, of the woman he knew she could be if given just a little more time to ripen.

Meanwhile, it was best to distract himself elsewhere before his increasing desire for his ward might lead him to do something he would undoubtedly regret afterward.

The arrangement with Azema was pleasant enough. She had openly flirted with him from the very beginning when he had first begun to visit the Ducole plantation back in the spring seeking her brother's advice on converting the Chausson plantation to sugarcane, and she most certainly was beautiful enough to appeal to any man. He knew he wasn't the first lover she had had, nor would he probably be the last. But then, he had never led her to believe that he was offering her his undying love, either.

Of course, she was no tavern slut and had every right to expect certain niceties from him, but that was all. He had no intention of marrying her, and he doubted she would have accepted the idea had he suggested it. No, Azema Ducole was the perfect mistress in every sense of the word.

Her brother Henri had long since accepted her as she was and even seemed to find a certain amount of humor in his sister's amorous caprices. They made quite a pair, those two. With their fiery red hair, intense green eyes, and delicately chiseled features, they could have almost passed for twins, although Azema was really several years younger than her brother. Like two peas in a pod, both were graced with extremely sharp wits, exquisite taste, and complete sensuality. They loved life and seemed determined to enjoy it to the fullest, with little regard for the rules that bound most people.

When Vidal had first begun to visit them, Henri had immediately suggested to him that he buy himself a young black slave girl to keep on hand for his pleasure, or perhaps even set up some free "woman of color" in a discreet little house near the ramparts where he could visit her whenever he wished. Many of the men in the colony—French and Spanish alike—had such mistresses and recommended them highly to Miguel, for their beauty as well as for their loyal and docile dispositions. Henri readily confessed that he had one himself and found her highly satisfactory, although he added with a sly wink that he seldom limited himself just to one woman, since he found "too much repetition of anything rather boring."

When Miguel had protested that he preferred to have nothing to do with slaves or prostitutes, Henri had laughingly assured him that those "free women of color" were far from being either one or the other. A class unto themselves, those quadroons, as Henri had gone on to explain, were mostly the offspring of rich Spanish and French colonists and their Negro concubines. Often supported and educated by their white fathers, such women were, consequently, extremely cultured and proud. The more beautiful ones were usually reared in strictest morality, each carefully trained and groomed from the cradle up to become the exclusive mistress of some fortunate Creole gentleman, who had to approach the girl first through her mother and meet with the latter's approval before any liaison could be established. Furthermore, it was the custom for a lover to give such a faithful mistress either a legacy or some cash settlement when he died or decided to break off with her, either to get married or simply because he was tired of her.

Henri warned Miguel that the men of the colony often vied for the favors of such women and even fought duels over them. "Of course, the prudish white women here are terribly jealous of their quadroon rivals," Ducole had added with a chuckle. "I understand that several years ago they became so furious when they began to see the colored wenches strutting about town in their jewels and plumes, often more elegantly dressed than they were and sometimes better-looking to boot, that they went and complained to the governor—I'm talking about Miró, naturally . . . the one before the baron. Well, to make a long story short, they finally got Miró and the council to pass a law forbidding any woman of color to wear her finery around in public. As a result, the quadroons have taken to wearing their hair bound up a special way in a kerchief—a *tignon*, they call it—in accordance with the law, so you can't miss them. Those headdresses are like badges that you can spot from blocks away . . . all in all, rather convenient, I'd say, since we can tell who's who right away! Personally, I think the old biddies did us a favor!"

Ducole had assured Miguel that there were literally hundreds of such potential mistresses around town to choose from and had even gone on to offer to take him to one of the famous quadroon balls so he could judge for himself, firsthand, the merits of such "dusky-skinned wenches."

Miguel, however, had surprised his friend by refusing his gracious invitation. Although he had tried to explain to Henri that he didn't like to feel a woman was with him simply because she had to be in order to survive, he doubted that Ducole really understood. But, as the Frenchman himself had laughingly pointed out, it wasn't in his nature to "split hairs over such things!"

Miguel smiled inwardly as he wondered what his rebellious wards might have said if they could have heard Ducole accusing him of being a "radical" in some of his ideas.

As things had turned out, however, it hadn't been necessary to look any further than the Ducole household itself for his needs, since Azema had made it clear that she, too, had some needs of her own, which she felt he could fill to perfection. Since she seemed to offer what he wanted—a liaison with very light strings attached to it—he had gone along with it and looked no further.

Miguel thought it best not to invite the Ducoles to the fiesta his wards were planning for that Tuesday afternoon. In the first place, the affair was really for the girls, and Vidal doubted the sophisticated Ducoles would have fit in very well. Also, out of respect for Grandmother Chausson and his young wards, he thought it wiser to keep the more intimate aspects of his life apart from them. After all, it wasn't as though he were going to marry Azema.

If only Monica were more mature, or at least more receptive to him, there would be no need to concern himself over mistresses and the like. Fortunately, Azema had proved to be a pleasant companion both

in bed and in the drawing room and was without
commitment, so it made the waiting until his little
ward grew up at least more tolerable.

From early Tuesday afternoon on, the guests
began to arrive for the party. Although the majority
were youngsters like Monique and Celeste, there
was a wide range of ages, since older or younger
brothers, sisters, and cousins, as well as parents and
guardians, also came to swell the ranks of the invited
guests.

The main rooms of the raised manor were gaily
adorned with colorful paper lanterns and clusters of
gilded pinecones, and the dining-room table was
laden with an appetizing assortment of refreshments, from roast beef, baked ham, and fried chick-
en to sweetmeats of all types—dried fruits, sugar
candies, and a wide assortment of bonbons. There
were liqueurs for the younger people and a choice of
imported wines for the older guests.

Between the proficiency of Celeste and two young
men on string instruments such as the guitar and
mandolin and the dexterity of one of the chaperons,
as well as Monique's, on the harpsichord, there was
more than enough music to keep the party lively.

The odor of citronella burning in little braziers
hung heavy in the air throughout the rooms, so that
the large double doors leading out onto the gallery
that circled the house might be left open to invite the
evening breezes without bidding welcome to the
mosquitoes as well.

Monique and Celeste had perked up considerably
by the time the guests had begun to arrive, and the
two sisters flittered about prettily in their new summer gowns—Celeste in a flounced organdy of sun-
flower yellow that brought out the highlights in her
honey-colored hair, and Monique in a whispering

multiskirted silk of soft blue-gray that echoed her eyes to perfection. There had been a few brief moments when Monique had first sallied forth from her room that she had looked so alarmingly pale that Vidal and her grandmother had feared she might have been coming down with something, but once Mlle. Baudier appeared on the scene lamenting over the amount of rice powder her charge had piled on her cheeks, everyone breathed a sigh of relief and the young girl was simply sent back to her room to wipe off some of her "fashionably pale complexion."

"I can't imagine what comes over the child sometimes!" Grandmother Chausson had exclaimed as Monique had stamped off under protest to obey their dictum. "One minute she wants to go around half naked and the next looking like a clown! Merciful heavens! What will the girl come up with next?"

Although Monique was annoyed over the reaction she had received for her efforts to cover up the pronounced rosiness of her cheeks, she did find some consolation in the fact that the decolletage of her new party dress was a little more provocative than usual.

As long as it was daylight, the guests ambled about the grounds, strolling arm in arm or playing games under the trees and in the garden. Only occasionally would they go inside to the dining room where neatly uniformed servants busily kept two huge tables, covered over with embroidered white linen, constantly replenished with tray after tray of fresh food and drink so that the guests could serve themselves whenever and as often as they wished.

As the afternoon waned, however, and dusk began to fall, the party moved indoors. The colorful lanterns hanging from the sturdy cypress-beamed ceilings swung gently now in the welcome currents of air wafting through the open gallery doors lining both sides of the large double parlor and dining room that spanned the width of the raised house, riding high on its massive brick pillars.

Two magnificent crystal chandeliers, pride of the plantation since Grandfather Chausson had imported them from France forty years ago, were lit, together with the many wall and floor candelabra scattered throughout the rooms, so that the main salons were aglow with myriads of candles and, as glimpsed from outside through the open gallery doors, gave the appearance of an island of light shining in the darkness . . . a shimmering fairyland hanging suspended in midair.

Miguel Vidal discreetly remained in the background, not coming out of his back bedroom to mingle freely with his cousins' guests until the party had moved indoors and little musical recitals and extemporaneous dance groups had begun to replace the outdoor games. For the most part, he deliberately kept himself among the older guests, trying to relieve Grandmother Chausson of some of the burden that had fallen on her to play hostess to the chaperons who had accompanied the younger guests. But there were several mothers who persisted in pushing him into the company of their eligible daughters, since it was obvious they considered the Chaussons' newly arrived relative from Spain to be one of the best catches of the season. Before long, therefore, Vidal found himself being forced to take a more active part in the festivities and, on several occasions, even compelled to participate in the dancing as the partner of some charmingly persistent young lady.

Monique's eyes followed her guardian's tall, lithe figure as he moved about the fiesta, begrudgingly noting how he looked more striking than ever in his olive-green frock coat and those clinging nankeen breeches that showed off to such advantage the hard, lean muscles of his thighs as he deftly went through the paces of a quadrille. Fleetingly she remembered how he had once taught her and Celeste those very steps during one of their music lessons. . . .

But even as she watched him, anger stirred in her again. First, that carrot-topped Azema Ducole, and now, those horrid little coquettes Camille LeBlanc and Emmaline Dossier hanging on to him like that all night! If she had needed any further evidence to back up her conclusion that her guardian was a woman chaser, that evening was proof enough for her!

At that moment she lifted her eyes to thank the owner of the white-gloved hand extending a glass of anisette toward her. It was Claude Roget, the older brother of one of her young friends at the party. Claude was the same age as Miguel, yet *he* didn't find her too young to treat like a full-grown woman. She could tell by the look in his dark blue eyes that he found her desirable. She had sensed his gaze fixed curiously on her all afternoon. Of average height, but well built, with his light brown hair neatly caught back and clubbed at the nape of his neck, he was clad in a lime-colored frock coat and sleek white breeches, set off by a matching vest of striped silk. There wasn't a marriageable girl in the colony who didn't want to snare Claude Roget, for he had been one of the most sought-after bachelors in New Orleans now for a number of years.

Not that she had any ambitions to be the one to snag him, but it did flatter her that he was showing so much interest in her. She hoped her guardian was duly noting that she was every bit as much a woman

as that Azema Ducole or any one of those giggling
girls fluttering around him at that moment.

With as enticing a glance as she could manage
from over the top of her rose-scented lace fan,
Monique rose, determined now to do a little flirting
herself.

Chapter Nineteen

THE FULL MOON HUNG HUGE AND HEAVY AGAINST THE darkened skies, casting a pale silvery streak down the length of the shadowy gallery. There at the far end of the raised porch, where the shuttered doors leading to the rear bedrooms were closed at the moment, a warm breeze gently stirred the midsummer night.

"Monique . . . you're so lovely . . . so lovely . . ." Claude was murmuring softly in her ear. His arm was easing about her waist.

The sounds of the fiesta seemed distant now as they wafted out through the open doors of the brightly lit front rooms. Monique wondered whether her guardian had seen her come out on the gallery with Roget. Perhaps he had been too busy being charming to that flighty little coquette he was dancing with even to notice what she was doing.

Claude was pressing her closer to him, trying to persuade the curves of her body to mold themselves all the better to his.

Suddenly Monique realized they were alone out there in the night and had strayed much farther away from the others than she'd really wanted to. After all, if she were too far away from her guardian's eyes, how would he know that Claude Roget was trying to court her?

"Please, Claude, we should be going back with the

others," she told him, trying to disengage herself from his embrace.

But he was not to be put off.

"Wait, my dear, not yet," he insisted. "Come here . . . behind these palmettos. No one can see us back here. Come, don't be afraid."

His arms were locked around her, and he was pulling her slowly but firmly into the shadowy niche behind the cluster of potted palmettos adorning that corner of the porch, all the while whispering meaningless phrases in her ear: "my little dove . . . my sweet cabbage . . ."

Although his breath was heavy with wine, there was that same masculine scent emanating from him . . . stirring her . . . reminding her of Miguel. Lavender and tobacco . . . it filled her nostrils and brought back memories . . . awakened desires. . . . If she closed her eyes she could almost imagine she was in her guardian's arms again. . . .

Passionate lips were clamping over hers now and swift, eager hands were beginning to explore her body. Oh, Miguel! Miguel! This is the way it always happens in my dreams. She began to tremble and instinctively parted her lips to that persistent tongue trying to push its way past them. There was heavy breathing in her ear . . . a hand was searching for her breast . . .

But no, somewhere in the midst of that wild confusion she knew something was wrong. That touch was wrong . . . that pulsating body pressed against hers was beating to a different rhythm . . . a rhythm she didn't recognize or want to follow!

Her eyes flew open and she saw the eager face of Claude Roget, moist with the heat of the summer night and his mounting passion, hovering above her with half-closed lids. The sight of him jarred her back to reality.

"Oh, no, Claude! No, I . . . I don't want . . . please, let me go!" She tried to push him away, but his arms only tightened all the more around her.

"Don't be a tease!" he chided. "You know you want me as much as I want you." His breathing was coming faster, and the strength of him suddenly frightened her. The tiny fists flying against his chest were as ineffective as falling raindrops on a mountainside.

"Come now, my dear, don't make me beg for it," pleaded Roget, pressing his loins harder yet against her and stifling her protests with still another kiss.

The potted palmettos quivered violently as she struggled with him in that crammed space where he held her trapped in his arms.

Suddenly the huge fanlike leaves parted and there, staring down at them like an avenging angel, was the dark, contorted face of Miguel Vidal.

For a moment both Monique and her overly amorous admirer stared back in complete confusion at the cold fury looming above them. Claude Roget's jaw dropped even as his arm dropped from the struggling girl.

Free at last, but wide-eyed and trembling, Monique broke away from the confinement of the potted plants and ran quickly to her guardian. She had never been so glad to see him as she was at that moment. But he only seemed to have eyes for Roget.

"Monica . . . go into the house," he told her acidly, without so much as a glance at her. He was like a dark panther ready to spring, not wanting to take his sights off his prey even for a second.

She stood there, however, paralyzed with an even greater fear now, for she had never before seen her guardian so furious. Even Roget was visibly shaken, his olive complexion ashen, as he saw that Vidal had donned his sword and was clutching its hilt restlessly.

"Now, now, Vidal . . . I . . . I hope you understand that your ward came out here of her own volition," he stammered.

"I suppose the young lady thought she could step out on her gallery with one of her guests without being mauled," retorted Vidal icily.

Despite the fear that obviously gripped him, Roget drew himself up as best he could and decided to brazen it out.

"I think you're misjudging this situation, senor," he insisted. "Your ward here gave me every indication that my advances would be most welcome . . ."

Vidal's knuckles whitened on the hilt of his sword. "Senor, take care. You're talking about my ward, who, as you well know, is not of age yet and, therefore, under my protection."

Roget smiled meaningly. "Mlle. Monique may be very young, as you say, senor, but she's woman enough to let a man know what she wants."

Monique gasped indignantly. "I told you to stop!" she exclaimed angrily. "I didn't think you'd . . . I never meant for you to . . ."

Vidal still didn't take his eyes off Roget, nor his hand from his sword hilt. "I told you to go into the house," he told her sharply. Then once more he addressed Roget, who continued to stand there cornered behind the palmettos.

"Let me make myself clear, senor," he said with calculated calm. "When a man takes advantage of a young, inexperienced girl, no matter how foolish she might be, it's called seduction."

The Frenchman gave a nervous laugh. "Aren't we making a mountain out of a molehill, Vidal?"

"That molehill happens to be my ward's reputation, senor, which you seem to take much too lightly."

Roget was growing increasingly uncomfortable with his back pressing against the plaster wall and the pointed tip of a palmetto leaf tickling his cheek.

"If I do, it's because the lady in question seems to place little value on it herself."

Livid now, Vidal swayed as though he had been struck. "I should run you through on the spot!" he exclaimed, his voice throaty with rage, as he began to unsheathe his sword.

Roget realized he had gone too far. The blood drained from his countenance. "I . . . I'm not armed, senor," he reminded Vidal feebly.

Even Monique held out a pleading hand to detain her guardian, but Vidal had already regained control of himself and, with a grunt of disgust, let his half-drawn sword drop back into place by his side once more.

"Bah! I see where there's no sense discussing anything with you," he growled angrily. "You're a boorish clod, senor, without even the conscience or sensitivity to apologize for your rude behavior to my ward while a guest in her home. You leave me no recourse except to send my seconds to you tomorrow morning."

Roget bowed stiffly and stepped out at last from

behind the potted palmettos, trying to preserve what little dignity he had left.

"I'm at your disposal, senor. Since I'm the challenged and have the right to choose weapons, I would prefer pistols."

The Frenchman eyed Vidal's blade apprehensively, obviously afraid that his adversary would be too formidable an opponent with the rapier that he seemed so eager to use on him at that moment.

"We can discuss the details in the morning," Vidal replied curtly. "For now I'll thank you if you just vacate the premises."

Roget bowed again with exaggerated pomp to both Vidal and his ward and then, turning rigidly on the heel of his boot, walked away.

For a few seconds there was an awkward silence on the gallery as Monique stood beside her irate guardian watching the retreating back of her would-be lover.

"Oh, Cousin Miguel, are . . . are you going to have to fight him?" she asked suddenly, her tear-stained cheeks whiter now than the rice powder could have ever made them.

He turned his dark, smoldering eyes at last to her.

"Yes, I am," he replied tartly. "For, in spite of your obvious determination to rush down the road to total ruin, I'm still your guardian and must answer for your reputation. But he has *la razón,* you know. I saw you flirting with him like the silly, thoughtless child you are, without any concern for the tragic consequences your reckless behavior could bring about. Well, I hope you're satisfied now!"

"But . . . but I never thought—"

"Of course not! When do you ever think, you foolish child?" he interrupted impatiently. "Do you realize that, because of your folly, two men are in peril now of losing their lives? Your thoughtless actions have provoked a senseless duel that will prove nothing except that you are a scatterbrained girl who puts no value on her reputation. Unfortunately, as your guardian, I have been placed in a situation where I am nevertheless obliged to defend it. *Bien*, perhaps this will be your way of finally ridding yourself of me. Now go back to your guests, and please try to behave yourself at least for the rest of tonight. I can only fight one duel at a time!"

Monique's eyes were brimming over with tears once more. "Please, you mustn't think I really wanted that horrid man to . . . to . . ."

"Then whatever possessed you to behave as you did? I know you're impulsive and headstrong sometimes, but I've never seen you flirting like a bawdy-house wench before. Are you in the habit of going around offering yourself to every man who murmurs a few pretty phrases in your ear?"

"Oh, no, of course not! I'd never let anyone take liberties with me."

"Well, he seemed well on his way to doing just that. I certainly hope you're not accustomed to letting men take you off into dark corners and have their way with you!"

His face was still livid.

"Oh, no . . . believe me, I've never . . ." The intensity of his rage awed her.

"Don't lie to me, Monica. What about your precious Maurice? If you let Roget, surely you've let him?" The nerve in his jaw was twitching as the knuckles of his hand went white over his sword hilt. He seemed to be wishing he had Foucher there, too, at that moment, so he could run him through along with Roget.

"Of course not!" she exclaimed indignantly. "What do you think I am? A fallen woman?"

He saw how offended she was, and the anger drained out of his eyes. He had never had any sisters, but after the courtesans of Europe and Azema Ducole, he had forgotten just how naive a seventeen-year-old girl in the provinces could be. He had to keep reminding himself that the sensuous woman standing there before him was really still a child in so many ways.

"All right," he acquiesced crossly. "At least it's a comfort to know I won't have died in vain if I should lose my life defending your virtue tomorrow."

The pale gold of her hair blended with the moonlight as she bowed her head. "That's what we were fighting about when you came out and found us," she confessed timidly. "He'd pulled me back of the palmettos and was trying to take liberties with me, but I wouldn't let him."

Vidal continued to eye her sternly. "Well, let that be one of your first lessons in womanhood," he said sharply. "Don't dangle the bait if you don't want to get caught. You see, my little ward, that's one of the big differences between a woman and a child. A woman considers the consequences of her actions. She doesn't just plunge headlong into trouble, pulling everyone else around her into the whirlpool with her as well. Now do as I say. Go inside to your party."

She turned to obey, her head still hanging dejectedly, the tears rolling unchecked now down her cheeks. Suddenly she paused and looked back at him from where she stood on the gallery.

"Miguel . . . Cousin Miguel . . ." She hesitated.

"Yes?" he asked impatiently.

"Please . . . please be careful tomorrow."

He lifted a dark, inquisitive brow. "I have every intention of doing so," he replied, but he was staring at her with renewed curiosity.

"I'm . . . I'm sorry . . . truly sorry you have to fight because of me."

"I hope you'll bear that in mind next time you feel tempted to act rashly."

She paused yet a moment more, as though loath to return to the party in progress within. The peals of carefree laughter and the tinkling of mandolins and guitars spilled out into the warm summer evening through the open doors farther down the gallery, but the merrymaking suddenly had a distant, unreal sound to the two motionless figures silhouetted there in the moonlight just then.

"I . . . I wouldn't want anything to happen to you because . . . because of me," she insisted.

"I wouldn't, either," he agreed, a faint smile tempering the annoyance in his dark eyes for the first time since he had found her behind the palmettos with Roget.

"Now go back in," he said, a little less severely, "and don't say anything for the moment. You don't want to worry your grandmother, and the less scandal the better. I'll be careful tomorrow, you can be certain of that much."

He watched her walk the rest of the way down the gallery and disappear into the house. The rustling of her silk skirts still echoed in his ears as he stood there in the semidarkness a few minutes longer, trying to collect his thoughts. He wondered whether

the day would ever come when he'd be able to
understand that bewildering little ward of his. He
could have sworn she seemed genuinely concerned
for him when she was leaving. But then, Monique
was a good-hearted girl underneath all that hostile
exterior. It was probably just her guilty conscience
reacting, once she realized how her foolish behavior
had put him in danger. Whatever made the girl act
the way she did sometimes?

The memory of her in Roget's arms came back to
haunt him, and his blood began to boil anew. The
damn bastard . . . pawing her like that! And Roget
hadn't been playing, either. He'd have taken her if
he could have gotten away with it!

Just the thought of another man's lips pressed
against that fleshy little mouth, of irreverent hands
caressing the fullness of those proud, hard-tipped
breasts, set him to trembling with rage. At least he'd
seen enough to know she'd been trying to fight him
off . . . that she hadn't wanted him to go on. The
foolish child! He'd have to keep his eye on her even
more from now on. She was at an age where her own
passions might betray her. The very thought of her
responding to another man's caresses, of someone
violating, even touching, the sweet wonder of that
warm, vibrant body, tormented him to the point of
madness. He had to come out of tomorrow's duel
alive . . . if only to protect her when she needed
him.

Chapter Twenty

MONIQUE WAS DESOLATE. SHE HAD WANTED TO SHOW her guardian that she was a full-grown woman but instead had only succeeded in making him look on her as more of a child than ever—and a foolish one, at that!

Worse yet, she had put him in danger of losing his life. Although it was true she'd often wanted to rid herself of her interfering guardian, she certainly had never wanted anything to happen to him, much less to be the cause of his misfortune!

During those long restless hours later in her room, she had lain awake tormented with visions of his seconds suddenly appearing at the front door carrying his bloody body between them . . . that fascinating, vibrant body she had felt pressed so close to hers, pulsating to the rhythm of her own! She'd never forgive herself if anything happened to him now because of her!

Shortly after dawn, unable to lie there sleepless any longer, she had risen from the twisted, tortured sheets of her bed and gone in search of her guardian. She had a great longing to see him again . . . to let him know how truly worried she was about him.

But he had already gone . . . gone to keep his appointment perhaps with death! If only she could have at least told him goodbye . . . seen him just one more time! Just the thought that she might never see him alive again made her physically ill.

Mlle. Baudier, noting the quiver of her charge's lower lip and the dark shadows under her eyes, called her quickly aside. Vidal had taken her into his confidence before leaving, she said, and had ordered her to say only that he had been called into the city on urgent business if Grandmother Chausson should ask why he wasn't there.

The governess's eyes seemed even larger than usual as she scolded Monique for her folly of the night before and repeated Vidal's warning that they were to say nothing to anyone about his real reasons for going into New Orleans.

By midday the last of the guests who had accepted the hospitality of Le Rêve for the night had gone. Normally Monique would have been sorry to see such festivities come to an end, but on this occasion she was only too happy to be relieved of her role as hostess.

Celeste sensed something was amiss and tried her best to find out from Monique what was wrong, but the older girl remained dolefully silent. Once she even broke out into unexplained weeping.

Grandmother Chausson immediately declared that Monique must be suffering from an attack of the vapors and told the governess to give the girl a good purgative and put her to bed. Monique would hear none of it, however, since she wanted to stay as close to the main entrance as possible. All that day she would start at every sound in the driveway and, heart pounding wildly, run to the front window to see who might be arriving.

But as night fell over the plantation and there was still no word of her guardian, she felt so ill that she finally retired to the refuge of the mosquito netting, where she could find welcome relief from prying eyes and let the tears flow freely.

That second sleepless vigil seemed longer than ever, for this time there was no distraction of guests to attend to until the early hours of the morning as there had been the night before. What's more, the fact that the duel had undoubtedly been fought by now only made her guardian's continued absence seem more ominous than ever with each passing hour.

When Celeste entered the bedroom to retire to her own four-poster, Monique pretended to be asleep so her sister wouldn't try to ask her anything more. She simply lay there wide-eyed behind the veil of netting, her back to the night candle on the table between the two beds, clutching her rosary in her hands and trying not to let the sob caught in her throat become audible.

As the second day wore on and there was still no news Monique was on the verge of letting the tears welled up inside of her burst their dam and confessing all to her grandmother and Celeste. Only the stern warning in Mlle. Baudier's watchful eyes forced Monique to keep the emotions churning inside of her in check.

It wasn't until near dusk Thursday afternoon that Miguel came riding up the long lane of oaks leading to the main house from the levee road. He came at a leisurely pace and even paused to say a few words to the stableboy, a quick-witted lad who took over the gelding he dismounted.

At the sight of her guardian Monique gave a little cry of delight and for a moment stood there by the window devouring his familiar tall figure with joyful eyes, while her heart pounded wildly and the blood raced through her veins, bursting the dam of her pent-up fears in a flood of relief. He was alive! Thank God, he had come back to her at last!

Unable to control herself any longer, she ran out on the gallery to meet him. She would have continued down the stairs to the driveway where he still stood talking to the boy if he hadn't seen her pert little figure in pale green muslin waiting for him and immediately gone up to join her on the porch.

He couldn't help noticing the vestiges of the two sleepless nights she had passed lingering on her woebegone, tearstained face, despite the fact that its paleness was momentarily flushed with the emotion of seeing him at last. The possibility that she could have been so upset did surprise him, but he chalked it up to remorse.

"How nice of you to come out and greet me," he said with a casualness that contrasted notably with her rush to the edge of the gallery as he reached the top step.

"I thought you'd never come!" she exclaimed breathlessly, all the while sweeping her eyes hungrily over his impressive figure in its rust-brown riding habit and black jackboots. She longed to throw herself into his arms and feel the hard reality of him once more!

"I didn't realize you were waiting so anxiously for my return," he replied, continuing to be maddeningly unruffled in the face of her effusive reception.

"I've been so worried!"

"Well, I'm glad to hear it." He smiled, beginning to enjoy the first real evidence of concern he had ever seen her show for him.

"I mean *really* worried!" she assured him emphatically.

"Well, if that's true, I'd say it was high time."

Anger and confusion crept into those wide gray eyes, swollen from weeping and lack of sleep, as they focused accusingly on him. "Then you just kept me hanging fire like this on purpose?"

"No, but since I didn't realize how upset you were, I decided to take care of some business in New Orleans while I was there so I wouldn't have to go back into town later on this week."

"Business? You could think of business at a time like that? What about the duel? I was so afraid you might have been . . . have been . . . You weren't hurt, were you?" Once more her eyes anxiously scanned him from head to foot, searching for signs of wounds.

"Fortunately, I wasn't," he assured her. "As you can see, I'm still all in one piece."

"And . . . and Roget? He isn't . . . you didn't . . . ?"

"I'm glad it's occurred to you to ask about him, too, for although he did behave very badly the other night, you must admit you led him into his predicament."

She blushed and lowered her eyes guiltily.

"I . . . I never meant for him to take me so seriously."

"But you *were* flirting." His dark eyes were uncomfortably penetrating at that moment.

She hesitated and then gave an impatient toss of her head. "Perhaps a little," she admitted reluctantly, "but women do sometimes flirt, don't they? I mean, that's all part of being a woman, isn't it?"

Vidal stifled his laughter. "Yes, I suppose you females are given to having a little sport with us men from time to time," he conceded, "but you shouldn't play the game unless you know the rules. And might I add that the game is, as you said, for women, not children!"

She smarted under that observation but bit her tongue since her curiosity was stronger than her pride at that moment.

"Well, aren't you going to tell me what happened?" she demanded impatiently.

"About the duel, you mean?" He was rather enjoying the opportunity of finally being able to do a little taunting himself.

"Of course, the duel! My, but you can be exasperating!"

"Well, by ten A.M. we were all assembled in the field back of the ramparts," he continued calmly, seeming to savor the suspense he was causing in her.

"Yes, yes . . . will you *please* get to the outcome!"

"Well, just when we got to the point where our seconds, as is the custom, asked us whether there was any possibility of reconciling our differences without resorting to bloodshed, Roget finally spoke up and acknowledged he'd been wrong. Rather shamefacedly, he confessed he'd been imbibing all afternoon long at the fiesta and blamed the wine for having made him forget how young you were by the time the two of you had stepped out on the gallery. The upshot of it, therefore, was that he offered me his apologies, and since he seemed sincere, and I thought it best not to encourage a scandal, I decided to accept them instead of going on with a senseless duel provoked by a senseless girl."

Monique was relieved to learn that no duel had been fought, after all, but she didn't appreciate that continual reference to her as a silly child. She was in no position to object at that moment, however, so she bit her tongue and followed her guardian into the house, resolving to settle that particular point with him at some later date.

Although Grandmother Chausson never knew

about the *affaire d'honneur* between Vidal and Roget, nor any of the circumstances that had led up to it, the elderly woman was, nevertheless, pleasantly surprised by her granddaughter's sudden recovery from her vapors and her obvious improvement in deportment thereafter. At least the girl was a little more subdued for the remainder of their stay at the plantation that summer.

Monique did confide the truth of what had happened, however, to Celeste, but only after she made her younger sister take their "sacred oath" not to repeat a word of it to Mémère or anyone else.

After listening with wide, incredulous eyes to the entire tale, Celeste had sighed and exclaimed, "Oh, Monique, do you realize Cousin Miguel was going to risk his life in a duel over you? Why, he could have been wounded or—or even killed!"

"Oh, they settled it without even firing a shot," she replied airily, reluctant to admit even to her sister how worried she had really been.

Suddenly Celeste giggled. "I'll wager Azema didn't like it any when she knew Cousin Miguel was fighting a duel with Claude Roget because of you!"

Monique's large, clear eyes lit up, and she began to laugh. She hadn't thought of that particular aspect of what, until then, had been a rather tragic incident in her seemingly dramatic young life, but now that Celeste had suggested it, the idea pleased her enormously.

Chapter Twenty-one

DURING THE WEEKS THAT FOLLOWED, VIDAL MADE very few trips to the city. Now that it was September, the time had come to plant his first crop of sugarcane. The cuttings were laid out in the furrows and then well covered with soil at a depth that would ensure them ample protection against any hurricanes or frosts that might threaten them during the long fall and winter months ahead. It wouldn't be until the spring before the cane would really begin to grow, but then it would shoot up by leaps and bounds.

He had decided to make arrangements with one or two nearby planters whose crops were failing to pay them for the services of their idle field hands during the month or two when he would need extra help with the planting and perhaps later for the harvest in the fall of the following year. Heaven knows, there were more than enough bankrupt planters around Louisiana these days only too happy to make a little extra money to help tide them over until their conditions improved. The rest of the time, Miguel felt, Roselle could manage well enough with the hands they already had.

He took the girls around with him once or twice so they could see how the cane was being planted in the furrows and learn some of the pertinent details about the process, but for the most part, with so much activity and strange workers on the grounds,

158

he preferred them to stay closer to the main house now. It was time to move back to their town house for the fall season anyway.

When Miguel announced that Don Andrés Almonester, the richest man in the colony, was planning a ball to open the social season the last day of the month, Monique and Celeste were unbearably excited.

As far as Vidal was concerned, about the only advantage of making the town house headquarters again was that he would be nearer his business contacts, since just about anyone of importance could be found in the city during the social season.

Of course, he had to admit that the fact that Azema's open arms would be more readily accessible to him was a pleasant enough prospect in itself. Henri's sister was a tantalizing wench who knew how to keep a man satisfied, especially in the bedchamber. Although sometimes there seemed to be an almost calculated perfection in her passionate lovemaking—a perfection born of years of experience in the art—there was, nevertheless, always the feeling of a certain challenge . . . as though each time he made love to her it was a conquest. For Azema was the type of woman who had that independent air about her which made love a sport. No matter how many times he had possessed her in the past, she always made him feel he had to win her anew whenever he wanted her favors again.

She had been furious over his near duel with Roget because of Monique, but, as he reminded her, he had never made any secret of the fact that his two wards would always have to come first with him.

Of course, she had been quite right when she'd

observed that he really had no need whatsoever to be spending so much of his time and energy cultivating a plantation when he had more than enough money of his own to permit him to spend the rest of his days doing exactly as he pleased, enjoying his leisure and pursuing more pleasant occupations, preferably with her.

Almonester's ball presented a problem for Vidal. He knew Monique and Celeste would never forgive him if he didn't take them, yet Azema had every right to expect him to escort her. She had been fuming ever since he had told her he'd already committed himself to his wards for that occasion.

When he suggested that perhaps she could go along with them, Azema only became angrier, declaring she had no intention of trailing along with him and his troublesome wards as though she were some kind of nursemaid. She reminded him that she could easily find someone else to accompany her from among the many other admirers she had been neglecting of late because of him, and Vidal was becoming so weary of her fussing and fuming that he was about to tell her to go ahead and do so. As a last resort, however, he appealed to Henri to help him out of his dilemma.

Ducole found the whole situation rather amusing and, knowing his sister, readily sympathized with Vidal.

"Go ahead and escort those spoiled brats of yours to the ball," he said with a laugh. "You can rest easy. I'll take Zee with me, and we'll meet there. But you'd better make it up to her once you're at the ball and attend her well, or there will be the devil to pay, if I know my sister. As for me, I'll be too busy trying to find myself a partner for the night—and I don't mean just for dancing, my friend—so don't expect much help from me once I get Zee to Don Andrés's for you."

With her brother's coaxing added to Vidal's, Azema finally agreed to the arrangement, but meanwhile she insisted that he spend more time with her than ever. As a result, his liaison with Azema became more evident than ever to his observing wards.

Not that he didn't try to be discreet. Out of respect to Grandmother Chausson and his wards, Miguel never passed a night away from the town house when he was supposed to have been there, leaving his more intimate visits to the Ducoles for either the beginning or the end of each of his excursions to Le Rêve. He felt the subterfuge was justified, although he had no intention of lying about it. If the subject came up, he was prepared to admit with complete openness that he had gone to the Ducoles', but in the meantime he saw no need to volunteer information. After all, he really owed no explanation to anyone for his personal movements.

Unfortunately, however, his testy little wards were already much more aware of his comings and goings than he could ever imagine. It was difficult for a man like Vidal, accustomed to moving about freely in cities the size of Madrid, Paris, and Rome, to remember how small and intimate New Orleans was by comparison. All it took was the sight of him riding by in the Ducole carriage with Azema by his side a day earlier than he was expected back in town, or a few indiscreet remarks from someone met at mass or while shopping, to keep the girls informed.

His ward's renewed hostility puzzled Vidal. Monique seemed to have forgotten all too soon her repentance of less than two months before. For a while he had begun to hope that the truce between them might have become permanent. Yet here she was defiant again, and he wondered what could have brought about that latest change in her.

To make matters worse, he knew Maurice Foucher would probably be at the ball, but there was no way he could strike the boy's name off Almonester's list as he had done when the girls had given their fiesta at the plantation.

From the very outset, the night of the Almonester ball forecast trouble. As far as Vidal was concerned, he dreaded the entire affair, but there was little he could do to avoid it without making matters worse.

To complicate things further, it was threatening rain, and the girls fretted the whole way to the party that it might be pouring down before the night was over and their elegant new gowns would be ruined.

At least Vidal had to admit that, if there was any pleasant aspect to the evening, it was the way his "pampered darlings," as Azema and Henri always referred to them, looked that night. He had never seen them lovelier.

Monique looked more desirable than ever with her abundant spun-gold hair spilling into a shimmering cascade down to her shoulders, and the full swell of her ripening breasts boldly pushing past the futile barrier of the discreetly draped neckline of her pale green muslin gown. A tiny bouquet of pink satin roses bobbed coquettishly atop the pert bustle where the full skirt of her gown was caught up by the bow of a darker green velvet sash to mark the delightful curve of her back.

When he saw her like that, hope sprang anew in him. Perhaps he would soon be able to leave off being her guardian and woo her as a woman. How he longed for the day when he could take her boldly into his arms and share at last with her that burning passion he carried deep within his being for her!

Even little Celeste, a copy of her older sister in pale lavender, with a dainty bouquet of satin forget-me-nots set in the bow of her matching velvet sash, seemed several years older than her fifteen summers that night as she proudly held her elaborate arrangement of chestnut-colored curls high for all to see.

Yes, from the look of his wards at that moment, Vidal suspected his days as guardian were numbered. Neither of them would be a child much longer.

Not to be outdone by his elegant young wards, he wore his own dark hair in the male version of the cadogan style, with the shorter side locks neatly framing his face and the fall in the back stylishly held in place by a black satin ribbon. Although some of the older men at the ball still persisted in using powder on such formal occasions, the younger ones like Vidal preferred now to wear their own hair or wigs in natural colors.

Although Monique had instantly begun to fume from the moment she realized that her guardian had arranged to meet Azema and her brother at the ball, she couldn't help stealing an appreciative glance at Miguel as he walked tall and proud beside her in his elegant frock coat of garnet velvet. She had to admit begrudgingly at the moment that he cut a fine figure from the tip of his high-crowned beaver hat to the soft polished leather of his black top boots. How jauntily his fine Toledo sword with its hilt of hammered gold swung against the molded perfection of his thighs in their sleek white breeches!

Grandmother Chausson had beamed her proud approval on her attractive grandchildren as she watched them go off to the ball. Since neither she nor Mlle. Baudier really cared about attending such elaborate functions anymore, they had readily agreed to stay home and keep each other company while Miguel and the girls went to represent the family.

The large hall on the ground floor of the manor had been turned into a spacious ballroom and it was ablaze with hundreds of candles reflected again and again in the dangling crystals of the chandeliers and the highly polished gold and silver of the countless candelabra. Some of the guests were already dancing, but others seemed to prefer the side of the room where the long tables of refreshments were being kept constantly overflowing with fresh food and drink by elegantly uniformed Negroes.

Despite the festive atmosphere, however, Vidal's hopes for a pleasant evening soon dimmed when he noted the manner in which his wards and his mistress greeted one another. From the moment the three of them came face to face, the temperature of that mild September night dropped by several degrees.

Azema, taller by several inches, looked disdainfully down her pretty aristocratic nose at Monique, while the young girl tilted the tip of her button nose all the higher and openly glared back. Little Celeste, like a faithful echo, immediately reinforced her sister with an equally seething stare.

All the while, Vidal stood uneasily to one side, silently cursing his bad luck to have become involved with three such ill-tempered females. Here he had made every effort to juggle them in such a way as to please, if possible, both "camps," yet he didn't seem to be succeeding with either one of them!

Chapter Twenty-two

NO SOONER HAD THE GREETINGS BEEN EXCHANGED THAN Azema, set off to advantage in a decollete gown of ice-blue satin, coyly rested her hand on Miguel's arm and announced she wished to dance the next set.

Feeling obliged to attend her without further delay, Vidal deposited his wards with a group of other young girls near their own age sitting on the sidelines and, with a hasty excuse, allowed Azema to whisk him off to the dance floor.

Bristling, Monique sat watching her guardian adeptly going through the paces of a sprightly cotillion with his disgustingly beautiful partner, while she fanned herself rapidly in frustrated rage and tried to fight back her tears of vexation.

How she detested that pasty-faced, long-nosed witch! Although two young men came up immediately to ask her and Celeste to join them in the next set, Monique refused them without even noting who they were. She kept her attention focused on her guardian and Azema Ducole most of the time, and the longer she watched them, the greater her chagrin. It had been bad enough to know about them, but to see them together like that right before her very eyes was insufferable! To have to sit there and watch her guardian dancing with that horrid woman only brought home the bitter truth more forcibly than ever to her. She could no longer deny the facts.

She tried closing her eyes for a moment, hoping to

blot out the sight of them together, but even worse pictures came to her mind—her guardian making love to that woman . . . kissing her . . . pressing his body close to hers. They were more vivid than ever now!

When Maurice finally arrived and came over to her, she gave him an especially warm welcome. Resolving to try to forget her obnoxious guardian and his equally obnoxious mistress for a little while, she readily accepted her friend's invitation to join the dancers.

Before long, however, it was Vidal who sought her out, curious to see how she and her sister were enjoying the ball thus far. He had seen Maurice Foucher dancing the last two selections with her, and now, taking advantage of the fact that he had seen Foucher go off to fetch some refreshment for her, Vidal had come over to talk to her.

"I hope you and Celeste are enjoying yourselves," he began, thinking how the misty green of her gown had penetrated her eyes as well. "From what I could see, you two have been dancing every set since we arrived."

"And I see you've been doing the same," she retorted coolly.

"Yes, I'm sorry to have neglected you until now, but I do have to attend Mlle. Ducole. She's my friend's sister and—"

"And your mistress!" she finished for him, almost hissing the word as she finally said it aloud to him.

Vidal stepped back as though she had struck him. "What . . . what makes you say that?" he asked bewilderedly.

Monique tossed her head in an effort to appear nonchalant about it all. "Oh, people gossip, you know," she replied airily, flipping open her frilly fan of dusty pink tulle and lace and fanning herself rapidly. "Besides, it's quite obvious . . . just the way she hangs on to you . . . that she considers you her personal property."

"Aha! Is that why you've been so belligerent toward me lately, hardly addressing a word to me, and then only snapping when you do?"

The little pink fan continued to flutter nervously.

"I don't like liars," she quipped.

"And when have I ever lied to you?"

"You say you're going out of town and you really just sneak off with that . . . that fallen woman! I saw you with my own eyes just this past Monday riding by with her in her barouche."

He flushed, but a twinkle was creeping into his dark eyes.

"Ah, yes, I forget sometimes that there's nothing more self-righteous than untried virtue." He smiled. "It's true I sometimes stop off at the Ducoles' before going home to the town house when I return to New Orleans from my trips to the plantation, but I don't recall lying about it. If you'd asked me, I wouldn't have denied it."

"But you always led us to believe you'd just arrived when you came home. . . ."

"I'm sorry, but I didn't realize I had to give a report of my every movement to you. Actually, it never occurred to me you were so interested in what I did every minute of my time."

It was Monique's turn to color. "It . . . it's not that I'm interested," she protested. "You can have all the mistresses you want. It's indifferent to me. What I . . . what Celeste and I resent is the subterfuge."

"I only meant to be discreet. Was that so wrong?"

"What's wrong is that you're in a situation where you have to hide anything in the first place."

"Touché!" He smiled. "I concede the point. Had I known you objected so vehemently, I might have been more inclined to mend my ways. Does my personal life really make so big a difference to you?"

She bit her lip and continued fanning herself.

"None whatsoever," she snapped crossly. "Your private life is your own, Cousin Miguel. Just don't be a hypocrite about it!"

He sighed and his smile saddened a little. "You're so young, little cousin. There are so many things you can't understand yet."

"I understand enough to know that long-legged carrot stick is your mistress, and that's more than I want to know already!" she replied scornfully. "Now I think you'd better go back to her before she comes over here to drag you off again."

He looked at her as one would at a petulant child who required infinite patience. "You probably won't believe me, but I came over here just now to ask you to be my partner for the next set. It's going to be a quadrille, and I thought you might remember that afternoon . . ."

Monique lowered her lids and fanned more violently than ever. Of course she remembered, and it made her furious whenever she thought how she had watched in secret those well-knit thighs flexing as he'd danced just for her and Celeste. How she had thrilled to the touch of those strong masculine hands as he had caught her and whirled her around in the turns! But that had been before she'd learned that those very same hands were caressing another woman and those fine thighs holding Azema Ducole between them!

"I'm sorry," she replied curtly, "but I'm already promised for the next dance."

"Then perhaps you can put me down for the next free one you have?"

"I'm sorry," she repeated, "but my dance card is filled. I'm promised for the rest of the night."

He stood looking down at her defiant little figure in frothy green trimmed with roses, trying to find some chink in that delicate yet impenetrable armor where he might be able to get through to her. Finally, with a sigh of resignation, he acknowledged defeat.

"I'm sorry to hear that," he said. "I'll leave you, then, to enjoy the evening. I won't disturb you until it's time for us to go home."

He turned and walked stiffly away while Monique sat watching his tall, proud figure, so elegantly etched in the long-tailed frock coat of dark red velvet. She brushed away the cloud of frustrated tears blinding her eyes. Let him go back to that horrid Azema, she thought angrily. After all, what could she expect of a Spaniard who was a libertine!

Her guardian had stopped now to talk to Celeste, who was still standing off to one side with the pudgy young boy who had been her partner for the last set. Even from across the large salon, Monique could see how delighted her sister was to accept her cousin's request for a dance. She was immediately extending the little card dangling from her wrist toward him so he could write his name on it. Celeste was too gullible, thought Monique, annoyed with her sister for so readily accepting their guardian's invitation.

At that moment, however, Maurice returned, holding a glass of punch in each hand. There was an eager grin on his freckled countenance. He had seen Monique's guardian conversing with her, so he had deliberately waited until Vidal had left before approaching, not wishing to have a confrontation with him if it could be avoided.

"I could see you seemed to be arguing with your guardian," he admitted as he apologized for his delay in bringing back her refreshment. "It seemed more prudent not to interrupt, knowing how your cousin feels about me. I hope you weren't having any words because of me."

With a start, Monique looked at her friend, standing there in his best finery, looking surprisingly aristocratic in his purple-colored swallow-tailed frock coat and nankeen breeches. He'd even made an attempt to comb his shaggy blond locks into some semblance of orderly disorder, and the effect gave him a rakish look that was rather appealing.

"No . . . no, it wasn't because of you," she replied absently. "I was confronting him with what I knew about him and that Ducole woman."

"I hope you didn't tell him I was noising it about?" he asked, the smile fading from his face.

"Of course not. Your name didn't even come up in the conversation."

Her eyes went back across the hall, singling out the slim, erect figure of her guardian as he made his way back to Azema's side through the couples milling around the dance floor. Maurice was saying something to her, but she suddenly realized she hadn't heard a word.

The orchestra began to play the opening chords of another quadrille, and she watched angrily as she saw Vidal leading the lissome redhead out on the floor again to complete a group of dancers. With a sigh she turned back to Maurice.

"I'm sorry I didn't hear you," she confessed. "You were saying?"

"That, all considered, your cousin does have a right to his private life. He's a bachelor and a free agent. But . . . but . . . you really didn't hear what else I said?"

"No, I'm sorry. I was momentarily distracted."

"Well, I . . . I was only trying to point out to you that, just as Vidal has a right to live his own life, so do you. After all, you'll be eighteen this coming January. You should begin thinking about making your own world . . . one more to your liking."

"Yes, I'd like that," Monique admitted. "But the courts wouldn't emancipate me unless my grandmother and guardian said they agreed to my being completely independent before I was twenty-one, and I doubt they'd do that."

"I do, too," agreed Maurice, "but there is another way."

Monique's eyes lit up. "I'd like that. If only I could . . . especially before that Azema Ducole completely dominates my guardian and succeeds in convincing him to make an honest woman of her. I hate to think of the day when he walks in with her on his arm as the new lady of the house! I use the term 'lady' lightly, of course!"

"If you were married yourself, neither he nor anyone he'd marry would have anything more to do with you," Maurice declared, anxiously watching her reaction to the idea.

The frilly pink fan stopped fluttering for a moment. "Yes," she said slowly. "I confess the thought has occurred to me, but . . ."

Foucher's freckled face became suddenly animated, and he went on quickly, the words pouring out of his mouth now in a fountain of hope. "Then why not? Why not marry? Surely you know I'd marry you in a minute if you'd just say yes, and I promise

I'd never try to dominate or mistreat you in any way. I'm so in love with you, Monique, I'd be your slave. I'd do your every bidding!"

Monique turned all her attention now to her enamored beau. Yes, she knew, with that womanly instinct awakening in her, that being married to Maurice would be the same as emancipation for her, if independence was all she really wanted.

"But I'm not of age yet, and the authorities here know Cousin Miguel. They wouldn't want to marry us without his consent, and my guardian has told me often enough that he has no intention of giving it as long as he holds that position, so there's no way. . . ."

"But there is," insisted Maurice, pressing his suit now that he saw she was at least receptive to the idea.

"It's not possible, I tell you . . . not now, anyway. Perhaps if I could convince my grandmother to recommend to the courts that my guardian be changed . . . But no, she'd never do that. She and Cousin Miguel are closer than ever now."

"We could elope!" he whispered in her ear, suddenly made bold by her seeming willingness to discuss at least the possibility of marrying him, something she had never before given him an opportunity to do.

On seeing that she still did not detain him, he rushed on softly in her ear, elaborating on the theme while the lilting music of the quadrille sounded in the background and Monique watched her guardian going through the paces of the dance with Azema. Reluctant as she was to admit it, they did make a striking couple. Azema Ducole was a joy to behold at that moment as she did the two-hand turns, her glorious red-gold mane streaming rhythmically behind her while her pale blue skirts whirled about those long, shapely limbs of hers, so tantalizingly glimpsed every time she gave a pretty turn.

Monique sighed. No wonder her cousin didn't even think of her as a woman when he compared her to a full-blown creature like that—with her sensuous breasts half exposed in the low sweep of her simple, unadorned neckline and the rest of her so emphatically marked by her tightly laced bodice! It didn't take much imagination to picture how alluring Azema Ducole must look to her guardian every time she lay naked in his arms responding to his caresses. . . .

Monique turned suddenly to Maurice, trying to blot out the image that had occurred to her, shocked and angry with herself for having even entertained such thoughts. She had only half heard what Maurice had been saying to her, but she had made her decision.

"If there really is a way it can be done, I'll marry you," she told him in a matter-of-fact tone.

Maurice Foucher's mouth hung open in the middle of a sentence. Her unexpected acceptance left him momentarily speechless. Still incredulous, yet not daring to give her time to change her mind, he caught her limp hand in his and, after a quick glance around them to be certain they couldn't be overheard, proceeded to discuss more fully the details of his proposal.

"If you really want to elope," he told her enthusiastically, "then the best time to do it is tonight."

Chapter Twenty-three

Monique slipped back into the ballroom while Maurice nervously waited for her in the foyer with their wraps.

"I don't want Celeste or my grandmother to be worried," she had explained to him. "Just yesterday the *Moniteur* had a note about the disappearance of another girl. That's the second one in only a few months, so Grandmother would think the worst right away. No, I couldn't go off like that without at least telling them I was going to be married and not to worry about me."

Celeste, however, was horrified by the whole idea. While the orchestra sounded still another quadrille and Azema Ducole kept their guardian busy going through his paces on the ballroom floor, Monique tried to convince her sister that what she was doing was for the best.

"We plan to leave a false trail by going out of the city by the North Gate, but we'll cut over to the west once we get to the fork farther up the river road about a half mile before Le Rêve. From there we can go on into the Acadian country and be married at the parish church in St. Martinville. Maurice says they're good-hearted people and should receive us well, especially when we tell them how we're fleeing from a cruel guardian."

Celeste shook her golden-brown head disapprovingly. "Oh, Monique, Cousin Miguel has never been cruel to us!"

"He's a despot, stifling us at every turn while he goes merrily along taking his pleasures where he pleases!"

"But to elope? I'm sure if you talked it over with Grandmother and Cousin Miguel, they'd take your wishes into consideration and would give you and Maurice their blessing. Wouldn't it be better to do it that way?"

"Oh, no, Cousin Miguel would never give his consent. He's told me time and again that he'll never permit me to marry as long as he's my guardian, and most certainly he'll never accept Maurice. I daresay he hates Maurice as much . . . as much as I hate that cat-eyed Azema!"

"But tonight? Merciful heavens! So soon? Why must it be precisely tonight? Shouldn't you . . . both of you . . . consider things just a little more? Marriage is such a big step!"

"We've been working out the details all evening," insisted Monique, "and I tell you, we'll never have a better opportunity to get away undetected than we do right now. No one will even notice we've gone until we're well on our way. What's more, with the ball, there's been so much activity at the gates all evening that one more carriage won't attract attention."

Celeste was near tears, her voice trembling with emotion. "Oh, Monique, please . . . *please* don't do this thing! You're so impulsive. Maurice is a good friend, I know, but to *marry* him? Are you sure? And there's a storm brewing outside, too. It's no night to travel."

"Now, Celeste, please don't try to stop me," begged Monique, but she was near to weeping now herself. She cast a final glance toward Miguel Vidal where he was still dancing with Azema. "I'm so miserable here," she said sadly. "I just want to go away from this horrid place . . . away from the Spanish yoke and . . . and Cousin Miguel and . . . and that horrid Ducole woman. I know I won't be satisfied until I'm free of them all, and the sooner the better. But you must promise me, on your sacred oath, that you won't tell anyone where we're going."

"I . . . I can't hide the truth from Grandmother. You know she'll be beside herself when she learns about this."

Monique lowered her eyes with momentary remorse. "All right," she acquiesced. "You can tell her, but at least give us a day or two before you do. By that time, there will be little Cousin Miguel will be able to do except accept the facts."

Celeste was weeping so uncontrollably that Monique feared someone might notice and come over to see what was the matter. "Please, my dear, don't fret so," she begged gently. "It's not as though we'll never see each other again. Maurice and I will come back when things are better here. I promise. Be sure to tell Grandmother that."

With a quick embrace, Monique brushed her wet cheek against her sister's in a discreet adieu. Then she dashed away, trying to keep her head turned so no one could see the hot tears scalding her flushed face. The ball was at its height at that moment, however, and everyone was too busy enjoying the dancing or the chatter on the sidelines near the buffet tables to concern themselves over a few excited youngsters running to and fro.

Monique was already beginning to have second thoughts by the time she had joined her impatient bridegroom nervously waiting for her in the entrance hall. But he immediately rushed to meet her and, throwing her long hooded cape around her shoulders, led her quickly toward the exit before she had time to think or hesitate any longer.

As soon as they stepped out into the heavy night air, a moist breeze greeted them and set her skirts to flapping about her legs. Tiny droplets of rain hit her face as they made their way toward Maurice's cabriolet, so she drew the hood of her cloak closer about her head. Her new ball gown would probably be ruined, but she was past caring about such things now.

Chapter Twenty-four

ON THE PRETEXT OF GOING TO FIND REFRESHMENTS, Vidal had at last managed to tear himself away from Azema. He walked rapidly over to where the youngsters seemed to be congregating the most.

He was anxious to see Monique again. She had been so furious about Azema. . . . The extent of her anger had surprised him. Could she possibly care about him as a woman cares about a man? Certainly she had looked like a desirable, sensual woman tonight with her flushed cheeks, her smoldering eyes, and those seductive curves of her young body. He longed to feast his eyes on her once more and, if possible, fathom the depths of that anger.

He hadn't seen Monique in well over an hour now, and all the time he had been dancing and conversing and then dancing again, he had been trying to catch a glimpse of that familiar head of wheat-colored curls bobbing about somewhere among the milling guests who filled the salon.

But his ward was nowhere to be seen. Just the fact that he couldn't see her filled him with apprehension. With that impulsive nature of hers, the girl had a knack for getting into trouble. He had left her in a spiteful mood . . . there was no telling what she might do if left to her own wiles.

He found himself trying to spot the shaggy blond

head of Maurice Foucher, fearful there might be another scene in the making like the one on the gallery that summer.

At last he caught sight of Celeste's slim little figure in lavender sitting over in a corner looking strangely doleful. By all the saints! What was the matter with the men of New Orleans to leave a pretty young girl like that sitting on the sidelines?

He made his way hurriedly over to her, determined to perk up his little ward by inviting her to dance. Why, the girl looked positively crushed. It annoyed him to see her neglected like that.

But even as he made his way over to her, he saw how she was refusing a young boy's invitation to dance at that very moment.

"Why, Celeste aren't you feeling well?" he asked solicitously, reaching her side just as her disappointed admirer was walking away from her.

The girl's amber eyes looked up at him like a startled fawn's. At the sight of him, she seemed to pale even more, and her reply was so disconnected that Vidal couldn't make any sense of it.

"Celeste, child, if you're ill, I'll take you home this minute," he offered, sitting down quickly in an empty chair beside her. The orchestra had begun to play a cotillion, and almost everyone was out on the dance floor once more. "You should have called me sooner," he told her.

"Oh, *mon Dieu! Mon Dieu!*" was all the girl could murmur as she sat there, her kerchief crumpled in her hand. She indeed looked ill—as though she were about to faint away at any moment.

Vidal took her by the arm. "Come, my dear, we'll go home this minute. Where's Monique?" He cast a glance curiously around the room once more. "Your sister should have never left you alone like this if you weren't feeling well."

He assumed the girl felt too ill to reply, for she simply continued to sit there in mute despair.

"Where in the world is Monique?" he asked her again. "I don't see her anywhere." The terrified look creeping into the young girl's eyes suddenly aroused his suspicions. Could it be his younger ward was indeed sick—very sick with fright? Something or someone seemed to have upset the young girl terribly, and Miguel Vidal had a fairly good idea now who was responsible.

"Come now, tell me, where's that sister of yours?" he insisted, his blood beginning to boil at the thought of his more adventurous ward wandering off somewhere in Almonester's mansion probably trapped behind another palmetto!

But Celeste only stared at him with large, frightened eyes and stubbornly shook her head. "I . . . I don't know," she faltered.

At that moment Azema came up to them rather impatiently.

"Really, Miguel! Whatever has been keeping you?" she asked crossly. "Here I am prostrate with thirst, waiting anxiously for you to bring me something, and all the while you're sitting here chatting with this child!"

But Vidal was in no mood to humor his mistress's tantrums. Ignoring her, he continued to direct his attention to Celeste. "I think you do know where your sister is," he persisted, "and for her own good, you must tell me."

"I . . . I can't. Please, Cousin Miguel, don't ask me!" pleaded the girl, twisting her kerchief nervously.

"If that other ward of yours is missing, you can be sure she's off in some dark corner with one of her beaux, that's all," volunteered Azema with an amused laugh. From what she had caught of their conversation, they were making a fuss over nothing.

But Vidal was not to be put off. "Now look, Celeste," he continued, addressing her in a sterner tone of voice now. "If you know anything, you'd better tell me. I'd prefer not to have to start searching Don Andrés's house from top to bottom for her. For Monica's sake, let's not make a scandal."

At his last words, Celeste burst into tears. "Oh, Cousin Miguel, she . . . she isn't here. She's gone!"

"Gone?" echoed Vidal, his jaw dropping in disbelief. "You mean she's left the premises?"

"Yes," came the muffled reply between sobs.

Vidal sputtered helplessly for a moment as his thoughts raced wildly ahead of his speech. "She . . . she's gone off with . . . with that Foucher boy, hasn't she?" He caught her almost roughly by the arm.

"Oh, yes," wailed Celeste. "She's with Maurice. They're eloping!"

"Eloping? *Qué barbaridad!* That's all I needed!" A flood of Spanish exclamations poured out of him. "But the girl is daft!"

"She . . . she told me to tell you and Grandmother not to . . . not to worry—that she'll be all right," Celeste added meekly, trying to soothe him a little, although it was evident she didn't fully believe her own words of consolation.

Suddenly the full impact of the news hit him. Only one thought was foremost in his mind now. He had to stop Monique before it was too late.

"Quick! Where did they go?"

His grip was on Celeste's tiny wrist, but she hesitated. "I . . . I don't know," she insisted.

"Come now, I'm sure she told you something of their plans."

The poor girl was sobbing uncontrollably now. "I . . . I don't know," she insisted.

Vidal pulled her up out of the chair and drew her aside so that those who were beginning to eye them with budding curiosity couldn't hear what they were saying. "Come now, Celeste," he coaxed more gently now, trying not to frighten the youngster more than she already was. "You must tell me what you know . . . for your sister's sake. She can't be permitted to do this idiotic thing."

"I . . . I can't." She stood there hanging her honey-colored curls in stubborn silence.

Vidal was beside himself. "Celeste, please! We're wasting precious time. You'll regret it to your dying day if you don't tell me."

"But I gave my sacred oath. She made me swear. . . ."

Vidal ran his hand desperately through the shock of dark ringlets framing his anguished face.

"Don't let false loyalty blind you to the greater things at stake here. Your sister's whole future is in jeopardy," he pleaded fervently. "And think of your grandmother. This could kill her."

Poor Celeste was weakening. The burden of so great a secret was too much for her scant years.

"They're . . . they're going to . . . to the Acadian settlement," she finally replied, seeming to be wringing the information out of her twisted handkerchief. "She said something about the parish church at St. Martinville."

Vidal seemed to be about to sprout wings, but he

paused a moment longer. "What time did they leave here? Quickly, how much head start do they have?"

"They left about an hour—no, an hour and a half ago, I think. Oh, I'm really not sure!"

Azema, who had been listening in aloof silence, suddenly caught Vidal by the sleeve to detain him. "Really, Miguel, you're not thinking of riding out into the night after them?"

"Of course I am!" he retorted, surprised she would even ask such a question. "I'm sure I can overtake them if I go on horseback." He turned again to Celeste.

"They're in a carriage, I suppose?"

"Yes, in Maurice's cabriolet."

Vidal gave an exasperated snort. "The fool! To attempt such a journey on a night like this in so light a vehicle!"

Azema blocked his way impatiently. "Miguel, aren't you being rather melodramatic?" she chided, a cool, half-amused tone in her voice. "After all, if your little cousin has chosen to elope, she may have good reasons for it."

Vidal looked down at her from his full height, making no attempt to hide his annoyance. "If you're implying what I think you are, senora, you're quite out of your mind. My ward is only a child . . . a foolish one, perhaps, but only a child. She may be naive and impetuous, but most certainly she isn't trying to cover up any transgression."

Azema laughed with a touch of sarcasm now. "Really, Miguel, for all your worldliness in so many things, you can be so blind where those little cousins of yours are concerned. Surely you've noticed by now that your ward is more of a woman than a child? If she wants to get married, why not let her do so and give her and the boy your blessing?"

Vidal pulled his sleeve almost angrily from her grasp. "I don't have time to argue fine points with you, senora," he snapped. "I'm sure that, under the circumstances, you won't mind if I ask Henri to take you and Celeste home for me. There simply isn't a minute to lose."

He turned again to his unhappy young cousin. "If she's going to Acadian territory, then I suppose they've taken the West Gate out of the city?"

Celeste vacillated. She saw the anguish on her guardian's face, ashen now above the snow-white folds of his high cravat. She couldn't let him go off chasing out into the night like that, frantically roaming the lonely roads of the dark wilderness looking in vain for her sister.

She could feel his dark eyes fixed on her—pleading —waiting for her reply.

"They . . . they left by the North Gate," she said at last. "Then at the fork on the levee road, just a little before Le Rêve, they plan to turn off and continue westward."

Vidal didn't wait to hear more. He went dashing off toward the exit, pausing only to say a few hurried words to Henri Ducole on his way out before clapping his beaver hat firmly down on his head and vanishing into the inclement night.

Celeste sank down into the nearest chair she could find, afraid that her legs would give way on her at any moment. She had broken her sacred oath and betrayed her sister's confidence in her. Monique would probably never speak to her again!

Chapter Twenty-five

THEY HAD BEEN RIDING FOR SEVERAL HOURS NOW, AND it was well after midnight. Although it hadn't begun to rain yet, the wind had been steadily increasing in velocity, and the small one-horse carriage swayed and creaked noisily as it made its way doggedly down the dark, winding road running beside the levee. The Mississippi looked like tarnished silver in the overcast night, for there was very little moonlight to reflect. Not even the lanterns bobbing on either side of the cabriolet had helped much to illumine the road as they had flickered and sputtered feebly to the rhythm of their feverish race against time.

Now, however, Foucher had drawn the carriage up to the side of the road in order to give their hard-pressed horse a momentary rest after their three-hour sprint on the wings of the wind. They were at the junction where the road either turned off to the west or continued straight north.

Monique sat huddled next to Maurice, the full skirts of her wilted ball dress crushed into the limited space of the small two-seater. If only the tumult raging inside of her would stop long enough to let her think! As they had ridden on and on into the damp, inclement night, with the wind rushing— almost pushing—them along their way, her confusion had continued to mount until now it overwhelmed her. Between Maurice and the wind and her own torment, she simply couldn't collect her thoughts. How she wished she could at least blot out that image of her guardian and Azema Ducole dancing together and shut out the sounds of Maurice's voice and the roaring wind in her ears! Somewhere amid the turmoil roaring around her and within her, she had begun to wonder whether she would really like everything that being married to Maurice Foucher would entail.

Now, as they paused on the lonely, dimly lit road, she was beginning to realize that, in the future, it would be like that—just she and Maurice. He was the one who would always be by her side now—not Miguel. Was Maurice Foucher the man, then, who would be holding her, making love to her for the rest of her life? It seemed that, although Miguel Vidal filled her dreams, the reality would be Maurice.

She wondered whether she would react the same way to him as she had with Claude that night on the gallery. When the moment came and Maurice would begin to kiss and fondle her, how would she feel on opening her eyes to see it was Maurice's face bending over her instead of her guardian's?

She tried to imagine how it would be to have Maurice kissing her and cupping his hands over her breasts and drawing her into the apex of his thighs, but the thought revolted her.

Suddenly she realized Maurice had put his arm around her shoulder and at that very moment was drawing her closer to him. She stiffened and drew away.

"What . . . what are you doing?" she demanded uneasily.

"I'd just like to kiss you," he said, bending eagerly toward her lips.

But she pushed him away so violently that the carriage vibrated all the more in the wind.

"Oh, don't you dare!" she exclaimed indignantly.

"But if we're to be married . . . All I want is a little kiss, my dear, nothing else. I mean no disrespect."

"Well, we're not married yet," she declared emphatically, "so don't think you can take liberties with me just because we're alone out here in the middle of the night."

Maurice flushed self-consciously. "I wouldn't dream of it!" he protested. "I . . . I just thought you might at least like me to kiss you. It's all rather romantic, don't you think? I mean, our eloping like this on the spur of the moment and all."

Monique frowned. She really didn't find anything very romantic about being parked on the side of a dark road at one o'clock in the morning on a damp, windy night with rain threatening to come down on them at any moment. Actually, much as she had always liked to share her feelings of patriotism and mutual hatred of Spaniards with Maurice, she had just about come to the conclusion that she didn't want to share any other kinds of feelings with him at all.

"I don't think we should try to go on any farther tonight," she told him crossly. "The weather seems to be getting worse. How populated is the road to Acadiana?"

"I'm not really sure," admitted her prospective bridegroom, rather crestfallen now over his bride-to-be's reaction to his efforts to add a little more romanticism to their flight. "But it does look as though we might be in for a bad storm, even a hurricane. Perhaps we should continue up the river road as far as Le Rêve and spend the night there. It's our nearest refuge from this point . . . just up the road a piece. Is there anyone there now? I mean, would we be able to get in?"

"Roselle and the field hands should be in their quarters out back, and usually grandmother leaves Old Meggie in charge of the main house when we're not there, but the poor old soul is almost deaf and usually sleeps in her room up in the attic."

"Do you think it would occur to your guardian to look for us there?"

"I doubt it. But you can never tell anything for sure about him. It's never easy to predict what my cousin will do."

"Perhaps we ought to backtrack to my place. I'm sure my family would welcome us."

Monique was pensive for a moment. "I still think it might be better to go on to Le Rêve," she said at last. "Even if Cousin Miguel were to find out about our elopement and that we took this road out of town, he'd probably go look for us at your place first."

There was the sound of horses' hooves coming toward them over the road they had just traveled.

"Listen . . . someone's coming!" exclaimed Monique, almost glad to know there were still other people abroad in that part of the world.

"Some lone traveler, I wager, probably trying to get to his destination before the storm breaks. We probably should be doing the same thing," declared Foucher.

"Oh, Maurice, let's hurry and stop off somewhere," she begged, suddenly feeling very alone and afraid. "I don't want to go any farther tonight!"

"All right, my dear, whatever you want," soothed Maurice. The weather does seem to be getting worse. What's more, I just remembered some friends of mine who live about two or three miles from here. They'll help us, I'm sure, and that's the least likely spot where Vidal would look for us."

He turned the carriage into the road forking off toward the west, but suddenly, without warning, the lone rider behind them came tearing out of the darkness.

The tall silhouetted figure on horseback rushed past them as though he were part of the wind itself, but all at once reined in abruptly and, catching the horse drawing the cabriolet by its bridle, forced it to come to a halt.

At that same moment the flickering lights of the carriage fell across a face as dark and stormy as the night.

"God in heaven! It's Miguel!" gasped Monique incredulously.

The two runaways sat in guilty confusion as they watched Vidal dismount and walk directly up to their carriage, leading his panting, snorting horse behind him by its reins, while the wind lapped at the long tails of his frock coat and his sword danced a menacing rhythm against his boot tops. The high-crowned black hat, pulled down tightly over his frowning brow, made him look all the taller and more imposing as he unceremoniously reached into the carriage and, without so much as a word, pulled his amazed ward brusquely out to the ground beside him. Then, with his hand on his sword hilt, he motioned to Foucher to step down, too.

Even the freckles on the young man's face paled. He had always had a healthy respect for Don Miguel Vidal de la Fuente, and his awe had never been greater than at that moment, but he realized he had no other recourse at this point except to descend from his cabriolet and brazen it out with his future bride's irate guardian.

"Now, Don Miguel, before you say or do anything we might both regret, I think you should know that your ward and I are on our way to St. Martinville to be married," he began in an unsteady voice, eyeing Vidal's sword hand all the while. "Monique is with me of her own accord."

"My ward is under age, Foucher, as you well know, so she can have no 'accord' of her own whatsoever," snapped Vidal. "Under the circumstances, I'd say it'll be generous of me if I don't run you through right here on the spot."

"I assure you I want to marry Monique."

"I wouldn't call running off with a girl in the middle of the night the best way to prove your good intentions."

"I'm afraid it's precisely because of your uncompromising attitude that Monique and I have had to resort to such unorthodox means," retorted the young man, finally beginning to muster enough courage to stand up to Vidal's wrath. "After all, if you'll permit me to remind you, once Monique and I are married, the courts will recognize my rights over her as her husband—rights that will supersede all others, including yours as her guardian."

Vidal smiled sardonically. "Perhaps, but you're *not* her husband yet, so there's nothing to recognize at this moment except my legal guardianship over Mlle. Monique, and I tell you, senor, I will never consent to this."

Monique, who had been standing beside Vidal listening in dismay to the two men discussing her future, suddenly found her tongue and dared to break in.

"I think I should have some voice in all of this," she ventured indignantly, but her guardian turned angrily toward her and cut her short.

"You just be quiet!" he snapped.

"Am I not to have any say-so, then?"

"If you don't hush, you'll have your say-so from a convent."

Monique glared at him from out of the ruffled frame of her black silk hood, which she was trying to hold close around her throat despite the nagging wind pulling at it. "Oh, but you're horrid! A despicable tyrant!" she hissed at him between clenched teeth.

"At this moment I feel every bit that and more," he warned her with equal fury. "I've been riding the wind at top speed now for well over two hours so I could reach you in time to save you from this latest childish caprice of yours. One thing is certain, I'm in no mood for any arguments in the middle of a deserted road in the wee hours of the morning with a thunderstorm about to come down at any moment!"

"Really, Vidal, my intentions toward your cousin are entirely honorable," interrupted Maurice, trying to keep a conciliatory tone in his voice. He, too, was sporting a fancy rapier by his side, but he was painfully aware of the fact that next to Vidal's finely tempered Toledo blade, his own seemed like a toy. Also, he was certain that his fair-to-middling swordsmanship would be found equally wanting if forced into competition with the Spaniard's. "If you'd but give your consent, all of this would be unnecessary," he pleaded.

Vidal tried to hold on to the last vestiges of his patience. "*Mira*, Foucher, I may as well be frank with you and settle this matter once and for all. First of all, I don't think Monica is mature enough to marry anyone right now, but even if she were, I'd never consent to her marrying you."

Maurice was taken aback. "But I love your cousin," he protested. "I swear to you, Don Miguel, it wasn't my intention just to run off with her. We were going to be married in—"

"I don't question your feelings, senor, nor do they interest me. Frankly, it's only Monique's future that concerns me."

"But what do you have against me? Is it simply because my loyalties are with the French instead of your country?"

"I don't give a damn about your loyalties, either, as long as you don't drag my ward into your foolhardy world of radicalism and fantasy. Your very actions tonight simply show that you are as irrational in your private life as you are in your politics."

"Many a true patriot has been slandered before. . . ."

Vidal gave a short sarcastic laugh. "Patriot of what, may I ask? You're simply a pigheaded fool, risking your life and the lives of those around you in treasonous activities on behalf of a country that doesn't even want you . . . that doesn't even know you exist! But permit me to remind you again, this is neither the time nor the place to be discussing politics or anything else. I'm afraid we're in for a bad storm and we'd better get going before we find ourselves caught out here in the mud and rain . . . another situation brought about by your idiotic behavior!"

Somewhat abashed, Foucher yielded. At least Vidal was right in one thing. They'd better get wherever they were going before the storm broke. The wind was increasing in force, and large drops of rain were beginning to fall.

"For Monique's sake, I agree we should get to some shelter," acquiesced Maurice.

"I don't know where you're going," Vidal corrected him acidly. "It can be to hell for all I care, but for what it's worth, I'd suggest that wherever you go, it be as far away as possible from me and my ward! And let me add that in the future you'll approach my cousin at your peril. I'd hate to have to take certain actions unless they were absolutely necessary."

Foucher's rain-spattered countenance colored despite his efforts to remain conciliatory. "Are you threatening me, senor?"

Vidal shrugged his rapidly dampening shoulders with an exasperated sigh. "I don't like making threats, and it's not my usual manner of doing things, but if it's a choice between your life or my ward's, I'm afraid I wouldn't hesitate for a moment in deciding which it would be. I'm sorry, but that's the way it is."

Monique shook a tiny fist up at her guardian.

"You're . . . you're ruthless and . . . and utterly detestable!"

He looked down at her calmly from where he towered over her, apparently unmoved by her outburst. "Yes, I'm afraid I could be both of those things if pushed far enough," he agreed, "so I suggest that you and your friend here remember that."

Foucher held his ground for one last moment. "I won't trouble you with my presence," he told Vidal stiffly, "but for Monique's sake, I'd still like to offer you my carriage so she can travel more comfortably."

Monique took a step toward the cabriolet, but Vidal caught her by the wrist and suddenly, without any preamble, hoisted her with one swift movement to the top of his horse. Then, before she could react, he had swung himself up behind her.

"Thank you, Foucher, but I think we can make better time on horseback," he replied curtly.

Monique was about to dismount in protest, but he clamped his arm firmly around her waist and pinioned her there in front of him. "The carriage would be too cumbersome to maneuver on a muddy road," he continued addressing himself to the young man, "and yet it would be too fragile to offer much protection if a heavy storm hit us. Frankly, if you'll permit me to point out, you, too, might do well to abandon the cabriolet and just make all speed on your horse to wherever you plan to go."

Monique was squirming restlessly in the crook of his arm, but he only tightened his grip on her.

"I think we've wasted enough time," he told Maurice as the latter stood there alone on the road looking up at them rather bewilderedly from beside his carriage. Under the circumstances, the young man didn't know what else to do except let her guardian take the girl wherever he wished.

"I think we're in for a bad one," Vidal observed from his perch atop his horse. "Time is of the essence now."

His last words trailed off behind him as he flicked his roan and was off, riding on again on the crest of the rain-laden wind, holding his indignant ward fast in his arms.

Chapter Twenty-six

"HOLD TIGHT," HE SAID TERSELY IN HER EAR. "WE must hurry."

Monique obeyed, but only because her instincts wouldn't let her do anything else. He was riding like a demon out of hell now. There was still so much she wanted to shout back at him, but she sensed that every moment counted at that point, so she sat there quietly fuming in his grip, while myriads of droplets stung her cheeks like tiny sharp arrows as they spattered against her face. The pending storm seemed like a huge invisible monster, howling and screaming in their ears, ready to overtake and devour them at any moment.

Vidal's arm was like a steel clamp around her waist, fusing her against his loins, as the added impetus of the wind pushed them ever forward, faster and faster, catapulting them through the night past the grass-covered levee on one side and the almost endless row of swaying trees on the other.

A flash of lightning zigzagged across the dark sky and a roar of thunder followed, sending a shudder through Monique's body as Vidal tightened his grip on both the reins and her waist. He was doubly glad now that he had decided in favor of just the horse instead of the cabriolet. The animal responded to him better. Nevertheless, he slowed down now into a more cautious trot, since not only was the steady drizzle beginning to make the road slippery, but he also calculated that they must be nearing the Chausson plantation by now. Between the wind and rain blinding his eyes and the darkness of the night as the moon drifted in and out of the blackened skies, he feared he might overshoot the entrance. One thing he knew for certain, he'd have to take refuge at the very first shelter they passed. He cursed the stupidity of Maurice Foucher to have chosen such a night as this to try to elope!

The roan was so skittish now, between the thunder and lightning and the increasing difficulty of the terrain, that he feared the frightened animal might lose its footing and throw them in a sudden fright. He was just beginning to consider dismounting and leading the horse, with Monique on its back, carefully by the reins over the pitfalls of the road, when suddenly he caught sight of the familiar gate in a flash of lightning.

"The saints be praised!" he exclaimed in her ear over the shrieking wind. "We're here!"

He rode a short distance more and then dismounted in front of the large black wrought-iron entrance with its lacy arch spelling out the name of the Chausson plantation.

Clutching her flying cloak around her as best she could against the angry, lashing wind, Monique continued to sit on the horse and steady it while through a curtain of rain she watched her guardian struggling to push open the gate.

When he had finally succeeded, he held it against the wind so she could ride the animal through. Then, after latching the gate once more behind him, he caught the reins from her and continued guiding the horse with her still on its back up the oak-lined driveway toward the main house.

High above the dark tumultuous lane, the trees tossed and twisted in agony as the wind howled and hacked its way through their tormented branches, sending the weaker limbs flying through the blackness like shrieking demons in the night. One of them came hurling against the already frightened roan with such force that it took the combined efforts of Monique and her guardian to calm it down once more before they could continue. But doggedly they pushed on against the wind . . . the manor, white and ghostly, their only guide, beckoning to them like a beacon at the end of that long black tunnel of gesticulating trees. They were in a shrieking inferno and there was no other way out but forward. . . .

By the time they finally came out into the clearing in front of the main house, the storm had burst in all its fury, and Miguel had all he could do to lead Monique and the horse to the first refuge at hand.

Afraid to risk running the gauntlet of that long open flight of stairs up to the entrance of the manor at that moment, he lifted Monique down from the roan and pulled her and the animal into the shelter formed by the overhanging gallery and the wide staircase slanting upward to it. There they at least found some protection from the wind, although it still sounded all around them like a pack of hungry wolves stalking its prey.

Miguel hitched the frightened horse to the nearest column supporting the gallery above them and stroked the length of its sleek wet body soothingly a few times to reassure it. Then, retiring even deeper into the relative safety of the niche under the stairs, he finally turned to his bedraggled ward.

She stood there, completely drenched, her cloak thrown back wet and limp behind her, while the damp, disheveled tendrils of her hair, free now of the confining hood, cascaded in a tangled mass about her shoulders. In the darkness, only the whiteness of her skin and the pale gold of her hair were faintly visible in the reflection of the whitewashed wall behind them.

It was pouring down rain now, and although the shelter offered them some protection, the wind lashed in at them from the sides, angrily spewing its spray against their faces.

The fury within Monique, however, matched that of the storm around her. If it hadn't been so dreadful outside, she wouldn't have stayed there another moment. As it was, she hated the confinement of those close quarters that forced her to be so uncomfortably close to her guardian.

Nor was Vidal in an especially understanding mood at that moment. After having spent three hours riding frantically across the countryside only to end up trapped under a staircase soaking wet with an ungrateful brat, he was not about to tolerate one of his ward's tantrums. His best beaver hat sacrificed now to the winds and the dark ringlets of his windblown hair dripping down his flushed cheeks, he stood there glaring down at her, the scowl on his face matching her own.

Monique shifted restlessly from one foot to the other, like a filly chafing at the bit to be off and away. "I suppose Celeste was the one who told you where to find me," she exclaimed at last, unable to hold back her rage any longer. "Wait till I see her!"

"You should thank her for it," replied her guardian. "If you'd gone with that jackass Foucher, you'd probably be stuck in the mud out in the middle of nowhere, or perhaps even lying on the road with the carriage turned over on top of you by now!"

The sound of the rain pounding on the gallery boards and stairs over their heads, together with the rush of the wind as it tried to search them out from their hiding place, was so deafening that they had to shout at each other just to be heard, yet somehow it all seemed to be in keeping with the mood of that moment.

"Merciful heavens! How humiliating! To be dragged off like that with no regard for my feelings or wishes in the matter! You're so arrogant! Maurice and I would have done very well without you. I wish that you'd stop your constant meddling in my life!"

"Perhaps the trouble is I haven't meddled enough," he flared back at her. "What you really need is for me to turn you over my knee and give you that spanking I warned might be forthcoming."

She paled and eyed him apprehensively. "You . . . you wouldn't dare!" she exclaimed, taking a step backward, as though fearful he might indeed carry out his threat.

"Don't count on it," he warned, "for I'm at the limit of my patience with you right now. You've done some foolish things these past few months, but you've surpassed even yourself tonight. Do you see where your folly has led you—or rather, both of us!—this time? By all that's holy! When are you going to grow up?"

"If being my guardian really disturbs you so much, why didn't you just let me go off with Maurice? Wouldn't that have been the best way to solve everything?"

"Best for me, perhaps," he agreed with an exasperated sigh, "but not for you. Unfortunately I'm your guardian, and I couldn't in all conscience let you go running off with someone like Foucher on just a whim."

"Why do you say whim? If I'd decided I loved and wanted to marry him—"

"Bah! You don't love that popinjay!"

Monique drew herself up indignantly. "And how do you know I don't? What do you know about me and my feelings?"

"If I thought you really loved him, I wouldn't have tried to stop you. But you're just a child. You have no idea whatsoever what love is all about."

"That's not true," she replied angrily. "The trouble with you is you can't see I'm a grown woman with a woman's feelings."

"Ah, so you think you're all grown up, do you? You want to behave like a woman, is that it?"

A flash of lightning brought a startled neigh from the horse nearby, and as the thunder roared its reply Monique caught a strange expression in her guardian's dark eyes—one she had never seen before. Once again his nearness disturbed her, and even though the darkness had immediately descended on them again, she lowered her eyes before that penetrating gaze she could still feel fixed on her, though she could no longer see him. How was it that, even in anger, she continued to feel those same emotions he always roused in her stirring again? She resented that strange hold her guardian seemed to have over her.

"Has it ever occurred to you that one of the main reasons for my running away might have been to escape from you?" she suddenly lashed out at him, tears of vexation mingling with the rain on her face.

"*Qué barbaridad!* Do you hate me so much that you'd marry someone you don't love just to get away from me?"

"Yes, yes, that's it! I hate you! Why didn't you just stay at the ball with that Ducole woman and go on dancing with her the rest of the night?"

"That's probably what I should have done," he agreed, "for all the thanks I've gotten."

"I never asked you to come after me. I despise you and I despise that horrid painted woman you make love to . . . I despise you both!"

Miguel tried to make out the features of that little round blob staring up at him with such smoldering intensity in the darkness. Suddenly incredulity swept over him.

"Don't tell me you're jealous—jealous of me and Azema?"

"I hate you!" she repeated lamely, not knowing how else to answer him. The hot tears coursing down her cheeks stung even more than the raindrops that the ever-increasing wind was hurling against her face.

He caught her by the shoulders and bent toward her. "You foolish child! You dear foolish child! So you really are jealous! Monica, Monica . . ." He drew her close and pressed the length of his body longingly against hers, murmuring her name again and again as his mouth sought her out eagerly in the darkness.

A fresh gust of wind lashed them together, whipping her wildly flapping skirts and cloak around them until they were entangled, bound together, their bodies molding instinctively one to the other, their lips pressing together long and hard through the misty veil of rain.

Monique swayed and reeled unsteadily against him, the sound of her pulse pounding louder in her ears than the storm raging around her. Her body was singing with the wind and swelling with the joy of the

new sensations sweeping over her. She was savoring
the taste of him at last! There was no need to open
her eyes and see his face. She knew it was Miguel.
Her whole being told her it was him!

Maurice had occasionally succeeded in robbing a
peck or two from her on the sly, and Roget had
boldly taken her mouth into his and given her a lusty
kiss. But this . . . this was something entirely different. Miguel's lips were pressing slowly, sensuously,
against hers until she sensed instinctively that he
wanted her to open them. Now his tongue was racing
past her parted lips into the hidden recess beyond.

She had never been so aware of her body before.
It seemed to be awakening, flexing itself, swelling
with expectancy. Like a leaf borne on the crest of the
wind, she felt as though she were being swept along
with the wave of emotions surging through her
being, overwhelming her, carrying her she knew not
where. The circle of his arms had suddenly become
her universe . . . the long lean hardness of his body
her only reality. She knew now she had never really
been kissed before . . . not really. This was her first
kiss—her first wondrous kiss of love!

Miguel could feel her rain-soaked body trembling
in his arms . . . swaying . . . readily yielding herself
to him. Every fiber of his being ached to go
on . . . to pour out at last all his pent-up longing for
her . . . to show her how foolish she was to be
jealous of Azema or any other woman. He bent to
savor the sweetness of those fleshy little lips again,
but even as he did, he knew how it would end if he
kissed her that second time.

The conflicting emotions churning within him
racked his being, even as the roaring wind without
continued to pound mercilessly against the boards of
the gallery and stairs above them.

Quickly, while he still had that last faint glimmer of reason to temper him, he tore himself away from the soft throbbing wonder of her and turned partially away, grateful now for the darkness that hid how those brief moments of intimacy had shaken him.

Still breathing heavily, he cursed himself for his impulsiveness. The moment wasn't right and he knew it. The fact that Monique had confessed a certain jealousy over Azema and responded with surprising ardor to his kiss had momentarily set his head spinning with wild hopes, but he realized he'd be foolish to act rashly because of one impulsive kiss. Though her woman's body had responded to him and her sweet tongue had leaped to his mouth as her breasts pushed eagerly against his chest, she was still only a child inside. And where Monique was concerned, he had to be certain, for he wanted all of her—not just that lovely, exciting little body, but the sweet passion of her all-consuming love.

He sensed her quickened breathing there in the darkness and knew she was still aroused. He'd been a fool to kiss her like that! His adorable, sensitive little ward was so vulnerable, so unaccustomed to the responses of her ripening body! Like a moth attracted to the flame of his passion, she was instinctively swaying toward him once more. If she only knew how that gesture of hers to return to his arms was setting him all the more on fire!

Quickly . . . desperately . . . he stepped back from her, trying to stifle that burning desire gnawing at his loins . . . a gnawing that would not leave him in peace, no matter how much he tried to reason it away. Deliberately he reminded himself that he ought to be concentrating on more pressing problems . . . like getting them to safety.

Chapter Twenty-seven

"WE'RE GOING TO HAVE TO MAKE A RUN FOR IT UP THE stairs to the door," he told her by way of explanation for his reluctance to continue any further intimacy with her at that moment. In a way, he was glad that the urgency of their situation didn't leave him any choice in the matter, for he doubted he would have had the strength to push her away like that again.

Once they were inside the house, with a few more feet between them, it might be easier to keep things under control. But being alone like that with her in such close quarters . . . feeling her so warm and inviting within his grasp . . . the best of his resolutions would be for naught if he had to spend much more time with her under those stairs!

"But the wind is still so strong, and the rain hasn't stopped," Monique objected with a skeptical glance outside to where the storm was still raging with frightening intensity. She was surprised her guardian would suggest that they leave the relative safety of their nook at such a moment. That niche under the stairs was so filled with Miguel's presence now that it seemed warm and protective to her, far removed from the realities of the world twisting in torment without.

"I know," he conceded, "but at least it's slackening a little, so I think we ought to get up the stairs now while we can. We may not get another chance."

"Couldn't we just stay and wait out the storm here?" There seemed to be a slight note of longing in her voice, but perhaps it was just his imagination.

"We're not really safe in this spot," he replied quickly, as much to explain the facts to her as to remind himself that there were also good practical reasons why he should resist the temptation to remain there alone with her. The passionate moments they had just shared still charged the atmosphere . . . the taste of her was still in his mouth.

"This storm could go on for hours and get much worse," he continued. "I don't want to frighten you, but if the wind picks up too much, we could be sucked out of here on a strong current or even be struck by lightning."

With the key to the main entrance ready in his front pocket, he ordered her to wrap her cloak about her again and hold on tightly to his arm.

"No matter what happens, don't let go," he cautioned her. "And remember, if we should get separated, grab on to anything solid you can find or try to crawl to the nearest shelter."

He led the horse even farther under the stairs where they had been standing, and then, putting one arm firmly around her well-cloaked shoulder and holding on tightly to her wrist with his other hand, he led her out from under the staircase and quickly around to the foot of the stairs. The force of the wind caught them by surprise, and he tightened his grip on her, fearful that her slight frame might be blown away from him if he were to let go even for an instant.

Despite the combined weight of their two bodies clinging together as one, the wind was so strong that it seemed to be an invisible wall blocking their progress. With a startled cry, Monique fell to her knees from the violent impact of that unseen force. It was like a living, palpable thing, lashing out at her in the darkness.

The rain was increasing in volume again and coming down in such torrents that she could no longer see the top of the stairs. She couldn't even see the next step. All she could do was blindly cling to Miguel's arm . . . his hand . . . his clothing. . . .

He was kneeling beside her now. "Crawl!" he yelled in her ear above the roar of the wind. "Keep crawling up and don't let go!"

She felt giant hands clutching at her, trying to tear her away from him, and she cried out his name to the wind. He was only a dark, barely visible shadow, devoid of form now, but she clung to him desperately. Her only sense of reality was the weight of his arm on her shoulders and the feel of his fingers digging into her wrist. They were bruising her flesh, but she didn't care . . . it was her only contact at that moment with something tangible in a world that had suddenly turned to chaos.

Somewhere off in the direction of the levee road, a bolt of lightning suddenly crackled across the dark heavens and left a blazing tree in its wake. For a few moments it illumined the night in a ruddy, hellish glow and then vanished as the downpour quenched its flames and the blackness of the night closed over it.

The rain was coming down so heavily now that it seemed to be pounding her mercilessly into the steps. She tried to lift her head toward Miguel but gulped so much water she nearly choked. Miguel was literally pulling her along with him now. Coughing and sputtering in a frantic effort to breathe, she no longer seemed to have the strength to resist the weight of the pounding rain and onrushing wind. Purgatory must be like this, she thought. Or perhaps she was already in the depths of hell, trying to climb out of the pit, but the demons were pulling her down, lashing out at her, tormenting her. . . .

Suddenly she realized she was on the gallery and Miguel was pulling her to her feet. He held her for a moment pressed close to the firmness of his body until he was certain she had regained her balance. Then, still holding on tightly to her, he fumbled with the key until he found the lock.

With a gush of wind, the massive oaken door suddenly flew open and the dark hallway in the interior yawned before them like the mouth of some hungry giant. She could feel herself being pushed by a huge invisible hand into those waiting jaws. She tried to clutch at Miguel or the doorjamb, to resist that mighty force, but it was too late. With a startled cry, she was suddenly torn from Miguel's grasp and sent hurtling headfirst into the inky blackness of the hallway.

The next thing she knew, she was lying wet and bruised on the floor, weary and gasping for breath but welcoming the reality of the solid cypress boards beneath her.

Miguel followed, groping and stumbling as he tried to keep his footing and close the door behind him against the wind and rain. The darkness was impenetrable now as he made his way cautiously down the hallway to where he calculated the console was, with its candelabrum and tinderbox always ready for any emergency.

"Monica, my dear, where are you?" he called out to her in the darkness. "Are you all right?"

She heard him call her name again, but she was so weary she could only mumble a weak reply—a reply

that the angry storm, pounding and shrieking to be
let in, completely drowned out.

Suddenly the toe of his boot brushed her leg, and
she called out a warning to him from where she lay
on the floor, but before he could catch himself, he
was falling forward, hopelessly entangled in her
cloak and skirts. Impulsively she lifted her hands to
protect herself from the impact of his fall. . . .

For a moment they lay there in a confused heap on
the floor, wet and spent, bruised and soaked to the
skin, yet somehow vibrantly alive. They had just
been through hell and back and were grateful to feel
the familiar nearness of each other's bodies once
more. The darkness that enveloped them suddenly
seemed friendly and protective . . . warm and
sensuous. . . . Memories of the moments they had
shared together earlier under the staircase returned.
Monique reached up to him and clung to the wet
velvet of his coat, weeping with the sheer joy of
being alive and knowing he was there.

For the first time, she murmured his name with no
prefixes or surnames and drew him closer. All the
hostility had drained out of her. Only the desire that
had lain submerged beneath it was left now.

His body was pressing longingly against hers, and
she could feel the hard core of him throbbing wildly
against her thigh. It excited her, set her pulsating to
its rhythm. His breath was warm and rapid on her
cheek as his lips found her in the darkness.

"Mona, my sweet, adorable little doll . . . I want
you so!" A flood of soft Castilian caressed her lips as
he cupped his mouth hungrily over hers. The scent
of him invaded her nostrils, penetrated the very
pores of her being. This time their kiss was long and
lingering, yearning for fulfillment. Her tongue

leaped to meet his, and the taste of him filled her mouth.

The hurricane had burst in all its fury outside, but it seemed distant compared to the storm raging within her, drowning out all other impressions except those racking her being at that moment.

She locked her arms around his neck and held fast, fearful he might pull away from her as he had done before under the staircase. But he was on fire now, and his lips were softly tracing the soft hollow of her neck down into the deep valley between her breasts, while he slipped his arm under the curve of her back and arched her even closer to the lean hardness of him.

"If you only knew . . . how I want you . . . only you . . ."

He groped momentarily in the darkness, exploring the decolletage of her gown. Eagerly he drew one of those soft firm breasts into the moist warmth of his mouth, caressing it rapidly with his lips, then the flutter of his tongue, again and again. She could feel the tip begin to harden and come to life as strange new sensations began to awaken deep within her.

Suddenly his mouth tightened over the swelling fullness of her breast and he began to suck long and hungrily until she felt the very essence was being drawn out of her and she was trembling wildly in the circle of his arms. It was like nothing she had ever felt before. Every corner of her body was throbbing with a thousand tiny pulses, all afire for want of him!

Her fingers gripped the damp thickness of his hair as she gave an involuntary moan of pleasure and she murmured his name again and again. Oh, yes, he was the one. She knew at last she loved him! All those nights of wondering . . . trying to imagine who it was going to be . . . how it was going to feel . . . yet never in her wildest dreams had she thought it could be like this! It had to be Miguel. There could be no other man now for her but him. Wars could rage . . . generations could hate . . . none of it mattered anymore. It all dissolved in the heat of their passion.

Miguel could feel her breast expanding and pulsating with mounting desire, pressing urgently upward through his fingers, eager to meet his lips once more. His whole being was on fire now for want of her. That gnawing knot in his loins had sprung to life and could no longer be denied. He pressed the burning ache of it desperately against her, and the feel of her soft and yielding beneath him set his pulse racing. He knew she wanted him. Her whole body was pleading for him to take her, and he could no longer deny the urgency of his own long-denied passion.

Quickly he felt beneath the wet, clinging skirts for her thighs and lightly stroked the smooth, firm lines of them, running his fingers again and again over their length until they were quivering uncontrollably to his every touch. Her lips murmured into his kisses . . . her breast pulsated wildly against the palm of his hand . . . slowly her trembling limbs began to part . . . ready . . . waiting. How he had dreamed of this moment . . . all those long months of aching, despairing . . . He was swollen with desire for her, eager to plunge at last into the innermost depths of her being and make her his own at last. He eased his knee between her thighs and gently, with the palm of his hand in the curve of her back, arched her toward him. . . .

A flash of lightning suddenly illuminated the hallway through the stained-glass window above the main entrance, and in that split second he saw that childlike face with its wide, trusting eyes bathed in ecstasy, those tiny little fists that she had so often lifted in anger against him clinging to him now, clenched with passionate longing. How terribly vulnerable she was at that moment . . . so young . . . so passionate . . . so completely aroused. . . . God help him! What was he doing? Here he was about to take her, driven only by the urgency of his own torment, his own needs, with no thought of the consequences for her! He had nearly killed two men to stop them from seducing her . . . to stop them from doing exactly what he himself was doing at that moment! And he was her guardian, sworn to protect her! *Qué barbaridad!*

He drew back and his loins went into a paroxysm of agony.

For a moment he knelt there on one knee above her in the darkness, trying to calm the turmoil twisting his insides into a thousand knots. Every fiber of his being screamed to go on to completion, and he could feel her voluptuous little body still stirring in his arms, begging to be taken.

But that momentary flash of lightning had brought him to his senses. This was Monique, his sweet, innocent little Monique whom he loved more than life itself. Also, this was his unpredictable little Monique who, up until less than an hour ago, had hated him with the same intensity as she was responding to his caresses now. No, even though he knew he could take her then and there, he didn't want it to be that way—not with her lying on the floor, wet and confused, worked into an emotional frenzy by the events of the night and his imprudent lovemaking. This was the woman he hoped to marry. He wanted their first time to be so different.

Most of all, he wanted her love. He wanted her to be as certain of her feelings for him as he was of his for her.

Clumsily he smoothed the damp curls back from her forehead with trembling fingers and tried to calm her, despite the fact that he was far from calm himself. Desperately he tried to ignore the raging furnace consuming him from within . . . the shrieking protests of his tormented loins.

"It . . . it's so dark," he mumbled huskily as he labored to catch enough breath to get past the constriction in his throat. In despair he kissed the outstretched hand that tried to detain him and moved back from her, momentarily fumbling in the dark with the yards of muslin tangled around his limbs. "Let me find the candle."

He rose carefully and groped for the table that he knew had to be nearby. He had to have light! In the light everything would take on more sensible proportions. He nearly knocked over the candleholder as he felt about blindly for it. His fingers were trembling uncontrollably as they struggled with the tinderbox.

Chapter Twenty-eight

THE FOUR-STEMMED CANDELABRUM SEEMED STAR-
tlingly bright as it illumined the blackness of the
hallway. Monique blinked bewilderedly as she rose
from the floor and self-consciously tried to arrange
her disheveled clothing.

Miguel seemed his usual cool, collected self once
more as he walked on into the parlor and continued
to light every candelabrum in sight. Then, mumbling
something about going to find Old Meggie to get
them some fresh clothing and a good meal, he
hurried off.

Monique sat down on the sofa, feeling strangely
exhilarated despite the physical weariness of her
battered body. The storm was still raging outside,
and the shutters rattled behind the drawn curtains as
the house vibrated in the demanding embrace of the
lusty wind.

The brightly lit room seemed familiar, yet she
knew that somehow things would never be quite the
same again for her after that night. The taste of him
was still on her lips . . . the feel of his body still
imprinted on her own. Every part of her seemed to
be tingling with a pulse of its own. Even as she sat
there vibrating to the familiar timbre of his voice as
he spoke to Old Meggie off in the rear of the house,
she longed to feel his caresses again, to yield to him
at last the very core of her being. She wasn't certain

what had been expected of her . . . what else she should have done. She wasn't even certain exactly how that passionate moment between them should have ended, but her instincts told her that he had brought his lovemaking to an abrupt halt . . . that he had drawn away from her again at the crucial moment, just when every fiber of her being had wanted to go on to fulfillment . . . to experience at last the very essence of him.

She felt a sense of incompleteness, as though she had opened her portals to him and been rejected. Had he been disappointed in her? Perhaps he had compared her to Azema and other women he had known and found her wanting. He had drawn away from her under the staircase, too, after their first kiss. . . .

Azema was so beautiful, so experienced in pleasing a man. How could she possibly expect to compete with such a woman? But no matter how perfect Azema Ducole was, one thing was certain. That horrid woman could never love Miguel the way she did. And she knew now that she loved him . . . loved him with every particle of her being. If only she could learn to please him so he'd never want Azema or any woman again but her! Now that she had known the feel of his hands coursing over her body, his lips suckling at her breast, his tongue seeking out the hidden recesses of her body, she could never bear the thought of him doing those things to any other woman. She had to let him know how much she loved and wanted him . . . that no one could possibly love him as much as she did!

But as the night wore on and her guardian returned with Old Meggie, he seemed to be avoiding her. They bathed and changed to some of the spare summer clothing stored in the massive bedroom armoires, and then sat down to an impromptu repast of chicken broth and cold venison that left her physical appetite satisfied but did little to assuage the deeper hunger still unslaked within her.

As soon as they had finished their meal, he suggested they retire immediately, pointing out that it was after four o'clock in the morning and time to get a few hours of much-needed sleep.

The storm had subsided now to a dismal drizzle, so just before going to his bedchamber, Miguel left orders for a messenger to be dispatched to the town house to tell Grandmother Chausson that he and Monique were all right and would be returning later that following day. He wanted to check first, however, on whatever damage the storm might have done there at the plantation, especially to the recently planted cuttings. If the soil wasn't well packed around them, they wouldn't be adequately protected when the cold weather set in. The planters had warned him that, hot as it was there in the summers, it sometimes got down to freezing temperatures during the colder months.

Although Monique realized her guardian was not only tired but worried about saving the crops, as well, she still couldn't understand why he hadn't at least made an effort to say a few words aside to her before retiring. True, he had been busy with Old Meggie and Roselle most of the time, but aside from his usual polite good night—which on this occasion he had said rather incongruously at five o'clock in the morning—there had been no hint in his manner that he even recalled the emotional experiences they had shared together earlier that night.

After tossing and turning for over an hour, her tingling, pulsating body still too vibrantly awake to let her relax long enough to sleep, Monique finally

slipped into her light sacque of pink cotton and went
down the gallery to her guardian's room. It was a
dismal, wet dawn, but she knew she wouldn't be able
to rest until she'd at least seen him alone again for a
few minutes.

When he opened the door, somewhat groggy from
his own first hour of fitful sleep, it was obvious he
had expected to see the overseer or Meggie and not
his restless ward staring up questioningly at him with
wide, confused eyes.

"Monica! In heaven's name, what are you doing
here? And in the damp morning air? Do you want to
catch your death of cold?" he exclaimed in amazement, grabbing his wine silk dressing gown and
quickly throwing it over his white linen nightshirt.
He pushed back the dark waves of his tousled hair as
he returned to the door where she still stood waiting.
"What's the matter, child? Why are you here?" he
asked again.

"I . . . I wanted to see you," she said simply.
"May I come in?"

Her request seemed to put him into a panic, but
he couldn't leave her standing out there. The dreary
gray morning air was still humid and heavy with the
aftermath of the recent storm.

"It . . . it's not proper for a young lady to be in a
man's bedchamber," he said lamely. "Servants gossip, you know."

"Meggie's out back in the kitchen, and no one else
is in the house right now," she assured him. "I . . . I
thought you'd want to see me."

He caught her by the hand and drew her quickly
into the room but left the door partially open. The
curtains and shutters of the chamber were still drawn
so the daylight wouldn't disturb his sleep.

"My sweet child, it's madness to come here like

this. Things can't be that way between us. Most
certainly not while I'm still your guardian." He was
more uneasy than ever.

"You were playing with me, then . . . mocking
me?"

"Of course not! You must believe me. It wasn't
my intention . . ." He ran his hand through his thick
dark hair in despair. Just the sight of her brought
back the agony of that moment when he had torn
himself away from her. He ached to take her in his
arms again and feel her lying beneath him responding to his caresses once more. "How can I make you
understand, my sweet darling?"

He turned aside, trying to veil the desire he was
sure must have been burning in his eyes at that
moment.

"That's it, isn't it? You still see me only as a
child!"

"A part of you is very much a woman, my dear,"
he assured her with a smile, "but the very fact that
you don't understand why I couldn't go on—why I
still can't—only proves you're still very much a child
in other ways. You're so young . . . so passionate
. . . God forgive me! What was I thinking of? When
I think how I could have taken you . . . I came so
close . . . *Qué barbaridad!*"

He cursed his weakness of the night before. He
had roused the woman dormant in her before she
was mature enough to handle such emotions.

"If I'd been Azema Ducole, I wager you wouldn't
have hesitated."

He laughed. "Azema? Why do you persist in
talking about her? What does she have to do with my
feelings for you? Believe me, my dear, I was only
thinking of you . . . I'm still thinking of you. I
couldn't have borne it if I'd taken you and then

you'd have regretted it afterward, perhaps even hated me all the more for having taken advantage of you like that. Why, only right before the storm you were eloping with that fellow Foucher and shaking your fist in my face telling me for the hundredth time how much you hated me. That's why I think we should wait a little. I want you to be sure of these new emotions of yours."

Tears were clouding over those enormous gray eyes, turning them to charcoal gray. He was just saying words, trying to spare her feelings. All the other men who had wanted to make love to her hadn't spent their time trying to rationalize why they shouldn't do so. She had had to fight them off. No, she knew why he'd stopped so abruptly and hadn't tried to come near her since then . . . not even now that she had gone so far as to come to his room and give him every opportunity to take her in his arms and kiss her again. He had compared her to his mistress and decided he preferred Azema. She wasn't woman enough for him. Azema was so much more beautiful than she was as a woman . . . and probably more expert as a lover, too.

Monique drew her dressing gown closer about her and her shoulders sagged as she turned back toward the door.

"I'm sorry to have disturbed you," she said coolly, trying to keep her voice steady and unemotional. She wondered how she could ever be nonchalant around him again when the memory of his caresses were so much a part of her now.

He hesitantly took a step toward her. Suddenly he took her by those drooping shoulders and turned her around to face him. The flame of the candle in the dimly lit room awakened gold flecks in the gray of her eyes, and he remembered how she had looked in that flash of lightning when her face had been aglow with ecstasy.

Gently he brushed a lock of her pale gold hair back from where it had fallen over her forehead, his finger trembling as he touched it.

"Monica—my sweet impatient little child with a woman's passions . . . a woman's body!" he murmured. "Please believe me, I want you so much! It's only because I really love you—*te quiero tanto*—that I don't want to hurt you, not now or ever. Everything must be right between us. Can you understand that?"

She lowered her lids to avoid the intensity of his gaze, despite the fact that he continued to hold her by the shoulders and look down into her face. "I . . . I think I do," she replied, but there was hesitancy in her voice.

"I want you to be sure . . . as sure as I am," he continued softly. "Then I promise I'll make love to you with all the passion of last night and then some. What happened between us has only convinced me more than ever that you're the woman I want. But I want you for a lifetime, so it's important that you feel the same way about me, too. Can you be patient just a little longer, my adorable *chiquilla*? I'd like to see how you feel in a few months from now . . . let's say in January when you turn eighteen. Who knows, you might feel quite differently toward me by then." He smiled sadly. "The fact is you may not even feel the same for me by tomorrow," he observed rather bitterly as he recalled how she had always been so hostile toward him until that fateful moment in the hallway when the storm had literally thrown them into each other's arms. "If in the three and a half months lacking from now to your birthday you can show me that the fact that I'm Spanish and not

French doesn't really matter to you . . . that you're no longer a petulant, impulsive child but a warm, loving woman who knows her own mind and can be steadfast in her emotions—then you'll make me the happiest man in all the Louisiana colony. Will you do that, my dear?"

It was she now who looked at him with open scrutiny. "Perhaps . . . but three and a half months seems like such a long time."

He smiled. "You have no idea how long it will be for me," he assured her. "So it's a pact, then? Our little secret, if you wish, so you'll feel no pressure from your family or anyone to do anything against your will?"

Her eyes were shining now. "Oh, yes, Miguel. You'll see how grown up I can be. I really don't hate you, you know. You'll never need Azema or any other woman but me!"

A twinkle glinted in his eye. "I'm sure I'll have my hands full with just you when the time comes," he conceded solemnly. "Meanwhile I suggest that we both try to remember I'm still your guardian and act accordingly."

He gave her as fatherly a kiss on the forehead as he could manage at that moment and hurried her out of his room before he wouldn't be able to follow his own advice.

Chapter Twenty-nine

DURING THE WEEKS THAT FOLLOWED, THE CHANGE IN Monique never ceased to amaze those around her. Grandmother Chausson reached the conclusion that it had been well worth the fright the girl's escapade had given them if the change in her had come about as the result of it.

Gone was the petulance and hostility of yore. Monique went about now with her luminous gray eyes reflecting an inner joy that seemed to bathe the world around her in a completely different light. Whenever her guardian spoke to her, she would lower her eyes and blush with proper maidenly modesty and submit to whatever he said without any further argument.

Even Mlle. Baudier was flabbergasted by the zest with which her charge suddenly attacked her studies, the most noteworthy of all being her progress in Spanish, which, until then, had been the girl's worst subject.

Celeste had expected her sister to tear into her for having violated their sacred oath, but instead Monique had been surprisingly forgiving about it all.

"It's just as well that Miguel found us," she had replied with an indifferent toss of her curls as Celeste had meekly tried to broach the subject the first time they had been alone again. "I realize now it would have been a mistake. Maurice is still so infantile."

Although her guardian had resumed his more formal attitude toward her, Monique saw a new tenderness in his eyes or a slight tremor in his touch that sent a delicious shiver down her spine and left her tingling with memories of past caresses and anticipation of those yet to come.

Just the sight of him was enough now to set her insides trembling. They had been in the darkness that night when he had made love to her in the hallway, but she had felt the long lean length of his body as he had molded it hungrily against hers. Now she looked at him in a new way. Even as she admired how handsome he looked in his elegant frock coat and breeches, she found herself recalling the hard firmness of the body she knew lay beneath them. Then the memory of that night would come flooding back, overwhelming her, and she could feel her breasts swelling again, their nipples hard and pulsating against her bodice.

It pleased her to fondle again and again in her mind that sweet secret they shared. She dreamed of the day when they would stand before Mémère and confess their love for each other and speak of plans for their marriage. Her newfound love so filled her heart now that there was no longer room in it for hatred or politics or old resentments.

Vidal, however, found the waiting almost more than he could bear. He cursed his lack of control that had prompted him to unleash the more passionate facets of his love for his young cousin that night of the hurricane, for those moments of intimacy with her had only fanned his desire to even greater heights. Yet he didn't completely regret what had happened. A powerful charge surged through his veins every time he remembered how she had responded to his caresses. All the ruffles and fichus in the world couldn't erase the impression of those full young breasts now from his mind . . . how they had felt cupped in his hand, palpitating to his caresses, swelling between his lips. Sometimes just the sight of them so perfectly molded by the tightness of her bodice was enough to set the knot in his loins pulsating again.

He knew that she remembered, too, just by the way she'd suddenly flush and steal a discreet glance in his direction whenever he was in the room and she thought no one was looking. He wondered whether she might also be lying awake at night, even as he was, wishing they could be together at that very moment. That bewitching little doll was every bit as passionate as Azema, but there was no calculation behind it. His little Monique was pure passion— ready to surrender completely with that innocent abandon of hers, so characteristic of everything she did.

Since their return to New Orleans, he had deliberately avoided being alone with that delectable little ward of his, for he felt he could no longer trust himself with her anymore. When he was near her, he couldn't be rational, and he didn't want a repetition of that episode in the hall. Delightful as it had been, that should not be the order of things where Monica was concerned. It would never do to seduce his ward and then ask for her hand in marriage. Grandmother Chausson had entrusted her to him, and it would be like betraying that trust if he protected Monique from everyone in the colony except himself!

Even little Celeste had been casting her lovely fawnlike eyes in his direction lately. The dear child was obviously having her first romantic fantasies, with him as her phantom hero. That role didn't especially disturb him, however, for it was one he knew he could handle with no harm done to anyone. After all, he was certain he would dissolve from those childish dreams the moment a flesh-and-blood beau entered the young girl's life, as was bound to happen before too long. But meanwhile, it was one more reason for him to be on tenterhooks and keep a short rein on that easily roused nature of his.

Unfortunately, he had never been in such a situation before. In that carefree existence as a bachelor that he had led until now, there had never been any need for him to hold his emotions in check. If he wanted a woman and she was willing, he took her. This holding back was a new and frustrating experience for him, especially since he had never desired any woman the way he desired Monique. Perhaps it was because he wanted so much more from her than just that voluptuous little body of hers.

On several occasions he'd been tempted not to wait a day longer and simply go to Grandmother Chausson, ask for the girl's hand in marriage, and be done with it. But in his heart he knew that the brief waiting period he had imposed upon himself and Monique was for the best. Marriage was for life, and he had to be sure that her feelings for him went beyond those of just a young girl's response to her first brush with the more pleasant sensations involved in making love.

Even if he spoke to Aimee Chausson about his *tendre* for his ward, Miguel was almost certain the latter would also insist that they wait a few months in order to give the girl time to be sure of her emotions. If he had been from any other country except Spain, perhaps it wouldn't be so necessary, but Monique's hostility toward anything and anybody Spanish seemed so ingrained in her that it would probably be better to proceed cautiously and not risk repenting a hasty marriage later. At Monique's age, a few months could make a great deal of difference. . . .

Of course, Grandmother Chausson would probably approve of the match, but Miguel preferred not to say anything to her about such a possibility yet, since he didn't want her or anyone else pressuring the girl and influencing her decision. He wanted Monique, but not in a marriage of convenience. A pox on those "arrangements"! He knew such matrimonies abounded, but he hadn't waited until he'd reached his twenty-seventh year to marry simply to enter that purgatory in which he had seen so many of his friends writhing. After all, he knew something better was possible between a man and a woman. Hadn't his father found it with his stepmother?

Now, after tonight, he knew no woman could ever satisfy him except his sweet, passionate little ward. With a woman like Azema—and he had known so many like her over the years!—it was always so superficial—pleasant enough at times, yet devoid of any real sentiment for either of them. He knew that with Monique, however, it would be an *entrega total*—a complete giving of one to the other—a perfect fusion of two beings. She was worth waiting for. With Monique he was learning the sweet torment of loving someone above all others . . . even himself.

Chapter Thirty

AFTER THE INTENSE HEAT OF THE SUMMER MONTHS, Miguel was surprised at how cold it was this first day of November—All Saints' Day. In keeping with the French custom of "Toussaint," or the Spanish one of "Day of the Dead," Monique and Celeste insisted that they attend the traditional picnic in the cemetery.

For in New Orleans, All Saints' Day was a social occasion—the fall counterpart of spring's Easter Sunday, when each one put on his or her new winter outfit and sallied forth to mass to pray for the souls of their dead and then went to the cemetery to visit or perhaps even spend the day with them.

Although their grandmother was satisfied with just getting out her best gray silk dress and matching woolen cape, Monique and her sister each had her "robe de la Toussaint" for the occasion, and even their lovely beaver-trimmed capes of royal-blue velvet with large matching fur muffs were new.

In the spirit of the occasion, Miguel also treated himself to a new black double-tiered cape, which Monique noted proudly only a man with a superb figure like her guardian could show off to advantage.

Since the five-year-old cemetery was on the fringes of the city, they had taken the family coach there, with Miguel riding up top beside the coachman and the women inside with the picnic baskets and the enormous bouquets of flowers that the girls had been growing all summer "for Mama, Papa, and our little brother."

Once at their destination, however, they left their coach at the gates and joined the continuous flow of townsfolk ambling about the cemetery. A holiday mood pervaded the atmosphere. Vendors were everywhere, offering refreshments and a wide assortment of real and aritificial floral pieces.

Although there were some graves in the new St. Louis Cemetery, the majority of the resting places were above ground, a lesson learned after the many disagreeable experiences the city had had with the old St. Peter burial grounds where corpses often used to come bobbing up to the surface after floods or excessive rains!

At that moment that strange City of the Dead, with its rows of little windowless "houses" of whitewashed brick and plaster, adorned with wrought-iron fences so similar to those of the city just outside its walls, looked like a veritable garden in bloom, belying the dreary wintry day.

There was a wrought-iron bench in front of the Chausson tomb, so Grandmother Chausson sat down with Mlle. Baudier to keep her company and, setting the picnic baskets beside her, began to hold court as many among that constant stream of people passing by stopped to pay their respects as they made their way up and down the lanes of whitewashed tombs.

A tall cross draped in black in the center of the grounds bore mute testimony to the ancient rites that had been held there the night before, when the priests had performed their imposing midnight chants for the response of the departed souls interred there. Some of the parishioners had kept votive candles burning on the resting places of their loved ones throughout the night, but many, including Grandmother Chausson, who hadn't been able to attend the ceremonies of the night before were simply asking one of the numerous monks strolling around the grounds to pause and give a special blessing.

After about an hour or so spent in receiving visitors at their family tomb, Monique and Celeste became restless and asked permission to go call on some of their friends in other parts of the cemetery; and since the place was thronging with so many friends and clergy, Grandmother Chausson saw no harm in letting them go off for a little while, as long as they didn't leave the grounds. Miguel had momentarily gone to do some visiting on his own with the governor and the Ducoles, and had promised to bring back some pineapple beer on his return.

Like children just out of school, the two girls left their grandmother with Mlle. Baudier and ran off down the rows of tall whitewashed tombs to see who else was there they knew. After pausing to greet a few of the families they had known since childhood, they suddenly heard a familiar voice greeting them from behind.

"Heavens! It's Maurice!" murmured Monique uneasily. Her first instinct was to try to avoid him, but Celeste, assuming that, as always, her sister would want to have a few words alone with her beau, immediately left them and took up vigil in front of the row of tombs behind which Maurice had led Monique so he could talk to her more privately.

Clad in his high-crowned hat with a dark gray cape

that Monique couldn't help thinking rather overwhelmed him, her friend looked appropriately fashionable for the occasion. His blue eyes had bright-
ened at the sight of her, and he pulled her even
farther behind the tall two-story tombs at the end of
the lane near a wall of crypts.

"I'm so happy to see you!" he exclaimed with
delight. "It's been over a month! I've waited for you
by the carriage entrance several times, hoping you'd
find a way to steal out as you used to, but I was
beginning to fear your guardian had made good his
threat and sent you to a convent."

Monique smiled and shook her hooded head. "Of
course not!" she replied. "I just haven't felt very
much like going out by myself anymore. Sneaking
out like that is for children. A lady doesn't go
stealing out of stable entrances."

Maurice looked at her curiously, as though he
could indeed see there was something different
about her.

"Yes, Monique, you really are a woman now," he
agreed, his eyes sweeping admiringly over her. "I've
never seen you look lovelier. I still get angry every
time I think of how your guardian thwarted our
elopement, but don't fret, my dear. I haven't given
up hope that the day will come when we can marry
right here in New Orleans with both our families'
consent. Your guardian can't stand in our way
forever."

"It was probably for the best that he stopped us,"
she told him. "It wasn't right to run away like that. I
realize that now."

"Yes, I suppose so," admitted Foucher reluctantly. "It would be better, as you say, to do things right
with everyone in accord. Perhaps after your cousin

himself marries, he'll be in a more amiable mood toward the idea of matrimony in general. Has he set a date yet?"

Monique lifted her brows in surprise. "A date?" she repeated in confusion. Maurice couldn't possibly know yet about her and Miguel. "Yes, Azema Ducole must be pressuring him to make an honest woman of her by now. She seems like the type of woman who gets what she wants."

"Azema? Oh, no, Maurice, you're mistaken. My guardian doesn't love that horrid woman anymore."

It was Maurice's turn now to be surprised. "Well, you could have fooled me," he replied. "I saw him with her just last week. It was Monday afternoon, I think . . . yes, that was it . . . last Monday. My father's business partner has his offices in the same block, so I go by there often."

Anger and disbelief welled up in her. "I . . . I'm sure you're mistaken," she reiterated, lashing out at him for having even suggested such a thing.

"I tell you it was him. I saw them with my own eyes. I was riding down Chartres and there he was standing in the carriage entrance of the Ducole town house, holding his horse by the reins and taking his leave of her. He was kissing her hand, and suddenly she bent forward and kissed him on the lips. I remember thinking that they were acting like an engaged couple."

"You're wrong . . . you're wrong!" insisted Monique as the row of crypts in front of her began to dissolve into a sea of tumultuous gray waves. Her eyes had lost their focus and everything seemed to be swimming in a distorted haze through the tears welling up in them.

"Oh, what does it matter anyway?" Foucher said

with a laugh, not wishing to make an issue of so trivial a matter. "Come quickly, my sweet, and slip me a little kiss. I've missed you so!"

He felt for her waist beneath her cape and pulled her lightly toward him, but she drew back impatiently. She seemed so angry he didn't dare insist, although the vehemence of her refusal bewildered him.

"By all that's holy, Monique! I mean no disrespect. After all, if we had succeeded in eloping that night, we'd be husband and wife now. Have you thought of that?"

"I . . . I have to go," she said feebly, wanting to run away from him . . . to run away from that horrid place . . . to run away from what he had just said. She broke free of his embrace and dashed off, running up the lane behind the row of tombs, forgetting about Celeste waiting at the end of the other path, forgetting everything except Maurice's words about her guardian and Azema. The memory of Miguel's caresses was searing her flesh . . . every spot he had touched was throbbing. Just the thought of his making love to Azema the way he had made love to her infuriated her. Maurice had to be wrong. Miguel couldn't still be seeing that horrid woman!

The stinging tears so blinded her eyes that she couldn't see where she was going. The dazzling white tombs with their gay flowers and decorations blended into a kaleidoscope of colors and patterns that she could no longer recognize. So distracted was she that she hardly noticed Padre Sebastian as he stepped out from behind a monument farther down the row of tombs and gave her a brief greeting. With unseeing eyes, she rushed past him, her dark blue cape flying behind her, its hood thrown back and her long gold hair glinting like a ray of sunlight on that otherwise dreary day. She never even noticed how the monk had continued to stand there, staring after her with dark, smoldering eyes long after she had gone by.

Chapter Thirty-one

MIGUEL WAS DESPERATE. HE COULDN'T UNDERSTAND the change that had come over Monique in the past two weeks. She had suddenly turned hostile toward him again. Perhaps his hopes of marrying her within a few months had been premature. She probably needed a year or two more yet. Some girls her age might be ready, but his ward had led such a sheltered, pampered existence up until now that it was probably too much to expect her to grow up so quickly. Lately she'd been so petulant toward him that he feared she might never declare a truce in her private war against him and Spain, no matter how the present hostilities between their respective countries might end.

He was glad he had insisted on giving their ever-fluctuating relationship a little more time to stabilize. One minute the girl would have him so exasperated that he'd be cursing himself for a fool to have ever been interested in such a spoiled brat; yet the next, there he would be smiling with tender indulgence at her caprices and thinking that, no matter now long it might take, it would be worthwhile waiting for so charming a child to ripen into the delightful woman he knew she could be. Then he would begin hoping all over again. . . .

His rebellious ward also seemed restless, but, as far as he could judge, for entirely different reasons.

That very afternoon, Mlle. Baudier had come bursting in on him while he was busy going over the household accounts to inform him that Monique had slipped out of the house again.

Racing off to the plaza, he found his unpredictable ward in one of her "patriotic demonstrations" with Foucher and some of his friends, promenading around the square singing the "Marseillaise" with the French tricolor on her blue bonnet and her gown of red and white stripes hanging loose "in the revolutionary mode"! He was beside himself with rage. Everything he thought he had gained over the past months suddenly seemed to have been for naught. There she was, more recalcitrant than ever. If anything, she seemed to be deliberately trying to provoke him!

Taking her by the arm, he literally dragged her away from her rebel friends, and not a moment too soon, for already a few gendarmes were coming out of the guardhouse to break up the demonstration, while several Spanish priests stood watching disapprovingly from the door of the church.

Now, at the town house once more, he marched his defiant ward straight into the parlor and, slamming the door angrily behind him, turned to look down accusingly at her.

"Will you please tell me, Monica, what in the world has come over you?" he demanded. "Have you forgotten our pact so soon?" There was torment now as well as anger in his dark eyes.

Monique flushed and turned away, unable to look another moment into the face that had been haunting her dreams ever since that night of the hurricane. "You should be the last one to speak to me of pacts!" she lashed back at him angrily. "Just like most of your countrymen, you're deceitful and say one thing while doing something else!"

He looked at her in bewilderment. "Whatever are you talking about? I meant what I said when we made our pact. If you'd only stop all this childish carrying-on and show me and your grandmother that you're mature enough, I'd marry you in an instant. But it's behavior like today's that makes me doubt you're ready to take a woman's role. . . ."

"And why should you worry about my qualifications as a woman when you already have one to fill your needs?" she suddenly flung back at him with all the venom she had been hoarding inside of her those past two weeks.

He shook his head, confusion beginning to corrode his anger. "I . . . I don't know what you mean," he faltered. "What woman are you talking about?"

"You know very well what woman. Azema Ducole. Who else?"

He put his hand to his forehead in despair. "God help me! Am I never to stop hearing that woman's name on your lips?"

"After all your fine talk of love and pacts, you've gone right on seeing her. You're nothing but a hypocrite!"

Miguel colored. "I swear I haven't been with Azema or any woman . . . not since that night . . ."

"How can you stand there and lie to me like that when you know very well you've been to see her heaven only knows how many times in these past two months?"

He blinked confusedly for a second; then he thought he understood. "It's true I've been by the Ducole town house a few times," he conceded, "but to see Henri, not Azema. You know very well he's my associate. I can hardly stop seeing him just because I've broken off with his sister."

"It's hard to believe that nothing passes between you and that sister when she's the one who kisses you goodbye at the exit!"

Miguel's dark eyes narrowed. "Who's been filling your head with such foolish gossip? It was that Foucher fellow, right? I wager that's why you've been acting so strangely recently. Have you been seeing that boy again behind my back?"

She held her ground defiantly. "What does it matter how I know? The fact is you're still seeing her!"

"Not in the way you're implying," he insisted. His mind was racing back over his recent visits to the Ducole town house, trying to remember what could have happened "at the exit" that someone might have seen and misconstrued or deliberately exaggerated.

Although Azema had seemed to accept with good grace his decision to leave off the more intimate aspects of their relationship, she had, nevertheless, made no secret of the fact that she would be quite willing to renew their liaison any time he felt so inclined. Miguel was beginning to remember now . . . that afternoon when she had insisted on seeing him to the door . . . she had coquettishly tried to kiss him goodbye. Someone must have seen them standing there in the entrance. . . . What rotten luck!

He took a pleading step toward Monique. "Please, my dear, believe me. There hasn't been anything between me and Azema for over two months now, and it's been that way because that's how I've wanted it . . . because the only woman I want is you." If she only knew how he ached to take her in his arms again! Even now, as he saw the swell of those fully ripened breasts pressing so exuberantly against her tightly laced bodice, he could remember the taste of those sweet nipples between his lips.

"Please, my dear, you must believe," he begged. She had turned her bonneted head away and only the high velvet crown with its rebellious French cockade confronted him.

"By all the saints, you have no reason to be jealous of anyone. God in heaven! How I wish you were just a little bit older!"

She whirled back to him, her gray eyes stormier than ever. "Yes, I know. You prefer more experienced women!" she exclaimed in bitter anger. "I've always suspected that was the real reason why you rejected me."

"Rejected you?" he echoed in disbelief. "*Qué barbaridad!* Is that what you've been thinking?"

Only the tragic expression on her face kept him from bursting out laughing at the impossible position in which he found himself. "Well, it seems I'm damned if I do, and damned if I don't!" he observed with an ironic chuckle.

But the tears of chagrin clouding her eyes bore witness to the fact that she could see no humor in the situation at all.

He moved in closer and gently lifted that angry little face so he could see it better. At that moment it looked more like a doll's than ever, he thought, with the ribbons of her blue bonnet so prettily framing it.

"Is that really what you think—that I rejected you that night of the storm?" he asked incredulously.

"It . . . it has occurred to me," she admitted, her chin quivering in the palm of his hand. "Especially in the light of recent events."

"God's my witness! If you only knew what it cost me . . . what it still costs me to keep my distance from you! I love you, you precious unruly child! Don't you know that yet? But you're robbing me of my wits. What am I to do with you?"

She continued to stand there, her tiny chin set, her figure drawn up indignantly, despite the limp skirts hanging so dejectedly about her limbs.

Bending down from his height, he peered beneath the brim of her hat, and at the sight of those huge gray eyes swimming in tears, a flood of mixed emotions surged through him.

"So you really do care!" he exclaimed. "Thank God, you love me a little!"

She lifted her head and gave him an indignant glare. "Do you think I'd have let you make love to me if I didn't?" Then suddenly she melted and threw herself against his chest. "Oh, Miguel, I do care!" she confessed passionately. "I only wish you really did, too! I can't bear it when you pull away from me. You see what I mean? You're doing it right now!"

Her words were like kindling thrown on the fire. He stopped drawing back and instead caught her to him, throwing all caution to the winds. "You think I don't want you? By all that's holy! If you only knew!" He pressed his body despairingly against hers, and the hard, throbbing reality of him sent a shiver of scalding desire racing through her veins.

"No one can satisfy me but you," he murmured as he bent his mouth to hers. "Just the sight of you . . . just the thought of you . . . You say you're a woman, my sweet child. Can't you feel how much I want you? God's my witness, I'm on fire for you day and night!"

His hands were rushing hungrily up and down the curves of her body now, his tongue boring desper-

ately through her lips. The force of his passion set
her head to spinning, her knees to dissolving.

"Oh, Miguel, you'll never have need of any other
woman . . . if you'll just teach me . . ."

His hand was on her breast and already it was
swelling to his touch. "My sweet passionate little
Monica, your doubts are so groundless! I'm yours.
Believe me, I'm saving myself only for you."

His breath was coming fast now, and the hard
reality of his desire pulsating wildly against her
seared her very being.

He was trembling, too, now. With his lips on hers,
his hand still cupping her bodice, he lowered her to
the sofa. He wanted to draw out that sweet breast
and savor the taste of it once more . . . to find
joyous relief from those long months of bridled
passion deep within the warm recesses of her.

But no . . . he tore his hands away from her and,
with the last vestige of willpower left him, forced
himself to his feet. "*Qué barbaridad!*" he gasped, his
breath labored with the passion racking his body at
that moment. "But this will never do! I started out
reprimanding you as your guardian, and here I am
making love to you again! I tell you, I'm bereft of my
senses when it comes to you!"

"And would it be so terrible if you did make love
to me?" she asked from where she still sat on the
sofa, breathless and somewhat bewildered by the
force of her own emotions.

"It's not the way things should be between us," he
replied, moving quickly over to the fireplace and
stoking the flames nervously in an effort to put some
distance between them and give himself time to
regain his control. "We made a pact, and I think it's
important we keep it. I'm simply letting my desire
for you as a man get out of hand, that's all."

"Doesn't what I feel count?"

He turned to her with a tender smile, the poker dangling in his hand. "Of course it does, my dear. That's the whole idea. I shouldn't be pressuring you this way. You need time to find out what it is you're really feeling. In part your jealousy springs from your doubting yourself as a woman. Our love must be built on trust and understanding, as well as passion. It would be folly for you to marry a man you say you love one moment and then hate and mistrust so intensely the next."

She started to rise in protest and go to him, but he held up a pleading hand. "No, my dear. Please don't misunderstand me and think I'm rejecting you, but I simply can't take any more proximity to you just now!"

He must be mad! Whatever had he been thinking of? Why, everyone in the household was probably just outside the door at that very moment waiting for him to finish reprimanding her. This certainly wasn't the time to let the situation between him and his ward get out of control. He knew his role as guardian had to come first, at least for now; yet how he longed to take her in his arms and make such passionate love to her that she'd never again doubt how much he really loved and wanted her!

Chapter Thirty-two

MIGUEL DREADED HAVING TO GO SEE HENRI, BUT IT was already a week into December, and he couldn't put it off any longer. He hoped this would be the last time he'd have to go to the Ducole town house. Perhaps he could persuade Henri to meet him elsewhere in the future—at the Chausson town house, Le Rêve, or some coffeehouse—any place where Azema wouldn't be.

It was embarrassing for both of them, especially since his ex-mistress obviously still nourished hopes of reviving their former liaison if she could. Most of all, there was no use fanning Monique's jealousy to even greater heights than it already was. They had enough obstacles between them without adding more! He hoped, however, that once the girl knew he was no longer going by the Ducoles' for any reason, she would accept the fact that her jealousy of Azema was unfounded now.

His visit had begun pleasantly enough, with Azema retiring after an effusive greeting to leave him and Henri alone to discuss their "tiresome business matters." He had just resolved the matter of their future meetings agreeably with a sympathetic Henri, when Azema returned with a tray of hot chocolate, which she insisted would be especially appropriate for such a cold, windy December afternoon.

. Miguel gulped down his chocolate hurriedly and, setting the cup on the tray again, rose to take his leave.

"I'm sorry to cut my visit short," he apologized, "but I'm anxious to get home. I haven't been there in almost four days now."

"Then you came here direct from Le Rêve?" asked Azema, obviously with the hope that he might remember how he used to stop off there on his way home from the plantation to spend the day or night with her.

"Yes," he replied, coloring in spite of himself. "I left the plantation early this morning, so I'm anxious to get home now and see what's been going on there."

Azema trilled a merry laugh. "My! But that ward of yours has put a short leash on you, hasn't she?" she taunted.

"It's not that," replied Vidal, trying to keep his tone polite despite his mounting impatience. "I'm the one who worries. Something might have come up while I wasn't there and they might need me, that's all."

"Your concern is truly touching!" observed Azema with a disdainful shrug of her shoulders as she took another sip of her chocolate. She looked exceptionally beautiful that afternoon in her rust-colored velvet dressing gown, which Miguel suspected she had put on for his benefit, and her long flaming hair falling freely about her shoulders.

"If you'll be kind enough to ring for my cape and hat?" he said, ignoring her sarcasm.

Henri rose uneasily. "Let me get you those figures I was working on last night, Miguel, so you can take them with you and look them over at your leisure. They're in my study."

He hurried out of the parlor while Miguel remained standing, waiting for Azema to ring for his wrap. Instead, she set her cup down languidly and took a few steps closer to him.

Miguel could tell she had perfumed herself a trifle more heavily than usual and he suspected that, too, had been deliberate. He realized it wasn't going to be as easy to leave as he had hoped.

"Really, Miguel, the way you run off from here these days, you'd think we had the pox!" she chided. "It wasn't always that way, *mon amour.*"

She reached up and toyed suggestively with a fold of his cravat. "Why don't you just sit back awhile and relax here by the fire?" she suggested coyly. "I'll pour you another cup of chocolate, if you like."

Miguel drew back stiffly. "Thank you, Zee, but I really am in a hurry," he said, adjusting the crease in his neckscarf back to the way it had been before she'd touched it.

Azema lowered discreet lids over the vivid green of her eyes. "I miss you, my dear," she murmured. "It grieves me to think you've forgotten all those happy hours we spent together so soon."

"I'll always remember fondly the time I spent in your company," he replied gallantly. "You're a very beautiful and charming woman, Zee. I hope we can at least remain friends."

"But you're so serious!" she scolded laughingly. "What need is there really, all considered, for us to stop seeing each other altogether? You know you're always welcome here. Of course, we can continue to be friends . . . and more, if you like, my sweet. After all, your getting married isn't the end of the world. What's between us needn't change."

"I'm afraid you don't understand, Zee. Mine won't be a marriage of convenience. It's a love match, and I hope to keep it that way by not provoking problems."

"My, but aren't you the lovesick swain! I thought you more sophisticated than that, Miguel, but we all make fools of ourselves over the ones who are hard to get, don't we? I hope you can keep all those fine resolutions once you're well yoked and begin to get bored with your naive little ward."

Miguel sighed. He had no intention of discussing Monique's more intimate qualities with his ex-mistress. He took Azema's hand politely and brushed it lightly with a parting kiss.

But suddenly she caught the hand that held hers and quickly drew him closer.

"Ah, *mon amour,* I can't let you go like this . . . so cold, so formal with me, your Zee who adores you so! At least let's say goodbye the way two lovers should. Come, lie with me one last time, no?"

She took the hand she held captive and deliberately cupped it over the mound of her breast, holding it there with a malicious smile as she watched him stiffen and flush uneasily.

"One more time, no?" she repeated coaxingly. "What difference will it make? Am I suddenly so repulsive to you?" She was trying to steer him back to the sofa where the fire was blazing away cheerfully in the chimney.

The feel of a woman's breast warm and pulsating in his hand momentarily stirred his long-denied carnal desires, but even in that split second, the memory of Monique's ripening body trembling with passion to his touch moved him all the more. Her sweet little face bathed in the ecstasy of her first and only love hung there in his mind's eye. . . .

Suddenly he heard a gasp. There in the open doorway, the face that had been floating like a phantom before his eyes seemed to have materialized. Monique was standing there staring at them, her face pale and anguished in the frame of her fur-lined hood.

He wrested his hand away from where Azema was holding it tightly pressed against her breast and stepped back, but it was too late. Without a word, Monique was gone.

It had all happened so quickly, so unexpectedly . . . for a moment he wondered whether she had been there at all. He called her name and tried to rush after her, despite Azema's obvious efforts to block his path, but only the slam of the front door answered him.

Chapter Thirty-three

MONIQUE RAN AND RAN . . . STRAIGHT DOWN CHARtres toward the main plaza. The biting north wind lashed at her cape until it whipped back the hood from her head and left her long hair flying loose in a golden stream behind her. She clutched the wrap closed at her neck to keep it from blowing away but didn't slacken her pace.

Some of the townspeople stopped and stared at her curiously as they stepped aside to let her race past them; others gave grunts of annoyance as she nearly knocked them off the wooden sidewalk in her blind haste.

But Monique was completely unaware of what was going on around her. Her clouded eyes saw nothing save the image of Miguel standing there in the Ducole parlor with his hand cupping Azema's breast.

She hadn't even realized where she was going until the huge flat-roofed cathedral with its hexagonal towers flanking it on either side suddenly loomed up in front of her. There was a quiet dignity in its simplicity, ornamented only by a balustrade around its terrace roof and a marble effect painted over the front of its plastered brick walls.

She stood there in the massive shadow undecided where to go next. She could continue down one of the streets on the other side of the square, but sooner or later she would come to the palisades, and outside lay only the swamps. Of course, if she went down the Rue Royale, it would lead her back home to the town house, but she hated facing anyone at that moment. It was bad enough to have been made a fool, but worse yet for all the world to know about it!

As she stood there vacillating, the brown-robed figure of Fray Sebastian suddenly emerged from the columned entrance of the church and held up a large bony hand to detain her.

"I see you're roaming the streets again, child," he admonished in that dry, cracked voice of his. "And it's blowing up colder, too. Perhaps you'd like to come in out of the wind for a minute and see our magnificent new cathedral, now that it's almost finished?"

She looked at him half dazed. He was only slightly taller than she was and looked as though he were slowly withering away within the dark recesses of his hooded habit. She wondered how long it had been since the light of day had struck him full on the face.

"I . . . I don't think . . ." she faltered, but the monk became more insistent. "It's all right," he assured her. "The church hasn't been dedicated yet, but you might want to say a little prayer and ask God to forgive you your sins."

Monique could see the gold leaf of the main altar glittering in the dim interior beyond the arched entrance, and she suddenly felt a great desire to enter. Perhaps spiritual balm was what she needed to soothe the tumult raging within her at that moment.

"Yes, I think I might like to go in and pray . . . just for a few moments, if you don't mind."

A spark glinted in the dark hollows of the monk's eyes as he stepped aside and motioned to her to go through the arched doorway.

The splendor that met her eyes was indeed impressive. The pews hadn't been placed yet, so the broad expanse of the marble floor, interrupted only by occasional white columns, was like a giant mirror, reflecting the colorful paintings and sculptures lining the walls and the ornate galleries and balustrades high above it.

Monique made her way slowly across the vast sheen of the empty church to where the main altar towered majestically above that sea of gleaming marble at the far end of the interior. Like one in a trance, she instinctively took her small lace headscarf from the pocket of her cape and set it atop her windblown hair while she gaped in wonder at the fresh, glittering beauty all around her.

Although as yet unfinished, the main altar was near enough to completion to be impressive, promising to become a veritable masterpiece of marble and gold. A scaffold still spanned it, but there were no artisans working on it at that moment, so Monique stood staring up at it, marveling at the enormousness of it.

There were few people in the cathedral just then, for it was not open to the public yet, but meanwhile the work continued. Off to one side of the entrance, two artisans were putting up a wrought-iron railing in front of a niche with a statue of St. Anthony, while two or three Capuchin friars were sauntering about leisurely in their brown homespun habits and peaked hoods like phantom shadows examining the progress of the work on the church and making random comments to one another. The murmur of their voices reverberated eerily in the vast emptiness of the interior, but their words were indistinguishable.

"Would you like me to hear your confession, child?" asked Padre Sebastian suddenly. "The confessional hasn't been installed yet, but—"

"No, no," she said quickly. "I'd prefer just to pray. May I?"

"You're in a building erected to the glory of God. That's what you should do," replied the friar dryly. "Today is the Feast of the Immaculate Conception, you know. I suggest you say a special prayer to the Virgin while you're at it."

He retreated a little from her as she made the sign of the cross and knelt at the railing in front of the main altar, but he remained discreetly behind a nearby column, never taking his eyes from her. Shafts of light from the high stained-glass windows made crisscross patterns over her blue-cloaked figure and turned the disheveled mass of her pale blond hair into a shining halo as it shimmered through the delicate lace of her scarf and poured over her shoulders like liquid gold.

Fray Sebastian stared at her in fixed fascination, glad that she was so engrossed in prayer that she was unaware of his scrutiny. He wondered how much longer he would have to wait before God would deliver the wench into his hands. He wished she didn't have that cape around her, but then he had been observing her for so long now that he knew every line of that sensuous little body of hers, fashioned, without a doubt, by the devil himself to lure men to the sins of the flesh.

Not that he wanted the girl for lustful purposes. To the contrary, his destiny was to cleanse women like that. He wasn't like so many of those sacrilegious French monks there in the colony with their concubines hidden away somewhere. They were as lax in their vows of celibacy as they were in their vows of poverty and fasting.

It wasn't by chance that the colony was suffering so many calamities—that dreadful year of '88 with its devastating flood and all-consuming fire, followed by famine and pestilence; then another lesser conflagration, in '92, and three hurricanes in the past year and a half! And as if that wasn't enough, even the crops were failing! How much more would it take to bring the sinful city of New Orleans to its knees? For it was an evil, seditious populace, rebelling against God and its rightful rulers.

What was needed was the firm hand of the Holy Inquisition to take over and root out the sin abounding there on all sides.

It had been a pity that his former superior, Padre Antonio de Sedella, had not been permitted to establish a branch of the Holy Tribunal in New Orleans as he had been commissioned to do by Madrid a few years back. But Miró, governor at that time, had wanted no part of the Inquisition in the colony and, at the risk of incurring the wrath of both the Church and his king, had ordered Padre Antonio deported back to Spain and hush-hushed the whole affair.

But if Miró and now the new governor, Carondelet, thought that was the end of it, they were greatly mistaken, for he—Sebastian Montez de Barcelona— was still there to carry on his superior's aborted work and keep the light of the Inquisition burning in New Orleans, undercover if need be, but at least carefully nurtured and ready to come out into the open just as soon as the right opportunity presented itself.

For he wouldn't be satisfied until he saw the Holy
Tribunal firmly established and active there in the
colony. A few autos in the Plaza de Armas were
what this wicked city needed to make it fall to its
knees and beg forgiveness for its sins. If its wayward
citizens knew they would be dragged before the Holy
Office to account for their acts of rebellion and
heresy, they would no longer be so quick to stray
from the fold.

Meanwhile in his humble way, thought Sebastian,
he would have to continue the work his unfortunate
superior had begun but had never been able to put
into effect. Of course, he'd have to be discreet until
the moment came when he could operate freely. The
fate of Padre Antonio had demonstrated the need
for caution.

Fortunately, however, no one seemed to suspect,
even now, that underneath the calabozo there still
lay that secret chamber he had helped his superior
prepare years ago for those singled out by the
Inquisition for special attention. Although there had
been one other friar who had assisted in the project,
the latter had died earlier that year, so now only one
person was left in the entire colony who knew about
that subterranean room. Fray Sebastian smiled com-
placently as he savored his secret in the dark recesses
of his mind. He was proud of the way he had kept his
silence and felt more than ever, with each passing
day, that the divine mission of bringing the Inquisition to New Orleans had fallen upon his shoulders.

Of course, until he could come out into the open,
he would have to continue doing the best he could
on his own. After the monastery had been destroyed in that devastating conflagration of '88,
he had deliberately built his hut over the entrance

to the passageway that led to that chamber under the calabozo, and there had been two or three times now that he had brought some sinner there and used the dungeon for the purpose it had been originally designed.

Of course, with the Chausson wench he would have to be more careful than with the others. She wasn't any street trollop like that last girl he had purged. This golden-haired temptress came from a distinguished family in the colony, with a guardian who had ties in Madrid. There would be an immediate fuss if a girl like that were to disappear. Whatever he did, it would have to be very carefully worked out. He'd have to have a good case against her when the time came to take her down to his secret chamber for questioning and purging . . . preferably a confession wrung out of her in which she herself admitted her complicity with the devil.

Chapter Thirty-four

MONIQUE CLASPED HER HANDS TIGHTLY TOGETHER over her rosary, fervently trying to keep her mind on her prayers, but Miguel's face kept blotting out the altar.

She found herself remembering how her mother had warned her never to put her trust in a Spaniard. How could she have forgotten and let Miguel Vidal make such a fool of her! That early Spanish captain-general had used deceit to trap her grandfather and the other French patriots. Now her guardian had deceived her, too. He had sworn to her that he'd broken off with Azema, yet less than half an hour ago she had seen him making love to that horrid woman.

After all his passionate declarations of love . . . all his assurances that no other woman could satisfy him except her . . . that he was saving himself only for their nuptial bed! How he had mocked her! He and Azema must be having a good laugh at that moment over what a gullible child she was.

She hated the thought of going home. How could she survive the pain of seeing Miguel again? Even knowing what she did about her guardian, her whole body still ached for him. A thousand fires were consuming her from within for want of him. She must ask the good Lord to take the anguish of that impossible love from her heart!

Suddenly the stillness of the cathedral was shattered by the sound of wild shouts and the frantic clanging of anvils and bells just outside the square. The two men working near the entrance of the church were the first to react. Abandoning their tools and paints on the spot, they dashed off quickly.

Unfortunately, that alarm had become all too familiar in New Orleans in recent years. That dreaded call for all able-bodied citizens to come help fight a fire or a flood always sent panic into the hearts of every man, woman, and child of the town. It could mean life or death . . . the loss of years of work and saving. In just a few moments, a lifetime—even life itself—could go up in a blaze of flames or be buried under torrents of water!

Monique rose from the prayer rail bewilderedly. The cries of *"Incendio!"* could be heard above the din of bells and frantic shouting. She wondered where the fire had struck and hoped her home would be spared this time.

The firehouse was there on the square, only a short distance from the church, next to the guard-house, but the city only had six pumps and those were operated by hand, so they usually had to be supplemented by lines of bucket brigades.

In those brief seconds that it had taken for her to rouse herself from her orations and realize what was happening, the church had emptied of its occupants. Only Father Sebastian remained now, standing there beside her with a strange elated look in his eyes.

She looked questioningly at him. "Merciful heavens! Don't tell me it's another fire?" she exclaimed in dismay. Her heart was still heavy, but she wanted to be with her loved ones now. Her own problems suddenly seemed to diminish in size next to the greater emergency that threatened everything and everyone she held dear.

Fray Sebastian stole a quick glance around him as he moved in closer to her. "Come, child, it's shorter if we go out the back," he said, grabbing her by the arm and beginning to lead her around to the rear of the altar. The grip of that bony hand was surprisingly strong, and instinctively Monique resisted, but the monk pulled her along with him.

"Come, we must hurry," he insisted.

"Please, I . . . I don't need any help," she told him, growing more annoyed by the minute over the monk's arbitrary manner. There was something about him that frightened her.

"Don't argue, do as I say!" he chided impatiently. They were behind the altar now, and he continued to pull her along by the arm.

Determined not to let him drag her any farther, Monique tried to break free and run away from him, but suddenly, with one sweeping gesture, he caught her to him, as though he were arresting the flight of a bird on wing. Deftly he twisted her arm behind her and pulled her back up against him, even as he clamped his other hand simultaneously over her mouth before she could utter a sound of protest.

"*Al fin!*" he exclaimed triumphantly in her ear. "At last I have you!"

The confused shouts just outside the church seemed to be echoing Monique's inner turmoil at that moment. With muffled protests against the hand that covered the lower half of her face, she tugged desperately at those steellike fingers clamped over her mouth while she struggled in vain to work herself free of him, but the wiry strength of the seemingly frail monk surprised her.

Her skirts whirled and her voluminous cloak tangled with the long loose habit and flowing sleeves of the Capuchin as she tried to kick and lash out blindly at him, but he wouldn't release his grip. Instead, he forced her to the floor facedown and, still keeping her arm pinioned behind her, held her there with one of his knees in the pit of her back while he shoved a gag into her mouth and quickly trussed her hands together behind her with the cord-belt from his own habit.

Finally he pulled her roughly to her feet and looked down at her jubilantly as she stood there swaying before him, whimpering and spent.

"This moment was heaven-sent!" he rejoiced. "God has delivered you into my hands at last! Now we must get you below immediately while everyone is busy with the fire."

He threw her voluminous cloak about her shoulders and pulled the hood down well over her head so that it covered her face almost completely. He adjusted the gag in her mouth more securely. It was dry and coarsely woven and tasted of sweat and incense. She murmured protests against it, but it stifled them. Terror paralyzed her. God help her! This couldn't be happening! It had to be some horrible nightmare. Soon she'd be awakening and Miguel would be there laughingly reassuring her that it had all been just a bad dream. Perhaps nothing of that dreadful afternoon had really happened. Perhaps she hadn't found Miguel caressing Azema. Perhaps there wasn't any fire at all outside. And perhaps that diabolical creature with the peaked hood wasn't really dragging her off at that very moment to she knew not where! The scream lodged in her throat was suffocating her . . . if only she could breathe! The blackness closed in and engulfed her.

Chapter Thirty-five

"PRAY, DAUGHTER OF SATAN, PRAY! LIFT UP YOUR voice to the heavens and confess your sins!"

Monique struggled desperately to emerge from the gray seas swirling around her. She had no idea where she was, but whatever the place, she had the vague memory of having been dragged, even carried there.

Contrary to her hopes, no one had tried to stop her or her abductor on their short walk from the back door of the church to Fray Sebastian's hut near the walls of the calabozo. It hadn't occurred to anyone that beneath the heavy folds of her cloak she had been bound and gagged.

True, a few people dashing by had shouted to them, but although Fray Sebastian's grip on her arm had tightened as he forced her to keep pace with him, he had called back casually enough. There hadn't seemed to be any reason to challenge them. Those who had seen her hooded figure with the monk had probably thought she'd been stumbling along like that because she had either been overcome with emotion or injured in the fire. After all, everyone had been too preoccupied with his or her own problems to be concerned over a friar helping some stricken woman get to wherever she was going.

She vaguely remembered Padre Sebastian leading her into the dark closeness of his one-room hovel, and then, as she had stumbled and fallen again, he had slung her over his shoulder as though she had been a sack of flour and continued down with her into a dark, damp passageway . . . down into what had seemed like the black caverns of Hades. The last thing she remembered before she had completely lost consciousness again had been a damp, musty odor mingled with incense stinging her eyes and nostrils. Now it was the first thing she was aware of as she came drifting back to reality.

She was lying on something hard and clammy, but when she went to get up, she was startled to find she couldn't. Her limbs seemed to be paralyzed. Frantically she tried to lower her arms, but they seemed to be frozen there high above her head. She tested her legs, but her ankles were held fast, too. Panic began to paralyze her now from within as she realized she was strapped down.

Although her cape had been removed and its hood was no longer pulled forward over her head blocking her view, she still couldn't make out at first where she was. As she grew accustomed to the dim light, however, the distorted shadows looming around her finally began to take on more definite forms, and she suddenly saw with horror that she was in a dungeon.

The air was damp and clammy and the crumbling bricks in the circle of light given off by the sputtering torch in the sconce on the wall glistened with huge drops of water. For a moment she thought she was seeing long black snakes crawling up and down the walls, but then, as her eyes began to focus better, she realized that what she was seeing was in reality a sinister assortment of long black whips hanging there ready for use!

Somewhere in the dim recesses of her confused mind Monique remembered rumors about the calabozo's hidden torture chamber—a deep, dark dungeon where prisoners were taken, never to emerge to the light of day again. But what had she to do with such things? Why would anyone want to bring her to such a place . . . most of all, someone like Fray Sebastian?

Even at that moment, the monk was bending over her and removing the gag at last. She coughed and sputtered as the air rushed in once more and seared her throat and lungs, but at least she could breathe again.

"No one can hear us here," he said in a matter-of-fact tone. "Many a scream has resounded in this chamber, but they have all remained buried here with their guilt."

"Why are you doing this to me?" she sobbed. "Why?" Her quivering lips kept mouthing the question, even after the sound would no longer come.

"So much the worse for you if you don't know the reason!" he admonished her. "That means we'll have to work all the harder to make you aware of the evil that lies within you before we can hope to bring you to repentance."

"If you mean to kill me, do so now and get it over with!" she exclaimed, suddenly defiant.

Fray Sebastian chuckled his dry, mirthless laugh and continued to stare down intently at her from where he stood beside the rack. His narrow, sunken face, partially shadowed by the hood of his homespun cowl, seemed longer than ever as he stroked his pointed beard pensively.

"No, no, child, we cannot go too quickly," he replied. "We must prolong each precious moment. You have no idea how many nights I've lain awake planning every exquisite step of your purification. We'll spend many a long hour here in holy commu-

nion during the days and nights to come, until the
devil has been drawn out of you completely and you
repent of all your sins."

"Mon Dieu! But what have I done that is so
terrible?" asked Monique tremulously from where
she lay helpless on the rack.

"The case against you is long, Monique Chausson.
All your transgressions have been duly noted in
detail for well over a year now, for you are most
surely a handmaid of the devil. You have exhibited
yourself brazenly in the streets, deliberately enticing
men to the temptations of the flesh. You have been
disobedient not only to your God and your elders,
but to his Catholic Majesty Carlos IV and the
authorities of this colony, publicly demonstrating
against them and inciting rebellion and sedition.
Women like you have been sent by Satan to cause
trouble in this world and lead those around them
into perdition. Your only hope for salvation is for
you to confess your guilt and accept your chastisement before it's too late."

"Am I truly so evil, then? God forgive me!"

"Don't lie to me, Monique Chausson. I have it all
written down with dates and details. But when I've
finished with you, you'll be crying out your guilt and
begging for forgiveness."

"Merciful God! If I've done so many wicked
things, then I beg forgiveness now, Padre!" exclaimed Monique, ready to burst into tears once
more. "There's no need to torment me. If I've
sinned, I want to atone."

"I'm glad to hear that," replied Fray Sebastian
with a wry smile, "but you daughters of Satan are sly
ones. You think that, by feigning repentance, you
can escape chastisement. But for those who have
sinned, there can be no true cleansing of the soul

without first suffering the pangs of the flesh . . . that flesh which harlots like you value more than your souls. So if you are sincere about wanting to be forgiven, you'll accept the purging that you must go through before true purity can be reached."

"What . . . what are you going to do to me, then?" Her voice was so tremulous that it was barely audible.

"We'll start with something I've wanted to do from the first time I saw you flaunting yourself in the plaza." He stepped off into the shadows for a moment and returned with what seemed to be a long iron bar in his hand. "I must first burn the mark of salvation into that sinful flesh of yours."

He reached down and, without further ado, whisked away the white lawn fichu that filled the low neckline of her gown. Monique gave a cry of dismay and turned her head away as the cleavage of her breasts suddenly gleamed white and bold in the dim torchlight.

The monk gave a sarcastic snort. "But why should you be so modest now?" he asked mockingly as he tugged impatiently at the bodice until it yielded the fullness of her breasts completely to his view. "Didn't I see you that time on the plaza pushing your collar apart so all men could see and lust after you?"

"Oh, no, I never meant to do that!" she protested, no longer able to control the trembling of her taut limbs as she stole a fearful glance at him and saw how his eyes gleamed with a strange light within the shadowy depths of his hood.

"Hush, child with the heart of a whore! Didn't I see you with my own eyes?" He held the tip of the brand close to the girl's face so she could see the cross it formed. "Do you see this—the sign of our

Lord and Savior?" He lowered the iron and pressed it between her breasts. She winced at the feel of the cold, hard metal against her flesh. "We'll brand these fine ripe breasts of yours . . . right here . . . like this. Then we'll see whether you'll ever bare them so brazenly again."

Monique watched in terrified fascination as the monk glided about the shadows like a silent phantom, lighting the ominous brazier in the center of the room. Its bricks blackened from the smoke and flames of past infamies, the open oven stood only an arm's span from where Monique lay suspended on the rack.

As the coals began to glow he stirred them with the long-handled iron and then left it lying there to continue heating while he turned once more to where she lay helpless and weeping. His eyes already seemed to be burning into the spot where he had decided the brand would first sear her flesh.

The monk began to mumble prayers over her, and instinctively she tried to murmur her own, but the words stuck in her throat. She couldn't take her eyes off the tip of the iron lying there amid the crackling flames and stared at it with hypnotic fascination as she watched the cross on its tip begin to glow. The tongues of fire licking hungrily at it seemed to be slowly imbuing it with a life of its own.

The chanting of the monk rose in volume until it reached a feverish pitch, the Latin phrases so accelerated now that the incantations were no longer distinguishable. Beads of sweat glistened on the ruddy blur of his features as the fire sought out his Mephistophelian features beneath the shadow of his hood, for the heat from the brazier had quickly warmed the chill of the room, making the stifling closeness of the atmosphere all the more intolerable.

A clammy sweat bathed Monique as she lay there numb with terror, her fear increasing with every moment as the cross glowed with greater and greater intensity among the burning coals.

Fray Sebastian pulled it out and held it up for closer scrutiny, peering at it critically and holding the palm of his hand near enough to feel the heat emanating from it. But he wasn't satisfied yet. He submerged it among the coals once more and turned back to her.

"Fire purges," he told her, in the manner that a teacher instructs a student. "Perhaps it's fitting that while that wicked city above us is being purged, you, the handmaid of Satan, be purged here below."

"My family will miss me," she warned her captor in a last desperate effort of defiance. "You'll have to answer to my grandmother and my guardian for whatever you do to me."

Fray Sebastian laughed humorlessly. "Oh, they'll miss you, all right," he agreed, "but they'll more than likely come to the conclusion that you were lost in the fire and give up looking for you after a day or two. No, child, the fire was a godsend. That's why I saw the opportunity to take you and seized it immediately."

"But what will you say when you release me? You'll have to give an accounting—"

"Silence, strumpet! The Holy Inquisition gives an accounting to no one! Suffice it to say I have very special plans for you. Meanwhile, we have time. There's no need for us to go too quickly." He seemed to savor the thought of the long, clandestine nights ahead of him when he could at last torment this wench whom the devil had sent to torment him.

"I have resolved to control myself and not be quite as zealous with you as I was with those other wenches I chastised in the past," he continued. "That last one I purged expired before she could recant. I don't want to make that same mistake with you, child, so I promise I won't torment the demons within you more than your flesh can tolerate, for I especially want you to live until you've confessed and repented. As I told you, I have important plans for you."

Despite the heat of the room, a cold chill gripped Monique from within. The man was mad! How could she reason with him? But then the whole idea of the Inquisition was mad! This diabolical monk was simply the venomous fruit of a weed that had been permitted to grow far too long in the garden of the Church. It should have been uprooted long ago, yet there was nothing so difficult to reason with as fanaticism.

"But what is it I must confess?" she ventured. "Exactly what is it you wish me to say?"

"You know full well the gamut of your sins," he snapped back, "and you must tell me everything. How many men you have led into sin . . . how many men you have let possess your body . . ."

"*Mon Dieu!* I'm not as bad as you think, Padre! I'm . . . I'm still a virgin—"

"Lying won't spare you, you know. You must confess to me every sinful deed you've ever done . . . every wicked thought that's crossed your mind."

"But I swear I . . ." She paused. "I . . . I've been kissed a few times, but . . . God forgive me! Is that so wicked?"

The monk walked over to the wall and chose one of the long multithonged whips hanging there. The metal tips on the ends of the one he held gleamed in the candlelight with the same intensity as his eyes as he passed the thongs almost caressingly between his fingers.

"Perhaps a good flogging will set you to remembering better," he told her. "Are you so depraved that your wickedness no longer even seems like sinning to you?"

"I . . . I'm so confused," protested Monique, anxiously eyeing the restless whip in his hands. "Just the thought of your doing so many terrible things to me fills me with such fear I can't think straight!"

The monk shrugged his scarecrowlike shoulders beneath his loosely fitting robes. "A few hours a night with me and my multiple persuaders should help stir your memory," he told her. "The days go by slowly here in the dark. You'll soon come to anticipate my nocturnal visits as the weeks go by, and before long you'll find yourself remembering many things to confess to me, I'm sure."

The brand was glowing red-hot now, and the flames sizzled and crackled about it, announcing its readiness. The monk hung the whip back up on the wall and went over to the brazier. This time there was no need to test it.

"Now we'll begin!" he announced with obvious pleasure at the prospect. He withdrew the glowing rod from the fire and reached down to steady her with his free hand.

She was twisting and turning in a frenzy of terror now, weeping hysterically. Already she could feel the heat radiating from the brand, but with her outstretched limbs strapped firmly to the rack, all she could do was writhe wildly, struggling desperately . . . vainly . . . to dodge the downward sweep of that sizzling cross. She was like a fluttering butterfly pinned fast to a board, futilely making its last stand against the inevitable.

The monk tried again to steady her to receive the full impact of the torch, but the feel of her breast brushing against his hand during the struggle seemed to disorient him. He suddenly paused and stood there, looking down at her in fascinated awe. His breath quickened, and the hand that had touched her breast began to tremble violently. Those dark, smoldering eyes were glowing now with more intensity than the red-hot brand he held suspended in midair.

After a moment he gave a start and seemed to come back to reality. Angrily he dug his fingers into her flesh until she moaned in pain.

"Cursed woman! Try your wiles on me, will you?" he roared.

Turning away in horror, he thrust the iron abruptly back into the fire while he tried desperately to regain control of himself. May God forgive him for his sinful thoughts! For the salvation of his soul, he must not give in to his desire for her. One more reason why he had to purge this spawn of the devil, for in so doing he would be cleansing himself of his own lust for her. But he knew now that he would never know peace until Monique Chausson was destroyed.

Chapter Thirty-six

Miguel was desperate. He had been searching frantically for Monique for over an hour, and she was nowhere to be found. Now, with the fire fast taking on the proportions of another major catastrophe for the city, it was even more difficult to look for her.

Everything had turned into a hellish nightmare since that moment he had turned to see Monique standing there in the Ducole hallway looking at him with wide, accusing eyes.

To make matters worse, Azema had made him lose precious minutes by blocking his way and insisting on arguing, until finally he had been obliged to thrust her aside and dash out despite her protests.

The irony of it all was that, since his pact with Monique the morning after the hurricane, he hadn't been near Azema's bedchamber, and that afternoon was to have been his last meeting with Henri at the Ducole town house. If only Monica hadn't suddenly appeared out of nowhere to complicate matters! Whatever had possessed the girl to go there in the first place? Poor sweet sensitive child! She had unwittingly given Azema the perfect opportunity to enjoy a brief moment of revenge against both her ex-lover and her rival.

Of course, Azema simply resented the fact

that he had been the first one to break off their liaison. Her vanity had been pricked, nothing more. And her pride was probably doubly wounded because it had been an inexperienced girl like Monique who had won out over her.

No, the only one he was worried about in that not-so-humorous comedy of errors was Monique. The memory of the look on her face wrung his heart. He didn't know how he would ever be able to convince her now that he hadn't betrayed her trust in him . . . that he had, in fact, broken off with Azema.

His sweet little ward—so young and passionate, so uncompromising in her judgments! All he wanted to do now was find her . . . kiss away her tears and make her understand. She had to know he hadn't deceived her, that she had misjudged the significance of what she had seen.

He had been so certain he'd find her at home that he had gone directly there. Instead, all he found was the overseer from Le Rêve waiting for him. He realized now that Monique had gone looking for him at the Ducoles' to advise him of Roselle's arrival at the town house. It seemed that an urgent matter had come up at the plantation shortly after he had left there that morning. But Miguel was too upset to discuss business at that moment. All he could do was beg Roselle's patience and explain he couldn't attend to anything until he'd found his missing ward.

On overhearing that Monique was missing, Grandmother Chausson was beside herself with fear. She began to weep hysterically and remind Miguel how the two other girls who had been missing recently had never been found. But Miguel tried his best to assure her he was going back out to comb the city, if need be, all the while trying to hide his own frantic misgivings.

No sooner had he stepped out of the front door, however, then the fire alarm sounded. Miguel looked up Rue Royale in dismay. The fire was only a few blocks away on the other side of the square. As if he didn't have enough to worry about already!

The strong wind that had been blowing all afternoon was rapidly fanning the flames, and the overcast sky to the opposite side of the city had taken on a reddish glow that had little to do with the sun.

Just to be on the safe side, Miguel gave hurried orders to Roselle to help the women and the household servants get whatever valuables they wished saved into the family coach and wagon and take them immediately to the plantation. He needed to be free to give his undivided attention to finding Monique. He didn't want to have to be worrying about the rest of the family's safety, as well, if the fire should reach the town house.

"Just leave the geldings and the houseboy here for me," he told Roselle hurriedly. "As soon as I find Monique, we'll join you at Le Rêve."

Even as Miguel rushed to the plaza, he continued to hope that the danger of the fire would make Monique come running back home, but meanwhile he decided to look around his ward's favorite haunts—the main square and the Orange Tree Walk.

The longer he walked the streets looking for her, however, the more difficult it became, for the people were milling about in a panic-stricken frenzy as memories of the destruction wrought by past conflagrations filled them with terror. Many were already trying to return to their homes, but the majority of the townsmen were rushing to the scene of the fire to help fight it before it reached tragic proportions.

All hell seemed to have broken loose. The soldiers were dragging out the town's pumps from the firehouse on the square, and several of the citizens, as well as one or two more elegantly dressed members of the city council, were urging them on to greater speed. There were only six pumps, and some of them had never really been put to the test, since they had only recently been acquired. Even the wooden building in which they were housed, with a door for each "engine," had just been built.

Miguel tried to stop two or three people he knew to ask them if they might have seen Monique during that past hour, but they simply gave him glazed looks and shook their heads.

With each passing moment his despair mounted. Where could she be? In some corner crying her eyes out, thinking he didn't love her and had only been deceiving her all the while? Or worse yet, perhaps trying to fend off the advances of some drunken Kaintock, like that time he had first met her and Celeste on the square? In a port where drinking and whoring were the favorite pastimes of two-thirds of the male population—townsmen and boatmen alike—a lone girl roaming the streets was fair game for any rake who chanced upon her.

He made his way quickly down the gravel path lined with trees that ran along the levee, deserted now of its usual afternoon strollers. The icy wind felt even colder up there, so close to the river and tunneled through the orange trees. He doubted the girl would have sought refuge in such a windy place, yet he could leave no stone unturned.

Quickly he made his way back toward the square, this time along Chartres, which had probably been the street Monique had traversed on first leaving the Ducole town house. The fire on Royale was only a block away and already the backs of several houses on that thoroughfare were beginning to shoot up in flames, as well. He wondered whether Henri and Azema were going to abandon their place or stay and try to fight it out. He would have liked to stop off to offer Henri help, but he didn't dare. Every minute now made his finding Monique more urgent than before.

Back on the plaza, with the crowds milling around him more frantic than ever now that it was evident the fire was out of control, Miguel made his way toward the cathedral. The thought occurred to him that the girl might have taken refuge there. As soon as he entered, however, his spirits sank, for he saw the place was empty.

With the faint hope that he simply might have missed Monique somewhere along the way and that she had returned home by that time, Miguel decided to return to the town house. Since the Rue Royale was the street that ran back of the church, he made his way across the polished marble floor toward the rear, wishing, as he went, that he could find some padre still on the premises who might have seen Monique around the plaza or even in the church earlier that afternoon.

Worried as he was over the girl, he couldn't help noting how splendid the new cathedral was. Of course, he had seen a few more lavish ones in Europe during his travels, but this one was especially elegant for a city the size of New Orleans.

The altar with its fine marble and gold work was particularly impressive in the late-afternoon light filtering in through the stained-glass windows. Perhaps it was because everything in the place was so

new—so shining and clean—that the dark clump of
delicately spun lace lying on the floor in sharp relief
against the light-colored tiles had immediately attracted his attention. Or perhaps it was because he
had recognized that particular wisp of lace from the
moment he had seen it. But whatever the reason, he
knew at once it was Monique's, even as he stooped
to pick it up.

After all, hadn't he brought two like it from
Madrid as gifts for his pretty young wards? He'd had
them handwoven just for them—little triangular
patches of black lace with delicate gold threads
running along their scalloped edges. He even remembered how he'd thought the gold of his Monica's curls had put those threads to shame the first
time he had seen her pale blond hair shining through
the gossamer weave of her headscarf.

The faint scent of crushed rose petals rising from
the shimmering triangle of black and gold lace
immediately evoked the girl's image and, with it, a
flood of countless questions that required answering.

Chapter Thirty-seven

"REALLY, VIDAL, I'D LIKE TO HELP YOU IF I COULD, but you can see what I'm up against. The fire is spreading by the minute, and I'm afraid Chartres—perhaps everything from Bourbon to the levee—will go before we even begin to get this damn fire under control."

The dynamic little Baron de Carondelet was in one of his more agitated moods. He had temporarily set up his center of operations on the ground floor of Almonester's palatial residence, the only formidable building flanking the square on the side of the fire. Once more on hand to help the city in its hour of need, Don Andrés had opened the portals of his home to the ever-increasing number of victims who had instinctively come clamoring at his doors seeking his aid.

The huge salon where the gala ball had been held only two months before was already beginning to overflow with haggard-eyed, tattered townspeople who were there, for the most part, simply because there was no place else to go. Amid the cross whimpering of frightened, soot-streaked children who didn't quite understand what was going on and the soft weeping of their tragic-faced mothers, who knew only too well what it all meant, the ever-increasing number of victims of the fire sat lining the walls. A few sought the privacy of some far corner, stunned and silent, contemplating the significance of what the complete loss of all their worldly belongings would mean to their futures, while others simply struggled to hold on to their very lives as, burned or injured, they moaned and anxiously waited for someone to come have a look at them and perhaps offer a few moments of relief until they could get to the hospital or back to their homes—homes they hoped would still be standing by the time they'd be able to return to them.

Miguel had found the governor in the center of all the turmoil, conferring with a knot of uniformed officers and several members of the city council, trying to decide what steps should be taken to head off the fire before it could advance any farther.

At first the baron had been delighted to see him and, assuming he had come to help them fight the fire, had invited him to join the group. But when Miguel had insisted that he needed to speak of an urgent yet confidential matter, Carondelet had finally taken him aside to the privacy of one of the front sitting rooms.

On hearing what the frantic young Spaniard had to say, the baron was glad he had had the foresight to withdraw to where no one could hear them.

"In God's name! Do you realize the situation we have here, Vidal? Between the damn wind and the low water pressure at this time of the year, we're in danger of losing the whole damn city! And all because of two brats playing with flint and tinder in a patio there on Rue Royale! A few sparks in some neighboring hayloft, and look what we have—a major catastrophe!"

The plump, energetic little man dabbed furiously at his brow with a lacy monogrammed handkerchief. "At least we got the alarm sounded sooner this time than they did in '88. They tell me the priest back then wouldn't let anyone ring the bells because it was Good Friday. Can you imagine? They let four-fifths of New Orleans burn down without sounding a single damn bell! God help us! The things that go on in this town! Now you want me to let you have one of my officers so you can go off looking for some mad monk that you think might have designs on your wayward ward! That's all I needed!"

"I assure you I have good reasons for making such a conjecture," Miguel replied, trying to remain calm in spite of the desperation welling up within him as he realized he probably wasn't going to find the cooperation he'd hoped to obtain from the governor.

"I'd like to help you, Vidal. If circumstances were different, I'd assign a man to aid you in your search; but, as you can see, I can't spare anyone right now. Actually, I need you here, too, helping to control the people out there on the street trying to fight the fire. They want to help, but they need direction."

Vidal hit the hilt of his sword impatiently. "There's nothing I'd rather do more than serve where I'm most needed in such an emergency," he assured Carondelet, "and I promise to report to you as soon as I've found my ward. But surely you understand my predicament. The girl may be in grave danger, and as her guardian and sole protector, my first duty is to her."

"Do you realize this city may burn to the ground?"

"I'll tear down this damn city myself house by house if I don't find my ward soon!" exclaimed Miguel, his exasperation increasing by the moment.

"Well, when you do find her, marry the wench and keep her pregnant so she'll quit running around loose in the streets. If ever a girl needed a man to settle her, that one does!"

"I'm afraid there were some . . . some rather unusual circumstances on this occasion—some that were probably more my fault than hers."

"In the name of heaven, Vidal! Go find the wench! If ever I've seen a man smitten, you are!"

"But if what I suspect is true, I'll probably need help . . . some officer of the law . . ."

"Are you certain the girl hasn't returned home by now?"

"I've just come from there, and my grandmother is near hysteria. I'm certain the girl would have been home by now if she could have gone there of her own volition. She's in trouble, I know it!"

"But the suspicions you've confided to me are too monstrous even to consider."

"It wouldn't be the first time a man of the cloth has found his vows of celibacy too heavy a burden to bear."

"Agreed, but Padre Sebastian? I can't believe that dried-up prune could roll a woman if he wanted to! Why, the man is one of the most notorious zealots of the Church! He usually has a reputation for going overboard."

"Perhaps so, but his own bridled passions might be the chink in his armor. I tell you I've seen lust in that man's eyes on more than one occasion. Every time I've caught him looking at my little ward, it was there."

"Good Lord, man, keep your voice down!" The baron drew Miguel even farther away from the door and continued in a lower tone. "If Fray Sebastian were one of those French monks, I'd be more inclined to accept such a possibility. I can tell you about a few of those Capuchins from the old regime who I know have their concubines on the side. But even if Padre Sebastian does have his secret vice, there are women enough around town who'd be only too willing to gratify him for a few bits. I doubt the monk would risk the complications involved by molesting a decent young girl like your cousin."

Vidal tried to remain patient, but he was in no mood to keep going over each point with the baron while precious time ticked away. "I admit I may be mistaken," he conceded, making an effort to keep his annoyance out of his voice, "but I know for a fact that Monica was in the church with him this afternoon, and I can't help but suspect that something happened to her while she was there.

"I've been stopping and asking people about her all afternoon, and one of the workmen who was in the new cathedral earlier this afternoon told me that when the alarm first sounded, he saw a young girl answering my ward's description talking to Padre Sebastian by the altar."

"Yes, but you can't be sure it really was her. It might have been some other young girl."

"But there's the headscarf I found as well," insisted Vidal. "I'm positive it belongs to Monica, and she'd never lose her headscarf like that. The girl is very careful about her things. She's always kept her headscarf neatly folded either in her reticule or in the pocket of her cloak. What's more, she wouldn't take it off while still by the altar.

"Of course, I'll grant you that there's always the possibility that some ruffian might have ventured into the deserted church and waylaid her, but frankly, I don't think we have to look any further than Padre Sebastian himself, when you consider that he was the last person seen with her just as the fire was breaking out and I've seen that very same monk ogling her with anything but a holy expression in his eyes! That's why I want an officer to accompany me to that Capuchin's hut to look around inside and, if possible, ask him some questions, as well."

"Vidal, you're relatively new here in New Orleans, so you don't know what you're asking," protested the baron. "That monk you're referring to is one of the pillars of the Church here in the colony, with connections that reach as high up as La Suprema in Madrid.

"Look, Vidal, all I can do is tell you that you're on your own. Go investigate the possibility that the girl might be with this Fray Sebastian in his hut or somewhere around the deserted church, but, in God's name, be discreet about it."

Chapter Thirty-eight

MONIQUE STRAINED AT HER BONDS, TRYING FEVER-ishly to break free, but Fray Sebastian continued to chant and turn the iron slowly in the flames as they rose higher and higher from the brazier.

"Don't fret, child. What we do is for the good of your immortal soul," he assured her as he paused a moment in his orations. "The devil has made you his pawn, but we will draw him out of you. Only through fleshly torment can you hope to be cleansed and forgiven. Satan is going to try his best to distract us from our task, but we must be firm and go forward."

The smooth perfection of the girl's skin glistened in the ruddy glow of the firelight, moist with the sweat of terror and the heat of the disagreeably humid air around them.

Fray Sebastian knew the iron was well up to temperature by now, but he was deliberately delay-ing the moment when he would approach the girl once more. Of course, after a few days of fasting on the rack and perhaps some lashes with the cat-o'-nine-tails, she wouldn't be so tempting anymore. Once he'd raised a few welts on that flawless skin of hers and marked her with two or three well-placed crosses, he'd be more easily reminded of the fact that it was his sacred duty to resist any desire he might feel for her over the weeks that lay ahead.

He wondered whether the fire was still spreading

throughout New Orleans at that moment. For what he cared, that wicked city could burn to the ground . . . all except the cathedral, of course. It would be a pity to see a house of God destroyed. He would have thought the colony had learned its lesson by now. How many more calamities would the Lord have to send down on that wicked city before it would realize that, even as the Egyptians had been brought low in Moses's day, the sinful citizens of New Orleans were going to have catastrophe after catastrophe heaped upon them until they ceased their rebellious activities and religious laxities? After all, the Supreme Council had proved time and again over the centuries that treason and heresy were often one and the same . . . simply the two sides of one coin.

He toyed thoughtfully with the branding iron, turning it about in the flames by its long handle as he watched the cross glowing there in the midst of the flames. The hand that had touched the girl's breast still smarted, as though the soft firmness of her flesh had singed his palm. His heart pounded at the memory of it. The very thought of touching her again, the anticipation of how it would feel, now that he had experienced it, sent the blood rushing wildly through his veins. Perhaps he should wait a bit before marring the perfection of that smooth young body.

The girl was softly weeping now, spent from the prolonged suspense of waiting for that inevitable moment of agony she knew to be forthcoming. In her mind he had branded her a dozen times over.

Sebastian lifted the iron cross at last from the flames, and it hissed and sputtered as though it were alive as he turned resolutely toward the trembling girl. Even at that moment he had to fight back the impulse to bend forward and taste the pink-tipped cone of her breast as he steadied her to receive the imprint of the iron. So engrossed was he with the task at hand and the turmoil of his inner conflict that he was completely unaware of the fact that the tall, slim silhouette of Miguel Vidal de la Fuente had emerged from the passageway and was standing there sword in hand.

Chapter Thirty-nine

A LOW GROWL—LIKE THE GROWL OF AN ANIMAL goaded into attack—sounded involuntarily from Vidal's throat as he swept his gaze across the room and saw the dark-cloaked figure bending over Monique's prostrate form.

"I'd rather not have to kill you," he told the monk icily through clenched teeth. "Just release the girl and let her leave peaceably with me."

But although Fray Sebastian was obviously startled by the unexpected interruption, he was not to be intimidated. "You're interfering with the work of the Holy Inquisition," he warned, turning the red-hot tip of the still-uplifted brand threateningly now in Vidal's direction. "You'll be damned to eternal hell if you stop me from doing God's work!"

"You mean the devil's work!" thundered Vidal, dangerously near the breaking point. "If you don't let her go, I'll dispatch you to hell this very moment."

He couldn't bear the sight of Monique lying there like that. Reaching over to where her wrists were fastened above her head, he tugged at the straps with his free hand while he kept his eyes and sword fixed on the monk.

Monique was sobbing and calling out to him, half in relief and half in fear for him now, as well as for herself.

The friar brandished the iron wildly at Miguel, lunging like a madman in an obvious effort to blind or burn him. "Hell and damnation!" he raged. "You must not interfere, I tell you. This is a matter for the Holy Tribunal!"

Miguel dodged the brand, but the heat from its still-sizzling tip nearly singed his cheek as he drew back. One look at Monique was enough to tempt him to forget all his fine resolutions and run the monk through on the spot, but he knew the repercussions of his actions at that moment might affect the lives of many people, perhaps even the future of the colony itself.

"The fire has reached the square," he told the friar. "We must get out of here before it's too late!"

"It's safe enough down here," retorted Padre Sebastian, "as long as the passage door is closed."

"We'll roast down here like pigs on a spit. We have to get out, I tell you."

He fumbled again with the straps around Monique's wrists, but it was difficult to loosen them with just one hand, and he didn't dare lower his guard against the friar.

"The only way I'll leave here will be if I see both you and the girl either dead or in chains!" The monk swished the long-handled branding iron above the flames to keep it deadly hot. Then, with one continuous movement, he lunged a second time.

Miguel parried the thrust with his sword, and their strange duel continued with even more deadly intent than before. Metal clashed against metal. Miguel threw his cape back out of his way as he set about defending himself in earnest.

Although his fine Toledo blade and expert swordsmanship made him by far the superior of the two, the wild frenzy of the monk made him an opponent to be reckoned with. Miguel remembered fleetingly, even as he thrust and parried desperately to keep that red-hot iron from finding its way into his eyes, how once he had heard someone say that the strength and cunning of one madman was equal to that of ten sane men, and now he knew it was true.

In the ruddy glow of the flames, the friar's face had taken on an even more diabolical aspect, his eyes smoldering in their deep sockets and his long brown robes whipping about his skinny frame as though he were a winged demon bolting out of hell.

Miguel recognized the fact that his reluctance to kill the monk was placing him at a disadvantage, since he was forced to fight defensively instead of aggressively. He had just about decided that the best way to bring their bizarre duel to an end would probably be to wound the friar just enough to disarm him, when suddenly the latter made another one of his sweeping movements over the brazier to keep the brand hot and then lunged forward. Holding the tip of the iron tilted high to reach his taller adversary's eye level, the monk thrust furiously . . . once . . . twice. He chuckled his satisfaction as Miguel instinctively retreated from him. But even as he moved in closer to press his advantage, the long sleeve of his habit trailed over the brazier.

Immediately the restless flames leaped up and snapped curiously at him.

In a split second, the fire was racing along the length of his uplifted arm and on toward the very peak of his hood. With a cry of amazement, he dropped the branding iron and clutched frantically at his blazing garment.

"Get it off! *Quítesela!*" Miguel shouted to him, even as the fire turned on itself and began racing down the other side of the monk's flowing robes. His figure was outlined in flames now from the top of his pointed hood to the hem of his habit.

There was no water to be found in the place, so Miguel quickly removed his own cape and stepped toward the friar, hoping at least to smother the swift course of the flames with it, but the monk shrieked wildly and drew back with threatening gestures.

Clawing, coughing and sputtering, he slapped at himself wildly in a vain effort to put out the flames. His hood fell back, exposing his tonsured head with its rim of dark hair circling the shaven crown. A human torch now, he ran toward the passageway, screaming as he went, leaving the odor of burning cloth and singed hair in his wake.

Long after he disappeared, his desperate cries of terror continued to echo throughout the tunnel.

At that moment, however, Miguel's first thought was for Monique. Sheathing his sword quickly, he ran to free her. But she was so stiff and sore when she slipped down from the rack and tried to stand that she couldn't sustain herself without his help.

He threw his cape around her shoulders and caught her eagerly to him, grateful just to feel her there at last in his arms. Weeping softly now, she clung to him like a confused, frightened child.

"Don't cry, my sweet," he kept murmuring as he showered her tearstained face with kisses. "You're safe now. You know I'd never let anyone hurt you."

"I . . . I was so afraid," she sobbed. "I thought I'd never see you or . . . or Grandmother . . . or anyone ever again. . . ." Her voice trailed off, smothered now by his lips.

"By all that's holy, I'll never let you get away from me again!" he told her as his own tears mingled now with hers.

Her body ached all the more as he crushed her to

him, and the taste of their kisses was salty, but she rejoiced in the sensations, for they told her she was alive and that Miguel was there holding her close once more.

"Are you hurt, my dear?" he was asking her gently. "Tell me the truth. Did that monster hurt you in any way?"

"He . . . he said horrible things to me and . . . and wanted to . . . to . . ."

But Miguel suddenly put a finger gently to her lips. "No, my dear, I shouldn't have asked you that. There's no time for such things now. We may be in danger here. We'll talk later when you're safe at home. Then you can tell me, but only me. You mustn't say anything to anyone else about any of this, do you understand? We're going to tell your grandmother and Celeste that you were caught in the fire, that's all . . . as little as possible. I promised the governor. It's for your sake, and for many others, too. Do you understand?"

She didn't really, but she nodded her assent. Whatever Miguel said. The important thing was that he was there taking care of her again and she knew everything would be all right now. At that moment nothing else mattered.

"We have to get out of this place," he continued anxiously. "We're in danger of being trapped down here." He didn't want to frighten her any more than she already was, but he knew there might also still be danger from Padre Sebastian himself. The man was a fanatic, and if he'd managed to put out his burning habit in time, he might be up there in his hut waiting for them . . . stalking them at that very moment.

He had finally spotted her cloak in a corner of the dimly lit chamber, so he went quickly to fetch it for her while she leaned against the rack, trying to rearrange her tattered gown and wondering where all her strength had gone.

Miguel's jaw clenched angrily as he helped her exchange his cape for her own and drew it protectively around her. He circled Monique's waist with his arm and firmly sustained her against him to steady her. For a moment just the feel of her vibrant warmth there in his arms again softened the cutting edge of his fury.

"I love you, Monica," he said huskily. "If anything had happened to you, I'd have never gotten over it."

She swayed a little, and he tightened his arm.

"My poor child!" he exclaimed anxiously. "Let me get you out of here right now. Can you walk if I support you this way?"

She tried a few steps and nodded. Slowly he led her over to the entrance of the tunnel, pausing only to take the torch from the wall bracket in order to light their way back.

As they stepped out of that chamber of horrors and pulled the rotting wooden door closed behind them, it was as though they were leaving the realms of Hades in their wake.

The passageway was so close that Miguel had to walk stooped, and their shoulders brushed the sides of the crumbling brick walls as they made their way pressed close together. The entire tunnel oozed and dripped with moisture. Huge droplets of water trickling from the ceiling fell into their faces, and the seepage coming through the brick-lined walls and flooring was so great that they had to pick their way over puddles of water as they went along.

The faint odor of smoke tinged the damp, clammy

atmosphere and seemed to grow stronger as they made their way closer to the other end, but there was only one way out, so they had to go on.

There were times when Monique stumbled and nearly fell, but Miguel's grip held her fast. At such moments all she could do was stand there clinging to him, weeping with fright and frustration.

"It's all right, my dear, it's all right," he kept reassuring her. "Come, we only have a little way more to go now. Hold on to me. I won't let you fall."

But the nearer they came to the end of the passageway, the more apprehensive Miguel became. The presence of fire permeated the atmosphere. Smoke was beginning to penetrate the tunnel, and its acrid odor was beginning to sting their eyes and sear their lungs. Miguel knew they had to get out of there at all costs before they were overcome.

With sword in one hand and torch in the other, he left Monique at the bottom of the short flight of tiny brick steps and climbed cautiously toward the trapdoor above them.

The saints be praised! It wasn't completely closed! One of his fears had been that the door wouldn't open and they'd find themselves trapped down there. Most certainly, if that fanatical monk hadn't been so occupied with his own troubles when he'd surfaced shortly before them, he would have tried to find some way to block their exit.

Partially sheathing his sword, Miguel carefully eased the trapdoor open. All his senses were on the alert for whatever lay waiting on the other side.

Suddenly a nauseating wave of heat rushed against his face. The entire hut over them was in flames! Miguel had the strange feeling that he was rising out of the bowels of the earth only to go from one hell to another!

Chapter Forty

"COVER YOUR HEAD!" MIGUEL CRIED AS HE LIFTED HER through the trapdoor into the fiery inferno of the burning hut. He swept her into his arms and began a desperate dash for the outer door, while the crackle and roar of the flames grew louder in their ears.

Monique clutched the hood of her cloak tighter about her to protect herself from the sparks of blinding light dancing around them in the smoke-filled haze like giant fireflies. She was aware of Miguel's chest heaving against her cheek as he carried her doggedly toward that slit of light shimmering off in the distance. The hut was not that large, yet at that moment the doorway seemed so far away. . . .

An oppressive, choking blanket of smoke enveloped them, and they began to cough and sputter, but Miguel toiled forward as swiftly as his panting, stifled breath would allow. Their hearts were pounding in a macabre union. . . . Had she escaped Fray Sebastian's fiery purge in the dungeon below only to perish in the hellfire of his blazing hut?

Suddenly one of those flaming darts of burning thatch from the roof came flying through the air and landed on the shoulder of her cloak. With lightning speed, however, before it could take hold, Miguel snuffed it out with a fold of his own damp cape. Thank God for that trek through the dripping tunnel! It had at least dampened their outer clothing enough to make them less vulnerable now to those insatiable flames around them! Straining every fiber of his being to the limits of his strength, Miguel ran those last few feet to the exit, relieved to see that the narrow slit of light that had been guiding him through the dark, smoke-filled hut had been indeed the partially open doorway.

He stumbled, hardly setting her to her feet, as he raced with her to a safe area near the still-smoldering ruins of a blackened brick wall, which had in all probability once been a part of the calabozo.

"The saints be praised!" exclaimed Miguel between heaving gasps as the chilly breath of that early-winter evening brought welcome respite to his agonizing lungs.

For a long moment they stood there merged with the darkening shadows of the ever-encroaching night, gulping in the cold brisk air while they laughed and exclaimed with the sheer joy of being alive and together again. Monique wept a little, and he kissed away her tears, murmuring reassuring phrases in her ear to calm her.

Then cries sounded close by and they were suddenly aware of their surroundings. Most of the huts there in back of the church and many of the larger buildings to one side of the square were still burning themselves out, and the Plaza de Armas itself was filled with screaming, shouting people trying to extend a bucket brigade into the square from the river, while the militia struggled desperately to keep the hand pumps working.

A man was looking curiously at them, so Miguel took Monique by the arm and decided they should get out of there as quickly as possible.

Suddenly someone called out above the din. "It's

stopped! The fire's stopped . . . right before the church! A miracle! A miracle!"

Another voice came from near the rear of the cathedral. "It's Padre Sebastian . . . the poor padre! God have mercy on his soul!"

Miguel paused. A stout elderly woman came waddling past them, shaking her head dolefully and making the sign of the cross again and again over her ample bosom.

"Did you say Padre Sebastian?" he asked her.

"Oh, yes, senor. The poor monk! They just found his charred body inside the church . . . lying there on the floor behind the altar! What a horrible way to die! God have mercy on his soul!"

Impulsively Monique began to speak. "He . . . he was evil . . . he . . ."

Miguel pressed her arm and hissed in her ear. "Be quiet!"

"But . . ." She tried to vent her anger. "But . . ."

Miguel squeezed her arm even tighter and turned to the woman, who hadn't heard the girl's weak voice amid all the noise and confusion around them.

"Yes, senora, it's really a pity," he said quickly, directing himself to the newcomer. "May the good friar receive his just reward in heaven."

The panting woman dabbed her eyes dramatically with her apron. "He must have caught fire while doing rescue work," she lamented. "God bless him! He died a hero's death . . . special masses should be said for him." She continued on her way, calling out her tragic news like a self-appointed town crier, while Monique turned a bewildered face up to her guardian.

"How could you say . . . Why?" she asked him incredulously.

"Remember what I told you below," he mumbled

to her under his breath as he steered her in the direction of the town house, grateful that it was less than two blocks away. "You must never say anything about Fray Sebastian and what happened . . . do you understand? You could bring the Inquisition down on all our heads if you did!"

He was gently hurrying her along as quickly as he could down the street toward the relative peace and quiet of the other side of the square where the fire had not reached.

"I won't say anything if I shouldn't, but it makes me furious," Monique complained somewhat breathlessly as she tried to keep up with Miguel, even though he was trying to reduce his long stride to a more leisurely pace for her. "To think they're calling Padre Sebastian a martyr when he was the one who really wanted to make martyrs of everyone else!"

"At least he'll never hurt anyone ever again!" Miguel mumbled between clenched teeth, equally angry over the injustice of it all, although he knew in his heart it had all turned out for the best.

"It's so ironic . . . so unfair!"

"I know, my dear, but perhaps there's some consolation in thinking that the death of one evil monk will probably serve to call attention to the good so many other friars—French and Spanish alike—have done for the colony over the years. Much as I hate to say it, for the sake of so many innocent people, including your own, we'll have to let the sins of one demented friar lie buried with him."

She sighed her resignation. "All right, you have my word on it. But surely someone will discover the entrance to the passageway when they rummage through the ashes of Padre Sebastian's hut?"

"Early tomorrow morning I'll meet with the governor and show him where the trapdoor is. I'm sure he'll have some trusted man seal off the tunnel and dungeon immediately before anyone is the wiser. There's too much at stake to take chances. That's why we must keep our little secret."

He looked down at the little cloaked figure plodding along beside him, and he paused a moment. "Here, my sweet, I'll carry you the rest of the way," he offered gently, but she shook her head.

"No, I'm all right," she assured him. "I'm just shaken, that's all, but I'm not hurt, really I'm not."

She was silent for the last half block of their short walk home. The events of the day had overwhelmed her. It was as though she had been forced to live several years of her life in the span of one afternoon. Although it was true what she had said about not being hurt, she was still trembling inwardly at just the thought of all that had happened in those past few hours. Most of all, she was awed by the realization of all that would have happened if Miguel hadn't been there to save her.

She cast a curious glance up at her guardian out of the tail of her eye as she walked beside him, clinging to his hand while he steadied her with an arm around her waist. Smudged with soot and grime, his face seemed leaner than ever at that moment. That fine black woolen cape and those knee-high boots that he wore so well were singed and spattered now. She looked down at the outline of his sword swinging jauntily by his side beneath the folds of his cloak and thought of how he had fought with Fray Sebastian . . . risked his life to save hers. It made the memory of him with his hand on Azema's breast all the more painful . . . like a two-pronged arrow lodged deep in her heart. Although it seemed that the scene in the Ducole parlor had taken place weeks, even months ago, the pain was still there. Only she couldn't hate him anymore. Her feelings for him were too complex now for that. All she could feel was one great hurt aching inside of her . . . a torment greater than any Padre Sebastian could have inflicted on her. No matter what had happened earlier that afternoon, she had to recognize that it was thanks to him she was safe and free again. She couldn't forget that. He may have failed her as a lover, but he had most certainly left nothing to be desired as her guardian. When she'd needed him, he'd been there to protect her. Always when she needed him he was there. . . .

The babble of the crowd behind them and fragments of conversations from isolated groups of townsfolk they passed along the way echoed down the street after them.

A group of men talking excitedly on the street only a few doors from the town house were waving their hands wildly and loudly discussing the fire.

"Hundreds homeless . . . not a store left in town . . ."

". . . no more wood . . . only brick and tile . . ."

"I tell you . . . worse than '88 . . . almost whole city's destroyed!"

Miguel shook his head. "The usual exaggerations," he muttered. Nevertheless, he gave a backward look at the smoking ruins of the fire-plagued city. It had burned swiftly, and it was truly a miracle that it hadn't been leveled with the swamps. But that paradox of a city had a stubborn spirit, which might often give its rulers headaches but would undoubtedly be its salvation in the end.

As far as he could judge at that moment, approximately a quarter of the town had been hit, including almost half of the square up to the cathedral. There would indeed be some shortages for a while in New Orleans, since the section that lay in ashes was where most of the shops had been located. Thank God they had the plantation to furnish them with their daily necessities!

He looked down tenderly at the bedraggled little figure of his weary ward and slackened his pace even more to accommodate her. The poor child! She'd been through so much that afternoon! Now that the danger was gone, memories of earlier that afternoon were beginning to flood back to him. He could still see the shock and disillusion on that dear little face as she had fled the Ducole town house in despair . . . only to run straight into the greater torment of Fray Sebastian's waiting dungeon!

He'd rather stand up to one of those fiery reprimands of hers than see her suffering so! As soon as he had her in the safety of the town house, he would at least try to set her mind at ease on one score. He couldn't bear to have her thinking he had betrayed her love. He only hoped he could make her believe him!

Chapter Forty-one

STILL WRAPPED IN HER CLOAK, MONIQUE RECLINED ON the sofa in the town house parlor, trying to sort out her confused emotions while she watched Miguel dash off a hasty note to the governor and give the houseboy his instructions.

" 'Regarding that matter . . . rest easy. But must see you in private. Will come to your home at dawn. Urgent.' "

Miguel quickly reviewed what he had written, then signed and sealed it. "You're to put this in the hands of His Excellency the Governor and no one else, is that clear?" he told the boy solemnly. "If there's no problem, go to your quarters when you return and get some rest. Tomorrow morning I'll need the horses groomed and ready to ride to the plantation. Remember, I'm trusting you to find the baron before the night is over, no matter where he is, and give this message to him. If you do well, I'll reward you handsomely, I promise. Now go . . . *pronto!*" He hurried the boy on his way and then bolted the door behind him.

With a sigh of relief he turned toward the sofa where he had left Monique resting. But, to his surprise, he saw she had risen and was already halfway up the staircase, a candle in hand and her tattered cloak trailing dejectedly behind her.

"Monica, what in the world are you doing?" he

chided solicitously, running to overtake her. "At least let me help you!"

"I . . . I'm all right now," she insisted. "I can manage."

But he swept her up quickly in his arms and carried her the rest of the way to the room where she and her sister always slept. Carefully he set her down on one of the four-posters and, taking the candle from her, put it on the nightstand beside her. Then he turned and lay her tousled head back on the pillow, and, making use of the bowl of water on the table that had been left for her usual nightly ablutions, he gently bathed her face and hands, all the while trying to soothe her.

The chamber was pleasantly warm with the crackle of a cheerful blaze in the fireplace, so Miguel made a move to remove her dusty, scorched cloak. But she drew away and instinctively pulled the wrap closer over her half-bared breasts, staring back at him with large, wounded eyes.

Respecting her gesture, he turned away and went on to refresh his own face and hands. But finally he turned and stood there looking down at her tense, unhappy little figure, so tightly wrapped in her tattered cloak . . . so afraid to be hurt again. . . . A wave of tenderness engulfed him. How he longed to take her in his arms and reassure her that she was surrounded by his love . . . that she need never be fearful of anything or ever doubt his love for her again! He yearned to kiss that adorable little body of hers from head to foot—every throbbing corner of it—and feel her warm pulse fluttering beneath his lips, responding to his every caress with that same passionate abandon, that same sweet trust, that she had given him before!

He bent toward her and, resting one knee on the

edge of the bed, gently lifted her into his arms. For a moment she let him hold her there, resting her pale gold head against the firmness of his chest like a frightened child longing to be comforted.

"Thank God you're safe again, little one," he murmured into the tousled curls. "I don't know what I would have done if I'd lost you!"

Gently he reached into the recess of her cloak and sought out one of those magnificent young breasts that Sebastian had been about to mar so cruelly, and, before she could stop him, he kissed its rosy tip reverently.

"I love you, Monica. Please believe me. I'd give my life for you."

But she had suddenly stiffened. Despite the pleasant sensations stirring within her at the feel of his lips on her breast, his action had reminded her all too vividly of how and why her torment of that afternoon had begun. That same hand cupping her breast so lovingly now had held Azema's only a few hours earlier!

Angrily she pushed him away. "Don't touch me!" she exclaimed. "Please don't come to me with the scent of that woman still on your hands . . . on your lips . . ."

"God as my witness, what you saw today was none of my doing," he protested. "Azema was trying to entice me precisely because I haven't wanted to be with her. You simply misconstrued what you saw. Actually, I'd stopped off to see Henri not only on business but to arrange with him that, in the future, we'd hold our meetings elsewhere. I didn't want to go to the town house anymore . . . I wanted to avoid scenes like that with Azema. The irony of it is that poor Henri doesn't even have a town house now. It was right in the heart of the section hit by the fire!"

But Monique only continued to sit there in the middle of the bed, clutching her cape around her and eyeing him with suspicion.

"If what you say is true, why wasn't Henri there, then?" she asked. "If you went there to see him, why were you alone with Azema in the first place?"

"He'd only stepped out for a moment," Miguel replied patiently. "I was taking my leave, and he went to his study to fetch some papers he wanted me to take with me."

"You're very glib." She smiled sadly. "Always you find a way to deny the evidence."

"It's easy to do, since I'm telling the truth," he assured her. He ran his hand despairingly through his hair, which was as tousled as hers was at that moment. What could he say or do to convince her? "You speak of evidence," he went on. "Haven't I given you enough proofs of my affection all these months . . . even this very evening?"

She hung her head and nodded. "I have to admit you've been a very conscientious guardian," she acquiesced, "and for that I realize I'm in your debt. I'm truly grateful for the way you risked your life to save me from Padre Sebastian. I—"

"I don't want your gratitude!" he interrupted, impatient for the first time that night. "My God, Monica! Don't you know I wouldn't have found my life worth living if I hadn't saved you? I love you, my dear, foolish child. For me, you're life itself!"

He caught her in his arms once more and, before she could stop him, kissed her with all the desperation of his long-denied passion, pressing his mouth long and hard against hers, his tongue pleading to be let through the pout of those fleshy little lips.

For a moment she resisted and tried to push him away, but he held her fast, and she could feel her lips parting in spite of herself. Why was it that, the moment he was near her, she couldn't hate him even when she knew she should?

"Monica, my life! My despair! If only I could make love to you! If only I could show you how much I really love you!" he murmured huskily against her lips. "God as my witness, I can't take your hate and distrust any longer! I'm not speaking as your guardian . . . I'm only the man who loves you now!"

His passion ignited her own. A surge of new energy was stirring through her veins. She longed for him to go on, yet dreaded that moment when he would draw back from her as he had always done in the past.

Suddenly she put out her hand and held him at bay. "I think what we need to do is go to the courts . . . as soon as possible . . . tomorrow perhaps, if we can," she said, trying to keep her tone as matter-of-fact as she could, despite the way her insides were trembling at that moment.

Chapter Forty-two

MIGUEL WAS TAKEN ABACK, HIS ARDOR MOMENTARILY dashed to the ground. "The courts?" he echoed incredulously. Her words were obviously a blow to him. "Then . . . then you've decided you want me to step down? You no longer want me to be your guardian?"

"No," she replied tartly. "I don't. For I'm afraid that as long as you're my guardian, you'll never really make love to me. You'll keep pushing me away, thinking of me as a child instead of a grown woman, and I can't bear that any longer!"

Miguel looked at her with mouth agape. He had all he could do to digest what she had just said. "Why, you mischievous little darling . . . to tease me so!"

"I'm not teasing," she said in the same tone. "I'm very serious. If your being my guardian is an obstacle between us, then I'd prefer you'd step down."

His arm tightened around her and he took that impish face between his trembling hands, scrutinizing it eagerly. "Are you sure, my dear, really sure?"

"Yes, I'm afraid I am. It might surprise you to know just how long I've been sure!"

"And you don't care anymore about my being Spanish and not French?"

"I find it increasingly difficult to go on hating someone I love so much," she confessed as the dimples in her cheeks began to deepen.

"By all the saints! I think the child really is a woman at last!" he exclaimed, the joy surging through his being giving renewed impetus to his passion. "Believe me, you'll never complain about my pushing you away again, I promise you that!"

His lips were on hers . . . hungrily . . . possessively. Eagerly she closed her arms around him and clung fast. She could no longer deny the longing she had carried in her heart for so many months. She loved this proud, fiery Spaniard and she could no longer fight her overpowering desire for him.

The tumult that had been raging within them since that night of the hurricane swept over them, stronger than ever now. This time there was no checking its momentum. They were caught up in the storm . . . carried along on the wave of their own churning emotions. Their tongues leaped to find each other, restlessly flicking and darting, even as the treetops bend and twist to the fury of the wind.

"Mona, *mi vida* . . . my life!" He was showering her with kisses . . . her eyes, her lips, her throat . . .

"Then you no longer see me as a child?"

"As an adorable, unruly child that I hope will always be in the heart of the woman I love!" His tongue was tracing the tracks of her earlobe, sending little flecks of delight up and down her spine. Weary as she had been only a short while ago, she was filled now with renewed life. Her whole being was vibrating . . . eager.

He was removing the singed cape, the tattered gown . . . tossing them impatiently aside. The cones of her breasts stood high and expectant, yearning for his lips.

He had waited for so long . . . he was swollen with desire, ready to burst from want of her, but he was resolved to be gentle . . . to lead her into womanhood with a tender passion that would make this, her first time—their first time together—a memory they would both treasure for the rest of their lives. He wanted to wait until he had that sweet body of hers awakened—every fiber of her singing—before he'd take her.

Slowly he lay her back against the pillow, one arm around that slim little waist, his free hand lightly cupping her breast. Already he could feel how she was responding . . . quivering to his slightest touch. What a wondrous, sensuous woman lay there in his arms ready to be born—an adorable, passionate woman who was to be the *alma de su alma*, the very heart of his innermost being!

Gently he circled one of her breasts with his hand and lifted its fullness to meet his lips, slowly coaxing its rosy peak to life with the flutter of his tongue. Finally he closed his mouth over it and didn't let go until the sweet torment racked her being . . . and even then it was only to catch the other between his lips and begin all over again. . . .

Monique buried her fingers deep into the dark mass of his thick black hair and pressed him eagerly, spasmodically, to her breast. She could feel him swiftly slipping off the rest of her clothing and his fingers running like quicksilver now over her bare skin, tracing the rounded contours of her hips and thighs, the soft swell of that patch of golden hair.

She closed her eyes the better to savor every delight-ful sensation all the more . . . to feel his lips explor-ing now every sensitive corner of her body, awaken-ing it with feathery thrusts of his tongue until her whole being was aglow, longing for him to go on to the very core of her and make her completely his at last.

"Oh, Miguel, I do love you . . . I love you so!" she murmured softly, her breath coming quickly now, matching the velocity of that restless, inquisi-tive tongue.

Suddenly the warm firmness of his flesh was brushing against her own, and she knew he had tossed aside his garments as well. It was a pleasant, exciting sensation, and she reached out impulsively to explore with trembling curiosity the wonder of those smooth, well-muscled forearms, the rise and fall of those broad shoulder blades, the rippling length of that long, supple spine. . . .

Timidly she opened her eyes to admire at last in the dim candlelight that tall, lean body she had so often tried to imagine flexing beneath the impecca-ble cut of his stylish garments. There were those dark curling hairs that had fascinated her whenever he'd open his shirt to the summer heat, and now there were new ones to intrigue her peeping out from the hollows under his arms. She brushed her lips over his bare shoulders and chest, delighting in the strength she could feel radiating from him. Her whole being was filled with the scent of him . . . the taste of him. He penetrated every pore of her body.

Slowly he was molding his flesh to hers, and the throbbing hardness of him set her afire. She didn't know exactly what she should do, but she ached to give herself completely to him.

"My precious, passionate little woman," he whispered breathlessly as he felt her body arching longingly against him. "So you really love and want me, then?"

She murmured her reply against his lips. There was an urgency in her now that matched his.

"Don't be afraid, my sweet," he said huskily. "I love you. Trust me."

The hard cords of his thighs pressed against hers, gently separating them. Her heart pounding wildly, she locked her arms instinctively around his neck and yielded, willing to follow him wherever he'd lead. The hardness of him was suddenly plunging into her being . . . thrusting forward . . .

She gave a startled gasp and her eyes flew open. He paused, his breathing labored, while he kissed her tenderly. "It's all right, my dear. You're a woman now, that's all," he reassured her. "Trust me."

She lay there tense, wondering whether that was all, yet strangely excited, still aware of that throbbing hardness deep within her. Then, to her surprise, he began to move again . . . slowly, sinuously, thrusting with a sensuous rhythm that seemed to invite her to follow his lead. They were pulsating as one now, that burning hardness deep in the core of her being setting the pace. A part of her was awakening that she'd never before suspected existed. She realized she'd never really been alive until that moment.

His rhythm was accelerating now, and she clung to him passionately, swept along on the powerful current of their unleashed passion, rushing at last to fulfillment. She knew this was the moment she'd been waiting for. Ever since that night in the blackness of the hallway, surrounded by the fury of wind and rain, this was the moment they had both been living for! It was as though he had plunged the eye of that storm into the very center of her being, where it would come to culmination at last!

That final thrust was like a shaft of lightning charging the heavens . . . bursting into a blinding climax that fused them at last into one!

A throaty cry of ecstasy burst from Miguel's lips, and with a husky sob he fell forward and buried his head between her breasts, momentarily spent with the force of his passion.

"You're mine, Monica . . . really mine!" he murmured, his breathing still labored but a great joy throbbing in his voice.

They lay there a few moments longer, locked in passionate embrace, the length of his body still molded to hers. Monique's whole being was one great sigh. She felt complete now. All the anguish and tears of earlier that day . . . all the prejudices and doubts of the past . . . they had all dissolved in that wave of passion that had swept over them.

It was as though a great weight had been lifted from her. The war that had raged within her for so long had finally ceased, and she was at peace now with the world . . . with Spain . . . with Miguel Vidal . . . and, most of all, with herself, for love had set her free.

She stirred a little, delighting in the feel of flesh against flesh, the imprint of Miguel's kisses still covering her body. She had felt not only his great desire for her but a deep abiding tenderness in every touch of his hand, in every pressure of his lips. She was sure now that he really loved her.

He turned a little and shifted her gently into the crook of his arm, resting her head on his shoulder.

"Are you all right, my dear?" he asked gently, brushing her temple with a kiss as he stroked her hair back from her forehead.

She snuggled in closer to him and gave a little purr of contentment in reply.

"I love you, Monica. God, how I love you!" His voice was still husky with emotion.

Suddenly she sat bolt upright in the bed as a thought occurred to her. "Oh, Miguel, do you think we'll have to wait very long before we can marry? I want to be with you like this always. . . ."

He chuckled. "Don't fret, my sweet. As your guardian, I certainly will give my most consent."

He ran his hand caressingly down the white smoothness of her back from where he still lay reclining against the pillow.

"But let's not fret over anything right now," he told her. "Tomorrow at dawn I have to see the governor, and in the afternoon I have to talk to your grandmother about us, but tonight . . . tonight, my dear, is ours."

He pulled her back down beside him and their passion surged anew.

Author's Note

In the story of New Orleans, the Spanish regime seldom receives the recognition it deserves. Yet it is an ironic fact that, in retrospect, many modern-day historians have come to the conclusion that the Louisiana colony often fared better under its Spanish rulers than it did under its French ones.

The year 1794 was particularly crucial for New Orleans. The colony was plagued not only by elements of nature—hurricanes, crop failures, and devastating fire—but also by the political upheavals of the times. France and Spain were at war, and, technically, Louisiana belonged to Spain, yet in spite of its elegant Spanish exterior, New Orleans was still fervently French at heart. Although *Iron Lace* is a historical romance, primarily meant to entertain, the symbolism is there for those who wish to look for it.

The changeover to the cultivation of sugarcane, begun skeptically in 1794, is, of course, a part of Louisiana history and was one of the major factors in giving birth to the Golden Era of the South that followed in the nineteenth century.

Less known, however, is the narrow escape New Orleans had from the Spanish Inquisition. In his personal correspondence to Spain, Governor Miró speaks of how and why he secretly deported a commissary sent to New Orleans to establish the Inquisition there. Nevertheless, the fact that a torture chamber, obviously meant to be used by such a tribunal, remained hidden beneath that city's old calaboose didn't come to light until fifty years after the Spanish regime there had come to an end.

Several leading Louisiana historians refer to the discovery of that dark secret in the mid-nineteenth century when the old calaboose was finally torn down.

Strange things came to light [says Lyle Saxon in his *Fabulous New Orleans*]. There were found secret rooms, iron instruments of torture, and other indications that a private court had held meetings there. These things were never explained satisfactorily. In addition to this, old newspaper files tell of the discovery of an underground passage which led from the rear of the Cathedral or from even beyond . . . [and] ended somewhere under the Calaboose. . . . One day the paper tells of the discovery and promises further disclosures. . . . But it is evident that some pressure was brought to bear on the Editor, for there is not a line in any of the later editions of the same paper regarding the discovery. One can only draw his own conclusions.

So, using these intriguing data as inspiration for its climax, *Iron Lace* draws its own conclusions. Who knows . . . perhaps it really did happen the way saucy little Monique Chausson "lived" it!

Lorena Dureau
New Orleans, La.

LORENA DUREAU lived for over 15 years in Mexico City before returning in 1977 to New Orleans, where she was born. She has pursued careers as an opera singer, editor, photographer and writer, and has published newspaper and magazine articles worldwide. She is the author of the historical romances *The Last Casquette Girl* and *Lynette,* and is currently at work on her fourth novel.

POCKET BOOKS PROUDLY INTRODUCES TAPESTRY ROMANCES

Breathtaking new tales of love and adventure set against history's most exciting times and places. Featuring two novels by the finest authors in the field of romantic fiction — <u>every month</u>.

TAPESTRY ROMANCES

496

THE BOOK PEOPLE WILL BE TALKING ABOUT AS LONG AS THINGS GO WRONG

"Stimulating, amusing reading ... The authors embark on one of the noblest endeavors of the human intellect: the search for and formulation of a fundamental principle of the universe. There have been few others who have successfully made this voyage, and history remembers them gratefully—Copernicus, Newton ... etc., etc."
—**Book World**

"It tells us as much about the world we live in as *Parkinson's Law* or *Games People Play* ... read this book and grow wise."
—Miles A. Smith, **Associated Press**

"As funny a book as has come along in a long while, and as serious a one ... This is a superbly funny—in spots, a brilliant—book."
—**Chicago Sun-Times**

"A hilarious piece of work, in every way comparable to that gem of ten years back, *Parkinson's Law*."
—**National Observer**

"So broadly applicable is Peter's Principle that its creator proposes it as 'the key to understanding the whole structure of civilization.' Not to mention the ABM student rebels and air pollution."
—**New York Post**

The Peter Principle

by *Laurence J. Peter*
&
Raymond Hull

A NATIONAL GENERAL COMPANY

THE PETER PRINCIPLE

*A Bantam Book / published by arrangement with
William Morrow and Company, Inc.*

PRINTING HISTORY

Morrow edition published February 1969

2nd printing	February 1969	9th printing	July 1969
3rd printing	February 1969	10th printing	August 1969
4th printing	April 1969	11th printing ..	September 1969
5th printing	April 1969	12th printing ..	September 1969
6th printing	May 1969	13th printing	October 1969
7th printing	June 1969	14th printing ..	November 1969
8th printing	June 1969	15th printing	January 1970

16th printing ...... March 1970

Chapters I and III appeared in MANAGEMENT REVIEW *February 1969*

Excerpts appeared in MEDICAL ECONOMICS *November 1969*

Literary Guild edition published November 1969

Serialized in NEWSDAY *Syndicate 1969*

Bantam edition published February 1970

2nd printing	February 1970	10th printing	April 1970
3rd printing	February 1970	11th printing	June 1970
4th printing	February 1970	12th printing	August 1970
5th printing	February 1970	13th printing	January 1971
6th printing	February 1970	14th printing	March 1971
7th printing	February 1970	15th printing	May 1971
8th printing	February 1970	16th printing ..	November 1971
9th printing	March 1970	17th printing	May 1972

18th printing

*Bantam Books are published by Bantam Books, Inc., a National
General company. Its trade-mark, consisting of the words "Bantam
Books" and the portrayal of a bantam, is registered in the United
States Patent Office and in other countries. Marca Registrada.
Bantam Books, Inc., 666 Fifth Avenue, New York, N.Y. 10019.*

PRINTED IN THE UNITED STATES OF AMERICA

This book is dedicated to all those who, working, playing, loving, living and dying at their Level of Incompetence, provided the data for the founding and development of the salutary science of Hierarchiology.

They saved others: themselves they could not save.

Contents

Introduction

by RAYMOND HULL

AS AN author and journalist, I have had exceptional opportunities to study the workings of civilized society. I have investigated and written about government, industry, business, education and the arts. I have talked to, and listened carefully to, members of many trades and professions, people of lofty, middling and lowly stations.

I have noticed that, with few exceptions, men bungle their affairs. Everywhere I see incompetence rampant, incompetence triumphant.

I have seen a three-quarter-mile-long highway bridge collapse and fall into the sea because, despite checks and double-checks, someone had botched the design of a supporting pier.

I have seen town planners supervising the development of a city on the flood plain of a great river, where it is certain to be periodically inundated.

Lately I read about the collapse of three giant cooling towers at a British power-station: they cost a million dollars each, but were not strong enough to withstand a good blow of wind.

I noted with interest that the indoor baseball stadium at Houston, Texas, was found on completion to be peculiarly ill-suited to baseball: on bright days, fielders could not see fly balls against the glare of the skylights.

I observe that appliance manufacturers, as regular policy, establish regional service depots in the expectation—justified by experience—that many of their machines will break down during the warranty period.

Having listened to umpteen motorists' complaints about faults in their new cars, I was not surprised to learn that roughly one-fifth of the automobiles produced by major manufacturers in recent years have been found to contain potentially dangerous production defects.

Please do not assume that I am a jaundiced ultra-conservative, crying down contemporary men and things just because they are contemporary. Incompetence knows no barriers of time or place.

Macaulay gives a picture, drawn from a report by Samuel Pepys, of the British navy in 1684. "The naval administration was a prodigy of wastefulness, corruption, ignorance, and indolence . . . no estimate could be trusted . . . no contract was performed . . . no check was enforced . . . Some of the new men of war were so rotten that, unless speedily repaired, they would go down at their moorings. The sailors were paid with so little punctuality that they were glad to find some usurer who would purchase their tickets at forty percent discount. Most of the ships which were afloat were commanded by men who had not been bred to the sea."

Wellington, examining the roster of officers assigned to him for the 1810 campaign in Portugal, said, "I only hope that when the enemy reads the list of their names, he trembles as I do."

Civil War General Richard Taylor, speaking of the Battle of the Seven Days, remarked, "Confederate com-

In the expectation that many of their machines will
break down during the warranty period.

manders knew no more about the topography . . . within a day's march of the city of Richmond than they did about Central Africa."

Robert E. Lee once complained bitterly, "I cannot have my orders carried out."

For most of World War II the British armed forces fought with explosives much inferior, weight for weight, to those in German shells and bombs. Early in 1940, British scientists knew that the cheap, simple addition of a little powdered aluminum would double the power of existing explosives, yet the knowledge was not applied till late in 1943.

In the same war, the Australian commander of a hospital ship checked the vessel's water tanks after a refit and found them painted inside with red lead. It would have poisoned every man aboard.

These things—and hundreds more like them—I have seen and read about and heard about. I have accepted the universality of incompetence.

I have stopped being surprised when a moon rocket fails to get off the ground because something is forgotten, something breaks, something doesn't work, or something explodes prematurely.

I am no longer amazed to observe that a government-employed marriage counselor is a homosexual.

I now expect that statesmen will prove incompetent to fulfill their campaign pledges. I assume that if they do anything, it will probably be to carry out the pledges of their opponents.

This incompetence would be annoying enough if it were confined to public works, politics, space travel and such vast, remote fields of human endeavor. But it is not. It is close at hand, too—an ever-present, pestiferous nuisance.

As I write this page, the woman in the next apartment is

talking on the telephone. I can hear every word she says. It is 10 P.M. and the man in the apartment on the other side of me has gone to bed early with a cold. I hear his intermittent cough. When he turns on his bed I hear the springs squeak. I don't live in a cheap rooming house: this is an expensive, modern, concrete high-rise apartment block. What's the matter with the people who designed and built it?

The other day a friend of mine bought a hacksaw, took it home and began to cut an iron bolt. At his second stroke, the saw blade snapped, and the adjustable joint of the frame broke so that it could not be used again.

Last week I wanted to use a tape recorder on the stage of a new high-school auditorium. I could get no power for the machine. The building engineer told me that, in a year's occupancy, he had been unable to find a switch that would turn on current in the base plugs on stage. He was beginning to think they were not wired up at all.

This morning I set out to buy a desk lamp. In a large furniture and appliance store I found a lamp that I liked. The salesman was going to wrap it, but I asked him to test it first. (I'm getting cautious nowadays.) He was obviously unused to testing electrical equipment, because it took him a long time to find a socket. Eventually he plugged the lamp in, then could not switch it on! He tried another lamp of the same style: that would not switch on, either. The whole consignment had defective switches. I left.

I recently ordered six hundred square feet of fiber glass insulation for a cottage I am renovating. I stood over the clerk at the order desk to make sure she got the quantity right. In vain! The building supply firm billed me for seven hundred square feet, and delivered nine hundred square feet!

Education, often touted as a cure for all ills, is apparently no cure for incompetence. Incompetence runs riot in the halls of education. One high-school graduate in three cannot read at normal fifth-grade level. It is now commonplace for colleges to be giving reading lessons to freshmen. In some colleges, *twenty percent* of freshmen cannot read well enough to understand their textbooks!

I receive mail from a large university. Fifteen months ago I changed my address. I sent the usual notice to the university: my mail kept going to the old address. After two more change-of-address notices and a phone call, I made a personal visit. I pointed with my finger to the wrong address in their records, dictated the new address and watched a secretary take it down. The mail still went to the old address. Two days ago there was a new development. I received a phone call from the woman who had succeeded me in my old apartment and who, of course, had been receiving my mail from the university. She herself has just moved again, and my mail from the university has now started going to *her* new address!

As I said, I became resigned to this omnipresent incompetence. Yet I thought that, if only its cause could be discovered, then a cure might be found. So I began asking questions.

I heard plenty of theories.

A banker blamed the schools: "Kids nowadays don't learn efficient work habits."

A teacher blamed politicians: "With such inefficiency at the seat of government, what can you expect from citizens? Besides, they resist our legitimate demands for adequate education budgets. If only we could get a computer in every school. . . ."

An atheist blamed the churches: ". . . drugging the people's minds with fables of a better world, and distracting them from practicalities."

A churchman blamed radio, television and movies: ". . . many distractions of modern life have drawn people away from the moral teachings of the church."

A trade unionist blamed management: ". . . too greedy to pay a living wage. A man can't take any interest in his job on this starvation pay."

A manager blamed unions: "The worker just doesn't care nowadays—thinks of nothing but raises, vacations and retirement pensions."

An individualist said that welfare-statism produces a general don't-care attitude. A social worker told me that moral laxity in the home and family breakdown produces irresponsibility on the job. A psychologist said that early repression of sexual impulses causes a subconscious desire to fail, as atonement for guilt feelings. A philosopher said, "Men are human; accidents will happen."

A multitude of different explanations is as bad as no explanation at all. I began to feel that I would never understand incompetence.

Then one evening, in a theatre lobby, during the second intermission of a dully performed play, I was grumbling about incompetent actors and directors, and got into conversation with Dr. Laurence J. Peter, a scientist who had devoted many years to the study of incompetence.

The intermission was too short for him to do more than whet my curiosity. After the show I went to his home and sat till 3:00 A.M. listening to his lucid, startlingly original exposition of a theory that at last answered my question, "Why incompetence?"

Dr. Peter exonerated Adam, agitators and accident, and arraigned one feature of our society as the perpetrator and rewarder of incompetence.

Incompetence explained! My mind flamed at the thought. Perhaps the next step might be incompetence eradicated!

Early repression of sexual impulses causes
a subconscious desire to fail.

With characteristic modesty, Dr. Peter had so far been satisfied to discuss his discovery with a few friends and colleagues and give an occasional lecture on his research. His vast collection of incompetenciana, his brilliant galaxy of incompetence theories and formulae, had never appeared in print.

"Possibly my Principle could benefit mankind," said Peter. "But I'm frantically busy with routine teaching and the associated paperwork; then there are faculty committee meetings, and my continuing research. Some day I may sort out the material and arrange it for publication, but for the next ten or fifteen years I simply won't have time."

I stressed the danger of procrastination and at last Dr. Peter agreed to a collaboration: he would place his extensive research reports and huge manuscript at my disposal; I would condense them into a book. The following pages present Professor Peter's explanation of his Principle, the most penetrating social and psychological discovery of the century.

Dare you read it?

Dare you face, in one blinding revelation, the reason why schools do not bestow wisdom, why governments cannot maintain order, why courts do not dispense justice, why prosperity fails to produce happiness, why utopian plans never generate utopias?

Do not decide lightly. The decision to read on is irrevocable. If you read, you can never regain your present state of blissful ignorance; you will never again unthinkingly venerate your superiors or dominate your subordinates. Never! The Peter Principle, once heard, cannot be forgotten.

What have you to gain by reading on? By conquering incompetence in yourself, and by understanding incompetence in others, you can do your own work more easily, gain promotion and make more money. You can avoid painful illnesses. You can become a leader of men. You can enjoy your leisure. You can gratify your friends, confound your enemies, impress your children and enrich and revitalize your marriage.

This knowledge, in short, will revolutionize your life—perhaps save it.

So, if you have courage, read on, mark, memorize and apply the Peter Principle.

*The Peter
Principle*

CHAPTER I

The Peter Principle

"I begin to smell a rat."
M. DE CERVANTES

WHEN I was a boy I was taught that the men upstairs knew what they were doing. I was told, "Peter, the more you know, the further you go." So I stayed in school until I graduated from college and then went forth into the world clutching firmly these ideas and my new teaching certificate. During the first year of teaching I was upset to find that a number of teachers, school principals, supervisors and superintendents appeared to be unaware of their professional responsibilities and incompetent in executing their duties. For example my principal's main concerns were that all window shades be at the same level, that classrooms should be quiet and that no one step on or near the rose beds. The superintendent's main concerns were that no minority group, no matter how fanatical, should ever be offended and that all official forms be submitted on time. The children's education appeared farthest from the administrator mind.

At first I thought this was a special weakness of the school system in which I taught so I applied for certification in another province. I filled out the special forms, enclosed the required documents and complied willingly with all the red tape. Several weeks later, back came my application and all the documents!

No, there was nothing wrong with my credentials; the forms were correctly filled out; an official departmental stamp showed that they had been received in good order. But an accompanying letter said, "The new regulations require that such forms cannot be accepted by the Department of Education unless they have been registered at the Post Office to ensure safe delivery. Will you please remail the forms to the Department, making sure to register them this time?"

I began to suspect that the local school system did not have a monopoly on incompetence.

As I looked further afield, I saw that every organization contained a number of persons who could not do their jobs.

A Universal Phenomenon

Occupational incompetence is everywhere. Have you noticed it? Probably we all have noticed it.

We see indecisive politicians posing as resolute statesmen and the "authoritative source" who blames his misinformation on "situational imponderables." Limitless are the public servants who are indolent and insolent; military commanders whose behavioral timidity belies their dreadnaught rhetoric, and governors whose innate servility pre-

In our sophistication, we virtually shrug aside
the immoral cleric.

vents their actually governing. In our sophistication, we virtually shrug aside the immoral cleric, corrupt judge, incoherent attorney, author who cannot write and English teacher who cannot spell. At universities we see proclamations authored by administrators whose own office communications are hopelessly muddled; and droning lectures from inaudible or incomprehensible instructors.

Seeing incompetence at all levels of every hierarchy— political, legal, educational and industrial—I hypothesized that the cause was some inherent feature of the rules governing the placement of employees. Thus began my serious study of the ways in which employees move upward through a hierarchy, and of what happens to them after promotion.

For my scientific data hundreds of case histories were collected. Here are three typical examples.

MUNICIPAL GOVERNMENT FILE, CASE NO. 17   J. S. Minion* was a maintenance foreman in the public works department of Excelsior City. He was a favorite of the senior officials at City Hall. They all praised his unfailing affability.

"I like Minion," said the superintendent of works. "He has good judgment and is always pleasant and agreeable."

This behavior was appropriate for Minion's position: he was not supposed to make policy, so he had no need to disagree with his superiors.

The superintendent of works retired and Minion succeeded him. Minion continued to agree with everyone. He passed to his foreman every suggestion that came from above. The resulting conflicts in policy, and the continual changing of plans, soon demoralized the department. Com-

---

* Some names have been changed, in order to protect the guilty.

plaints poured in from the Mayor and other officials, from taxpayers and from the maintenance-workers' union.

Minion still says "Yes" to everyone, and carries messages briskly back and forth between his superiors and his subordinates. Nominally a superintendent, he actually does the work of a messenger. The maintenance department regularly exceeds its budget, yet fails to fulfill its program of work. In short, Minion, a competent foreman, became an incompetent superintendent.

SERVICE INDUSTRIES FILE, CASE NO. 3   E. Tinker was exceptionally zealous and intelligent as an apprentice at G. Reece Auto Repair Inc., and soon rose to journeyman mechanic. In this job he showed outstanding ability in diagnosing obscure faults, and endless patience in correcting them. He was promoted to foreman of the repair shop.

But here his love of things mechanical and his perfectionism become liabilities. He will undertake any job that he thinks looks interesting, no matter how busy the shop may be. "We'll work it in somehow," he says.

He will not let a job go until he is fully satisfied with it.

He meddles constantly. He is seldom to be found at his desk. He is usually up to his elbows in a dismantled motor and while the man who should be doing the work stands watching, other workmen sit around waiting to be assigned new tasks. As a result the shop is always overcrowded with work, always in a muddle, and delivery times are often missed.

Tinker cannot understand that the average customer cares little about perfection—he wants his car back on time! He cannot understand that most of his men are less interested in motors than in their pay checks. So Tinker cannot get on with his customers or with his subordinates.

He was a competent mechanic, but is now an incompetent foreman.

MILITARY FILE, CASE NO. 8   Consider the case of the late renowned General A. Goodwin. His hearty, informal manner, his racy style of speech, his scorn for petty regulations and his undoubted personal bravery made him the idol of his men. He led them to many well-deserved victories.

When Goodwin was promoted to field marshal he had to deal, not with ordinary soldiers, but with politicians and allied generalissimos.

He would not conform to the necessary protocol. He could not turn his tongue to the conventional courtesies and flatteries. He quarreled with all the dignitaries and took to lying for days at a time, drunk and sulking, in his trailer. The conduct of the war slipped out of his hands into those of his subordinates. He had been promoted to a position that he was incompetent to fill.

An Important Clue!

In time I saw that all such cases had a common feature. The employee had been promoted from a position of competence to a position of incompetence. I saw that, sooner or later, this could happen to every employee in every hierarchy.

HYPOTHETICAL CASE FILE, CASE NO. 1   Suppose you own a pill-rolling factory, Perfect Pill Incorporated. Your foreman pill roller dies of a perforated ulcer. You need a replacement. You naturally look among your rank-and-file pill rollers.

Miss Oval, Mrs. Cylinder, Mr. Ellipse and Mr. Cube all show various degrees of incompetence. They will naturally be ineligible for promotion. You will choose—other things being equal—your most competent pill roller, Mr. Sphere, and promote him to foreman.

Now suppose Mr. Sphere proves competent as foreman. Later, when your general foreman, Legree, moves up to Works Manager, Sphere will be eligible to take his place.

If, on the other hand, Sphere is an incompetent foreman, he will get no more promotion. He has reached what I call his "level of incompetence." He will stay there till the end of his career.

Some employees, like Ellipse and Cube, reach a level of incompetence in the lowest grade and are never promoted. Some, like Sphere (assuming he is not a satisfactory foreman), reach it after one promotion.

E. Tinker, the automobile repair-shop foreman, reached his level of incompetence on the third stage of the hierarchy. General Goodwin reached his level of incompetence at the very top of the hierarchy.

So my analysis of hundreds of cases of occupational incompetence led me on to formulate *The Peter Principle:*

IN A HIERARCHY EVERY EMPLOYEE TENDS
TO RISE TO HIS LEVEL OF INCOMPETENCE

A New Science!

Having formulated the Principle, I discovered that I had inadvertently founded a new science, hierarchiology, the study of hierarchies.

The term "hierarchy" was originally used to describe the

system of church government by priests graded into ranks. The contemporary meaning includes any organization whose members or employees are arranged in order of rank, grade or class.

Hierarchiology, although a relatively recent discipline, appears to have great applicability to the fields of public and private administration.

This Means You!

My Principle is the key to an understanding of all hierarchal systems, and therefore to an understanding of the whole structure of civilization. A few eccentrics try to avoid getting involved with hierarchies, but everyone in business, industry, trade-unionism, politics, government, the armed forces, religion and education is so involved. All of them are controlled by the Peter Principle.

Many of them, to be sure, may win a promotion or two, moving from one level of competence to a higher level of competence. But competence in that new position qualifies them for still another promotion. For each individual, for *you*, for *me*, the final promotion is from a level of competence to a level of incompetence.*

So, given enough time—and assuming the existence of enough ranks in the hierarchy—each employee rises to, and remains at, his level of incompetence. Peter's Corollary states:

In time, every post tends to be occupied by an employee who is incompetent to carry out its duties.

---

* The phenomena of "percussive sublimation" (commonly referred to as "being kicked upstairs") and of "the lateral arabesque" are not, as the casual observer might think, exceptions to the Principle. They are only pseudo-promotions, and will be dealt with in Chapter 3.

A few eccentrics try to avoid getting involved
with hierarchies.

Who Turns the Wheels?

You will rarely find, of course, a system in which *every* employee has reached his level of incompetence. In most instances, something is being done to further the ostensible purposes for which the hierarchy exists.

Work is accomplished by those employees who have not yet reached their level of incompetence.

CHAPTER II

The Principle in Action

"To tell tales out of schoole"
J. HEYWOOD

A STUDY of a typical hierarchy, the Excelsior City school system, will show how the Peter Principle works within the teaching profession. Study this example and understand how hierarchiology operates within every establishment.

Let us begin with the rank-and-file classroom teachers. I group them, for this analysis, into three classes: competent, moderately competent and incompetent.

Distribution theory predicts, and experience confirms, that teachers will be distributed unevenly in these classes: the majority in the moderately competent class, minorities in the competent and incompetent classes. This graph illustrates the distribution:

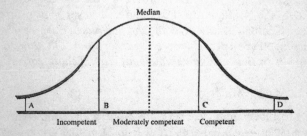

The Case of the Conformist

An incompetent teacher is ineligible for promotion. Dorothea D. Ditto, for example, had been an extremely conforming student in college. Her assignments were either plagiarisms from textbooks and journals, or transcriptions of the professors' lectures. She always did exactly as she was told, no more, no less. *She was considered to be a competent student.* She graduated with honors from the Excelsior Teachers' College.

When she became a teacher, she taught exactly as she herself had been taught. She followed precisely the textbook, the curriculum guide and the bell schedule.

Her work goes fairly well, except when no rule or precedent is available. For example, when a water pipe burst and flooded the classroom floor, Miss Ditto kept on teaching until the principal rushed in and rescued the class.

"Miss Ditto!" he cried. "In the Name of the Superintendent! There are three inches of water on this floor. Why is your class still here?"

She replied, "I didn't hear the emergency bell signal. I pay attention to those things. You know I do. I'm certain you didn't sound the bell." Flummoxed before the power of her awesome *non sequitur,* the principal invoked a provision of the school code giving him emergency powers in an extraordinary circumstance and led her sopping class from the building.

So, although she never breaks a rule or disobeys an order, she is often in trouble, and will never gain promotion. Competent as a student, *she has reached her level of incompetence as a classroom teacher, and will therefore remain in that position throughout her teaching career.*

The Eligible Majority

Most beginning teachers are moderately competent or competent—see the area from B to D on the graph—and *they will all be eligible for promotion.* Here is one such case.

A Latent Weakness

Mr. N. Beeker had been a competent student, and became a popular science teacher. His lessons and lab periods were inspiring. His students were co-operative and kept the laboratory in order. Mr. Beeker was not good at paper work, but this weakness was offset, in the judgment of his superiors, by his success as a teacher.

Beeker was promoted to head of the science department where he now had to order all science supplies and keep extensive records. *His incompetence is evident!* For three years running he has ordered new Bunsen burners, but no tubing for connecting them. As the old tubing deteriorates, fewer and fewer burners are operable, although new ones accumulate on the shelves.

Beeker is not being considered for further promotion. *His ultimate position is one for which he is incompetent.*

Higher up the Hierarchy

B. Lunt had been a competent student, teacher and department head, and was promoted to assistant principal. In this post he got on well with teachers, students and parents, and was intellectually competent. He gained a further promotion to the rank of principal.

Till now, he had never dealt directly with school-board members, or with the district superintendent of education. It soon appeared that he lacked the required finesse to work with these high officials. *He kept the superintendent waiting* while he settled a dispute between two children. Taking a class for a teacher who was ill, *he missed a curriculum revision committee meeting* called by the assistant superintendent.

He worked so hard at running his school that *he had no energy for running community organizations*. He declined offers to become program chairman of the Parent-Teacher Association, president of the Community Betterment League and consultant to the Committee for Decency in Literature.

His school lost community support and he fell out of favor with the superintendent. Lunt came to be regarded, by the public and by his superiors, as an incompetent principal. When the assistant superintendent's post became vacant, the school board declined to give it to Lunt. He remains, and will remain till he retires, unhappy and incompetent as a principal.

THE AUTOCRAT   R. Driver, having proved his competence as student, teacher, department head, assistant principal and principal, was promoted to assistant superintendent. Previously he had only to interpret the school board's policy and have it efficiently carried out in his school. Now, as assistant superintendent, he must participate in the policy discussions of the board, using democratic procedures.

But Driver dislikes democratic procedures. He insists on his status as an expert. He lectures the board members much as he used to lecture his students when he was a classroom teacher. He tries to dominate the board as he dominated his staff when he was a principal.

The board now considers Driver an incompetent assistant superintendent. He will receive no further promotion.

SOON PARTED   G. Spender was a competent student, English teacher, department head, assistant principal and principal. He then worked competently for six years as an assistant superintendent—patriotic, diplomatic, suave and well liked. He was promoted to superintendent. Here he

He got on well with teachers, students and parents.

was obliged to enter the field of school finance, in which he soon found himself at a loss.

From the start of his teaching career, Spender had never bothered his head about money. His wife handled his pay check, paid all household accounts and gave him pocket money each week.

Now Spender's incompetence in the area of finance is revealed. He purchased a large number of teaching machines from a fly-by-night company which went bankrupt without producing any programs to fit the machines. He had every classroom in the city equipped with television, although the only programs available in the area were for secondary schools. Spender has found his level of incompetence.

Another Promotion Mechanism

The foregoing examples are typical of what are called "line promotions." There is another mode of upward movement: the "staff promotion." The case of Miss T. Totland is typical.

Miss Totland, who had been a competent student and an outstanding primary teacher, was promoted to primary supervisor. She now has to teach, not children, but teachers. Yet *she still uses the techniques which worked so well with small children.*

Addressing teachers, singly or in groups, she speaks slowly and distinctly. She uses mostly words of one or two syllables. She explains each point several times in different ways, to be sure it is understood. She always wears a bright smile.

Teachers dislike what they call her false cheerfulness and her patronizing attitude. Their resentment is so sharp that, instead of trying to carry out her suggestions, they

Miss Totland had been an outstanding primary teacher.

spend much time devising excuses for *not* doing what she recommends.

Miss Totland has proved herself incompetent in communicating with primary teachers. She is therefore ineligible for further promotion, *and will remain as primary supervisor, at her level of incompetence.*

You Be the Judge

You can find similar examples in any hierarchy. Look around you where you work, and pick out the people who have reached their level of incompetence. You will see that in every hierarchy *the cream rises until it sours.* Look in the mirror and ask whether . . .

No! You would prefer to ask, "Are there no exceptions to the Principle? Is there no escape from its operation?"

I shall discuss these questions in subsequent chapters.

CHAPTER III

Apparent Exceptions

"When the case goes bad, the guilty man Excepts, and thins his jury all he can."

J. DRYDEN

MANY people to whom I mention the Peter Principle do not want to accept it. They anxiously search for—and sometimes think they have found—flaws in my hierarchiological structure. So at this point I want to issue a warning: *do not be fooled by apparent exceptions.*

APPARENT EXCEPTION NO. 1: THE PERCUSSIVE SUBLIMATION

"What about Walt Blockett's promotion? He was hopelessly incompetent, a bottleneck, so management *kicked him upstairs* to get him out of the road."

I often hear such questions. Let us examine this phenomenon, which I have named the *Percussive Sublimation.*

Did Blockett move from a position of incompetence to a position of competence? No. He has simply been moved from one unproductive position to another. Does he now undertake any greater responsibility than before? No. Does he accomplish any more work in the new position than he did in the old? No.

The percussive sublimation is a pseudo-promotion. Some Blockett-type employees actually believe that they have received a genuine promotion; others recognize the truth. But the main function of a pseudo-promotion is *to deceive people outside the hierarchy.* When this is achieved, the maneuver is counted a success.

But the experienced hierarchiologist will never be deceived. Hierarchiologically, the only move that we can accept as a genuine promotion is a move *from a level of competence.*

What is the effect of a successful percussive sublimation? Assume that Blockett's employer, Kickly, is still competent. Then by moving Blockett he achieves three goals:

1) He camouflages the ill-success of his promotion policy. To admit that Blockett was incompetent would lead observers to think, "Kickly should have realized, before giving Blockett that last promotion, that Blockett wasn't the man for the job." But a percussive sublimation *justifies the previous promotion* (in the eyes of employees and onlookers, not to a hierarchiologist).

2) He supports staff morale. Some employees at least will think, "If *Blockett* can get a promotion, *I* can get a promotion." *One percussive sublimation serves as carrot-on-a-stick to many other employees.*

3) He maintains the hierarchy. Even though Blockett is incompetent, *he must not be fired:* he probably knows enough of Kickly's business to be dangerous in a competitive hierarchy.

A Common Phenomenon

Hierarchiology tells us that every thriving organization will be characterized by this accumulation of deadwood at the executive level, consisting of percussive sublimatees and potential candidates for percussive sublimation. One well-known appliance-manufacturing firm has twenty-three vice-presidents!

A Paradoxical Result!

The Waverley Broadcasting Corporation is noted for the creativity of its production department. This is made possible through percussive sublimation. Waverley has just moved all its non-creative, non-productive, redundant personnel into a palatial, three-million-dollar Head Office complex.

The Head Office contains no cameras, microphones or transmitters; indeed, it is miles away from the nearest studio. The people at Head Office are always frantically busy, drawing up reports and flow charts and making appointments to confer with one another.

Recently a reshuffle of senior officials was announced, aimed at streamlining the headquarters operation. Four vice-presidents were replaced by eight vice-presidents and a co-ordinating assistant to the president.

So we see that the percussive sublimation can serve *to keep the drones out of the hair of the workers!*

APPARENT EXCEPTION No. 2: THE LATERAL ARABESQUE

The lateral arabesque is another pseudo-promotion. Without being raised in rank—sometimes without even a pay raise—the incompetent employee is given *a new and longer title* and is moved to an office in a remote part of the building.

R. Filewood proved incompetent as office manager of Cardley Stationery Inc. After a lateral arabesque he found himself, at the same salary, working as co-ordinator of interdepartmental communications, supervising the filing of second copies of inter-office memos.

AUTOMOTIVE MANUFACTURING FILE, CASE NO. 8 Wheeler Automobile Parts Ltd. has developed the lateral arabesque more fully than most hierarchies. The Wheeler operations are divided into many regions, and at last count, I found that twenty-five senior executives had been banished to the provinces as regional vice-presidents.

The company bought a motel and ordered one senior official to go and run it.

Another redundant vice-president has been laboring for three years to write the company's history.

I conclude that *the larger the hierarchy, the easier is the lateral arabesque.*

A CASE OF LEVITATION　The entire 82-man staff of a small government department was moved away to another department, leaving the director, at $16,000 a year, with *nothing to do* and *nobody to supervise.* Here we see the rare phenomenon of a hierarchal pyramid consisting solely of the capstone, suspended aloft without a base to support it! This interesting condition I denominate the *free-floating apex.*

APPARENT EXCEPTION NO. 3: PETER'S INVERSION

A friend of mine was travelling in a country where the sale of alcoholic beverages is a government monopoly Just before returning home he went to a government liquor store and asked, "How much liquor am I allowed to take back home with me?"

"You'll have to ask the Customs officers at the border," said the clerk.

"But I want to know *now*," said the traveller, "so that I can buy all the liquor that is permissible, and yet not buy too much and get some of it confiscated."

"It's a Customs regulation," replied the clerk. "It's nothing to do with us."

"But surely *you know* the Customs regulation," said the traveller.

"Yes, I know it," said the clerk, "but Customs regulations are not a responsibility of this department so I'm not allowed to tell you."

Have you ever had a similar experience, ever been told, "We don't give out that information"? The official knows the answer to your problem; you know that he knows it; but for some reason or other, he won't tell you.

Once, taking a professorship at a new university, I received a special identification card, issued by the payroll department of the university, entitling me to cash checks at the university book store. I went to the store, presented my card, and proffered a twenty-dollar American Express traveller's check.

"We only cash payroll checks and personal checks," said the book-store cashier.

"But this is better than a personal check," I said. "It's better even than a payroll check. I can cash this in any store even without this special card A traveller's check is as good as cash."

"But it's not a payroll check or a personal check," said the cashier.

After a little more discussion, I asked to see the manager. He listened to me patiently, but with a faraway expression, then stated flatly, "We do not cash traveller's checks."

You have heard of hospitals which spend precious time filling in sheaves of forms before helping accident victims. You have heard of the nurse who says, "Wake up! It's time to take your sleeping pill."

You may have read of the Irishman, Michael Patrick O'Brien, who was kept for eleven months on a ferryboat plying between Hong Kong and Macao. He did not have the correct papers to get off at either end of the trip, and nobody would issue them to him.

Particularly among minor officials with no discretionary powers, one sees an obsessive concern with getting forms filled out correctly, whether the forms serve any useful purpose or not. No deviation, however slight, from the customary routine, will be permitted.

Professional Automatism

The above type of behavior I call *professional automatism*. To the professional automaton it is clear that means are more important than ends; the paperwork is more important than the purpose for which it was originally designed. He no longer sees himself as existing to serve the public: he sees the public as the raw material that serves to maintain him, the forms, the rituals and the hierarchy!

The professional automaton, from the viewpoint of his customers, clients or victims, seems incompetent. So you will no doubt be wondering, *"How do so many professional automatons win promotion? And is the professional automaton outside the operation of the Peter Principle?"*

To answer those questions I must first pose another: "Who defines competence?"

A Question of Standards

The competence of an employee is determined *not by outsiders but by his superior in the hierarchy*. If the superior is still at a level of competence, he may evaluate his subordinates in terms of the performance of useful work—for example, the applying of medical services or information, the production of sausages or table legs or achieving whatever are the stated aims of the hierarchy. That is to say, *he evaluates output*.

But if the superior has reached his level of incompetence, he will probably rate his subordinates in terms of institutional values: he will see competence as the behavior that supports the rules, rituals and forms of the status quo. Promptness, neatness, courtesy to superiors, internal paperwork, will be highly regarded. In short, such an official *evaluates input*.

"Rockman is *dependable*."

"Lubrik contributes to the *smooth running* of the office."

"Rutter is *methodical*."

"Miss Trudgen is a *steady, consistent* worker."

"Mrs. Friendly *co-operates* well with colleagues."

In such instances, *internal consistency is valued more highly than efficient service:* this is *Peter's Inversion*. A professional automaton may also be termed a "Peter's Invert." He has inverted the means-end relationship.

Now you can understand the actions of the Peter's Inverts described earlier.

If the liquor-store clerk had promptly explained the Customs regulations, the traveller would have thought, "How courteous!" But his superior would have marked the clerk down for breaking a rule of the department.

If the book-store cashier had accepted my traveller's check, I would have considered him helpful: the manager would have reprimanded him for exceeding his authority.

Promotion Prospects for Peter's Inverts

The Peter's Invert or professional automaton has, as we have seen, little capacity for independent judgment. He *always obeys, never decides*. This, from the viewpoint of the hierarchy, is competence, so the Peter's Invert is eligible for promotion. He will continue to rise unless some mischance places him in a post where he has to make decisions. Here he will find his level of incompetence.*

We see therefore that professional automatism—however annoying you may have found it—is not, after all, an exception to the Peter Principle. As I often tell my students, "Competence, like truth, beauty and contact lenses, is in the eye of the beholder."

APPARENT EXCEPTION NO. 4: HIERARCHAL EXFOLIATION

Next I shall discuss a case which to untrained observers is perhaps the most puzzling of all: the case of the brilliant, productive worker who not only wins no promotion, but is even dismissed from his post.

Let me give a few examples; then I will explain them.

In Excelsior City every new schoolteacher is placed on one year's probation. K. Buchman had been a brilliant English scholar at the university. In his probationary year of English teaching, he managed to infuse his students with his own enthusiasm for classical and modern literature. Some of them obtained Excelsior City Public Library

---

* There are two kinds of minor decisions which I have sometimes seen made by promoted Peter's Inverts:
  a) to tighten up on enforcement of regulations
  b) to make new regulations covering a marginal case which does not exactly fit existing regulations.
These actions only serve to strengthen the inversion.

cards; some began to haunt new- and used-book stores. They became so interested that they read many books that were not on the Excelsior Schools Approved Reading List.

Before long, several irate parents and delegations from two austere religious sects visited the school superintendent to complain that their children were studying "undesirable" literature. Buchman was told that his services would not be required the following year.

Probationer-teacher C. Cleary's first teaching assignment was to a special class of retarded children. Although he had been warned that these children would not accomplish very much, he proceeded to teach them all he could. By the end of the year, many of Cleary's retarded children scored better on standardized achievement tests of reading and arithmetic than did children in regular classes.

When Cleary received his dismissal notice he was told that he had grossly neglected the bead stringing, sandbox and other busy-work which were the things that retarded children should do. He had failed to make adequate use of the modelling clay, pegboards and finger paints specially provided by the Excelsior City Special Education Department.

Miss E. Beaver, a probationer primary teacher, was highly gifted intellectually. Being inexperienced, she put into practice what she had learned at college about making allowances for pupils' individual differences. As a result, her brighter pupils finished two or three years' work in one year.

The principal was very courteous when he explained that Miss Beaver could not be recommended for permanent engagement. He knew she would understand that she had upset the system, had not stuck to the course of studies, and had created hardship for the children who would not fit into the next year's program. She had disrupted the official marking system and textbook-issuing system, and had caused severe anxiety to the teacher who would next year have to handle the children who had already covered the work.

The Paradox Explained

These cases illustrate the fact that, in most hierarchies, *super-competence is more objectionable than incompetence.*

Ordinary incompetence, as we have seen, is no cause for dismissal: it is simply a bar to promotion. Super-competence often leads to dismissal, *because it disrupts the hierarchy,* and thereby violates *the first commandment* of hierarchal life: *the hierarchy must be preserved.*

You will recall that in Chapter 2 I discussed three classes of employees: the incompetent, the moderately competent and the competent. At that time, for simplicity's sake, I chopped off the two extremes of the distribution curve and omitted two more classes of employees. Here is the complete curve.

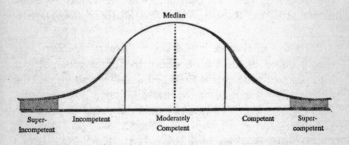

Employees in the two extreme classes—the super-competent and the super-incompetent—are alike subject to dismissal. They are usually fired soon after being hired, for the same reason: that they tend to disrupt the hierarchy. This sloughing off of extremes is called *Hierarchal Exfoliation.*

Some Horrible Examples

I have already described the fate of some super-competent employees. Here are some examples of super-incompetence.

Miss P. Saucier was hired as a salesgirl in the appliance department of the Lomark Department Store. From the start she sold less than the average amount of merchandise. This alone would not have been cause for dismissal, because many other salespeople were below average. But Miss Saucier's record keeping was atrocious: she punched wrong keys on the cash register, accepted competitors' credit cards and—still worse—inserted the carbon paper with the wrong side up when filling in a sales-contract form. She then managed to give the customer the original of the contract. He left with the two records (one on the front of the contract and the other in reverse on the back) and she was left with none. Worst of all, she was insolent to her superiors. She was dismissed after one month.

W. Kirk, a Protestant clergyman, held radical views on the nature of the Deity, the efficacy of the sacraments, the second coming of Christ, and life after death—views sharply opposed to the official doctrines of his sect. Technically, then, Kirk was incompetent to give his parishioners the spiritual guidance they expected. He received no promotion, of course; nevertheless he retained his post for several years. Then he wrote a book which condemned the stodgy church hierarchy and propounded a reasoned argument favoring taxation of all churches. He asked that ecclesiastical recognition be extended to such social problems as homosexuality, drug abuses, racial injustices and the like. . . . He had moved, at one jump, from incompetence to super-incompetence, and was promptly dismissed.

The super-incompetent exfoliate must have two important characteristics:

W. Kirk held radical views on the nature of the Deity.

1) he fails to produce (output).
2) he fails to support internal consistency of the hierarchy (input).

Is Exfoliation for You?

We see, then, that super-competence and super-incompetence are equally objectionable to the typical hierarchy.

We see, too, that hierarchal exfoliates, like all other employees, are subject to the Peter Principle.

They differ from other employees in being the only types who, under present conditions, are subject to dismissal.

Would you like to be somewhere else? Is your present placement in military service, school or business your choice or are you a victim of legal or family pressure? With planning and determination *you, too,* can make yourself either super-competent or super-incompetent.

APPARENT EXCEPTION No. 5: THE PATERNAL IN-STEP

Some owners of old-fashioned family businesses used to treat their sons like regular employees. The boy would start at the bottom of the hierarchy and rise in accordance with the Peter Principle. Here, of course, the owner's love for his hierarchy, his desire to keep it efficient and profitable, and his stern sense of justice, outweighed his natural familial affections.

Often, though, the owner of such a business would bring his son in at a high level with the idea that in time, without rising through the ranks, he should take over the supreme command or, as the phrase went, should "step into his father's shoes."

This type of placement, therefore, I call *The Paternal In-Step*.

There are two principal means by which the Paternal In-Step is executed.

P.I-S Method No. 1

An existing employee may be dismissed or removed by lateral arabesque or percussive sublimation, to make a place for the In-Stepper. Used less often than Method No. 2, this technique may cause considerable ill-feeling toward the new appointee.

P.I-S Method No. 2

A new position, with an impressive title, is created for the In-Stepper.

The Method Explained

The Paternal In-Step is merely a small-scale example of the situation that exists under a class system, where certain favored individuals enter a hierarchy above the class barrier, instead of at the bottom.*

The infusion of new employees at a high level may sometimes increase output. The Paternal In-Step, therefore, arouses no ill-feeling outside the hierarchy.

Yet the arrival of the In-Stepper is to a degree resented by other members of the hierarchy. Employees actually have a sentimental feeling (Peter's Penchant) for the promotion process by which they themselves have risen and

---

* For full discussion of the operation of hierarchies under a class system, see Chapter 7.

by which they hope to rise further. They tend to resent placements made by other means.

The Paternal In-Step Today

The family business, controlled by one man with the authority to place his sons in its higher ranks, is nowadays something of a rarity. Nevertheless, the Paternal In-Step is still executed in just the same way, except that the In-Stepper need not be related to the official who appoints him.

Let me cite a typical example.

PATERNAL IN-STEP FILE, CASE NO. 7   A. Purefoy, Director of the Excelsior City Health and Sanitation Department, found that by the end of one financial year he was going to have some unexpended funds. The citizens had suffered no epidemics; the Excelsior River had not, as it often did, overflowed its banks and silted up the drainage system; both his assistant directors (one for health, the other for sanitation) were earnest, competent, economically minded men.

So the budgeted funds had not been spent. Purefoy realized that unless he took rapid action he would suffer a cut in the coming year's budget.

He determined to create a third assistant directorship whose incumbent would organize an Anti-Litter and City Beautification Program. To fill the new post he engaged W. Pickwick, a young graduate from the School of Business Administration of his own alma mater.

Pickwick, in turn, created eleven more new posts: an anti-litter supervisor, six litter inspectors, a three-girl office staff, and a public relations officer.

N. Wordsworth, the P.R.O., organized essay contests for

school children, adult contests for jingles and poster designs, and commissioned two films, one of anti-litter propaganda, the other on city beautification. The films were to be made by an independent producer who had been with Wordsworth and Pickwick in the university dramatic society.

Everything worked out well: Director Purefoy exceeded his budget and was successful in obtaining a larger budget for the following year.

Modern Father Substitutes

Nowadays governments set up the "Father's Shoe Situation." Federal grants are offered for many new purposes— war on pollution, war on poverty, war on illiteracy, war on loneliness, war on illegitimacy and research into the recreational potential of interplanetary space travel for the culturally disadvantaged.

As soon as money is offered, a way must be found to spend it. A new position is created—anti-poverty co-ordinator, head-start director, book-selection advisor, organizer for Senior Citizens' Welfare and Happiness Projects, or what have you. Someone is recruited to occupy the position, to wear, if not necessarily to *fill,* the shoes.

The In-Stepper may or may not solve the problem that he was set to solve: that does not matter. The important point is that he must be able and willing to spend the money.

The Principle Not Breached

Such a placement is in accordance with the Peter Principle. Competence or incompetence is irrelevant so long as the shoes are filled. If they are filled competently the In-

Stepper will in time be eligible to step up and out of them and find his level of incompetence on a higher plane.

CONCLUSIONS

The apparent exceptions *are not exceptions*. The Peter Principle applies to all employees in all hierarchies.

CHAPTER IV

Pull &
Promotion

*"A long pull, and a strong pull,
and a pull all together."*
C. DICKENS

YOU have seen that the Peter Principle is immutable and universal but you may still want to know how long your hierarchal ascension will take. Chapters 4 and 5 will help reveal this to you. First let us turn our attention to accelerated elevation through pull.

"PULL" DEFINED IN SIXTEEN WORDS

I define Pull as "an employee's relationship—by blood, marriage or acquaintance—with a person above him in the hierarchy."

Unpopularity of the Pullee

Winning promotion through Pull is a thing we all hate— *in other people.* Co-workers dislike the beneficiary of Pull (the Pullee) and usually express that dislike in comments on his incompetence.

Soon after W. Kinsman became superintendent of schools in Excelsior City, his son-in-law, L. Harker, was promoted to the post of music supervisor. Some teachers criticized this appointment on the ground that Harker was *hard of hearing!* They said the music supervisor's post belonged by right of seniority (input) to D. Roane.

ENVY KNOWS NO LOGIC D. Roane had listened so long to so many school choirs and orchestras that *he hated music and children!* Obviously, he would have been no more competent (in terms of output) than Harker as music supervisor.

The teacher's resentment, then, was not really against Harker's incompetence, but against his violation of the time-honored seniority system.

Employees in a hierarchy do not really object to incompetence (Peter's Paradox): they merely gossip about incompetence to mask their envy of employees who have Pull.

HOW TO ACQUIRE PULL

One may study the careers of many employees who had Pull (Pullees), comparing them with employees of equal ability who had none. The results of my research can be reduced to five practical suggestions for the would-be Pullee.

1. Find a Patron

A Patron is a person above you in the hierarchy who can help you to rise. Sometimes you may have to do a good deal of scouting to find who has, and who has not, this power. You may think that your promotion rate depends on the good or bad reports written about you by your immediate superior. This *may be* correct. But management *may be* aware that your immediate superior is already at his level of incompetence, and therefore may attach *little importance* to his recommendations, favorable or otherwise! So do not be superficial: dig deep, and ye shall find.

2. Motivate the Patron

"An unmotivated Patron is no Patron." See that the Patron has *something to gain* by assisting you, or *something to lose* by not assisting you, to rise in the hierarchy.

My research has yielded many examples of this motivation process, some charming, some sordid. I shall not cite them. I would rather make this point a test for the reader, a test which I call *Peter's Bridge*. If you cannot cross it under your own steam, you have already reached your level of incompetence and no advice from me can help you.

3. Get Out from Under

"There's no road like the open road."

Imagine you are at a swimming pool, trying to climb to the high diving board. Halfway up the ladder, your ascent is blocked by a would-be diver who began to climb but has now lost his nerve. Eyes shut, he clings desperately to the handrail. He will not fall off, but he cannot go higher, and you cannot pass him. Encouraging shouts from your friend already on the top board are of no avail in this situation.

Similarly, in an occupational hierarchy, neither your own efforts, nor the Pull of your Patron, can help you if the next step above you is blocked by someone at his level of incompetence (a Super-incumbent). This awkward situation I denominate *Peter's Pretty Pass*. (Things have come to a pretty pass, etc.)

Let us return mentally to the swimming pool. To reach the top of the diving board, you would get off the ladder that is blocked, cross over to the ladder on the other side, and climb without hindrance to the top.

To move up the job hierarchy, you get out from under the Super-incumbent and move into a promotion channel that is not blocked. This maneuver is called *Peter's Circumambulation.*

Before investing time and effort in Peter's Circumambulation, make sure that you really are in Peter's Pretty Pass— *i.e.*, that the man above you is a genuine Super-incumbent. If he is still eligible for promotion, he is not a Super-incumbent: you need not dodge round him. Simply exert a little patience, wait a while; he will be promoted, a gap will open up and Pull will be able to do its wondrous work.

To discover, without any doubt, whether your superior is a Super-incumbent, look for the medical and non-medical indices of Final Placement, which are described in Chapters 11 and 12 of this book.

4. Be Flexible

There is only so much that any one Patron can do for you. To draw an analogy, an experienced mountaineer can pull a weaker climber up to his level. Then the leader must himself climb higher before he can exert more pull.

But if the first Patron *cannot climb higher,* then the Pullee must find another Patron who can.

So be prepared, when the time comes, to switch your allegiance to another Patron of higher rank than the first.

"There's no Patron like a new Patron!"

A patron is a person above you in the hierarchy
who can help you to rise.

5. *Obtain Multiple Patronage*

"The combined Pull of several Patrons is the sum of their separate Pulls multiplied by the number of Patrons." (Hull's Theorem.) The multiplication effect occurs because the Patrons talk among themselves and constantly reinforce in one another their opinions of your merits, and their determination to do something for you. With a single Patron, you get none of this reinforcement effect. "Many a Patron makes a promotion."

WHY WAIT? ESCALATE!!!

By following these hints, *you can obtain Pull*. Pull will speed your upward motion through the hierarchy. It can bring you to your level much sooner.

CHAPTER V

Push &
Promotion

*"Slump, and the world slumps with you.
Push and you push alone."*

NEXT let us see how far an employee's promotion rate can be affected by the force of Push.

There has been much misunderstanding about the function of Push, largely because of the persistence of Alger* in exaggerating the efficiency of Push as a means to promotion. One must indeed deplore the unscientific, misguided zeal of Alger's work, and its retarding effect on the science of hierarchiology.

Peale,† too, seems to overestimate the effect of Push.

A Fallacy Exploded

My surveys show that, in established organizations, the downward pressure of the Seniority Factor nullifies the up-

---

* Alger, Horatio, Jr. (1832–99). *Struggling Upward, Slow and Sure,* and many other works.

† Peale, Norman V. (1898–19——). *The Power of Positive Thinking,* New York: Prentice-Hall, 1952, and many other works.

ward force of Push. This observation, by the way, shows that Pull is stronger than Push. Pull often overcomes the Seniority Factor. Push seldom does so.

Push alone cannot extricate you from Peter's Pretty Pass. Push alone will not enable you to successfully execute Peter's Circumambulation. Using the Circumambulation without the aid of Pull simply makes superiors say, "He can't apply himself to anything for very long." "No stick-to-itiveness!" etc.

Neither can Push have any effect on ultimate placement level. That is because all employees, aggressive or shy, are subject to the Peter Principle, and must sooner or later come to rest at their level of incompetence.

Signs and Symptoms of Push

Push is sometimes manifested by an abnormal interest in study, vocational training and self-improvement courses. (In marginal cases, and particularly in small hierarchies, such training may increase competence to a point where promotion is slightly accelerated. The effect is imperceptible in large hierarchies, where the Seniority Factor is stronger.)

Perils of Push

Study and self-improvement may even have a negative effect if increased areas of competence result in the employee's requiring a larger number of promotional steps to reach his level of incompetence.

Suppose, for example, that B. Sellers, a competent local sales representative for Excelsior Mattress Co., managed, by hard study, to master a foreign language. It is quite possible that he would then have to fill one or more posts in the company's overseas sales organization before being brought home and promoted to his final position of incompetence as sales manager. Study created a detour in Sellers' hierarchal flight plan.

The Final Verdict

In my judgment, the positive and negative effects of study and training tend to cancel each other. The same applies to other manifestations of Push such as starting work early and staying late. The admiration inspired in some colleagues by these semi-Machiavellian ploys will ultimately be balanced by the detestation it elicits from others.

An Exception That Proves the Rule

You do occasionally find an exceptionally pushful employee who manages, by fair means or foul, to oust a Super-incumbent, and so clear a place for himself on a higher rank, sooner than natural processes would have done it.

W. Shakespeare cites an interesting example in *Othello*. In Act I, Scene 1, the ambitious Iago bemoans the fact that promotion is determined by Pull, not by strict rules of seniority:

> . . . *'tis the curse of service,*
> *Preferment goes by letter and affection,*
> *And not by old gradation, where each second*
> *Stood heir to the first.*

The promotion that Iago wants is given instead to Michael Cassio. So Iago contrives a double plan, to murder Cassio and to discredit him in the eyes of the commanding officer, Othello.

The plan comes near to success, but Iago's wife, Emilia, is an incorrigible blabbermouth:

> *Let heaven and men and devils, let them all,*
> *All, all cry shame against me, yet I'll speak.*

She gives the game away, and Iago never receives the coveted promotion.

We should learn by Iago's fate that *secrecy is the soul of Push.*

Pushfulness of this degree, however, is quite rare; it cannot seriously alter my assessment of the Push Factor.

A Dangerous Delusion

There are two reasons why the power of Push is so often overestimated. First is the obsessive feeling that a person who pushes harder than average deserves to advance farther and faster than average.

This feeling, of course, has no scientific basis: it is simply a moralistic delusion that I call *The Alger Complex.**

The Medical Aspect

Second, to unskilled observers, the power of Push sometimes seems greater than it really is because *many pushful persons exhibit the Pseudo-Achievement Syndrome.*

They suffer from such complaints as nervous breakdowns, peptic ulcers and insomnia. An ulcer, the badge of administrative success, may only be the product of pushfulness.

Colleagues who do not understand the situation may classify such a patient as an example of the Final Placement Syndrome (see Chapter 11) and may think that he has achieved final placement.

In fact, these people often have several ranks and several years of promotion potential ahead of them.

---

* *Ibid.*

An Important Distinction

The difference between cases of Pseudo-Achievement Syndrome and Final Placement Syndrome is known as *Peter's Nuance*. For your own guidance in classifying such cases, you should always ask yourself, "Is the person accomplishing any useful work?" If the answer is:

   a) "YES"—he has not reached his level of incompetence and therefore exhibits only the Pseudo-Achievement Syndrome.

   b) "NO"—he *has* reached his level of incompetence, and therefore exhibits the Final Placement Syndrome.

   c) "DON'T KNOW"—*you* have reached *your* level of incompetence. Examine yourself for symptoms at once!

LAST WORDS ON PUSH

Never stand when you can sit; never walk when you can ride; never Push when you can Pull.

CHAPTER VI

*Followers &
Leaders*

"Consider what precedes and what follows."

P. SYRUS

Bang! Bang!

One urgent task I have had to face is the exploding of various fallacies that still linger on from the pre-scientific era of hierarchiology.

What could be more misleading, for example, than "Nothing succeeds like success"?

As you already understand, hierarchiology clearly shows that *nothing fails like success,* when an employee rises to his level of incompetence.

Later, when I discuss Creative Incompetence, I shall show that *nothing succeeds like failure.*

But in this chapter I shall particularly discuss the old saw, "You have to be a good follower to be a good leader."

This is typical of the hierarchiological fallacies bandied about in administrative circles. For instance, when asked to comment on how her son achieved his military prowess, George Washington's mother answered, "I taught him to obey." America was thus presented with one more *non sequitur*. How can the ability to lead depend on the ability to follow? You might as well say that the ability to float depends on the ability to sink.

From Underdog to Upperdog

Take the simplest possible case: a hierarchy with two ranks. The employee who proves himself good at obeying orders will get promotion to the rank where his job is to give orders.

The same principle holds true in more complex hierarchies: competent followers show high promotion potential in the lower ranks, but eventually reveal their incompetence as leaders.

A recent survey of business failures showed that 53 percent were due to plain managerial incompetence! These were the former followers, trying to be leaders.

MILITARY FILE, CASE NO. 17 Captain N. Chatters competently filled an administrative post at an army base. He worked well with all ranks and obeyed orders cheerfully and exactly. In short, he was a good follower. He was promoted to the rank of major, and now had to work largely on his own initiative.

But Chatters could not endure the measure of solitude that necessarily accompanies a position of authority. He would hang around his subordinates, gossiping and joking with them, interfering with the performance of their work. He was quite unable to give someone an order and *let him get on with it:* he had to butt in with unwanted advice. Under this harassment, Chatters' subordinates became inefficient and unhappy.

Chatters also spent much time loitering around the office of his colonel. When he could find no legitimate reason for talking to the C.O., he would gossip with the C.O.'s secretary. She could not very well tell him to clear out and leave her alone. Her work slipped into arrears.

To get rid of Chatters the colonel would set him running errands all over the base.

In this instance, a good follower promoted to a position of leadership:

a) Fails to exercise leadership
b) Reduces efficiency among his subordinates
c) Wastes the time of his superiors

SELF-MADE MEN FILE, CASE NO. 2   In most hierarchies, as a matter of fact, employees with the greatest leadership potential cannot become leaders. Let me cite an example.

W. Wheeler was a bicycle delivery boy in the Mercury Messenger Service. Wheeler systematized his delivery work to an unprecedented degree. For example, he explored and mapped every passable lane, alley and short-cut in his territory; he timed with a stop watch the periods of all the traffic lights, so that he could plan his route to avoid delays.

As a result, he always delivered his daily quota of packages with two hours or more to spare, and spent the time sitting in cafés reading books on business management. When he began reorganizing the routes of the other messenger boys, he was fired.

For the moment, he seemed to be a failure, an example of the super-incompetent hierarchal exfoliate, a living testimony to the "poor-follower-poor-leader" theory.

But soon he formed a concern of his own, Pegasus Flying Deliveries, and within three years drove Mercury out of business.

So we see that exceptional leadership competence cannot make its way within an established hierarchy. It usually breaks out of the hierarchy and starts afresh somewhere else.

Wheeler systematized his delivery work to an
unprecedented degree.

Famous Names File Case No. 902   T. A. Edison, fired
for incompetence as a newsboy, founded, and successfully
led, his own organization.

A Rare Exception

Occasionally, in special circumstances, leadership potential may be recognized. For example, in an army at war,
all the officers of a certain unit were killed in a night attack.
L. Dare, a corporal, assumed command, repulsed the
enemy and led his comrades to safety. He was promoted
in the field.

Dare would not have gained such a promotion in peace-
time: he showed too much initiative. He was promoted
only because the normal system of ranks and seniority had
been disrupted and the hierarchy destroyed or temporarily
suspended.

But How about the Principle?

At this point you may be feeling baffled, wondering
whether I am not undermining the Peter Principle, which
of course states that a competent employee is always eligible for promotion. There is no contradiction!

As we saw in Chapter 3, an employee's competence is
assessed, not by disinterested observers like you and me,
but by the employer or—more likely nowadays—by other
employees on higher ranks of the same hierarchy. In their
eyes, leadership potential is insubordination, and insubordination is incompetence.

Good followers do not become good leaders. To be sure,
the good follower may win many promotions, but that does
not make him a leader. Most hierarchies are nowadays so
cumbered with rules and traditions, and so bound in by
public laws, that even high employees do not have to lead

anyone anywhere, in the sense of pointing out the direction and setting the pace. They simply follow precedents, obey regulations, and move at the head of the crowd. Such employees *lead* only in the sense that the *carved wooden figurehead leads the ship*.

It is easy to see how, in such a milieu, the advent of a genuine leader will be feared and resented. This is called *Hypercaninophobia* (top-dog fear) or more correctly by advanced hierarchiologists the *Hypercaninophobia Complex* (fear that the underdog may become the top dog).

CHAPTER VII

Hierarchiology & Politics

"The history of mankind is an immense sea of errors in which a few obscure truths may here and there be found."

C. DE BECCARIA

WE have seen how the Peter Principle operates in some simple hierarchies—school systems, factories, auto-repair shops and so on. Now let us examine the more complex hierarchies of politics and government.

During one of my lectures a Latin-American student, Caesare Innocente, said, "Professor Peter, I'm afraid that what I want to know is not answered by all my studying. I don't know whether the world is run by smart men who are, how you Americans say, putting us on, or by imbeciles who really mean it." Innocente's question summarizes the thoughts and feelings that many have expressed. Social sciences have failed to provide consistent answers.

No political theorist so far has satisfactorily analyzed the workings of governments, or has accurately predicted the political future. The Marxists have proved as wrong in their analysis as have the capitalist theoreticians. My studies in comparative hierarchiology have shown that capitalistic, socialistic, and communistic systems are characterized by the same accumulation of redundant and incompetent personnel. Although my research is incomplete at this time, I submit the following as an interim report. If funds are made available, I will complete my research on comparative hierarchiology. When this is done I intend to study *universal hierarchiology.*

INTERIM REPORT

In any economic or political crisis, one thing is certain. *Many learned experts* will prescribe *many different remedies.*

The budget won't balance: A. says, "Raise taxes," B. cries, "Reduce taxes."

Foreign investors are losing confidence in the dollar: C. urges tight money, while D. advocates inflation.

There are riots in the streets. E. proposes to subsidize the poor; F. calls for encouragement of the rich.

A foreign power makes threatening noises. G. says, "Defy him." H. says, "Conciliate him."

Why the Confusion?

1) Many of the experts have actually reached their level of incompetence: their advice is nonsensical or irrelevant.

2) Some of them have sound theories, but are unable to put them into effect.

3) In any event, neither sound nor unsound proposals can be carried out efficiently, because the machinery of

government is a vast series of interlocking hierarchies, riddled through and through with incompetence.

Let us consider two of the branches of government—the legislature which frames laws, and the executive which, through its army of civil servants, tries to enforce them.

THE LEGISLATURE

Most modern legislatures—even in the undemocratic countries—are elected by popular vote. One might think that the voters would, in their own interests, recognize and elect the most competent statesmen to represent them at the capital. That is, indeed, the simplified theory of representative government. In reality, the process is somewhat more complicated.

Present-day politics is dominated by the party system. Some countries have only one official party; some have two; some have several. A political party is usually naïvely pictured as a group of like-minded people co-operating to further their common interests. This is no longer valid. That function is now carried on entirely by *the lobby,* and there are as many lobbies as there are special interests.

A political party now exists primarily as *an apparatus for selecting candidates* and getting them elected to office.

A Dying Breed

To be sure, one occasionally sees an "independent" candidate get elected by his own efforts, without party endorsement. But the enormous expense of political campaigning makes this phenomenon rare enough at the local and regional levels, and unknown in national elections. It is fair to say that parties dominate the selection of candidates in modern politics.

The Party Hierarchy

Each political party, as any member knows, is a hierarchy. Admittedly, most members work for nothing, even pay for the privilege, but there is nevertheless a well-marked structure of ranks and a definite system of promotion from rank to rank.

I have so far shown the Peter Principle in its application to paid workers. You will see now that it is valid in this type of hierarchy, too.

In a political party, as in a factory or an army, competence in one rank is a requisite for promotion to the next. A competent door-to-door canvasser becomes eligible for promotion; he may be allowed to organize a team of canvassers. The ineffective or obnoxious canvasser continues knocking on doors, alienating voters.

A fast envelope stuffer may expect to become captain of an envelope-stuffing team; an incompetent envelope stuffer will remain, slowly and awkwardly stuffing envelopes, putting two leaflets in some, none in others, folding the leaflets wrongly, dropping them on the floor, and so on, as long as he stays with the party.

A competent fund raiser may be promoted to the committee which nominates the candidate. Although he was a good beggar, he may not be a competent judge of men as lawmakers and may support an incompetent candidate.

Even if a majority of the nominating committee consists of competent judges of men, it will select the candidate, *not for his potential wisdom as a legislator, but on his presumed ability to win elections!*

The Big Step: Candidate to Legislator

In bygone days, when great public meetings decided the results of elections, and when public speaking was a high art, a spellbinding orator might hope for nomination by a

In a political party competence in one rank is a requisite
for promotion to the next.

party, and the best orator among the candidates might win the seat. But of course the ability to charm, to amuse, to inflame a crowd of ten thousand voters with voice and gesture did not necessarily carry with it the ability to think sensibly, to debate soberly and to vote wisely on the nation's business.

With the development of electronic campaigning a party may give its nomination to the man who looks best on TV. But the ability to impress—with the aid of makeup and lighting—an attractive image on a fluorescent screen is no guarantee of competent performance in the legislature.

Many a man, under the old and the new systems, has made the upward step from candidate to legislator, only to achieve his level of incompetence.

Incompetence in the Legislature

The legislature itself is a hierarchy. An elected representative who proves incompetent as a rank-and-file member will obtain no promotion.

But a competent rank-and-file legislator is eligible for promotion to a position of greater power—member of an important committee, committee chairman or, under some systems, cabinet minister. At any of these ranks, too, the promotee may be incompetent.

So we see that the Peter Principle controls the entire legislative arm of government, from the humblest party worker to the holders of the loftiest elective offices. Each tends to rise to his level and each post tends in time to be occupied by someone incompetent to carry out its duties.

THE EXECUTIVE

It will be obvious to you by now that the Principle applies also to the executive branch: government bureaus, departments, agencies and offices at the national, regional and local level. All, from police forces to armed forces, are rigid hierarchies of salaried employees, and all are necessarily cumbered with incompetents who cannot do their existing work, cannot be promoted, yet cannot be removed.

Any government, whether it is a democracy, a dictatorship, a communistic or free enterprise bureaucracy, will fall when its hierarchy reaches an intolerable state of maturity.*

Equalitarianism and Incompetence

The situation is worse than it used to be when civil service and military appointments were made through favoritism. This may sound heretical in an age of equalitarianism but allow me to explain.

Consider an imaginary country called Pullovia, where civil service examinations, equality of opportunity and promotion by merit are unknown. Pullovia has a rigid class system, and the high ranks in all hierarchies—government, business, the armed forces, the church—are reserved for members of the dominant class.

You will notice that I avoid the expression "upper class"; that term has unfortunate connotations. It is generally considered to refer to a class which is dominant by reason of aristocratic or genteel birth. But my conclusions apply also to systems in which the dominant class is marked off from the subordinate class by differences of religion, stature, race, language, dialect or political affiliation.

It does not matter which of these is the criterion in Pull-

---

* The efficiency of a hierarchy is inversely proportional to its Maturity Quotient, M.Q.

$$MQ = \frac{\text{No. of employees at level of incompetence} \times 100}{\text{Total no. of employees in hierarchy}}$$

Obviously, when MQ reaches 100, no useful work will be accomplished at all.

ovia: the important fact is that the country has a dominant class and a subordinate class. This diagram represents a typical Pullovian hierarchy which has the classical pyramidal structure.

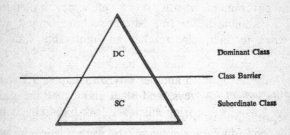

The lower ranks—the area marked SC—are occupied by employees of the subordinate class. No matter how brilliant any of them may be, no one is eligible to rise above CB, the class barrier.

The higher ranks—the area marked DC—are occupied by dominant-class employees. They do not start their careers at the bottom of the hierarchy, but at the level of the class barrier.

Now, in the lower area, SC, it is obvious that many employees will never be able to rise high enough, because of the class barrier, to reach their level of incompetence. They will spend their whole careers working at tasks which they are able to do well. No one is promoted out of area SC, so this area keeps, and continually utilizes, its competent employees.

Obviously, then, in the lower ranks of a hierarchy, the maintenance of a class barrier ensures a higher degree of efficiency than could possibly exist without the barrier.

Now look at area DC, above the class barrier. As we have already seen, an employee's prospects of reaching his level of incompetence are directly proportional to the number of ranks in the hierarchy—the more ranks, the more incompetence. The area DC, for all practical purposes, forms a closed hierarchy of a few ranks. Obviously, then, many of its employees will never reach their level of incompetence.

Moreover, the prospect of starting near the top of the pyramid will attract to the hierarchy a group of brilliant employees who would never have come there at all if they had been forced to start at the bottom.

Look at the situation another way. In Chapter 9 I shall discuss efficiency surveys, and shall show that the only effective way of increasing efficiency in a hierarchy is by the infusion of new blood at its upper levels. In most present-day systems, such infusion takes place at intervals, say after a reorganization, or during periods of rapid expansion. But in Pullovian hierarchies, it is a continuous process: new employees are regularly entering at a high level, above the class barrier.

Obviously, then, in areas SC and DC, below and above the class barrier, Pullovian hierarchies are more efficient than those of a classless or equalitarian society.

A Contemporary Class System

Before I am accused of recommending the establishment of a class system here, let me point out that we already have one. Its classes are based, not on birth, but on the prestige of the university which one has attended. For example, a graduate of Harvard is referred to as "A Harvard Man" but a graduate of Outer Sheepskin College is not referred to as "A Sheepskin Man." In some hierarchies, the graduate of the obscure college—no matter how competent he may be—does not have the same opportunities for promotion as the graduate of the prestigious establishment.

The situation is changing. There is a strong trend toward making university graduation a prerequisite for more and more positions, even in the lowest ranks of certain hierarchies. This should increase the promotion potential of all degree holders, and therefore diminish the class value of the prestige degree.

My personal studies of this phenomenon are incomplete, due to that most lamentable dearth of funds, but I will hazard a prediction that with every passing year, each university graduate will have greater opportunities for reaching his level of incompetence, either in private employment, or in government.

CHAPTER VIII

Hints &
Foreshadowings

*"Poets are the hierophants of an
unapprehended inspiration."*

P. B. SHELLEY

IT is the custom to ornament every
scientific work with a bibliography,
a list of earlier books on the same subject. The aim may
be to test the reader's competence by laying out for him
an awe-inspiring course of reading; it may be to prove the
author's competence by showing the mountain of dross
he has sifted to win one nugget of truth.

Since this is the first book there is no formal bibliography.
I confess to this apparent shoddiness of scholarship, since
guile is not my long suit, in firm belief that the future shall
vindicate my unorthodoxy.

With these considerations in mind, I have decided to
mention some authors who, although they never wrote on
this subject, might have done so, had they thought of it.
This, then, is a bibliography of proto-hierarchiologists.

The unknown originators of several proverbs had some
intuitive understanding of incompetence theory.

"Cobbler, stick to your last" is clearly a warning to the journeyman cobbler to be wary of being promoted to fore-man of the boot-repair shop. The hand that skillfully wielded awl and hammer might well fumble pen, time sheet and work schedule.

"Too many cooks spoil the broth" suggests that the more people you involve in any project, the greater are the odds that one of them, at least, has reached his level of incom-petence. One competent vegetable peeler, promoted to his level of incompetence as cook, may add too much salt and ruin the good work of the other six cooks who helped make the broth.

"Woman's work is never done" is a sad commentary on the high proportion of women who reach their level of in-competence as housewives.

In his Rubáiyát, O. Khayyám remarked sourly on the high incidence of incompetence in educational and religi-ous hierarchies:

> *Myself when young did eagerly frequent*
> *Doctor and Saint, and heard great argument*
> *About it and about: but evermore*
> *Came out by the same door where in I went.*

I have mentioned elsewhere the existence of a "hier-archal instinct" in men: their irresistible propensity to arrange themselves by ranks. Some critics have denied the existence of this instinct. However, A. Pope noticed it over two centuries ago, and even saw it as the expression of a divine principle.

> Order *is Heav'n's first law; and this confest,*
> *Some are, and must be, greater than the rest.*
> (Essay on Man, *Epistle IV,* ll. 49–50)

He accurately observed the satisfaction that is obtained from doing one's work competently:

> *Know, all the good that individuals find,*
> *Or God and Nature meant to mere Mankind,*
> *Reason's whole pleasure, all the joys of Sense,*
> *Lie in three words, Health, Peace, and Competence.*
> (*Ibid.*, ll. 77–80)

Pope enunciates one of the key principles of hierarchiology:

> *What would this man? Now upward will he soar,*
> *And little less than angel, would be more.*
> (Essay on Man, *Epistle I*, ll. 173–74)

In other words, scarcely an employee is content to remain at his level of competence: he insists upon rising to a level that is beyond his powers.

S. Smith's description of occupational incompetence is so vivid that it has lingered on as the basis of a cliché.

> If you choose to represent the various parts in life by holes upon a table, of different shapes—some circular, some triangular, some square, some oblong—and the persons acting these parts by bits of wood of similar shapes, we shall generally find that the triangular person has got into the square hole, the oblong into the triangular, and a square person has squeezed himself into the round hole. The officer and the office, the doer and the thing done, seldom fit so easily that we can say they were almost made for each other.*

W. Irving points out that "Your true dull minds are generally preferred for public employ, and especially promoted to city honors." He did not realize that a mind may well be bright enough for a subordinate position, yet appear dull when promoted to prominence, just as a candle is all very well to light a dinner table, but proves inadequate if placed on a lamppost to illuminate a street corner.

K. Marx undoubtedly recognized the existence of hier-

---

* Smith, Sydney (1771–1845). *Sketches of Moral Philosophy*, 1850.

archies, yet seemed to believe that they were maintained by the capitalists. In advocating a non-hierarchal society, he obviously failed to see that man is essentially hierarchal by nature, and must and will have hierarchies, whether they be patriarchal, feudal, capitalistic or socialistic. On this point his insight is vastly inferior to that of Pope.

Then, with glaring inconsistencey, Marx proposes, as the ruling principle of his non-hierarchal dream society, "From each according to his abilities and to each according to his needs." This suggests the creation of twin hierarchies of ability and neediness.

Even if we overlook this inconsistency in the Marxian scheme, the Peter Principle now shows that we cannot hope to obtain work "from each according to his ability." To do that, we should have to keep employees permanently at a level of competence. But that is impossible: each employee must rise to his level of incompetence and, once arrived at that level, will *not* be able to produce according to his ability.

So we see Marxist theory as a pipe dream and another opiate of the masses. No government which has tried to apply it has ever been able to make it work. Marx must be dismissed as an unscientific visionary.

We seem to find better science among the poets, E. Dickinson's aphorism

> *Success is counted sweetest*
> *By those who ne'er succeed*

is psychologically sound when "success" receives its hierarchiological meaning of final placement at the level of incompetence.

C. W. Dodgson, in *Through the Looking-Glass,* refers to life at the level of incompetence when he makes the Queen say, "Now *here,* you see, it takes all the running you can do to keep in the same place." In other words, once an em-

ployee has achieved final placement, his most vigorous
effort will never win him any further promotion.

S. Freud seems to have come closer than any earlier
writer to discovering the Peter Principle. Observing cases
of neurosis, anxiety, psycho-omatic illness, amnesia, and
psychosis, he saw the painful prevalence of what we might
call the Generalized Life-Incompetence Syndrome.

This life-incompetence naturally produces sharp feelings
of frustration. Freud, a satirist at heart, chose to explain
this frustration mainly in sexual terms such as penis envy,
castration complex and Oedipus complex. In other words,
he suggested that women were frustrated because they
could not be men, men because they could not bear children, boys because they could not marry their mothers
and so on.

But Freud missed the point in thinking that frustration
comes from the longing for a change to a more desirable
position (man, father, mother's husband, father's wife,
etc.), in other words, a longing for a promotion! Hierarchiology now shows us, of course, that frustration occurs
as a result of promotion.

This oversight of Freud's occurred because of his extremely introspective nature: he persisted in studying what
was going on (or what he imagined was going on) inside
his patients. Hierarchiology, on the other hand, studies what
is going on *outside* the patient, studies the social order in
which man operates, and therefore realistically explains
man's function in that order. While Freud spent his time
hunting in the dark recesses of the subconscious, I have
devoted my efforts to examining observable and measur-
able human behavior.

Freudian psychologists, in their failure to study the function of man in society, might be compared with a man seeing an electronic computer and trying to understand it by

speculating on the internal structure and mechanism without trying to find out what the instrument was used for.

Still, let us not minimize Freud's pioneering work. Although he misunderstood much, he discovered much. Always looking within the patient, he became famous on the strength of his theory that man is unconscious of his own motivations, does not understand his own feelings and so cannot hope to relieve his own frustrations. The theory was unassailable, because nobody could consciously and rationally argue about the nature and contents of his unconscious.

With a stroke of professional genius he invented psychoanalysis, whereby he said he could make patients conscious of their unconscious.

Then he went too far, psychoanalyzed himself and claimed to be conscious of his own unconscious. (Some critics now suggest that all he had ever accomplished was to make *his patients* aware of *his own*—Freud's—unconscious.) In any event, by this procedure of self-psychoananalysis he kicked the ladder from under his own feet.

If Freud had understood hierarchiology, he would have shunned that last step, and would never have arrived at his level of incompetence.

By thus undermining the grand structure, which he had built on the impenetrability of the unconscious, Freud prepared the way for his great successor, S. Potter.

Potter, like Freud, is a satirical psychologist (or a psychological satirist), and he can fairly be ranked with Freud for keenness of observation and boldness in creating a picturesque and memorable terminology to describe what he saw.

Like Freud, Potter observed and classified many phenomena of human frustration. The basic condition of being frustrated he calls being "one-down," and the exhilarated feeling caused by removal of frustration he calls "one-up." He assumes that men have an innate urge to advance from the former state to the latter. The technique for making this move he calls "one-upmanship."

The main difference between the two men is that Potter rejects Freud's doctrine of unconscious motivation. He explains human behavior in terms of a conscious drive to outdo other people, triumph over circumstances, and so become one-up. Potter also repudiates Freudian dogma that the frustrated patient must receive professional aid, and expounds a do-it-yourself brand of psychology. He teaches various plots, ploys and gambits that, if properly used, will enable the patient to become one-up.

The One-upman, the Lifeman, the Gamesman, to summarize Potter's elegantly expressed theories, are all using various forms of obnoxious behavior to move themselves up the ranks of social, commercial, professional or sporting hierarchies.

Potter writes so entertainingly that we tend to overlook the central weakness of his system, the assumption that, if only the One-upman can learn enough ploys, he can keep on rising, and can be permanently one-up.

In reality, no amount of One-upmanship can raise a man above his level of incompetence. The only result of the technique will be to help him reach that level sooner than he would have done otherwise. And, once there, he is in a one-down situation which no amount of lifemanship can cure.

Lasting happiness is obtainable only by avoiding the ultimate promotion, by choosing, at a certain point in one's progress, to abandon one-upmanship, and to practice instead what he might have called *Staticmanship*. I shall point out later, in the chapter on Creative Incompetence, how this can be done.

Meanwhile, I must salute Potter as a truly great theoretician who ably bridged the gap between the Freudian Ethic and the Peter Principle.

C. N. Parkinson, eminent social theorist, accurately observes and amusingly describes the phenomenon of staff accumulation in hierarchies. But he tries to explain what he calls the rising pyramid by supposing that senior employees are practicing the strategy of divide and conquer, that they are deliberately making the hierarchy inefficient as a means of self-aggrandizement.

This theory fails on the following grounds. First, it assumes intent or design on the part of persons in supervisory positions. My investigations show that many senior employees are incapable of formulating any effective plans, for division, conquest or any other purpose.

Second, the phenomena that Parkinson describes—overstaffing and underproduction—are often directly opposed to the interests of the supervisory and managerial personnel. Efficiency becomes so low that businesses collapse, and the responsible employees find themselves out of work. In governmental hierarchies they may be badgered and humiliated by legislative committees, or commissioners, investigating waste and incompetence. It is scarcely conceivable that they would deliberately injure themselves in this way.

Third, other things being equal, the less money that is spent on the wages of subordinates, the larger will be the profits of the business, and the more money will be available for salaries, bonuses, dividends and fringe benefits for the high-ranking staff. If the hierarchy can function efficiently with a thousand employees, management has no motive for employing twelve hundred.

But suppose the hierarchy is not operating efficiently with its thousand employees. As the Peter Principle shows, many, or most, senior employees will be at their levels of incompetence. They cannot do anything to improve the

No amount of One-upmanship can raise a man above his level of incompetence.

situation with their existing staff—everyone is already doing the best he can—so in a desperate effort to attain efficiency, they hire more staff. As pointed out in Chapter 3, a staff increase may produce a temporary improvement, but the promotion process eventually produces its effect on the newcomers and they, too, rise to their levels of incompetence. Then the only apparent remedy is another staff increase, another temporary spurt and another gradual lapse into inefficiency.

This is the reason why there is no direct relationship between the size of the staff and the amount of useful work done. Staff accumulation cannot be explained by Parkinson's conspiracy theory: it results from a sincere, though futile, quest for efficiency by upper-level members of the hierarchy.

Another point: Parkinson based his law on the Cheopsian or feudal hierarchy.

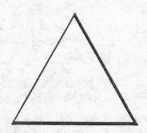

The Cheopsian or Feudal Hierarchy

The reason for this is that Parkinson made his discovery in the armed forces, where obsolete traditions and modes of organization have the strongest foothold.

To be sure, the feudal hierarchy has not disappeared, but a complete hierarchiological system must also recognize the existence and explain the operations of several other hierarchal forms.

For example, the *Flying T Formation*

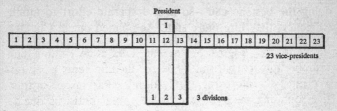

This diagram clearly illustrates that a company with 3 major divisions, 23 vice-presidents and 1 president does not fit the traditional pyramidal model.

The Automated Model

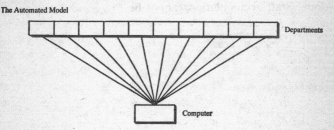

In this recent modification the broad pyramidal base of employees is replaced by a computer.

Many departments are supported by one computer, producing an inverted pyramid. A similar form results when numerous executive, supervisory and sales staff are supported by a highly automated production process.

I have already described, in Chapter 3, the Free-Floating Apex—a condition which exists when a director is in charge of a non-existent department, or when a staff is assigned to another department leaving the administrator to his lonely office.

⋀ Administrator

Free-Floating Apex

Unfortunately Parkinson's investigation does not go far enough. It is true that work can expand to fill the time allotted but it can expand far beyond that. It can expand beyond the life of the organization and the company can go bankrupt, a government can fall, a civilization can crumble into barbarism, while the incompetents work on. We must therefore regretfully dismiss Parkinson's attractive-sounding theory. Nevertheless, great praise is due to him for drawing attention to those phenomena which are now, for the first time, scientifically explained by the Peter Principle.

CHAPTER IX

The Psychology of Hierarchiology

> *"Alas! regardless of their doom
> The little victims play."*
>
> T. GRAY

AFTER one of my hierarchiology lectures a student handed me a note which included the following questions. "Why did you not give us some insight into the mind of the incompetent loafer type you described so vividly? After final placement, does the employee realize his own incompetence? Does he accept his own parasitism? Does he know that he is swindling his employer, frustrating his subordinates, and eating like a cancer at the economic structure of society?" Recently I have received many questions of this type.

A DISPASSIONATE SURVEY

I must first emphasize that *hierarchiology is a social science* and as such employs objective criteria in its evaluation rather than emotion-laden terms like "loafer," "parasite," "swindling" or "cancer." The question of insight, though, is worthy of consideration. My approach to behavioral science has been that of an objective observer. I discovered the Peter Principle through observing overt behavior and have avoided introspection or inferences regarding what is going on in the minds of others.

Mirror, Mirror, on the Wall

Yet the question of insight is, in essence, an interesting one: "What understanding does the individual attain into his own copelessness?" My answers to this question are subjective and lack the scientific rigor of the balance of this work.

In most cases I have found little indication of real insight. However, a few cases in my study were in analysis, and I was able to obtain psychiatric reports. These showed that patients rationalized and blamed other people for their difficulties.

Where depth analysis was achieved, there was more acceptance of self. Yet I never observed, in an individual, any understanding of the hierarchal system, or of *promotion as the cause of occupational incompetence*.

PSYCHIATRIC FILE: CASE No. 12   S. N. Stickle was a competent stock clerk with Bathos Brothers Lead Weight and Sinker Company. By hard night-school study, Stickle gained diplomas in warehouse management and elementary non-ferrous metallurgy. He was promoted to assistant warehouse foreman.

After six years in this post, Stickle asked for another promotion. He was told that he lacked leadership ability: he could not make the warehousemen obey his commands; so he was not eligible for promotion to warehouse foreman.

But Stickle could not accept the truth about his own incompetence as a supervisor. He rationalized that the big, burly warehousemen scorned him because he was only five feet six inches tall.

He bought elevator shoes, and took to wearing a hat in the warehouse; this made him look taller. He attended a body-building studio, gained weight and developed bulging muscles. Still the warehousemen did not obey him.

Stickle brooded over his physical deficiencies, developed a severe complex, and eventually sought psychiatric advice.

During therapy Dr. Harty tried to help Stickle by telling him about small men who had achieved fame and fortune. This made Stickle more depressed: now he saw himself not only as small, but as an obscure failure. His self-confidence deteriorated further, and he became still less competent as a supervisor.

Psychiatry, Like Love, Is Not Enough

The Stickle case shows that, without an understanding of the Peter Principle, psychiatry is at a severe disadvantage in trying to treat problems arising from occupational incompetence.

Dr. Harty was diverted by an irrelevancy, Stickle's stature. Stickle's situation was simply that, within the Bathos Brothers' hierarchy, he had reached his level of incompetence. No psychiatric treatment could alter that fact.

But Stickle might have been consoled had he been shown that his coming to rest in the position of assistant warehouse foreman was *not failure, but fulfillment*.

He might have been happier had he realized that his was not a solitary example of misfortune, but that everyone else, in every hierarchal system was, like him, under the sway of the Peter Principle.

I do feel that an understanding of the principle will aid

**He saw himself not only as small,
but as an obscure failure.**

the analysis of all cases exhibiting any degree of copelessness.

Insight Is Not Enough, Either!

Sometimes, after granting a promotion, *management attains insight* and realizes that the promotee cannot properly fulfill his new responsibilities.

"Grindley *isn't working out too well* as foreman."

"Goode *wasn't quite big enough,* after all, to fill Betters' shoes."

"Miss Cardington *isn't shaping up* as filing supervisor."

Occasionally *the employee* also attains this insight and accepts his own incompetence for the higher rank. Here, too, insight produces much regretful thought, but little or no action.

INSIGHT FILE, CASE NO. 2   F. Overreach, a competent school vice-principal in Excelsior City, was promoted to principal. Before one term was over, he realized that he was incompetent for the job.

He asked to be demoted. His application was refused!

He remains, unhappy and resentful, at his level of incompetence.

OUTSIDE INVESTIGATORS

I mentioned that management and employees do sometimes achieve insight into occupational incompetence but do little to counteract it. You may now be thinking, "But what about vocational aptitude tests? What about efficiency surveys? Surely disinterested outside observers can diagnose incompetence and can prescribe appropriate remedies."

Can they? Let us look at these experts and see how they run.

Placement Methods, Old-fashioned and Newfangled

In olden days, entry into most careers was governed by random placement, based on the employer's prejudices, on the employee's wishes or on chance (an applicant happens to turn up seeking work just at the moment when a vacancy occurs). Random placement is still operative in some hierarchies, particularly the smaller ones.

Random placement often puts an employee into a position that he is barely competent to fill. His mediocre work is blamed on a vicious character, flabby will-power or plain laziness. He is exhorted to work harder. He is edified with such adages as "Where there's a will, there's a way," and "If at first you don't succeed, try, try again."

In bad favor with his superiors, his first promotion is long delayed. (He may even come to believe that he is worthless, undeserving of any advancement at all: I call this condition *The Uriah Heep Syndrome.*)

Random placement is now largely superseded by examinations and aptitude tests. The prevailing attitude is best expressed in the saying, "If at first you don't succeed, try something else."

Of course, it is no use giving aptitude tests if you have no competent person to mark the papers and interpret the scores. With incompetent handling, the test system is only a disguised form of random placement.

But, if competently handled, aptitude tests have their uses. We have general aptitude or intelligence tests, which sample ability with language, ingenuity, computational facility and so on. There are clerical tests which indicate skill in remembering numbers, copying names and addresses and so forth. There are tests which rate a person for mechanical ability, artistic ability, physical skill, social intelligence, scientific reasoning and persuasiveness

Test results are commonly expressed in a "profile," a

graphic representation of the employee's competence in various skills. Here is such a profile.

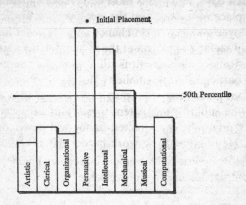

The purpose of this testing is to place the employee, as soon as possible, in a job which will utilize the highest competence level on his profile. Obviously, *any promotion will be to an area of less competence.*

Let us see how this works in practice.

PLACEMENT TECHNIQUES FILE, CASE NO. 17 The profile shown above actually resulted from the testing of C. Breeze, a young commerce graduate, who applied for a post with the I. C. Gale Air Conditioning Company. You will notice that Breeze is above average in persuasive ability, and also has high general intelligence.

Breeze was hired as a salesman and in time achieved two promotions: first to District Sales Manager, where he still spent much of his time selling, and then to General Sales Manager, a supervisory and organizational post.

Note that his lowest score, much below average, is in organizational ability. This is the very faculty that he now uses daily. For example, his salesmen are assigned arbitrarily. Hap Hazard, an inexperienced salesman, was sent to call on two new important clients and managed to lose both sales and goodwill. Conn Manly, a new employee who had achieved an impressive sales record, was promoted to district sales manager. He showed little sincere interest in his salesmen. His calculated, crafty methods of manipulation have reduced morale of his men to a new low.

C. Breeze also mismanaged paperwork. The size and topography of sales territories had no relationship to transportation, volume of business or salesmen's experience and ability. His memos and records are beyond comprehension and his desk looks like a litter pile.

As the Peter Principle predicts, his career has proceeded from competence to incompetence.

Aptitude Testing Evaluated

The main difference between tested and untested employees is that the tested people reach their levels of incompetence in fewer steps and in a shorter time.

Efficiency Surveys

We have seen that outside intervention at the time of initial placement cannot prevent but in fact hastens achievement of incompetence levels. I will now examine the operations of efficiency experts who, of course, usually appear on the scene at a later stage, when a hierarchy has achieved a high Maturity Quotient. (M.Q. defined, Chapter 7.)

First, we must remember that the investigating experts, too, are subject to the Peter Principle. They have reached their position by the same promotion process that has crippled the organization they are surveying. Many of the experts will be at their level of incompetence. Even if they can see deficiencies, they will be unable to correct them.

EFFICIENCY SURVEY FILE, CASE NO. 8 Bulkeley Cold Store and Transfer Ltd. hired Speedwell and Trimmer, Management Consultants, to survey its operation. Speedwell and Trimmer found that the Bulkeley organization was no more inefficient than most firms in the same line of business. By discreet questioning they discovered the real reason why the survey had been ordered: several directors felt that they could not sufficiently influence the firm's policy.

What could Speedwell and Trimmer do? Suppose they said, "Gentlemen, there is not much wrong with your firm. You are as efficient as your competitors."

There is good reason to believe that Speedwell and Trimmer fear dismissal in such an instance. They may feel they would get the reputation of being inefficient management experts; they would see the Bulkeley survey taken over by a rival firm.

Under this emotional stress they felt obliged to say, "Gentlemen, you are understaffed, and many of your existing employees are wrongly placed. We recommend the creation of certain new posts, and the promotion of a number of your employees."

Once the organization was thoroughly stirred up, the dissident directors could place or promote protégés just as they wished, thereby strengthening their influence at various levels and in various departments of the hierarchy. The board was satisfied, and Speedwell and Trimmer received their fee.

Management Surveys Evaluated

1) An efficiency survey, in effect, temporarily weakens, or even suspends, the operation of the Seniority Factor in a hierarchy. This automatically hastens promotion, or facilitates initial placement, for employees who have Pull (Pullees).

2) A favorite recommendation of efficiency experts is the appointment of *a co-ordinator between two incompetent officials or two unproductive departments.** A popular fallacy among these experts and their clients is that "Incompetence co-ordinated equals competence."

3) *The only recommendation* that actually produces an increase of output is "Hire more employees." In some instances, new recruits will do work which is not being done by the old employees who have reached their level.

The effective management consultant realizes this and recommends various lateral arabesques and percussive sublimations of high-ranking incompetents and hierarchal exfoliation of super-incompetent low-ranking employees. Competent consultants also make useful recommendations regarding personnel practices, production methods, color dynamics, incentive schemes and so forth, which can improve the efficiency of the competent employees.

COMPULSIVE INCOMPETENCE

While reviewing depth studies of a few cases of competence at the top levels of hierarchies, a remarkable psychological phenomenon presented itself to me and I will here describe it.

Summit Competence is rare, but not completely unknown. In Chapter 1, I wrote, "Given enough time—and assuming the existence of enough ranks in the hierarchy—each employee rises to, and remains at, his level of incompetence."

Victorious field marshals, successful school superintend-

---

* A survey of efficiency experts reveals that co-ordinator appointments, lateral arabesques and percussive sublimations are always acceptable to management.

ents, competent company presidents and such persons have simply not *had time* to reach their levels of incompetence.

Alternatively, the emergence of a competent trade-union leader or university president simply shows that, *in that particular hierarchy, there are not enough ranks* for him to reach his level.

These people exhibit *Summit Competence.**

I have observed that these summit competents are often not satisfied to remain in their position of competence. They cannot rise to a position of incompetence—they are already at the top—*so they have a strong tendency to side-step into another hierarchy*—say from the army into industry, from politics into education, from show business into politics and so on—*and reach, in the new environment, that level of incompetence which they could not find in the old*. This is *Compulsive Incompetence.*

Compulsive Incompetence File, Selected Cases

Macbeth, a successful military commander, became an incompetent king.

A. Hitler, a consummate politician, found his level of incompetence as a generalissimo.

Socrates was an incomparable teacher, but found his level of incompetence as a defense attorney.

---

* Our records contain a few outstanding cases of *Multi-modal Summit Competence*—individuals who could be at the summit of several hierarchies at one time. A. Einstein is an example of this phenomenon. He wa⌐ a highly competent thinker who provided science with a special and general theory of relativity. It was also obvious that Einstein was highly competent in the area of men's fashions. His hair style and casual clothing established a trend followed by young people to this day. Considering what he accomplished in the fashion world without effort, one wonders what he might have achieved if he had really tried.

Why Do They Do It?

"The job lacks challenge."

This, or some variant of it, is the reason invariably given by summit competents at the time when they are considering the move which will eventually lead them to compulsive incompetence.

Need They Do It?

There is in fact a greater, more fascinating challenge in remaining below one's level of incompetence. I shall discuss that point in a later chapter.

CHAPTER X

Peter's Spiral

"We all of us live too much in a circle."

B. DISRAELI

I pointed out in Chapter 9 that hierarchiology is not moralistic with regard to incompetence. Indeed, I must say that, in most cases of incompetence, there appears to be a definite *wish to be productive*. The employee *would be competent if he could*.

Most incompetents realize, however dimly, that the collapse of the organization would leave them jobless, so they try to keep the hierarchy going.

Let me give an illustration.

INTRA-HIERARCHAL FILE, CASE NO. 4

Health for Wealth

In twenty years at Perfect Pewter Piano Strings Inc., Mal D'Mahr had worked his way up from lead ingot handler to general manager. Shortly after occupying the chief executive office he suffered a series of health problems associated with high blood pressure and peptic ulcers. The company physician recommended that he slow down and learn to relax. The board of directors recommended that an assistant general manager be appointed to relieve Mal of some of the strain. Although both of these recommendations were well intentioned they failed to deal with the cause of the problem. Hierarchiologically Mal D'Mahr had been promoted beyond his physiological competence. As chief executive at P.P.P.S.I. he had to deal with and accommodate conflicting codes or values. He had to please the stockholders and board by making money. He had to please the customers by maintaining a high-quality product. He had to please the employees by paying good wages and by providing comfortable, secure working conditions. He had to please his community by fulfilling certain social and family responsibilities. In attempting to accommodate these conflicting codes he broke down physically. No increase in staff or advice about relaxing could reduce this requirement of the office of the chief executive.

Calculate the Unknown

The board's recommendation was carried out and J. Smugly, a competent engineer and mathematical genius, was promoted to assistant general manager. Smugly, competent in dealing with things, was incompetent at dealing with people. He had no appropriate people-formulas to help him decide about personnel matters. Not wishing to act on incomplete data, he postponed personnel decisions until pressure became so great that he made unwise, snap decisions. Smugly reached his level of incompetence

In attempting to accommodate these conflicting codes
he broke down physically.

through social inadequacy. It was recommended that he be assisted through the appointment of a personnel manager.

Compassion Is Its Own Reward

Roly Koster was promoted to the position of personnel manager. A competent psychology student, he soon became so empathetic with his clients that he was perpetually on an emotional binge. When he listened to Smugly's complaint about an inaccurate report from Miss Count, his sympathy was with the assistant general manager and he was filled with anger toward Miss Count for her carelessness. When he heard Miss Count's story about Smugly's cold, calculating, inhuman approach toward her and her colleagues he was brought to tears of sorrow and indignation at Smugly's heartlessness. Roly achieved his level of incompetence through emotional inadequacy. To resolve some of the personnel problems it was decided to create a new position of personnel supervisor and to promote someone from the plant who had the confidence of the men.

Mind Over Matter

B. Willder was popular with the men and had distinguished himself as chairman of the social committee. Now as personnel supervisor he is required to see that the policy decisions of management are carried out. But, as he does not really understand the policy, B. Willder is ineffective in this role. He lacks the intellectual capacity to deal effectively with abstraction and therefore makes illogical decisions. He has reached his level of incompetence through mental inadequacy.

INCOMPETENCE CLASSIFIED

I have reported this study, conducted at Perfect Pewter Piano Strings Inc., because it illustrates the four basic classes of incompetence.

Mal D'Mahr was promoted beyond his *physical competence.*

J. Smugly was promoted beyond his *social competence.*

Roly Koster was promoted beyond his *emotional competence.*

B. Willder was promoted beyond his *mental competence.*

A Vain Effort

This example, typical of many, shows that even a sincere attempt to relieve high-level incompetence may only produce multi-level incompetence. In such circumstances, staff accumulation is inevitable. Each time around *Peter's Spiral,* the number of incompetents increases, and *still there is no improvement of efficiency.*

THE MATHEMATICS OF INCOMPETENCE

Incompetence plus incompetence equals incompetence.

CHAPTER XI

The Pathology
of Success

"Troubles never ccme singly."

I T should be clear by now that when an employee reaches his level of incompetence, he can no longer do any useful work.

INCOMPETENT, YES! IDLE, NO!

This in no way suggests that the ultimate promotion suddenly changes the former worker into an idler. Not at all! In most cases he still *wants to work;* he still makes a great show of activity; he sometimes thinks he is working. Yet actually little that is useful is accomplished.

Sooner or later (usually sooner) these employees become aware of, and feel distressed at, their own unproductivity.

A Bold Step

Here we must venture into the field of medicine! I will describe the physical condition which has been alluded to earlier as the Final Placement Syndrome.

An Exhaustive Research Program

A number of medical doctors in general practice were asked:

1) "What physical conditions, if any, do you find to be most commonly associated with success?"*

2) "What advice or treatment, if any, do you give to patients in the success-group?"

AN ALARMING REPORT (1)

On collating the doctors' replies, I found that the following complaints from A to Z were common among their "successful" patients.

a) Peptic ulcers
b) Spastic colitis
c) Mucous colitis
d) High blood pressure
e) Constipation
f) Diarrhea
g) Frequent urination
h) Alcoholism
i) Overeating and obesity
j) Loss of appetite
k) Allergies
l) Hypertension
m) Muscle spasms
n) Insomnia
o) Chronic fatigue
p) Skipped heartbeats
q) Other cardiovascular complaints
r) Migraine headaches
s) Nausea and vomiting
t) Tender, painful abdomen
u) Dizziness
v) Dysmenorrhea
w) Tinnitus (ringing in the ears)
x) Excessive sweating of hands, feet, armpits or other areas
y) Nervous dermatitis
z) Sexual impotence

All of these are typical "success" complaints, and may occur without the existence of organic disease.

I saw—and by now you will be able to see—that such

---

* What the ordinary sociologist or physician calls "success," the hierarchiologist, of course, recognizes as *final placement*.

symptoms indicate the constitutional incompetence of the patients for the level of responsibility they have attained.

A CASE STUDY IN DEPTH For example, T. Throbmore, vice-president in charge of sales of Clacklow Office Machine Company, is frequently prevented from attending the company's weekly executive meeting by a migraine headache that occurs fairly regularly on Monday afternoons at 1:30 P.M.

DEPTH STUDY OF ANOTHER CASE Because of the delicate condition of his heart, C. R. Diack, president of Grindley Gear and Cog Ltd., is permanently shielded by his staff from any news that might excite or irritate him. He has no real control over the company's affairs. His main function is to read glowing reports of its progress at annual meetings.

NOTE THIS IMPORTANT DEFINITION The ailments I have named, usually occurring in combinations of two or more, constitute the Final Placement Syndrome.*

AN ALARMING REPORT (2)

Unfortunately, the medical profession has so far failed to recognize the existence of the Final Placement Syndrome! In fact, that profession has displayed a frigid hostility toward my application of hierarchiology to the pseudoscience of diagnostics. However, truth will out! Time and the increasingly tumultuous social order inevitably will bring enlightenment.

---

* Refer to Chapter 5 for an infallible means of distinguishing the Final Placement Syndrome from the Pseudo-Achievement Syndrome.

Three Medical Errors (a)

Final Placement Syndrome patients often rationalize the situation: they claim that their occupational incompetence is the result of their physical ailments. "If only I could get rid of these headaches, I could concentrate on my work."

Or "If only I could get my digestion fixed up . . ."

Or "If I could kick the booze . . ."

Or "If I could get just one good night's sleep . . ."

Some medical men, my survey reveals, accept this rationalization at face value, and attack the physical symptoms without any search for their cause.

This attack is made by medication or surgery, either of which may give temporary, *but only temporary, relief*. The patient cannot be drugged into competence and there is no tumor of incompetence which can be removed by a stroke of the scalpel. *Good advice* is equally ineffective.

"Take it easy."

"Don't work so hard."

"Learn to relax."

Such soothing suggestions are useless. Many F.P.S. patients feel anxious because they know quite well that they are doing very little useful work. They are unlikely to follow any suggestion that they should do still less.

Another futile approach is that of *the friendly philosopher:*

"Stop trying to solve all the world's problems."

"Everybody has troubles. You're no worse off than lots of other people."

"You have to expect some of these problems at your age."

Few F.P.S. patients are susceptible to such crackerbarrel wisdom. Most of them are quite self-centered: they show little interest in philosophy or in other people's problems. They are only trying to solve the problems of their jobs.

Threats are often employed:

"If you carry on like this, you will end up in the hospital."

"Unless you slow down, you're going to have a really serious attack."

This is futile. The patient cannot help but "carry on like this." The only thing that would change his way of life would be a promotion, and he will not get that, because he has reached his level.

Another much-used line of advice is the *exhortation to self-denial*.

"Go on a diet."

"Cut down on your drinking."

"Stop smoking."

"Give up night life."

"Curb your sex life."

This is usually ineffective. The F.P.S. patient is already depressed because he can take no pleasure in his work. Why should he give up the few pleasures he has outside of work?

Moreover, many men feel that there is a certain aura of competence associated with heavy indulgence in bodily pleasures. It is reflected in such phrases as "He has a *wonderful* appetite," "He's a *great* ladies' man," and "He can hold his liquor." Such praise is doubly sweet to the man who has little else to be praised for; he will be reluctant to give it up.

Three Medical Errors (b)

A second group of physicians, finding nothing organically wrong with an F.P.S. patient, will try to persuade him that *his symptoms do not exist!*

"There's really nothing wrong with you. Just take these tranquillizers."

"Get your mind off yourself. These symptoms are only imaginary. It's your nerves."

Such advice, of course, produces no lasting improvement. The patient *knows that he is suffering,* whether the physician will admit it or not.

A common result is that the patient loses faith in the physician, and runs to another one, seeking someone who "understands his case" better. He may lose faith altogether in orthodox medicine and start consulting pseudo-medical practitioners.

Three Medical Errors (c)

After medication and surgery have failed, psychotherapy is sometimes tried. It seldom succeeds, because it can have no effect on the root cause of the F.P.S., which is the patient's vocational incompetence.

A Smattering of Sense

The only treatment, my survey shows, which gives any relief for the F.P.S. is distraction therapy.

"Learn to play bridge."

"Start a stamp collection."

"Take up gardening."

"Learn barbecue cookery."

"Paint pictures by numbers."

Typically, the doctor senses the patient's copelessness with regard to his job, and so tries to divert his attention to something that he can cope with.

AN ILLUMINATING CASE HISTORY   W. Lushmoor, a department-store executive, spent every afternoon at his club,

W. Lushmoor spent every afternoon at his club.

rather than return to his office. An advanced F.P.S. case, Lushmoor was a near-alcoholic, had survived two mild coronary attacks, was grossly overweight and chronically dyspeptic.

On his physician's advice, he took up golf. He became obsessed by the game, devoted all his afternoons and most of his energy to it, and was making rapid progress until he suffered a fatal stroke while driving his electric golf cart.

The point is that, although Lushmoor's symptoms were not relieved, he had been transformed from an F.P.S. case in relation to his job—since he no longer worried about the job—to a mere Pseudo-Achievement Syndrome case in relation to golf! The treatment was therefore successful.

Physicians who give this sort of advice do seem to understand, even though dimly, the pathogenic role of incompetence; they try to give the patient a feeling of competence in some non-occupational field.

A Sinister Sign

One more point about the Final Placement Syndrome: it has an ever-increasing sociological importance, because its component ailments have acquired high status value. An F.P.S. patient will boast of his symptoms; he will show a perverse kind of competence in developing a bigger ulcer or a more severe heart attack than any of his friends. In fact so high is the status value of the F.P.S. that some employees who have none of its ailments will actually simulate them, to create the impression that they have achieved final placement.

CHAPTER XII

Non-Medical
Indices of
Final Placement

"How can I tell the signals and the signs?"
H. W. LONGFELLOW

A LONG-FELT WANT

It is often useful to know who, in a hierarchy, has and has not achieved final placement. Unfortunately, you cannot always get hold of an employee's medical record to see whether he is a Final Placement Syndrome case or not. So here are some signs which will guide you.

ABNORMAL TABULOLOGY

This is an important and significant branch of hierarchiology.

The competent employee normally keeps on his desk just the books, papers and apparatus that he needs for his work. After final placement, an employee is likely to adopt some unusual and highly significant arrangement of his desk.

Phonophilia

The employee rationalizes his incompetence by complaining that he cannot keep in close enough touch with colleagues and subordinates. To remedy this, he installs several telephones on his desk, one or more intercommunication devices with buttons, flashing lights and loudspeakers, plus one or more voice-recording machines. The phonophiliac soon forms the habit of using two or more of these devices at the same time; this is an infallible sign of galloping phonophilia. Such cases degenerate rapidly and are usually considered incurable.

(Phonophilia, by the way, is nowadays increasingly seen among women who have reached their level of incompetence as housewives. Typically, an elaborate microphone-loudspeaker-switchboard-telephone system is installed in the kitchen to enable such a housewife to keep in constant, close, simultaneous contact with her neighbors, her dining nook, her laundry room, her play room, her back porch and her mother.)

Papyrophobia

The papyrophobe cannot tolerate papers or books on his desk or, in extreme cases, anywhere in his office. Probably every such piece of paper is a reminder to him of the work that he is not able to do: no wonder he hates the sight of it!

But he makes a virtue out of his phobia and, by "keeping a clean desk," as he calls it, hopes to create the impression that he despatches all his business with incredible promptitude.

Papyromania

Papyromania, the exact opposite of papyrophobia, causes the employee to clutter his desk with piles of never-used papers and books. Consciously or unconsciously, he thus tries to mask his incompetence by giving the impression that he has *too much to do*—more than any human being could accomplish.

Fileophilia

Here we see a mania for the precise arrangement and classification of papers, usually combined with a morbid fear of the loss of any document. By keeping himself so busy with rearranging and re-examining bygone business, the fileophiliac prevents other people—and prevents himself—from realizing that he is accomplishing little or nothing of current importance. His preoccupation with records fixes his vision on the past so that he backs reluctantly into the present.

Tabulatory Gigantism

An obsession with having a bigger desk than his colleagues.

Tabulophobia Privata

Complete exclusion of desks from the office. This symptom is observed only at the very highest hierarchal ranks.

PSYCHOLOGICAL MANIFESTATIONS

In my researches I spent much time in waiting rooms, interviewing clients and colleagues as they left executive offices. In this way I discovered several interesting psychological manifestations of final placement.

Self-Pity

Many executive conferences consisted of the high-ranking employee telling hard-luck stories about his present condition.

"Nobody really appreciates me."

"Nobody co-operates with me."

"Nobody understands how the incessant pressure from above and the incurable incompetence below make it utterly impossible for me to do an adequate job and keep a clean desk."

This self-pity is usually combined with a strong tendency to reminisce about "good old days" when the complainant was working at a lower rank, at a level of competence.

This complex of emotions—sentimental self-pity, denigration of the present and irrational praise of the past— I call *the Auld Lang Syne Complex.*

An interesting feature of the Auld Lang Syne Complex is that although the typical patient claims to be a martyr to his present position, he never on any account suggests that another employee would be better able to fill his place!

Rigor Cartis

In employees at the level of incompetence, I have often observed Rigor Cartis, an abnormal interest in the construction of organization and flow charts, and a stubborn insistence upon routing every scrap of business in strict accordance with the lines and arrows of the chart, no matter what delays or losses may result. The Rigor Cartis patient will often display his charts prominently on the office walls, and may sometimes be seen, his work lying neglected, standing in worshipful contemplation of his icons.

Compulsive Alternation

Some employees, on achieving final placement, try to mask their insecurity by keeping their subordinates always off balance.

An executive of this type is handed a written report; he pushes it aside and says, "I've no time to wade through all that garbage. Tell me about it in your own words—and briefly."

If the subordinate comes in with a verbal suggestion, this man chokes him off in mid-sentence with, "I can't even begin to think about it until you put it in writing."

A confident employee will be deflated with a snub; a timid one will be flustered by a display of familiarity. One may at first confuse Compulsive Alternation with Potter's One-upmanship but they are quite different. Potter's method is designed to advance the user to his level of incompetence. Compulsive Alternation is primarily a defensive technique employed by a boss who has reached his level. This man's subordinates say, "You never know how to take him."

The Teeter-Totter Syndrome

In the teeter-totter syndrome one sees a complete inability to make the decisions appropriate to the sufferer's rank. An employee of this type can balance endlessly and minutely the pros and cons of a question, but cannot come down on one side or the other. He will rationalize his immobility with grave allusions to "the democratic process" or "taking the longer view." He usually deals with the problems that come to him by keeping them in limbo until someone else makes a decision or until it is too late for a solution.

I notice, by the way, that teeter-totter victims are often papyrophobes as well, so they have to find some means of getting rid of the papers. *The Downward, Upward and Outward Buckpasses* are commonly used to effect this.

In the Downward Buckpass the papers are sent to a subordinate with the order, "Don't bother me with such trifles." The subordinate is thus bullied into deciding an issue that is really above his level of responsibility.

The Upward Buckpass calls for ingenuity: the teeter-totter victim must examine the case until he finds some tiny point out of the ordinary which will justify sending it up to a higher level.

The Outward Buckpass merely involves assembling a committee of the victim's peers and following the decision of the majority. A variant of this is *The John Q. Public Diversion:* sending the papers to someone else who will conduct a survey to find what the average citizen thinks about the matter.

One teeter-totter victim in government service resolved his problem in an original manner. When he got a case that he could not decide, he would simply remove the file from the office at night and throw it away.

A Classical Case

W. Shakespeare describes an interesting manifestation of final placement: an irrational prejudice against subordinates or colleagues because of some point of physical appearance in no way related to the performance of their work. He quotes Julius Caesar as saying:

> *Let me have men about me that are fat. . . .*
> *Yon Cassius has a lean and hungry look;*
> *He thinks too much: such men are dangerous.*

It is reliably reported that N. Bonaparte, toward the end of his career, began judging men by the size of their noses, and would give preferment only to men with big noses.

Some victims of this obsession may attach their baseless dislikes to such trifles as the shape of a chin, a regional accent, the cut of a coat or the width of a necktie. Actual competence or incompetence on the job is ignored. This prejudice I call *The Caesarian Transference*.

Cachinnatory Inertia

A sure mark of final placement is the habit of *telling jokes* instead of getting on with business!

Structurophilia

Structurophilia is an obsessive concern with buildings—their planning, construction, maintenance and reconstruction—and an increasing unconcern with the work that is going on, is supposed to be going on, inside them. I have observed structurophilia at all hierarchal levels, but it undoubtedly achieves its finest development in politicians and university presidents. In its extreme pathological manifestations (*Gargantuan monumentalis*) it reaches a stage where the victim has a compulsion to build great tombs or memorial statues. Ancient Egyptians and modern Southern Californians appear to have suffered greatly from this malady.

Structurophilia has been referred to, by the uninformed, as the Edifice Complex. We must be precise in differentiating between this simple preoccupation with structures and the Edifice Complex which involves a number of elaborately interrelated, interconnected and complicated attitudes. The Edifice Complex tends to afflict philanthropists wishing to improve education, health services or religious instruction. They consult experts in these fields and discover so many at their respective levels of incompetence that formulation of a positive program is impossible. The only thing they agree on is to have a new building. Frequently the advising educator, doctor or minister suffers

A sure mark of final placement is the habit of telling jokes
instead of getting on with business.

from structurophilia and therefore his recommendation to the donor is, "Give me a new building." Church committees, school trustees and foundation boards find themselves in the same *complex* situation. They see so much incompetence in the professions that they decide to invest in buildings rather than people and programs. As in other psychological complexes, this results in bizarre behaviour.

RELIGIOUS PROGRAM IMPROVEMENT FILE #64   The congregational committee of the First Euphoria Church in Excelsior City became concerned with declining church attendance. Various proposals were investigated. One faction recommended a change of minister. They were tired of Reverend Theo Log's traditional sermons that had little to say about the contemporary human condition. As a result guest clergy were invited. Questions were raised regarding the sexual revolution, generation gap, the futility of war, and the new morality. Some of the more conservative church members threatened to quit if these "far-out" sermons continued. The committee finally agreed that a building drive and new church would be the most acceptable solution. The old minister was retained at his low salary. After completion of the new building it came to the committee's attention that the small congregation seemed even smaller in the large new church. The recommendation for a more dynamic ministry was reconsidered but was rejected because it was decided that it would be impossible to get a better man for such a low salary. Furthermore, it was concluded, this might seriously hamper the funding of the new organ and the building of the new social centre.

Which Is Which

Usually the structurophilia victim has a pathological need to have a building or monument named in his honor,

whereas the Edifice Complex afflicts those who are trying
to improve the quality of some human endeavor but end
up by only producing another building.

TICS AND ODD HABITS

Eccentric physical habits and tics often develop soon
after final placement has been achieved. A noteworthy example is *Heep's Palmar Confrication,* so acutely observed
and vividly described by C. Dickens.

I would also mention under this head such habits as nail
biting, drumming with fingers or tapping with pencils on
desks, cracking knuckles, twiddling pens, pencils and paper
clips, the purposeless stretching and snapping of rubber
bands, and heavy sighing with no apparent cause for grief.
Often F.P.S. goes unnoticed because the sufferer adopts
the pose of staring off into the middle distance for indefinite
lengths of time. Untrained observers are inclined to think
he is absorbed in the awesome responsibility of high office.
Hierarchiologists know otherwise.

REVEALING SPEECH HABITS

Baffling the Listener

Initial and Digital Codophilia is an obsession for speaking
in letters and numbers rather than in words. For example,
"F.O.B. is in N.Y. as O.C. for I.M.C. of B.U. on 802."

By the time, if ever, that the listener realizes that Fred-
erick Orville Blamesworthy is in New York as Operative
Co-ordinator for the Instructional Materials Center of
Boondock University conducting business concerning Federal Bill 802, he has lost the opportunity to observe that

the speaker did not really know much. Codophiliacs manage to make the trivial sound impressive, which is what they want.

Many Words, Few Thoughts

Some employees, on final placement, stop thinking, or at least sharply cut down on their thinking. To mask this, they develop lines of *General Purpose Conversation* or, in the case of public figures, *General Purpose Speeches*. These consist of remarks that sound impressive, yet which are vague enough to apply to all situations, with perhaps a few words changed each time to suit the particular audience.

My Executive Wastebasket and Trash Can Research Project* turned up the following notes, obviously fragments from the rough draft of an all-purpose speech. The writer has problems enough without my identifying him. My cause is education, not humiliation. Here are his notes:

> Ladies and/or Gentlemen:
> In these troublous times, it gives me great pleasure to speak to you on the important topic of ——. This is a subject in which fantastic advances have been made. We naturally—and rightly—take pride in our accomplishments locally, yet we must not omit a word of tribute to those individuals and groups who have made outstanding contributions on a larger scale, at the regional, national, yes, and—dare I say it?—the international level. . . .
> While we must never underestimate the marvels that can be achieved by personal devotion, resolution and persistence, yet I suggest that it would be presumptuous

---

* This research method has been restricted. Some firms have installed locked trash cans in their offices to prevent piracy of ideas by competitors. A trash-disposal firm loads the trash cans' contents into a truck each day where at once all is turned into a grayish, unpiratable sand.

for us to think that we can solve problems which have baffled the best brains of bygone and present generations. In conclusion, then, let me state my position without qualification or equivocation. I stand solidly behind progress; I call for progress; I expect to see progress! Yet what I seek is true progress, not simply a chopping and changing for the mere sake of novelty. That true progress, friends, will be made, I suggest, only if, as and when we fix our minds, and keep them unshakably fixed, on our great historical heritage, and those magnificent traditions in which, now and forever, our real strength lies.

A WORD TO THE SUFFICIENT IS WISE

Look about you for the signs described above. They will greatly help you to analyze your fellow workers. But your most difficult task will be self-analysis. Hierarchiologist: heal thyself!

CHAPTER XIII

Health & Happiness at Zero PQ—Possibility or Pipe Dream?

*"No sense have they of ills to come
Nor care beyond today."*

T. GRAY

W HEN an employee reaches his Level of Incompetence (Peter's Plateau) he is said to have a Promotion Quotient (PQ) of zero.* In this chapter I shall show how different employees react to the situation.

FACE THE SORDID TRUTH (NOT RECOMMENDED)

The employee realizes consciously that he has achieved final placement, reached his level of incompetence, bitten

---

* The Promotion Quotient: a numerical expression of the employee's promotion prospects. When PQ declines to zero, he is completely ineligible for promotion. The PQ is fully explained in *The Peter Profile*, an unpublished monograph on the mathematical aspects of incompetence.

off more than he can chew, is out of his depth or "arrived." (These terms are synonymous.)

The type of employee who is capable of realizing this truth tends to equate incompetence with laziness; he assumes that he is not working hard enough, so he feels guilty.

He thinks that, by working harder, he will conquer the initial difficulties of the new position, and become competent. So he drives himself mercilessly, skips coffee breaks, works through his lunch hour and takes work home with him on evenings and weekends.

He rapidly falls victim to the Final Placement Syndrome.

Ignorance Is Bliss

Many an employee *never* realizes that he has reached his level of incompetence. He keeps perpetually busy, never loses his expectation of further promotion, and so remains *happy* and *healthy*.

You will naturally ask, "How does he do it?"

SUBSTITUTION: THE LIFESAVER

Instead of carrying out the proper duties of his position he substitutes for them some other set of duties, which he carries out to perfection.

I will describe several Substitution techniques.

Technique No. 1: Perpetual Preparation

Faced with an important task, the competent employee simply begins it. The Substituter may prefer to busy himself with preliminary activities. Here are some well-tried methods.

a) CONFIRM THE NEED for action. The true Substituter an never get enough evidence. "Better be safe than sorry," s his watchword, or "More haste, less speed."

Spend sufficient time in confirming the need, and the eed will disappear. (Peter's Prognosis.)

For example, in organizing famine relief, study the need ong enough, and you will eventually find that there no onger is any need for relief!

b) STUDY ALTERNATE METHODS of doing whatever is to e done. Suppose that, after suitable preliminary investiga- ion, the need is confirmed. The Substituter will want to be ure that he chooses the most efficient course of action, no natter how long he may take to find it. The "alternate nethod" technique is in itself a substitute and a less panicky orm of the Teeter-Totter syndrome.

c) OBTAIN EXPERT ADVICE, in order that the plan finally :hosen may be effectively carried out. Committees will be ormed, and the question referred for study. A variant of his technique, looking to bygone experts instead of live ones, is to *search for precedents*.

d) FIRST THINGS FIRST. This technique involves mi- ute, painstaking, time-consuming attention to every phase of preparation for action: the building-up of abundant re- serves of spare forms, spare parts, spare ammunition, noney, etc., in order to *consolidate the present position* before beginning an advance toward the goal.

Perpetual Preparation: An Instructive Example

Here is an interesting case which shows several of these :echniques in use. Grant Swinger, deputy director of Deep- est Welfare Department, was regarded as highly competent because of his outstanding ability to coax government and charitable foundations into parting with money for worthy local causes.

War was declared on poverty. Swinger was promoted to the post of co-ordinating director of the Deeprest Anti-Disadvantagement Program, on the principle that since he so well understood the mighty, he should be highly competent to help the weak.

As this goes to press, Swinger is still busily raising funds to erect an Olympian office building to house his staff and to stand as a permanent monument to the spirit of aiding the needy. (First Things First.)

"We want the poor to see that they have not been forgotten by their government," explains Swinger. Next he plans to convene a Deeprest Anti-Disadvantagement Advisory Council (obtaining expert advice), raise money for a survey of the problems of the disadvantaged (confirming the need) and tour the Western world to inspect similiar schemes in preparation and operation elsewhere (studying alternate methods).

It should be pointed out that Swinger is busy from morning till night, is happy in his new post, and sincerely feels that he is doing a good job. He modestly turns away invitations to capitalize on his good image by running for elective office. In short he has achieved a highly successful *Substitution.*

Technique No. 2: Side-Issue Specialization

P. Gladman was promoted to manager of a rundown, inefficient plant of the Sagamore Divan and Sofa Company, with the specific task of increasing production and making the branch pay.

He was incompetent for this task, realized it immediately and so quickly ceased to apply his mind to the question of productivity. He *Substituted* a zealous concern with the internal organization of the factory and office.

He spent his days assuring himself that there was no friction between management and labor, that working conditions were pleasant and that all employees of the branch were, as he put it, "one big, happy family."

Fortunately for Gladman he had taken with him, as assistant manager, D. Dominy, a young man who had not yet reached his level of incompetence. Thanks to Dominy's energetic action, the branch was revitalized and earned a handsome profit.

Gladman received the credit, and felt proud of his "success." He had appropriately *Substituted,* and achieved happiness in so doing.

The watchword for Side-Issue Specialists is *Look after the molehills and the mountains will look after themselves.*

U. Tredwell was a competent assistant principal in an Excelsior City elementary school, intellectually capable, maintaining good discipline among students and good morale among teachers. After promotion, he found his level of incompetence as principal: he lacked the tact necessary to deal with parents' organizations, newspaper reporters, the district superintendent of schools, and the elected members of the school board. He fell out of favor with the officials, and the reputation of his school began to decline in the eyes of the public.

Tredwell launched an ingenious Side-Issue Specialization. He developed an obsessive concern with the human traffic problems—with the swirls, eddies and bumps caused by movement of students and staff about halls, corridors, corners and stairways.

On large-scale plans of the building he worked out an elaborate system of traffic flow. He had lines and arrows painted in various colors on the walls and floors. He insisted on rigid observance of his traffic laws. No student was allowed to cross a white line. Suppose that one boy, during a lesson period, was sent from his classroom to take a message to a room immediately across the corridor. He could not cross the line down the middle: he had to walk right to the end of the corridor, go around the end of the line, then back down the other side of it.

Tredwell spent much time prowling the building looking for violations of his system; he wrote many articles about it for professional journals; he escorted visiting groups of Side-Issue-Specialist educators on tours of the building; he is at present engaged in writing a book on the subject, illustrated with many plans and photographs.

He is active and contented, and enjoys perfect health, with not the slightest sign of the Final Placement Syndrome. Another triumph for *Side-Issue Specialization!*

Technique No. 3: Image Replaces Performance

Mrs. Vender, an Excelsior City high-school mathematics teacher, spends a great deal of class time telling her pupils how interesting and important mathematics is. She lectures on the history, present state and probable future development of mathematics. The actual work of learning mathematics she assigns to the students as home study.

Mrs. Vender's classroom periods are bright and interesting; most of her pupils think she is a good teacher. They do not get on very well with the subject, but they believe that is just because it is so difficult.

Mrs. Vender, too, firmly believes that she is a good teacher; she thinks that only the jealousy of less competent teachers above her in the hierarchy bars her from promotion. So she enjoys a permanent, pleasant glow of self-righteousness.

Mrs. Vender is *Substituting*. Her technique is not uncommon, and it may be employed consciously or unconsciously. The rule is: for achieving personal satisfaction, *an ounce of image is worth a pound of performance*. (Peter's Placebo.)

Note that although this technique provides satisfaction to the user, it does not necessarily satisfy the employer!

Peter's Placebo is well understood by politicians at all levels. They will talk about the importance, the sacredness, the fascinating history of the democratic system (or the monarchic system, or the communist system or the tribal system as the case may be) but will do little or nothing toward carrying out the real duties of their position.

The technique is much used, too, in the arts. A. Fresco, a painter in Excelsior City, produced a few successful canvases and then appeared to run out of artistic inspiration. He then established his career as a speaker on the value of art. Typical is the *Saloon Writer* who sits in a bar all day, at home or overseas, talking about the importance of writing, the faults of other writers and the great works he himself is going to write some day.

Technique No. 4: Utter Irrelevance

This is a daring technique, and often succeeds for that very reason.

The *Perpetual Preparer,* the *Side-Issue Specialist* and the *Image Promoter,* as we have seen, are not accomplishing any useful work—at least, not what they should be doing— yet they are doing, or talking about, something that is in some way connected with the job. Sometimes casual observers—even colleagues—will not realize that these people are *Substituting* instead of producing results.

But the *Utter Irrelevantist* makes not the slightest pretense of doing his job.

F. Helps, president of Offset Wheel and Axle Inc., spends all his time serving on the directorates of charitable organizations: spearheading fund-raising campaigns, planning the philanthropic activity, heartening the volunteer workers and supervising the professionals. He comes to his own office only to sign a few important papers.

In his *Irrelevance,* Helps constantly rubs shoulders with a former antagonist—now a good friend—T. Merritt, life vice-president of the Wheel Truers' and Axle Keyers' Union. Merritt is on most of the same charitable committees as Helps and he, too, does nothing useful in his own office.

University boards of governors, government advisory panels and investigative commissions are happy hunting grounds for the *Utter Irrelevantists*.

In industrial and commercial hierarchies, this technique is usually seen at the upper levels only. However, in domestic hierarchies, it is exceedingly common at the housewives' level. Many a woman who has reached her level of incompetence as wife and/or mother achieves a happy, successful *Substitution* by devoting her time and energy to *Utter Irrelevance* and leaving husband and children to look after themselves.

Technique No. 5: Ephemeral Administrology

Particularly in large, complex hierarchies, an incompetent senior employee can sometimes secure *temporary appointment* as acting director of another division, or pro tem chairman of some committee. The temporary work is substantially different from the employee's own regular job.

See how this works. The employee no longer has to cope with his own job (which he cannot do, anyway, having

Leaving husband and children to look after themselves.

reached his level of incompetence), and he can justifiably refrain from taking any significant action in the new post.

"I can't make that decision: we must leave that for the permanent director, whenever he is appointed."

An adept *Ephemeral Administrator* may continue for years, filling one temporary post after another, and achieving sincere satisfaction from his *Substitution.*

Technique No. 6: Convergent Specialization

Finding himself incompetent to carry out all the duties of his position, the *Convergent Specialist* simply *ignores* most of them and concentrates his attention and efforts on one small task. If he is competent to do this, he will continue with it; if not, he will specialize still more narrowly.

F. Naylor, director of the Excelsior City Art Gallery, paid no attention to acquisition, exhibitions and financial policies, neglected building maintenance and spent all his time either working in the gallery's framing shop or researching for his *History of Picture Framing*. My latest information is that Naylor has realized that he will never learn all there is to know about framing; he has decided to concentrate on studying the *various types of glue* that have been used or may be used in picture framing.

A historian became the world's foremost authority on the first thirty minutes of the Reformation.

Several physicians have made reputations by studying some disease of which there are only three or four known cases, while others have become specialists who deal only in one small area of the body.

An academician who is incompetent to understand the meaning and value of a literary work may write a treatise titled, "A Comparative Study of the Use of the Comma in the Literary Works of Otto Scribbler."

Substitution Recommended

The examples I have cited, and others that doubtless occurred to you, show that, from the employee's point of view, *Substitution* is far and away the most satisfactory adjustment to final placement.

The achievement of an effective *Substitution* will usually prevent the development of the Final Placement Syndrome, and allow the employee to work out the rest of his career, healthy and self-satisfied, at his level of incompetence.

CHAPTER XIV

Creative
Incompetence

*"Always do one thing less than
you think you can do."*

B. M. BARUCH

DOES my exposition of the Peter Principle seem to you like a philosophy of despair? Do you shrink from the thought that final placement, with its wretched physical and psychological symptoms, must be the end of every career? Empathizing with these questions, I should like to present the reader with a knife that allows him to cut through this philosophical Gordian knot.

BETTER TO LIGHT A SINGLE CANDLE THAN TO CURSE THE EDISON CO.

"Surely," you may say, "a person can simply refuse to accept promotion, and stay working happily at a job he can do competently."

An Interesting Example

The blunt refusal of an offered promotion is known as Peter's Parry. To be sure, it sounds easy enough. Yet I have discovered only one instance of its successful use.

T. Sawyer, a carpenter employed by the Beamish Construction Company, was so hard-working, competent and conscientious that he was several times offered the post of foreman.

Sawyer respected his boss and would have liked to oblige him. Yet he was happy as a rank-and-file carpenter. He had no worries: he could forget the job at 4:30 P.M. each day.

He knew that, as a foreman, he would spend his evenings and weekends worrying about the next day's and the next week's work. So he steadily refused the promotion.

Sawyer, it is worth noting, was an unmarried man with no close relatives and few friends. He could act as he pleased.

Not So Easy for Most of Us

For most people, Peter's Parry is impracticable. Consider the case of B. Loman, a typical citizen and family man, who refused a promotion.

His wife at once began to nag him. "Think of your children's future! What would the neighbours say if they knew? If you loved me, you'd want to get ahead!" and so on.

To find out for sure what the neighbours would say, Mrs. Loman confided the cause of her chagrin to a few trusted friends. The news spread around the district. Loman's young son, trying to defend his father's honor, fought one of his schoolmates and knocked out two of the other boy's teeth. The resulting litigation and dental bills cost Loman eleven hundred dollars.

Loman's mother-in-law worked Mrs. Loman's feelings up to such a pitch that she left him and secured a judicial separation. In his loneliness, disgrace and despair, he committed suicide.

No, refusing promotion is no easy route to happiness and health. I saw, early in my researches that, for most people, *Peter's Parry does not pay!*

An Illuminating Observation

While studying hierarchal structure and promotion rates among the production and clerical workers of the Ideal Trivet Company, I noticed that the grounds around the Trivet Building were beautifully landscaped and maintained. The velvety lawns and jewel-like flower beds suggested a high level of horticultural competence. I found that P. Greene, the gardener, was a happy, pleasant man with a genuine affection for his plants and a respect for his tools. He was doing what he liked best, gardening.

He was competent in all aspects of his work except one: he nearly always lost or mislaid receipts and delivery slips for goods received by his department, although he managed requisitions quite well.

The lack of delivery slips upset the accounting department, and Greene was several times reprimanded by the Manager. His replies were vague.

"I think I may have planted the papers along with the shrubs."

"Maybe the mice in the potting shed got at the papers."

Because of this incompetence in paper work, when a new maintenance foreman was required, Greene was not considered for the post.

I interviewed Green several times. He was courteous and co-operative, but insisted that he lost the documents accidentally. I questioned his wife. She told me that Greene kept comprehensive records for his home gardening operations, and could calculate the cost of everything produced in his yard or greenhouse.

A Parallel Case?

I interviewed A. Messer, shop foreman at Cracknell Casting and Foundry Company, whose little office seemed to be in grotesque disorder. Nevertheless, my time-and-motion study showed that the tottering piles of old account and reference books, the cardboard cartons bursting with tattered work sheets, the cabinets overflowing with un-indexed files and the sheaves of long-disused plans pinned to the walls were really not a part of Messer's basically efficient operation.

I could not tell whether he was or was not consciously using this untidiness to camouflage his competence, in order to avoid promotion to general foreman.

Madness in His Method?

J. Spellman was a competent schoolteacher. His professional reputation was high, yet he never got the offer of a vice-principalship. I wondered why, and began to make inquiries.

A senior official told me, "Spellman neglects to cash his pay checks. Every three months we have to remind him that we would like him to cash his checks, so that we can keep the books straight. I just can't understand a person who doesn't cash his checks."

I questioned further.

"No, no! We don't distrust him," was the reply. "But

Was it only coincidence that Spellman was happy
in his teaching work?

naturally one wonders whether he has some private source of income."

I asked, "Do you suspect that he might be involved in some illegal activities?"

"Certainly not! We don't have a shred of evidence against him. A fine teacher! A good man! A sterling reputation!"

Despite these disclaimers, I drew the inference that the hierarchy cannot trust a man who manages his finances so well that he does not rush to the bank and cash or deposit his pay check in order to cover his bills. Spellman, in short, had shown himself incompetent to behave as the typical employee is expected to behave; hence he had made himself ineligible for promotion.

Was it *only* coincidence that Spellman was happy in his teaching work, and had no desire for promotion to administrative duties?

Is There a Pattern?

I investigated many similar cases of what seemed to be deliberate incompetence, but I could never certainly decide whether the behavior was the result of conscious planning, or of a subconscious motivation.

One thing was clear: these employees had avoided advancement, not by refusing promotion—we have already seen how disastrous that can be—but by contriving never to be offered a promotion!

EUREKA!

This is an infallible way to *avoid the ultimate promotion;* this is *the key to health and happiness* at work and in private life; this is *Creative Incompetence*.

A Proven Policy

It does not matter whether Greene, Messer, Spellman and other employees similarly situated are consciously or unconsciously avoiding the ultimate promotion. What does matter is that we can learn from them how to achieve this vitally important goal. ("Vitally important" is no figure of speech: the correct technique may save your life.)

The method boils down to this: *create the impression that you have already reached your level of incompetence.*

You do this by exhibiting one or more of the non-medical symptoms of final placement.

Greene the gardener was exhibiting a mild form of Papyrophobia. Messer, the foundry foreman, to a casual observer, seemed to be an Advanced Papyromaniac. Spellman the schoolteacher, procrastinating over the deposit of his pay checks, showed a severe, though unusual, form of the Teeter-Totter Syndrome.

Creative Incompetence will achieve best results if you choose an area of incompetence *which does not directly hinder you in carrying out the main duties of your present position.*

Some Subtle Techniques

For a clerical worker, such an unspectacular habit as leaving one's desk drawers open at the end of the working day will, in some hierarchies, have the desired effect.

A show of niggling, officious economy—the switching off of lights, turning off of taps, picking up paper clips and rubber bands off the floor and out of the wastebaskets, to the accompaniment of muttered homilies on the value of thrift—is another effective maneuver.

Stand Out from the Crowd

Refusal to pay one's share of the firm's or department's Social Fund; refraining from drinking coffee at the official coffee break; bringing one's own lunch to a job where everyone else eats out; persistent turning off of radiators and opening of windows; refusing contributions to collections for wedding and retirement gifts; a mosaic of standoffish eccentricity (the Diogenes Complex) will create just the modicum of suspicion and distrust which disqualifies you for promotion.

AUTOMOTIVE TACTICS   One highly successful department manager avoided promotion by occasionally parking his car in the space reserved for the company president.

Another executive always drove a car one year older, and five hundred dollars cheaper in original price, than the cars of his peers.

PERSONAL APPEARANCE   Most people agree *in principle* with the dictum that fine feathers don't make fine birds, but *in practice* an employee is judged by his appearance. Here, then, is ample scope for Creative Incompetence.

The wearing of unconventional or *slightly shabby* clothes, irregularity of bathing, *occasional* neglect of haircutting or *occasional* carelessness in shaving (the *small* but conspicuous wound dressing adjoining a *small* blob of congealed blood, or the small patch of stubble missed by the razor) are useful techniques.

Ladies may wear *a shade too much* or *too little* makeup, possibly combined with the *occasional* wearing of an unbecoming or inappropriate hair style. Overly strong perfume and overly brilliant jewelry work well in many cases.

MORE REAL-LIFE EXAMPLES Here, for your guidance and inspiration, are some superb instances of Creative Incompetence which I have observed* in my studies.

Mr. F. proposed to the boss's daughter at the firm's annual Founder's Birthday Party. The girl had just graduated from a European finishing school, and F. had never seen her before that occasion. Naturally, he did not get the daughter and naturally, too, he rendered himself ineligible for promotion.

Miss L. of the same firm, contrived to offend the boss's wife at the same party by imitating the older woman's peculiar laugh within her hearing.

Mr. P. got a friend to make *one* fake threatening phone call to him at the office. Within earshot and sight of his colleagues P. reacted dramatically, begged for "mercy" and "more time" and pleaded, "Don't tell my wife. If she finds out this will kill her." Was this just one of P.'s typically stupid jokes, or was it an inspired piece of Creative Incompetence?

An Old Friend Revisited

I recently reviewed the case of T. Sawyer, the carpenter whose successful use of Peter's Parry I described at the beginning of this chapter.

In the last few months he has been buying cheap paper-bound copies of *Walden*† and giving them away to his workmates and superiors, in each case with a few remarks

---

* At least I *think* I have observed them. The mark of *perfect* Creative Incompetence is that no one, *even the trained hierarchiologist,* can ever be *sure* it is not just plain incompetence.

† Thoreau, Henry D. (1817–62). *Walden, or Life in the Woods,* 1854.

Mr. F. proposed to the boss's daughter.

on the pleasures of irresponsibility and the joys of day labor.

He follows up the gift with persistent questioning to see whether the recipient has read the book and how much of it he has understood. This meddlesome didacticism I denominate *The Socrates Complex*.

Sawyer reports that the offers of promotion have ceased. I naturally felt a little disappointment at the disappearance of the only living example of a *successful* Peter's Parry (successful in the sense that it had averted proffered promotion without causing him unhappiness). Yet this disappointment was counterbalanced by pleasure at seeing an elegant proof of the fact that

CREATIVE INCOMPETENCE BEATS PETER'S PARRY—
EVERY TIME!

An Important Precaution

A thoughtful study of Chapter 12 will give you plenty of ideas for developing your own form of Creative Incompetence. Yet I must emphasize the paramount importance of *concealing the fact that you want to avoid promotion!*

As camouflage, you may even indulge in the occasional mild *grumble* to your peers: "Darned funny how *some* people get promotion in this place, while others are passed over!"

DARE YOU DO IT?

If you have not yet attained final placement on Peter's Plateau, you can discover an irrelevant incompetence.

Find it and practice it diligently. It will keep you at a level of competence and so assure you of the keen personal satisfaction of regularly accomplishing some useful work.

Surely creative incompetence offers as great a challenge as the traditional drive for higher rank!

CHAPTER XV

The
Darwinian
Extension

"The meek . . . shall inherit the earth."
JESUS OF NAZARETH

IN discussing competence and incompetence we have so far dealt mainly with vocational problems—with the toils and stratagems men use to make a living in a complex, industrialized society.

This chapter will apply the Peter Principle to a broader issue, to the question of *life-competence*. Can the human race hold its position, or advance, in the evolutionary hierarchy?

THE PETERIAN INTERPRETATION OF HISTORY

Man has achieved many promotions in the life-hierarchy. Each promotion thus far—from tree dweller to caveman, to fire lighter, to flint knapper, to stone polisher, to bronze smelter, to iron founder and so on—has increased his prospects of survival as a species.

The more conceited members of the race think in terms of an endless ascent—or promotion *ad infinitum*. I would point out that, sooner or later, *man must reach his level of life-incompetence.*

Two things could prevent this happening: that there should not be enough time available, or not enough ranks in the hierarchy. But, so far as we can ascertain, there is infinite time ahead of us (whether we are here to take advantage of it or not), and there are an infinite number of ranks in existence or in potential (various religions have described whole hierarchies of angels, demigods and gods above the present level of humanity).

Other species have achieved many promotions, only to reach their levels of life-incompetence. The dinosaur, the saber-toothed tiger, the pterodactyl, the mammoth developed and flourished by virtue of certain qualities—bulk, fangs, wings, tusks. But the very qualities which at first assured their promotion eventually brought about their incompetence. We might say that *competence always contains the seed of incompetence.* General Goodwin's vulgar bonhomie, Miss Ditto's unoriginality, Mr. Driver's dominant personality—*these were the qualities which gained them promotion; these same qualities eventually barred them from further promotion!* So various animal species, after eons of steady promotion, have reached the levels of incompetence and have become static, or have achieved super-incompetence and have become extinct.

This has happened to many human societies and civilizations. Some people who flourished in colonial status, under the tutelage of stronger nations, have proved incompetent when promoted to self-government. Other nations that competently ruled themselves as city-states, republics or monarchies, have proved incompetent to survive as imperial powers. Civilizations that thrived on adversity and hardship proved incompetent to stand the strains of success and affluence.

What of the human race as a whole? *Cleverness* is the quality which has won for mankind promotion after promotion. Will that cleverness prove a bar to further promotion? Will it even reduce mankind to the condition of super-incompetence (see Chapter 3) and thus ensure his speedy dismissal from the life-hierarchy?

Two Ominous Signs

1. Hierarchal Regression

It is through the schools that society begins its task of molding and training the new members of the human race. I have already examined a typical school system as it concerns the teachers who staff it. Now let us look at school as it affects the pupils.

The old-fashioned school system was a pure expression of the Peter Principle. A pupil was promoted, grade by grade, until he reached his level of incompetence. Then he was said to have "failed" Grade 5 or 8 or 11, etc. He would have to "repeat the grade"; that is, he would have to remain at his level of incompetence. In some instances, because the child was still growing mentally, his intellectual competence would increase during the "repeating" year, and he would then become eligible for further promotion. If not, he would "fail" again, and "repeat" again.

(It is worth noting that this "failure" is the same thing that, in vocational studies, we call "success," namely, the attainment of final placement at the level of incompetence.)

School officials do not like this system: they think that the accumulation of incompetent students lowers the standard within the school. One administrator told me, "I wish I could pass all the dull pupils and fail the bright ones: that would raise standards and grades would improve. This hoarding of dull students lowers the standard by reducing the average achievement in my school."

Such an extreme policy will not be generally tolerated. So, to avoid the accumulation of incompetents, administrators have evolved the plan of promoting everyone, *the incompetent as well as the competent*. They find psychological justification for this policy by saying that it spares students the painful experience of failure.

What they are actually doing is *applying percussive sublimation* to the incompetent students.

The result of this wholesale percussive sublimation is that high-school graduation may now represent the same level of scholastic achievement as did Grade 11 a few years ago. In time, graduation will sink in value to the level of the old Grade 10, Grade 9 and so on.

This phenomenon I designate *hierarchal regression.*

Results of Hierarchal Regression

Educational certificates, diplomas and degrees are losing their value as measures of competence. Under the old system we knew that a pupil who "failed" Grade 8 must at least have been competent in Grade 7. We knew that a pupil who "failed" first-year university must at least have been a competent high-school graduate, and so on.

But now we cannot assume any such thing. The modern certificate proves only that the pupil *was competent to endure a certain number of years' schooling*.

High-school graduation, once a widely accepted certificate of competence, is now only a certificate of incompetence for most responsible, well-paid jobs.*

So it goes at the post-high-school level. Bachelors' and masters' degrees have regressed in value. Only the doctorate still carries any notable aura of competence, and its value is rapidly being eroded by the emergence of post-doctoral degrees. How long will it be before the post-doctorate, too, becomes a badge of incompetence for many posts, and the earnest striver will have to plow on through post-post and post-post-post doctorates?

Escalation of educational effort speeds the process of degradation. Many universities, for example, now use the very same pupil-teacher system (older students teaching younger students) which fifty years ago was being condemned in the grade schools!

Escalation of effort in any other field produces comparable results. Under the pressure to get *more* engineers, scientists, priests, teachers, automobiles, apples, spacemen or what have you, and to get them faster, the standards of acceptance necessarily sink: hierarchal regression sets in.

You, as a consumer, an employer, an artisan or teacher, no doubt see the results of hierarchal regression. I shall return to the subject later, to suggest ways in which it might be controlled.

2. Computerized Incompetence

A drunken man is temporarily incompetent to steer a straight course. So long as he is on foot, he is a danger

---

* It is noteworthy that hierarchal regression is not entirely a modern phenomenon. Many years ago, literacy was itself regarded as a certificate of competence for most important positions. Then it was found that there was an increasing number of literate fools, so employers began to raise their standards—fifth grade, eighth grade, and so on. Each of these standards began as a certificate of competence; each was finally regarded as a certificate of incompetence.

chiefly to himself. But put him at the wheel of an automobile and he may kill a score of other people before he breaks his own neck.

The point needs no laboring. Obviously, the more powerful the means at my disposal, the greater good or harm I can do by my competence or incompetence.

The printing press, radio, television have in turn expanded man's power to propagate and perpetuate his incompetence. Now comes the computer.

Computer Use File: Case No. 11

R. Fogg, founder and managing director of Fogg Interlocking Blocks, Inc., was an inventor-engineer who had reached his level of incompetence as an administrator. Fogg constantly complained about the poor performance of his office manager, clerks and accountants. He did not realize that they were about as efficient as most similar groups of employees. Some of them were not yet at their levels of incompetence; they turned out some work and kept the business going. They managed to take Fogg's muddled instructions, separate what had best be ignored from what would be of some use to the company, and then took appropriate action.

A salesman convinced Fogg that a computer could be programmed to do much of the work of his office staff as well as improve efficiency of the plant. Fogg placed the order, the computer was installed, and the "surplus" staff was dismissed.

But Fogg soon found that the work of the firm was not being handled so fast or so well as before. There were two points about a computer that he had not understood. (At least, he had not understood that they would apply to his operations.)

a) A computer balks at any unclear instruction, simply blinks its lights and waits for clarification.

b) A computer has no tact. It will not flatter. It will not use judgment. It will not say, "Yes, sir; at once, sir!" to wrong instructions, then go away and do the job right. It will simply follow the wrong orders, so long as they are clearly given.

Fogg's business ran rapidly downhill and within a year his company was bankrupt. He had fallen victim to *Computerized Incompetence*.

MORE HORRIBLE EXAMPLES   The Quebec Department of Education wrongly paid out $275,864 in student loans. The mistake was made by computer-directed multi-copying services.

In New York a bank computer went on the blink; three billion dollars' worth of accounts went unbalanced for twenty-four hours.

The computer belonging to an airline printed 6,000 instead of ten replenishment notices. The airline found itself with 5,990 surplus orders of mint chocolates.

A study made in 1966 shows that over 70 percent of computer installations made to that time in Britain must be considered commercially unsuccessful.

One computer was so sensitive to static electricity that it made errors every time it was approached by a female employee wearing nylon lingerie.

Three Observations

1) The computer may be incompetent in itself—that is, unable to do regularly and accurately the work for which it was designed. This kind of incompetence can never be eliminated, because the Peter Principle applies in the plants where computers are designed and manufactured.

2) Even when competent in itself, the computer vastly magnifies the results of incompetence in its owners or operators.

3) The computer, like a human employee, is subject to the Peter Principle. If it does good work at first, there is a strong tendency to promote it to more responsible tasks, until it reaches its level of incompetence.

The Signs Interpreted

These two signs—the rapid spread of hierarchal regression and computerized incompetence—are only part of a general trend which, if continued, will escalate inevitably to the Total-Life-Incompetence level. In Chapter 3 you saw that the obsessive concern for *input* could eventually destroy the purpose for which the hierarchy existed (*output*). Here we see that the thoughtless escalation of educational effort and the automation of outmoded or incorrect methods are examples of this mindless kind of input. Our leaders in politics, science, education, industry and the military have insisted that we go as fast as we can and as far as we can inspired only by blind faith that *great input* will produce *great output*.

As a student of hierarchiology you now realize that society's continued escalation of input is simply *Peter's Inversion* on a grand scale.

MAN'S FIRST MISTAKE: THE WHEEL

Look at the results. Conceivably we are all doomed by our own cleverness and devotion to escalation. Our land, a few decades ago, was dotted with crystal-clear lakes and laced with streams of cool, clear water. The soil produced wholesome food. Citizens had easy access to rural scenes of calm beauty.

Citizens had easy access to rural scenes of calm beauty.

Now lakes and streams are cesspools. Air is noxious with smoke, soot and smog. Land and water are poisoned with pesticides, so that birds, bees, fish, and cattle are dying. The countryside is a dump for garbage and old automobiles.

This is progress! We have made so much progress that we cannot even speak with confidence about the prospect of *human* survival. We have blighted the promise of this century and converted the miracles of science into a chamber of horrors where a nuclear holocaust could become a death-trap for the entire human race. If we continue feverishly planning and inventing and building and rebuilding for more of this progress, we will achieve the level of *Total-Life-Incompetence*.

New Social Science Shows the Way

Do you sometimes feel you have a rendezvous with oblivion but would prefer to break the date? Hierarchiology can show you how.

Of all proposals for betterment of the human condition and survival of the human race only one, the Peter Principle, realistically embodies factual knowledge about the human organism. Hierarchiology reveals man's true nature, his perpetual production of hierarchies, his quest for means of maintaining them, and his countervailing tendency to destroy them. The Peter Principle and hierarchiology provide the unifying factor for all social sciences.

PETER'S REMEDIES

Must the whole human race achieve life-incompetence and earn dismissal from the life-hierarchy?

Before you answer this question, ask yourself, "What is the purpose (output) of the human hierarchy?"

In my lecture, *Destiny Lies Ahead,* I tell my students, "If you don't know where you are going, you will probably end up somewhere else."

Obviously, if the purpose of the hierarchy is total human exfoliation, Peter's Remedies are not needed. But if we wish to survive, and to better our condition, Peter's Remedies, ranging from prevention to cure, will show the way.

I offer:

1. Peter's Prophylactics—means to avoid promotion to the level of incompetence.

2. Peter's Palliatives—for those who have already reached their level of incompetence, means for prolonging life and maintaining health and happiness.

3. Peter's Placebos—for suppression of the symptoms of the Final Placement Syndrome.

4. Peter's Prescriptions—cures for the world's ills.

1. PETER'S PROPHYLACTICS—AN OUNCE OF PREVENTION

A prophylactic, in the hierarchiological sense, is a preventive measure applied before the Final Placement Syndrome appears, or before Hierarchal Regression sets in.

The Power of Negative Thinking

I strongly recommend the health-giving power of negative thinking. If Mr. Mal d'Mahr had thought about the negative aspects of the chief executive's post, would he have accepted the promotion?

Suppose he had asked, "What will the directors think of me? What will my subordinates expect? What will my wife expect?"

If Mal had dwelt steadily on the negative aspects of promotion, would he have halted the course of action that destroyed his health?

He was intellectually competent; he could have added up the negatives, including the conflict of codes described earlier, the changed relationships with his friends, the pressure to join the country club, the need to own a dress suit, his wife's demands for a new wardrobe, the community's request that he head fund-raising drives, and all the other pressures associated with the promotion.

He might well have decided that life at his old level was actually fulfillment, that he was satisfied where he was, and that his status, social life, avocations and *health* were worth protecting.

You can apply the power of negative thinking. Ask yourself, "How would I like to work for my boss's boss?"

Look, not at your boss, whom you think you could replace, but at *his* boss. How would you like to work directly for the man two steps above you? The answer to this question often has prophylactic benefits.

In dealing with incompetence on the civic, national or world-wide scale, the power of negative thinking has great potential.

Consider the merits of a costly undersea exploration program, for example. Contemplate the discomforts and hazards of life on the sea bed; contrast them with the comfort and safety of an afternoon beside the swimming pool or an evening party at the beach.

Consider the stench, bad flavors and perils involved in spraying the entire globe with pesticides: compare them with the simple pleasure, and the therapeutic exercise, of hand-spraying the garden.

The power of negative thinking can help us avoid escalating ourselves to a level of life-incompetence, and so help prevent destruction of the world.

Another Prophylactic—Creative Incompetence

As another approach to the great problem of man's life-incompetence, let us consider application of creative incompetence. We need not give up the *appearance* of striving for promotion in the life-hierarchy, but we could deliberately practice *irrelevant incompetence* so as to bar ourselves from obtaining that promotion.

(By "irrelevant" I mean "not connected with getting food, keeping warm, maintaining a healthful environment, and raising children, the essential elements for survival.")

Here is an example. Man has competently solved many problems of transport on and about the world he inhabits. At no great expenditure of time, he can travel to any part of the globe, with no more hardship or danger than he endures in walking the streets of his own town. (With considerably *less* danger, if he happens to live in a major city!)

Promotion in the travel-hierarchy would be expected to advance man from earth traveller to space traveller. But this would be escalation for its own sake. Man has no need to explore the moon, Mars or Venus in person. He has already sent radar, TV and photographic instruments which transmit vivid descriptions of these heavenly bodies. The reports suggest that they are inhospitable places.

Man would be better off without the promotion to space traveller. But, as we have seen, it is no easy thing to *refuse* a promotion. The safe, pleasant, effective way is to seem *not to deserve it:* this is creative incompetence.

Man now has the chance to exhibit creative incompetence in this field of space travel.* He has the chance to

---

* The bungles, delays and disaster associated with space travel indicate that the people concerned with it *may,* indeed, be exercising creative incompetence. I emphasize "may" because the test of real creative incompetence is that an observer cannot certainly tell whether the incompetence is deliberate or not.

curb his dangerous cleverness and show a little wholesome incompetence.

THE MALADY LINGERS ON　　Let us look at another example. Man has moved up the therapeutic hierarchy, through magic, voodoo, faith healing, to modern, orthodox medicine and surgery. He is now very near to fabricating human beings out of spare parts, natural and synthetic. This step would promote him from healer to creator.

But, faced with a population explosion and with widespread starvation, what need has man to accept that promotion?

Would it not be timely to exhibit creative incompetence at this point, to bungle the creative technique, and so avoid the useless, the potentially dangerous, promotion?

It's Up to You

By a little thought, you will be able to find other areas in which this creative incompetence—this meekness—might well be applied.

Faced with the possibility of promotion to the level of Total-Life-Incompetence—say through atmospheric pollution, nuclear war, global starvation or invasion of Martian bacteria—we would be well advised to use Peter's Prophylactics.

If we practice negative thinking and creative incompetence, and thereby avoid taking the final step, the possibility of human survival would be enhanced. *Peter's Prophylactics prevent pathological promotions.*

2. PETER'S PALLIATIVES—AN OUNCE OF RELIEF

Although the human race, as a whole, has not yet reached its level of Total-Life-Incompetence, many individuals, as we saw earlier, do reach that level, and fairly rapidly remove themselves from this world.

I have already discussed some palliatives for these people—measures that can enable them to live out their lives in comparative happiness and comfort. Now let us see how such palliatives can be applied on a large scale.

Hierarchal Regression Stopped!

As we saw earlier, hierarchal regression in an educational system is caused by mass percussive sublimation of pupils who, in olden days, would have been allowed to "fail."

I propose, instead of using percussive sublimation, to give such students the *lateral arabesque*.

At present, a student who "fails" Grade 8 is sublimated to Grade 9. Under my plan, he would be arabesqued from Grade 8 to a year, say, of Freshman Academic Depth Study. He could then repeat his year's work, preferably with special emphasis on the points that he failed to understand before. The extra experience, his own growing maturity and—with luck—more competent teaching, might prepare him for Grade 9.

If not, his parents could hardly object to his "winning" a two-year Fellowship in Higher Academic Depth Study.

Eventually, if the pupil made no further progress by school-leaving age, he would be awarded a certificate making him a Life Fellow of Academic Depth Study.

Thus the lateral arabesque lets him out sideways. It does not interfere with the education of the pupils who are still moving upward, and it does not diminish the worth of the grades and degrees which those upward-moving pupils achieve.

The technique has proved successful with individuals at

work. Why not try it on a big scale in the educational field? *Peter's Palliative prevents percussive sublimation.*

3. PETER'S PLACEBO—AN OUNCE OF IMAGE

Hierarchiologically speaking, a Placebo is the application of a neutral (non-escalatory) methodology to suppress the undesirable results of reaching a level of incompetence.

I would like to refer again to the case of Mrs. Vender, cited in Chapter 13. Mrs. Vender, at her level of incompetence, did not spend her time teaching mathematics, but in extolling the value of mathematics.

Mrs. Vender was *substituting image for performance.* Peter's Placebo: an ounce of image is worth a pound of performance.

Now let us see how the Placebo can be applied on the grand scale. Incompetent workers, instead of striving for promotion, would lecture eloquently on *the dignity of labor.* Incompetent educators would give up teaching and spend their time extolling *the value of education.* Incompetent painters would promote *the appreciation of art.* Incompetent space travellers would *write science fiction.* Sexually incompetent persons would *compose love lyrics.*

All such practitioners of Peter's Placebo might not be doing much good, but at least, *they would be doing no harm,* and they would not be interfering with the operations of competent members of the various trades and professions. *Peter's Placebo prevents professional paralysis.*

4. PETER'S PRESCRIPTION—A POUND OF CURE

What might be the results, for the human race, of applying Peter's Prescription?

Peter's Prophylactics would prevent millions of people from ever reaching their levels of incompetence. Consequently those same millions who, under the present system, are frustrated and unproductive, would remain, all their lives, happy and useful members of society.

Peter's Palliatives and Placebos would ensure that those who had achieved their levels of incompetence were kept harmlessly busy, happy and healthy. This change would set free for productive work the millions of people presently employed in looking after the health, and repairing the blunders, of all those incompetents.

The net result? An enormous store of man-hours, of creativity, of enthusiasm, would be set free for constructive purposes.

We might, for instance, develop safe, comfortable, efficient rapid-transit systems for our major cities. (They would cost less than moonships and serve more people.)

We might tap power sources (*e.g.,* generator plants powered by smokeless trash burners) which would not pollute the atmosphere. Thus we would contribute to the better health of our people, the beautification of our scenery and the better visibility of that more beautiful scenery.

We might improve the quality and safety of our automobiles, landscape our freeways, highways and avenues, and so restore some measure of safety and pleasure to surface travel.

We might learn to return to our farm lands organic products that would enrich, without poisoning, the soil.

Much waste that is now dumped might be salvaged and converted into new products, using collection systems as complex as our present distribution systems.

Otherwise useless waste might be dumped to fill abandoned open-pit mines and reclaim the land for constructive purposes.

You Figure It Out

Space permits no further elaboration. You, as a serious reader, will be able to see the application of Peter's Prescription* in your life and work, and in the life and work of your city, country and planet.

You will agree that man cannot achieve his greatest fulfillment through seeking quantity for quantity's sake: he will achieve it through improving the *quality of life,* in other words, through avoiding life-incompetence.

Peter's Prescription offers life-quality-improvement in place of mindless promotion to oblivion.

HIERARCHIOLOGY IN THE ASCENDANT

I have said enough to indicate that your happiness, health and joy of accomplishment, as well as the hope for man's future, lies in understanding the Peter Principle, in applying the principles of hierarchiology, and in utilizing Peter's Prescription to solve human problems.

I have written this book so that you can understand and use the Peter Principle. Its acceptance and application is up to you. Other books will doubtless follow. In the meantime, let us hope that a philanthropist somewhere will soon endow a chair of hierarchiology at a major university. When he does I am qualified and ready for the post, having proven myself capable in my present endeavours.

---

* I have applied this to education. (See *Prescriptive Teaching,* by Laurence J. Peter, New York: McGraw-Hill Book Co., 1965.)

Man will achieve his greatest fulfillment through
improving the quality of life.

Glossary

Alger Complex—a moralistic delusion concerning the effect of Push on promotion. Chap. 5.

Alternation, compulsive—a technique for flustering subordinates. Chap. 12.

Aptitude tests—a popular means of hastening final placement. Chap. 9.

Arrived—achieved final placement. Chap. 3.

Auld Lang Syne Complex—sentimental belittlement of things present and glorification of things past· a sign of final placement. Chap. 12.

Buckpass, Downward, Upward and Outward—techniques for avoiding responsibility. Chap. 12.

Cachinnatory Inertia—telling jokes instead of working. Chap. 12.

Caesarian Transference—irrational prejudice against some physical characteristic. Chap. 12.

Codophilia, Initial and Digital—speaking in letters and numbers instead of words. Chap. 12.

Comparative Hierarchiology—an incomplete study. Chap. 7.

Competence—the employee's ability, as measured by his superiors, to fill his place in the hierarchy. Chap. 3.

Compulsive Incompetence—a condition exhibited by Summit Competents. (See "Summit Competence.")

Computerized Incompetence—incompetent application of computer techniques or the inherent incompetence of a computer. Chap. 15.

Heep Syndrome—a group of symptoms indicating the patient's belief in his own worthlessness. Observed by D. Copperfield, reported by C. Dickens. Chap. 9.

Hierarchal Exfoliation—the sloughing-off of super-competent and super-incompetent employees. Chap. 3.

Hierarchal Regression—result of promoting the incompetent along with the competent. Chap. 15.

Hierarchiology—a social science, the study of hierarchies, their structure and functioning, the foundation for all social science.

Hierarchy—an organization whose members or employees are arranged in order of rank, grade or class.

Hierarchy, Cheopsian or feudal—a pyramidal structure with many low-ranking and few high-ranking employees. Chap. 8.

Hull's Theorem—"The combined Pull of several Patrons is the sum of their separate Pulls multiplied by the number of Patrons." Chap. 4.

Hypercaninophobia Complex—fear caused in superiors when an inferior demonstrates strong leadership potential. Chap. 6.

Image Replaces Performance—a Substitution technique. Chap. 13.

Incompetence—a null quantity: incompetence plus incompetence equals incompetence. Chap. 10.

Input—activities which support the rules, rituals and forms of a hierarchy. Chap. 3.

John Q. Diversion—undue reliance on public opinion. Chap. 12.

Lateral Arabesque—a pseudo-promotion consisting of a new title and a new work place. Chap. 3.

Leadership Competence—disqualification for promotion. Chap. 6.

Level of Competence—a position in a hierarchy at which an employee more or less does what is expected of him.

Level of Incompetence—a position in a hierarchy at which an employee is unable to do what is expected of him.

Life-Incompetence Syndrome—a cause of frustration. Chap. 8.

Maturity Quotient—a measure of the inefficiency of a hierarchy. Chap. 7.

Medical Profession—a group showing apathy and hostility toward hierarchiology. Chap. 11.

Meekness—a technique of Creative Incompetence. Chap. 15.

Obtain expert advice—a Substitution technique. Chap. 13.

Order—"Heav'n's first law": the basis of the hierarchal instinct. Chap. 8.

Output—the performance of useful work. Chap. 3.

Papyromania—compulsive accumulation of papers. Chap. 12.

Papyrophobia—abnormal desire for "a clean desk." Chap. 12.

Party—a hierarchal organization for selecting candidates for political office. Chap. 7.

Patron—one who speeds the promotion of employees lower in the hierarchy. Chap. 4.

Percussive Sublimation—being kicked upstairs: a pseudo-promotion. Chap. 3.

Peter Principle—In a hierarchy, every employee tends to rise to his level of incompetence.

Peter's Bridge—an important test: can you motivate your Patron? Chap. 4.

Peter's Circumambulation—a circumlocution or detour around a super-incumbent. Chap. 4.

Peter's Circumbendibus—a veiled or secretive circumambulation (see above).

Peter's Corollary—In time, every post in a hierarchy tends to be occupied by an employee who is incompetent to carry out its duties.

Peter's Inversion—internal consistency valued more highly than efficiency. Chap. 3.

Peter's Invert—one for whom means have become ends in themselves. Chap. 3.

Peter's Nuance—the difference between Pseudo-Achievement and Final Placement Syndromes. Chap. 5.

Peter's Palliatives—provide relief for incompetence symptoms. Chap. 15.

Peter's Paradox—employees in a hierarchy do not really object to incompetence in their colleagues. Chap. 4.

Peter's Parry—the refusal of an offered promotion. (Not recommended.) Chap. 14.

Peter's Placebo—An ounce of image is worth a pound of performance. Chap. 13.

Peter's Plateau—the level of incompetence.

Peter's Prescriptions—CURES for individual or world ills. Chap. 15.

Peter's Pretty Pass—the situation of having one's road to promotion blocked by a super-incumbent. Chap. 4.

Peter's Prognosis—Spend sufficient time in confirming the need, and the need will disappear. Chap. 13.

Peter's Prophylactics—an ounce of prevention. Chap. 15.

Peter's Remedies—means of preventing total-life-incompetence. Chap. 15.

Peter's Spiral—the non-progressive course followed by organizations suffering from high-level incompetence. Chap. 10.

Peterian Interpretation—the application of hierarchiological science to the facts and fictions of history. Chap. 15.

Phonophilia—an abnormal desire for possession and use of voice transmission and recording equipment. Chap. 12.

Professional Automatism—an obsessive concern with rituals and a disregard of results. Chap. 3.

Promotion—an upward movement from a level of competence.

Promotion Quotient—numerical expression of promotion prospects. Chap. 13.

Protégé—see "Pullee."

Proto-hierarchiologists—authors who might have contributed to hierarchiological thought. Chap. 8.

Proverbs—as repositories of hierarchiological fallacies. Chap. 8.

Pseudo-Achievement Syndrome—a complex of physical ailments resulting from excessive Push. Chap. 5.

Pull—an employee's relationship—by blood, marriage or acquaintance—with a person above him. Chap. 4.

Pullee—an employee who has Pull. Chap. 4.

Random Placement—a cause of delay in reaching the level of incompetence. Chap. 9.

Rigor Cartis—abnormal interest in charts, with dwindling concern for realities that the charts represent. Chap. 12.

Saints—good men but incompetent controversialists. Chap. 8.

Secrecy—the soul of Push. Chap. 5.

Seniority Factor—downward pressure which opposes the upward movement of competent employees. Chap. 5.

Side-Issue Specialization—a Substitution technique. Chap. 13.

Socrates Complex—a form of Creative Incompetence. Chap. 14.

A Note on the Illustrations

The authors and the publishers of *The Peter Principle* appreciate the special permission granted by the Managing Director of *Punch* to reproduce the drawings without the original captions. For anyone who might be interested, in addition to the name of the artist and the year of publication, we are providing as follows the complete text that accompanied each illustration when it first appeared:

Page xi Charles Keene (1888)

REPRISALS!

Tradesman (to Old Gentleman, who has purchased Lawn-Mower). "Yes, sir, I'll oil it, and send it over imm—"
Customer (imperatively). "No, no, no!—It mustn't be oiled! I won't have it oiled! Mind that! I want noise! And, look here—pick me out a nice rusty one. My neighbour's children hoot and yell till ten o'clock every night, so"—*(viciously)*—"I mean to cut my grass from four till six every morning!!"

Page xvi G. du Maurier (1889)

AN AWKWARD REPARTEE TO DEAL WITH.

Head Master. "It's disgraceful, sir! Why, your brother, who is two years younger than yourself, knows his Greek grammar better than you do!"

Dunce. "Ah, but my brother's not been here so long as I have, sir. It's only his first term!"

Page 3   G. du Maurier (1889)

TROP DE ZÈLE.

Clerical Customer. "I want to buy a nice diamond brooch for my better half."

Over-anxious Shopkeeper. "Certainly, sir. We have just the very thing. We can accommodate you also for your other half, if you wish."   [*They did not trade.*

Page 9   Charles Keene (1864)

AN EXCELLENT EXCUSE.

This is Jack Sparkles, who used to be such a thorough preraphaelite, as we came upon him "at work" the other day—at least he called it so. He said he had come to the conclusion that "painting was, after all, more or less a matter of memory, and that he was studying skies!!"

Page 15   W. Ralston (1871)

PRACTICAL.

Fond Father. "I see ye've put my son intil graummer an' jography. Noo, as I neither mean him tae be a minister or a sea-captain, it's o' nae use. Gie him a plain bizness eddication."

Page 17   G. du Maurier (1887)

A DAY IN THE COUNTRY.

Little Tommy (*who has never been out of Whitechapel before*). "Oh! Oh! Oh!"
Kind Lady. "What's the matter, Tommy?"
Little Tommy. "Why, what a big sky they've got 'ere, Miss!"

Page 30   Charles Keene (1874)

VERY MUCH CARED FOR.

Chorus of Ladies (*to comely Curate*). "O, Mr. Sweetlow, do take care! Don't go up!—So dangerous! Do come down! O!"

Rector (*sarcastically*). "Really, Sweetlow, don't you think you'd better let a married man do that?!!"

Page 41   Charles Keene (1886)

A PESSIMIST.

Exemplary Clerk. "Can I have a week's holiday, if you please, sir? A—a domestic affliction, sir—"

Employer. "Oh, certainly, yes, Mr. —— Dear me, I'm very sorry! Near relative?"

Clerk. "Ah—ye'—n'—that is—you misunderst— What I mean, sir—I'm going to be married!"

Page 52   A. C. Corbould (1885)

LIKE HIS CHEEK.

" 'Old yer 'oss, sir?"

Page 59   E. T. Reed (1892)

ELECTION INTELLIGENCE.

Brilliant Elector (*at the Polling Station*). "It's a stoutish koind of a man, with a bald 'ead, as ar wishes to vote for, but ar'm blessed if ar know 'is naame!!"

Page 73   W. T. Maud (1891)

IT'S A GREAT THING FOR A MAN TO KNOW WHEN HE'S WELL OFF.

Page 80   G. du Maurier (1883)

A FAIR RETORT.

Mrs. Mountjoy Belassis (*after several Collisions*). "It strikes me, Mr. Rudderford, you're much more at home in a boat than in a ball-room!"

Little Bobby Rudderford (*the famous Oxbridge Coxswain*). "Yes, by Jove! And I'd sooner steer eight men than one woman *any* day!"

Page 91   Charles Keene (1874)

SHOCKING!

Dr. Jolliboy (who had been called away from a social Meeting at his Club). "Thirteen, fourteen, f'fteen-two, f'fteen-four, f'fteen-six—pair eight—nob'sh nine——" *(Drops off.)*

["*We draw a Veil*," &c., &c.

Page 101   John Leech (1862)

OLD SCHOOL.

Mr. Grapes (helping himself to another glass of that fine old Madeira). "Hah! We live in strange times—what the dooce can people want with drinking fountains!"

Page 110   E. T. Reed (1891)

DRAWING THE LINE.

Judge. "Remove those barristers. They're drawing!"
Chorus of Juniors. "May it please your Ludship, we're only drawing—pleadings."

Page 123   A. C. Corbould (1885)

"RUS IN URBE."

Fair Equestrian (from the Provinces, her first turn in the Row). "Good gracious, Sam! You can't ride out with me like that! Where are your boots and things?"
Country Groom. "Lor', Mum, I didn't bring 'em up. But it don't matter. Nobody knows me here!"

Page 131   Charles Keene (1880)

DEFINITIVE.

Board Schoolmaster (desiring to explain the word "Conceited," which had occurred in the course of the Reading Lesson). "Now, Boys, suppose that I was always boasting of my Learning—that I knew a good deal o' Latin for instance, or that my personal appearance was—that I was very Good-looking, y'know—what should you say I was?"

Straightforward Boy (*who had "caught the Speaker's eye"*). "I sh' say you was a Liar, S'!"

Page 136   G. du Maurier (1890)

STUDIES IN REPARTEE.

She. "How silent you are! What are you thinking of?"
He. "Nothing!"
She. "Egotist!"

Page 147   G. du Maurier (1882)

A GOOD-BYE TO JOLLY WHITBY.

The Browns and their Family drag their Luncheon-Baskets over the Dam on the Esk for the last time, alas! And for the last time, Brown Senior attempts a feeble French Joke, beginning "Esker la Dam——" and, as usual, falls down on the slippery Stones before he can finish it!

Page 157   G. du Maurier (1882)

"NOT FOND OF STEERING? JUST AIN'T WE THOUGH!"

ABOUT THE AUTHORS

LAURENCE J. PETER was born in Canada and received an Ed.D. from Washington State University. With wide experience as a teacher, counselor, school psychologist, prison instructor, consultant and university professor, he has written more than thirty articles for professional journals, and a book, *Prescriptive Teaching* (1965). He is now Associate Professor of Education, Director of the Evelyn Frieden Center for Prescriptive Teaching, and Coordinator of Programs for Emotionally Disturbed Children at the University of Southern California.

RAYMOND HULL, the son of an English Methodist minister, has lived in British Columbia since 1947. He has had thirty TV and stage plays produced and four stage plays published. His articles have been featured in such magazines as PUNCH, MACLEANS, and ESQUIRE.

Wait 'til you see what *else* we've got in store for you!

Send for your FREE catalog of Bantam Bestsellers today!

This money-saving catalog lists hundreds of bestsellers originally priced from $3.75 to $15.00—yours now in Bantam paperback editions for just 50¢ to $1.95! Here is a great opportunity to read the good books you've missed and add to your private library at huge savings! The catalog is FREE! So don't delay—send for yours today!